THE SONG OF IMMARU

EARTH'S DOOR

By

PJ DUDEK

Ballast Books, LLC
www.ballastbooks.com

Copyright © 2024 by PJ Dudek

ISBN: 978-1-962202-60-2

Printed in Hong Kong

Published by Ballast Books
www.ballastbooks.com

For more information, bulk orders, appearances, or speaking requests, please email: info@ballastbooks.com

To Nova, Kathy, and Becky—not all lights that go out grow dim.

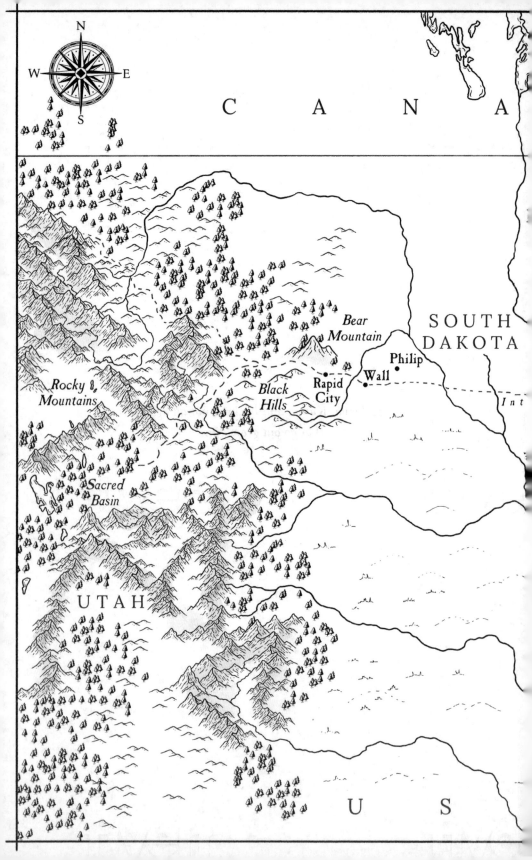

D   A

NESOTA

Wind
Farm

N i n e t y

Lake
***S**uperior*

Lake
Huron

Lake
Ontario

Lake
Michigan

Madison •

Chicago •

Lake
Erie

• Cleveland

East •
Fairfield

OHIO

SSOURI

Mississippi River

Appalachian
Mountains

When all is nearly lost and the world has reached its end, it is from the end of the world that the kingdoms shall reunite. Three will arise, heralds of the light. Three will follow, warriors of the light. One emerges. And then there is Light.

—*Annals of Illuminara,*
author unknown

CHAPTER 1

Tarin sprung from his bed with a scream. The haunting melody still swirled between his ears, even as the vision of the four necks within four nooses started to fade. Usually, he managed at least a few nights' gap between these awful dreams. But now they were plaguing him with far more regularity.

He stumbled into his trailer's tiny bathroom. A trash bin next to the sink sat full of empty amber bottles. Tarin splashed water on his face and looked into the dusty mirror. His sandy brown hair lay matted onto his pale forehead. Maybe a drink would help. Sure, it was early, but his heart was still beating fast, and he needed to calm down.

"What's the time?" he murmured to the mirror.

Four three-dimensional digits appeared near the top of the glass, revealing it was already ten in the morning. Tarin cursed. He needed to be at the ranch in fifteen minutes to feed the horses and lead them out to pasture. Howard would be angry if he was late again, and he couldn't afford to get fired.

He groaned and splashed more water on his face. After grabbing his coat, he headed out into the chilly November air for the twenty-minute walk—or today, ten-minute jog—to the ranch.

An hour later, he was leading the final horse from the barn toward a fenced enclosure set upon the gently rolling hills of western South

Dakota when the horse whinnied and lurched its head back. "Shhh, girl," Tarin said, "what's wrong?"

The horse's wild eyes stared into the sky. He held tightly to the lead line to steady the animal, then winced. The texture of the rope on the palm of his hand brought him back to his dream—to the nooses.

To the poor family about to be killed.

He clenched his eyes shut. "Why do I always run when I hear the music? Why don't I help them?"

Because you're a coward.

The inner voice that answered was not his own. It seemed to be made from the dream's familiar and haunting melody. He tried to think of something else, but the sound refused to relent. It joined with the voices of a battalion of what appeared to be medieval soldiers, always echoing the accusation as he fled an apparent battle. He was this battalion's leader, though he had no idea why. He appeared to be only eleven or twelve years old.

He focused on this detail and allowed its absurdity to bring him comfort. He knew the dream was just a manifestation of some trauma he must have experienced as a child, something he'd repressed. That's why he didn't remember anything from before he was twelve. It was the time after that that gave him pause. The voices and images reminded him of something he'd run from, something far more real than that battle. As he focused on that memory, the dreadful music quieted, but not the ache in his heart.

He managed to steady the horse and led it back out to pasture. As he let it go, a cold wind blew across his face, chilling him. The scent of the oncoming winter reminded him of the day he'd left Ohio on a similarly cold night years ago.

"Mom," he found himself whispering. He choked back tears. But there was nothing he could have done. It was too late. He just had to get out of there, away from the chaos, away from his father.

The wind blew faster, colder.

There was nothing I could have done.

The music was back. *Coward*, it sang.

A humming, like that of a transformer, buzzed somewhere in the distance. The horses whinnied, then started a frantic gallop across the field. Tarin searched for the source of the sound. He'd not heard anything like it before at the ranch. There were no power lines nearby, and the fence was wooden, not electric. Was it coming from the sky?

He looked up, and in the corner of his eye, he thought he saw something dart behind a cloud, something oblong and dark. A bird, perhaps? But that would have been a massive bird. He squinted, and the humming went away. The horses, too, stopped their charge and returned to looking for any lingering green grass in the otherwise brown fields.

Odd, he thought. He scanned the sky for another moment, shrugged, and headed back to the barn to start cleaning the stalls. Howard also wanted him to fix any broken fence railings before winter fully set in. There were many, so that would take the rest of the day. As he worked, he tried to force his mind from his dream and from Ohio, but both continued to taunt him. He decided that after work, he'd have to get some liquid help.

As the sun set, he approached Old Cotton's bar. It stood alongside the dimly lit main roadway in the small South Dakotan town of Philip, about one hour's drive east of Rapid City and even less from Badlands National Park. Tarin sat inside, idly listening to the conversation of three townsfolk whispering about the war in Europe as they smoked. He didn't care much about the war, at least not right now. He just cared about . . . forgetting. And hopefully getting a good night's sleep.

He brought his third beer in less than an hour to his lips and peered past his wiry arms at the two empty glasses on the table. If he drank too much more—and he intended to—it might get hard to walk straight. He was glad that his trailer was just outside town and that all of Philip was within walking distance, barely a mile in diameter—a tiny island within an ocean of prairie.

"Seeing a lot more bad news about the war," one of the smokers said. He was a grizzled man with a brown beard, and he took a long swallow of his beer after he spoke, as if he needed it even more, given the news.

Tarin continued to listen in. He doubted he'd hear anything new, but at least it was a distraction.

"Looking more likely the Alliance might use nukes to gain more territory," the man continued.

"Glad I finally got my bomb shelter finished," another man at the same table said. He blew some smoke out of his mouth. "Also got three months of food stocked away, just in case."

The first man laughed. "You think three months is enough! If the war spreads out of Europe, or even if just a few Alliance nukes land nearby, then it's going to take years before there's uncontaminated food again."

The second man puffed harder on his cigarette. "Well, it'll at least be enough for me and the family to hide out until the fallout isn't as bad. I don't want to start glowing or anything," he said with a nervous chuckle.

Tarin rubbed a hand through his hair and groaned. He hadn't come here to drink away worries about the war. But the men were right. Things seemed to be getting worse. Maybe that was at least one good thing about his dreams. They kept him distracted from the mess the rest of the world was in.

The door to the bar opened, pulling him from his ominous musings. A careworn woman entered. She appeared to be in her late forties. Blue nurse's scrubs hung from her slim build. She glanced briefly at Tarin, then sat at a barstool near the smokers. The bartender walked over.

"Haven't seen you here in a while, Samantha," he said. "What'll it be?"

"Need something a bit stronger than the usual," she said. Her voice sounded tired. "Abigail passed last night. I thought she still had a few more weeks. It took me a bit by surprise." She paused, staring down at her feet. "I really wanted more time to have a chance to say goodbye properly." She sighed and then looked back up at the bartender. "That's what you get when you allow yourself to become friends with hospice patients, I guess."

Abigail? Tarin didn't recall the name, which surprised him given the town's small size. He continued to eavesdrop, though he kept his eyes focused on his beer.

The bartender filled a glass and handed it to Samantha. "Sorry to hear that. I know she was pretty young. No family, from what I recall?"

Samantha took a sip of her beer. "Nope, no family nearby. She grew up Amish, then moved to Pittsburgh after leaving the community during her Rumspringa, you know, the time when Amish youth have a chance to try the real world. After tasting the big city, she decided she preferred the 'English' way. But after a couple of years, her life didn't go as she'd hoped. So she came here to try the small-town life again as a non-Amish." She smiled. "Said she hoped to find a nice man. She was a fan of those silly romance books—you know, the ones that are more like fairy tales than reality, where the city girl falls in love with the country guy, then they get married and live happily ever after. Nice kid, but so naive."

"Not a bad thing to have a dream, I suppose," the bartender said.

"Yeah," Samantha agreed, "but the dream didn't come true for her, just like most folks, myself included." She took a full sip of beer and then set her glass down. "I'm so sad for her. I wish things could have been different. But at least she didn't end up in a bad divorce like I did. The only positive I can see in passing so young is you're less likely to see your dreams die first."

Samantha's somber gaze moved toward Tarin. He'd barely noticed his eyes had drifted upward and now stared directly at her. A name entered his mind. *Chelsy.*

Samantha's face seemed to morph into that of a young woman, one he used to know—an old friend from Ohio, but maybe more than that . . . at least, to him. He felt a warmth behind his eyes and mumbled a curse. The alcohol was calming the anxiety about his dreams but at the cost of making him more susceptible to other feelings, those better left repressed.

"Don't let me bring you down, hun," Samantha said.

The image of Chelsy snapped away, replaced by Samantha's reflective expression. He felt his face grow hot.

"You look pretty young too," Samantha continued, "around Abigail's age. I've seen you here before, and the fact that you're here again and alone means you've probably already seen your share of hurt." She gulped down the rest of her drink. "Put that guy's last beer on my account," she said to the bartender before giving Tarin a warm smile.

Tarin felt more blood flow into his cheeks but managed to sputter, "That's . . . that's very kind of you. Thank you." He noticed smeared mascara beneath her eyes.

"Don't let life get you down too much," she added. "Some of us, by sheer luck, will have some dreams come true. You got time. Don't waste it like I did, and don't take it for granted either." With that, she grabbed her purse, chatted with the folks smoking in the corner for a few minutes, then left.

Samantha's words stung Tarin. Wasting time was all he did right now. His life was an endless iteration of working, drinking, and playing cards with his friends. But all of that was better than giving his mind space to dwell on other things.

"You going to want any more, or should I close out your tab?" the bartender asked.

"I'm done," Tarin said. It was time to go home and try to sleep while his anxiety was mostly muted.

The bartender tapped on a computer screen embedded in the counter. "Guess you only owe me for two of the three drinks."

Tarin nodded and reached for his wallet.

The bartender stopped tapping. "You don't want me to pull from your Lattice account?"

"I'm over quota for alcohol."

The bartender groaned and then mumbled, "The Lattice is going to put me out of business for *The Greater Good*." He sighed. "I guess you can pay under the table with cash—again."

Tarin took out some money and set it on the table. He prepared to get up when the door opened, and a man walked in.

All heads turned. The newcomer was dressed in a dark brown tunic and hood. He wore tall boots that came to his knees and covered medieval-style black pants. He was bearded, with dark brown hair, his face partially shrouded in his hood.

"Is this Old Cotton's?" he said.

Tarin's eyes narrowed and his chest tightened. That outfit . . . it reminded him a little of what those men in the battalion wore in his—

"Yeah, this is Old Cotton's," said the bartender. He looked the stranger up and down. "But it's not Halloween, in case you didn't know."

The men in the corner chuckled beneath their cloud of smoke, but Tarin could sense they also felt concerned. Visitors were generally getting more and more eccentric as the war dragged on, and occasionally, someone would wander into town and cause some trouble. But none of them had been dressed like this man.

"My apologies for the garb," the stranger said. "It is a complicated story that I will spare you for the moment. I was told someone by the name of Tarin was here. Do you know him?"

CHAPTER 2

Tarin squirmed in his seat. The bartender glanced at him, provided a knowing look, then returned his gaze to the newcomer. "And who's asking?"

Tarin considered making a hasty exit, but as he stared at the hooded stranger, he couldn't shake an odd feeling of familiarity. Tarin searched his memories but found nothing other than the familiar garb from the people in his dreams.

The man took off his hood and looked around the room. His rugged face held enough lines to place him in his early forties, though there were no visible greys in his hair or beard.

"I asked, who are you?" the bartender said again, this time his voice stern.

"I'm Tarin," Tarin suddenly answered, surprising himself. His voice came out shaky and with a slight squeak. What was he doing?

Letting the beer cloud my better judgments, he thought. *That's what I'm doing*. But it was too late now to pull back the words. The man was staring directly at him. Tarin leaned back in his chair and put his hands behind his head. Maybe that would make him look more confident after his weak introduction.

The bartender grunted and asked the stranger, "Do you want a drink?"

"Not at the moment," the man replied, "but thank you." He walked to Tarin's table. "May I sit?"

"Please," Tarin said. He studied the man while he kept his hands behind his head. Tarin cleared his throat. "So, who sent you to find me?"

The man sat down. "I was sent by your friends," the man said, "who I met earlier today while looking for you throughout this town."

"My friends wouldn't send a stranger looking for me without trusting you." He locked his gaze with the man, starting to feel more curious than nervous. "How did you earn their trust?"

"I know a lot about you," the man said. "You are right. They were somewhat taken aback by my request and my attire." He peered around the room at all the staring eyes, "as most people I have encountered have been. But once I shared with them what I knew, it was impossible for them to doubt that I know you."

"How on earth could you know me? I've never met you in my life."

"That is partially true."

What did that mean? The man was starting to sound crazy. Tarin stood and gestured toward the door. "Okay, this has been a fun conversation, but unless you want to start making sense and tell me a little bit more about yourself, I'm done here."

The man also stood and reached out his hand in a reassuring gesture. "I would be happy to share more, but you must understand it is a complicated matter. Before I can explain fully, I will need to show you some things you may find odd. And after that, I will be able to tell more. Please, can we sit again?"

For a few moments, Tarin didn't move. But finally, he let his shoulders relax and sat back down. "Okay, give me the details."

"Your friends said once I found you that I could accompany you to their house, not far from here, as I understand. They said you could call them to prove my story." He handed Tarin a piece of paper. "They gave me this number. You can call it, and they will tell you something they shared with me that I can verify."

"And why wouldn't they have just called me to let me know you were coming?"

The man leaned forward. "One of your friends—Allen, if I recall— was concerned you may not be willing to meet with me if they contacted you first. He seemed to be quite interested in my connection to you."

Tarin wondered why Allen, his best friend, would be so interested in this meeting taking place. Of course, this man could still be lying, but then how would he know Allen's name?

His curiosity got the best of him. "Fine," he said. "I'll give them a call."

He dialed the number. The faint sound of ringing, barely audible above the background noises of the bar, gave way to a quiet voice on the other end. "It's Tarin." He looked up at the man. "I'm at Old Cotton's with someone from out of town who says he knows me. He also said he talked to you all earlier and that you guys told him I should head over to your house with him. He said you could tell me something to prove you talked to him." Tarin listened and fixed his eyes on the man in front of him. "Okay, thanks." Tarin hung up and shook his head. "Okay, what's the password you all agreed on?"

The man replied, "Bostt, legendary creature, immune to viruses, yet with an insatiable appetite." He smiled. "I was told it was from the game you played with them, Legendarium of Beasts, and that it was a powerful card."

Tarin crossed his arms. Although he still felt tipsy from the drinks, he was now convinced that the man was telling the truth, or at worst, a harmless nerd looking to find others who enjoyed the game of Legendarium of Beasts, which was not easy in such a small, agricultural town. Perhaps that's why Allen was so eager for this meeting.

"Okay, I'll go with you to Allen's." He double-checked that he'd left enough cash when a holographic projection emerged from the screen embedded in the counter near the bartender. The bartender stood next to it, watching what appeared to be a female news reporter, standing two feet tall above the counter, staring forward as if into a camera. Eyes previously still fixed on the mysterious newcomer moved to focus on her.

The reporter wore body armor and a military helmet. She stood in front of what looked like a European town in ruins. She began reporting on evacuation plans and what steps people living near the most likely target zones around the center of the conflict should take.

By now, Tarin had grown used to such reports and mostly numb to the idea that neither the small sanctuary he'd discovered in Philip, South Dakota, nor his old hometown in northeast Ohio would be safe if an all-out nuclear war erupted. However, the thought of a mushroom cloud over the latter bothered him less than he'd like to admit.

"Turn it off!" the smoker with the brown beard yelled. "I don't want to see any more about the war tonight. We all know it's getting worse. All we can do now is get ready for what's next."

"Sorry," the bartender said. "I thought you'd all want the latest update." He tapped on the screen and turned off the projection.

"Interesting," the man in front of Tarin said. "It appears your world is on the precipice of war." He looked down at the table and whispered, "Could he potentially be involved in this?"

Tarin tilted his head and said, "You know someone who's involved in the tensions in Europe?"

The man looked up and said quickly, "Perhaps." He smiled. "But the rumblings of war from a faraway land are not my primary concern at the moment."

Tarin raised his eyebrows. "Faraway land? You're being a bit theatrical, don't you think? Or is this part of your whole medieval persona or whatever this is?" he said, motioning to the man's outfit.

"I do not know what this *medieval persona* is you speak of," the man said. "But it is of no matter. Right now, it is you and your friends who I am most concerned about. When can we depart to make council?"

Tarin sighed. "Fine, you're one of those folks who takes their role-playing very seriously, I see. It's another reason why my friends probably didn't take long to trust you. They're into cosplay too. Anyway, I'm ready to leave for Allen's house now."

"Wonderful!" the man said. "Then let us be off."

Wary stares followed them as Tarin and the man stepped out of the bar and into the brisk night.

"Could you at least tell me your name?" Tarin asked as they left the dimly lit windows of Old Cotton's and headed toward the outskirts of Philip beneath the glow of scattered streetlights.

"You may call me Gil."

I was expecting something a bit more exotic, Tarin thought, but at least Gil was easy enough to remember.

They headed east, passed by the town grocery store, and soon were under the few trees lining Pine Street in a residential neighborhood. Not many in Philip went out in November past nine o'clock, and it was now ten. The two men moved silently through the darkness, the muffled thumping of their footfalls against the concrete the most notable sound in the darkness.

"How long have you been in town?" Tarin asked Gil.

"I only just arrived," Gil said. "I have traveled here from a place called Utah, a twenty-day journey."

Tarin stopped. "Utah is at most a two-day drive. Are you saying it took you twenty days to get here? What did you do, hike?"

Gil nodded. "Primarily—how else would I have gotten here?"

"By car or plane."

"I am not yet familiar with all the forms of travel in this place. I found a horse at one point, but it was only useful for a short while over some flatlands."

Tarin held out his hand. "Now look, I told you I was okay playing along with your whole cosplay act, but I'm not an idiot. There's no way you walked here or rode a horse. You must have hitched a ride or something."

Before he could continue, Tarin noticed a figure ahead of them. An old man in a tattered overcoat and a wide-brimmed hat stood on the corner of the street. On closer inspection, Tarin recognized him and grimaced. "Hold up," he said to Gil. "That's Old Bill. He's one of the town crazies. Don't interact with him or we'll never get away."

"You mean he will try to slay us?" said Gil. "Is he very powerful?"

"Come on, Gil, seriously? I mean that he'll talk our ear off about one of his stupid conspiracies. He believes in a lot of weird stuff." He tapped Gil on his chest. "So don't interact."

Tarin and Gil continued walking down the sidewalk toward Bill. His eyes were fixed on something in the sky above him. He seemed on edge, fidgeting and running his hand through his long grey beard.

As they approached him, Gil said, "Is everything all right?"

Tarin slapped his shoulder, but Gil took no heed.

Bill just kept staring up into the sky with a nervous expression on his face.

"You seem afraid," Gil said. "Is there anything we can do to help?"

Bill finally spoke in a trembling voice: "Did you see that? There was something strange up there about ten minutes ago . . ."

Gil looked up to where Bill was pointing. Tarin followed his gaze. Nothing was there but a starlit expanse.

"What did you see?" Gil asked. Tarin saw real concern on his face and rolled his eyes.

"Well, boy, you're going to call me crazy, but I swear I just saw a UFO."

"What do you mean by UFO?"

"Well, it was something in the sky that wasn't a plane, and it wasn't a bird, and I swear it wasn't a cloud. It was something I couldn't explain." Bill turned to Tarin. "Have you or your friends seen anything recently? I know at least Josh and Rob say they sometimes see strange things in these parts and have lots of stories from their Lakota upbringing."

Tarin thought briefly about the humming he'd heard back at the ranch earlier that day and the object he saw dart away in the sky. But he doubted it was anything unusual.

"Sorry, Bill," Tarin said. "I haven't seen any UFO, and Josh and Rob haven't mentioned anything to me about seeing one either." Bill was right, though: they both were very intrigued by anything paranormal, particularly Rob.

14

"Please describe this thing in the sky to me," Gil interrupted, with urgency in his voice.

Bill stood silently for another moment, then looked back up into the darkness. "I'd come out for my evening stroll when I noticed it. At first, I thought it might have just been a big satellite. But satellites move and look like stars. This was hovering and cigar-shaped . . . definitely not something you'd see in the sky on an ordinary night, or any night." He rubbed his beard. "I felt like I was frozen in time. It was strange—like I was unable to move. I also felt like some mysterious force was calling to me, taunting me in some way. Made me feel both drawn in and horrified at the same time." He pointed west. "Then it shot like a bullet over the horizon."

Tarin couldn't help but follow Bill's gaze. As much as he'd wanted to avoid Bill, there was something different in his voice now from when he usually told stories, often at Old Cotton's, about aliens, secret government programs, and other conspiracies. Tonight, did Bill actually see something?

No, this was ridiculous. The alcohol was clouding his good senses. He wouldn't allow himself to get sucked into this. "Well, Bill," he said as he took Gil by the shoulder and pulled him along. "Hope you don't see anything else too crazy tonight. But we need to get going."

Bill raised a thick grey brow at Tarin. "I know you're a skeptic, but keep a lookout. I'm telling you: that thing I saw, I think it's bad news."

"I'll be careful," Tarin said. He turned to Gil. "Ready to go?"

Gil looked at Bill, then back into the sky. "Yes."

A few moments later, and out of earshot of Bill, Gil said, "I sense you did not believe that man's story. Why?"

Tarin sighed. "Because he's a bit of a fanatic. I think he probably does believe he saw something, but he's always been so caught up in conspiracies that I'm worried he's beginning to lose sense of reality. And it's only been getting worse since the war started a few years back and got him even more worked up. Though, in fairness, it's got lots of people worked up."

"But not you?"

Tarin closed his eyes. In his mind, he heard angry shouts directed at him as he stood catatonic next to about a hundred soldiers armed with swords and bows. That eerie music was playing, telling him he was weak, urging him to run. Tarin shook his head, and the vision passed. "I have other things distracting me from the war," he said. He noticed an odor and sniffed. "Have you been working in a horse barn? You smell like I do after I've been cleaning stalls all day. How long has it been since you've showered . . . or bathed?"

"I have not bathed for days. I have been on a relatively long journey. I had to make haste to find you and another, both of whom I observed lived in this area after I first arrived in Utah."

"There's another person you know from here?" Tarin said.

"I did not know her," Gil answered. "But I came to be aware she was someone of apparent importance, as are you."

"If you say so," Tarin said. "Maybe you can tell me more about that when we get to Allen's. More importantly, I'm sure he'll let you use his shower." He sniffed again and grimaced. "And wash your clothes."

"I would not refuse this offer if Allen agrees. My travels have wearied me, and washing off the dust of the last many days would be quite pleasant."

"Oh, he'll oblige. Trust me. He's somewhat obsessive about cleanliness."

They walked down the sleepy street with no more distraction and finally made it to Allen's small, white, ranch-style two-bedroom home near the eastern edge of town. It was quaint, as were most of the houses in Philip, and its porch light cast an inviting glow, a welcome sight after the odd encounter with Bill. The house was nestled between two decorative bushes twice as tall as the house, both in need of a trim, and the front yard also needed tending. Although Allen liked things clean, it only applied to inside his house.

Tarin and Gil stepped up onto the small porch leading to the front door. The living room window glowed with a soft yellow light from behind a set of closed blinds, and they could hear the faint sound of laughter within. Tarin knocked, and a moment later, a tall, gangly man opened the door. He appeared to be in his late twenties, with dark, shoulder-length hair and the beginnings of a beard.

"Gil!" he said. "So happy you've come!" He looked at Tarin with excitement in his eyes. "And you've managed to convince Tarin that you know him." He turned and yelled into the living room, "Guys! Gil and Tarin are here!"

Two other men, both a bit younger than Allen, jumped up from a couch behind a card table and shouted, "You came!" They hurried over and stood behind Allen.

"I honestly didn't think you'd agree to come over with Gil!" the shorter and stockier of the two said, his eyes beaming at Tarin through round glasses.

"Well, Rob," Tarin said, "I guess it's your lucky day."

"Come on in," the other man, this one with a tight black pony tail, said hastily as he nudged past Allen and ushered both Tarin and Gil into the house.

Rob rubbed both his hands on his own much shorter black hair and said, "No, no, no, Josh." He pointed to the couch. "Gil should have the seat of honor!"

"Ah, you're right, pardon my manners. Please take the couch, Gil."

Tarin and Gil sat on the couch, and Tarin whispered to Gil, "I see you've already made a good impression with them."

"They rather liked my outfit," Gil said, then turned to Allen as he closed the front door. "I was told you might have a washroom of some sort I could use to clean up a bit from my travels. If that is so, I would be very obliged if you would let me make use of it, and even more so if you had some clean clothes I could borrow just until mine could be brushed and aired out."

Allen opened his arms in a welcoming gesture. "Absolutely! Follow me and I'll get you situated."

"That would be quite appreciated," Gil said. He followed Allen down a hall toward the bathroom.

Josh and Rob sat across from the couch, grinning ear to ear, clearly thrilled by how seriously Gil seemed to be taking on the caricature of a medieval traveler.

Tarin fingered through the cards lying on the table. After a few moments, he heard water running in the bathroom as the shower came on. Allen came back into the living room. "Weird," Allen said. "I had to show Gil how to use the shower."

The smell of recently brewed coffee replaced Gil's smell of a horse stall as all eyes turned to Tarin. "Weird is an understatement for that man," Tarin said. "I still haven't completely decided if it was a good idea for me to bring him here. But so far, he seems harmless."

"So far," Josh said with a smirk.

"Do you think he could be dangerous?" Rob asked. The wide grin on his face had been replaced with a tight frown.

Allen took a seat next to Tarin. "He'd probably have killed one of us by now if he was dangerous. But I assumed you all might be worried, so just to be safe, I checked his clothes after he tossed them out of the bathroom to be cleaned, and there's nothing in there, no knife or gun or anything else dangerous."

"What if he kept his weapons in the bathroom with him?" Josh asked, eyeing Rob with a grin.

"Stop trying to scare your brother!" Allen said. "We all agreed he seemed safe when he told us what he did about Tarin. And since Tarin seems to trust him too, I don't think there's anything to worry about."

"I just didn't think it through much until now," Rob said. "Should we really be letting a stranger in the house like this, as cool as he seems? What if he's actually a Mistai or Skinwalker?"

"Calm down," Josh said, patting Rob's shoulder. "I was teasing you earlier. It'll be fine." He turned to Tarin. "Has he told you what he told us yet . . . about what he knew about you?"

"He hasn't," Tarin said. "But he was convincing enough that I wanted to learn more." He looked down the hall where the sound of the shower continued, then back at his friends. "So—what did he know about me?"

The group silently looked at each other until Allen finally said, "Tarin, he knew about your dreams."

CHAPTER 3

Tarin's mouth gaped open. "He knew about my dreams? The only way he'd know about those is if you all told him! I told you not to tell anyone about those. If people found out, they'd think I'm crazy!"

Allen held out his hands. "I swear, we didn't tell him anything about your dreams . . . or anything else he told us about you that we've only discussed here in our little group."

"What do you mean? He knew more?"

Allen wrung his hands together. "Tarin. He knew about your past—about Ohio. He even knew about your father—and your mother."

Tarin's face grew flushed. The room was silent. Then everyone realized the water in the shower had stopped running.

Gil walked into the room, his dark brown, shoulder-length hair still damp. He looked very different outside of his medieval-style tunic and breeches. In fact, he looked like he'd fit in fine with the group, all of whom were wearing old hoodies or T-shirts with baggy sweatpants, except for Tarin, who wore jeans.

"I have never experienced such a remarkable contraption as that hanging water dispenser," Gil said with a smile. He gave a small bow. "Thank you for your hospitality. I cannot tell you how much better I feel after that wonderful experience." He pointed to the couch. "May I?" he said, motioning to the gap between Tarin and Allen.

Tarin rubbed his temples and feigned a smile. He didn't have much choice at the moment but to oblige without creating a scene. He scooched over a little farther from Allen and patted the empty space. "Sure thing, Gil."

Gil sat down and admired the cards on the table in front of him. "So this must be the game of Legendary Beasts you speak of."

"It's actually called Legendarium of Beasts, or LOB," Rob corrected, with a very serious expression on his face.

Gil carefully fingered some of the cards that were strewn across the table. "Please tell me more about it." He stopped at one particular card: a great bearlike monster with mouth agape in a fearsome snarl and batlike wings spread open in flight.

Rob's eyes twinkled behind his glasses. "Well, as I'm sure you can see, it's a card game. Each card is either a noun or a verb. Nouns are things like a beast, virus, food, or shelter. Verbs are things like types of attack or defense. Your job is to choose three beast cards, then stack a deck with thirty other noun or verb cards. There are chips in the cards, so when, say, a virus with particular attributes is played against an opponent's beast, it will gradually hurt that beast and decrease its stats." He pointed at a card with the bearlike creature. "See those numbers on the top of that card?"

Gil nodded.

Rob dropped a card next to it and said, "I'm going to attack it." One of the numbers near the top of the bear card dropped by three.

"Amazing," Gil said. "That number changed before my very eyes. Are these cards governed by some sort of magic?"

Rob shook his head, his smile widening. "I wish. It's just cheap tech. But it's way better than having to track stats manually like with pen and paper."

Josh dropped a card with what looked like a kettle of stew next to the bear card. A number on the bear card ticked up, while a number on the food card dropped. "Here you go, fella," Josh said. "Feel better."

"How does one win?" Gil asked.

"See that blank card in the middle of the table?" Rob said.

"Yes."

"Once all players have dropped their final card, it uses some heuristics to reveal which beast would have come out on top given all the cards on the table. If that beast is yours, you win. Things like the remaining strength of a virus card, the heartiness of a food card, or the strength of a shelter all play into the final result. Because the conclusion is based on probabilities with some random chaos thrown into the calculation, a tad of the game is based on luck. But there are ways to maximize your beasts' chances once you get really good because the order you play cards and how fast you play them is very important."

"Fascinating," Gil said. "We play games of cards where I come from as well, yet none with these capabilities." He picked up the card with the bearlike monster on it. "Is this the Bostt you told me about earlier? We have these where I come from too, though, thankfully, sightings are rare."

The full group stared at Gil with confused expressions for what seemed like many minutes. Finally, Tarin broke the silence. "Okay, Gil, let's stop this charade of yours." He narrowed his eyes. "My friend told me more about the stuff you know about me. How did you know all of that? And how do you know me? Because I still don't remember ever seeing or meeting you before."

Gil continued to study the Bostt card, then set it down. His hair had dried tangled, and his new attire looked sloppy and foolish as Allen's clothes were tight on him. He'd not put his socks on correctly, and the ends hung loosely from his feet. After a few long moments, Gil said, "I will show you," and reached down toward his left side near his waist, where the long t-shirt hung over the sweatpants.

Rob jolted and jumped out of his seat. "Oh no! He did bring a gun!" He toppled backward, tripped over his chair, and scrambled to the door.

Undeterred, Gil pulled out a round glass phial. "Please do not be afraid," he said, and set it on the table. He held out his hands. "It will not hurt you."

"Rob, you idiot!" Josh yelled. "Settle down! You nearly gave us all heart attacks!" He got up and helped his brother to his feet and back into his chair, though Rob kept a wary eye on both Gil and the object.

"I'm sorry about that," Josh said. "Rob's a bit neurotic."

Gil smiled at Rob like one might to a nervous child. "Please forgive me for startling you. It was not my intent."

Panting, Rob said, "It's okay . . . just glad, you know . . . that . . . that . . ."

"That I'm not here to hurt you?" Gil said. "I can imagine how you feel about my presence, and I can only hope, in time, I will gain your trust." He gestured to the phial. "But this might help with that." He looked around at the group. "May I show you?"

"Please," said Tarin, noticing his frustration turn to intrigue as he studied the smooth glass object.

"Would it be possible to darken the room?"

Rob stiffened and looked at the others. Josh rolled his eyes, got up, turned off the two lamps lighting the living room, and sat back down. All that now lit the room was the ambient glow from the front porch light beyond the window blinds.

The phial began to glimmer, at first barely noticeable, then brighter, until its brightness grew stronger than the light from the porch.

"What is that thing?" Rob asked slowly, mesmerized by its soft glow, as was everyone else in the room, save Gil.

The object continued to glow with a gentle, ethereal radiance that illuminated its surroundings like an otherworldly candle. Its light emanated from an apparent void, not a liquid or some other substance, and it seemed to cast waves of mystical energy outward, almost like a warmth, though there was no heat.

Tarin felt drawn to it, desiring it with a fervor he'd never known while also feeling the urge to run away, an urge he knew all too well. Rob was sweating. Josh quaked. Allen seemed spellbound.

"You have asked me how I know of your life here on this earth," Gil said to Tarin. "It is through this. It became a window for me from my world to yours after a battle . . . from which you disappeared."

"I told you he knew about your dreams," Allen whispered.

Tarin remained motionless, barely noticing Allen's comment. Was Gil insinuating that his dreams were . . . more than dreams? He felt bile rise in his throat. That wasn't possible. This was crazy.

Gil continued. "I saw how you were cast forth upon the top of a tower, still only a boy, to awaken here with no memories of the world you came from."

World I came from? This was getting even weirder, but the phial held his attention so much so that he felt no urge to argue. Also, Gil was right. Tarin didn't have any memories from before he was twelve. But that was just a medical disorder. Right?

The light grew brighter, glistening on Gil's stoic face. He continued speaking. "I saw you as you awoke within a circle of rocks and were found by a stranger. I watched when you were brought to be cared for at a place for youth with no homes and also when you found a new home."

The phial continued to draw Tarin's eyes deeper into it. The light inside began to swirl and dance to form a sort of shining mist. He saw two figures forming within this fog, slowly at first but then faster as the light embraced them, almost as if molding them into being. He leaned in closer until their now nearly formed faces turned to him with know-ing eyes.

Tarin's heart lurched as he recognized the man and the woman peering at him through the phial. "Stop it!" he shouted. He jumped forward and knocked the object off the table. It flew across the room until it hit the hardwood floor with a thud. It spun around a few times, making shadows of furniture dance along the walls. Finally, it rolled to a stop by the front door. It flickered, then dimmed to a gentle glow.

Tarin hastily turned on all the lights in the living room, nearly knocking Rob over in the process. He went to the front door, struggled to open it as his hands shook, and ran outside after pulling the door closed behind him.

"Tarin!" Allen yelled from behind the door, but Tarin ignored him. He sat on the last stair of the porch and brushed aside an angry tear, his heart still beating fast from the encounter with those figures inside the phial.

What was that light? And how could it and Gil know so much about him? There was no way it was a hologram, unless it was some very new tech he'd never seen before that could pull memories from those around it. Maybe he'd drank too much. Yes, that was it—he drank too fast and too much at the bar. He just needed to get a good night's sleep, and tomorrow, everything would be back to normal.

A moment later, Allen came outside. Slowly, he approached Tarin before placing his hand on his quaking shoulder. "You okay, buddy?"

Tarin continued to shake. "No, Allen! I'm not okay! I thought this was just some game that would end with Gil telling me he was a friend of someone I used to work with back in Ohio and that you all had somehow gotten excited and accidentally given him some information about my dreams. But I didn't expect him to be able to show me exact images of my mom and dad in some magical glass jar!"

"We didn't tell him anything," Allen said. "I swear."

"Well, I believe you now," Tarin said. "Unless you slipped me some sort of hallucinogen, and you and Gil are pulling some weird prank on me."

"Tarin!" Allen said. "This is real! I didn't believe him at first. But when he told us about the battle and the tower—just like in your dreams—and about your parents and your life in Ohio . . . well, I didn't know what else to think, other than maybe he was somehow the key to help you with your past. I've never known how to actually help you. I've always wanted to—so badly. But I don't know how!"

"I'm fine, Allen! I don't need help!"

"You're lying to yourself! I know you want to be able to live again after what happened to your mom and what your dad did to her—and to you. And what about Chelsy?"

"Don't say her name!"

Allen took a step back. "I'm . . . I'm sorry. I—you have no idea how much I just want you to be happy again."

"What do you mean? When have I ever been happy?"

Allen didn't respond.

Tarin clenched his fists, took in a deep breath, and let it out as a slow sigh. "I get what you were trying to do when you sent Gil to look for me. But Allen, you can't help me." He pointed at the house. "And Gil can't help me either." His voice cracked. "That phial, it's bringing it all back." He stared deeply at Allen. "I don't want it back. I don't want any of it to be real—the dream, what happened in Ohio, none of it!"

Before Allen could respond, the front door opened again, and Josh and Rob came out and each took a seat next to Tarin. Allen stepped back to give them room.

"We gave Gil some coffee," Rob said, "and he seems to really like it. He's not mad about you knocking his magical light across the room. Thankfully it didn't break. Who knows what would have happened if it had! I still can hardly believe this is all really happening. But Gil does feel terrible that he upset you so much. He'd like to talk to you again when you're ready."

"I'm going to need a minute," Tarin said, taking a few more slow deep breaths. He noticed the tension in his body begin to ease.

"We're here for you, buddy," Josh said, patting his shoulder. "Sorry, this got out of hand. I swear we thought he was just going to tell you what he told us. We were so amazed by what he knew. But that shining glass . . . we weren't expecting that."

"Wasn't it amazing?" Rob blurted. "I mean . . . it was like something from LOB, but it's real. We got to see a real-life magical artifact in our own house! And oh . . . you know what this means, don't you?"

"What does it mean?" Josh asked, sounding annoyed.

"It means that Gil must be a wizard! You know, like from a book or movie or something. Maybe he's Gandalf. He did say he's from another world."

"Gandalf's not real," Josh said, rolling his eyes.

"Do we really know what's real and what's not anymore?" Tarin asked.

The group didn't respond. But their presence was bringing his heart rate down. Ever since he'd come looking for Allen on his way west to escape the pain and heartache in Ohio, these guys had become the family he'd never had and the support structure he needed. As they sat on the porch together, silently, looking up at the vastness of the South Dakotan sky, he felt gratitude for this brief moment of calm in the turbulent emotional sea that Gil and the light had brought back up to the surface. Later, he'd have to apologize to Allen for his outburst.

"I think I'm ready to head back in," Tarin said. "Let's offer to get Gil a hotel or something. I don't really want to hear any more of what he has to say."

"But . . ." Rob stuttered.

Josh elbowed him, and Rob said, "Ok, ok, I get it. Yep, that's fine. After all, we probably don't want to ask a stranger to spend the night." But he didn't sound convinced.

Tarin prepared to stand but stopped midway. A hum was reverberating through the air just past the neighbor's rooftop—a familiar hum. He looked at the sky, but all he could see was an empty, star-filled expanse.

Allen pointed toward the south. "What's that?"

Tarin followed his finger and squinted. A cigar-shaped object was gliding above the trees on the other side of the street. Its smooth, elongated structure, about the size of a semitruck trailer, reflected the starlight off its ebony exterior. It gave off a ghostly glow, and the humming grew louder. *Coward.* Tarin grimaced as the pain of the accusation from his dreams now seemed to emanate from the craft.

It turned and began to approach Allen's house. Tarin's mind raced as he recalled Bill's earlier story about a UFO. He also remembered his experience back at the ranch—the humming, the object that had darted away. As much as he didn't want to believe, he couldn't deny what he was seeing—and feeling.

Allen gagged and held his stomach. "I don't feel good," he said.

Tarin backed up a step and then looked at the others. "We need to get inside—now."

Josh and Rob seemed transfixed as they continued to stare at the approaching craft.

The humming amplified. "Now!" Tarin reiterated.

"Got it," Josh said, as if he'd just been woken up. He tugged at Rob and pulled him toward the front door. Tarin and Allen followed. As Tarin shut the door behind them, Gil jumped up from the couch, nearly spilling a mug full of coffee.

"What is wrong?" he said.

"There's something out there," Tarin said, his voice quaking.

"It's a UFO!" Rob yelled. "And it's right across the street, maybe a hundred or so feet above the neighbor's house!"

Allen collapsed onto the floor near the front door. He held his stomach. Tarin knelt next to him. Allen's face was ashen.

"I feel so sick," Allen said. "There's something very bad about that thing." The strange humming grew louder. Allen squinted his eyes. "What's going on?" he whispered.

"I . . . I don't know," Tarin said. He placed his own hand over Allen's. At the same time, the melody from his dreams began to play in his mind. He thought of the nooses and of the crowds screaming in the background. What was happening? Why was the humming triggering those thoughts?

"Stay here," Gil told the group. He reached for his side. "I can feel some sort of evil." He pulled out the phial and whispered something. The object's radiance burst forth. It lit up the room with the intensity of the midday sun. Tarin closed his eyes as Gil rushed outside. The door slammed behind him.

○ ○ ◇ ○ ○

Gil jumped from the porch and onto Allen's front lawn. A burst of sound, like the drone of a million wasps, knocked him to the ground. He held his ears and screamed in pain. It was a sound he'd heard before when he'd first arrived on Earth weeks ago and again when he'd found a little white house not far from here.

Gil pushed himself to his feet and held his phial into the air, focusing on the dark object looming just above. "*Edin Na Zu, Utuk Xul!*" An arrow of white light exploded from the phial and struck the craft. It paused its descent and emitted another hum, almost like a cry of pain.

In his mind, he saw the woman inside that little white house. She'd been lying on a bed—dying. He recalled her pain, her sadness. It had moved him. But then—the shadows had come.

The craft restarted its descent and erupted with another powerful drone, again knocking Gil to the ground. It began lowering toward Allen's roof. Gil studied the house and saw the bushes. He ran to one and, using it and a nearby drain pipe, managed to climb onto the roof.

As his feet touched the metal slab at the top, he again saw the woman. Her soul was struggling against the shadows. He grimaced. They were trying to take her away.

The craft continued to drop closer. Gil could now easily see its smooth and leathery exterior, more like skin than metal. He felt a heat radiating from its surface. The light in his phial grew brighter. He sensed his foe's excitement even as he could feel the fear of Tarin and his friends somewhere below him. The object seemed to be feeding off their energy, radiating more heat while also pushing a strange dark energy Gil perceived as a painful despair.

Gil prepared to send another burst of light into the sky when he heard a voice—ominous and evil. It flowed through the heavens as if the sky itself was speaking.

"*Ina Etuti Asbu,*" it hissed. Gil's stomach churned. He'd heard it before, just as the woman had died.

He held his phial tighter and whispered something into it. The unease subsided, though the object was now close enough that he could almost touch it. He was nearly out of time. He raised his phial, and directed it toward his enemy. One last time he thought of the woman. The shadows were pulling her soul toward an ominous tear in the sky.

Tarin heard a muffled shout. A brilliant flash of light flooded through the still-closed blinds and into the room as if it were noon outside. The humming stopped.

Tarin felt Allen's hand release its tension. "My nausea's gone," Allen whispered. At the same time, Tarin watched the terrible images from his dream retreat.

He helped pull Allen to his feet. Footsteps clanked overhead, followed by the sound of scuffling toward the corner of the house. The front door opened. Gil stood framed in the doorway. He was sweating in Allen's old t-shirt and sweatpants, his hair as disheveled and wet as when he'd first gotten out of the shower.

"Water," he whispered. He stumbled onto the couch and collapsed on it. There was no sign of his phial. Tarin assumed he must have returned it to the waistband under his shirt.

Without a word, Josh ran into the kitchen, filled a glass with water, and handed it to Gil. He drank it greedily. Meanwhile, Tarin and Allen sat next to Gil on the couch and looked at him in wonderment. Josh and Rob took seats by the card table. They all waited a moment until Rob finally said, "Did you win?"

Gil managed a laugh. "Indeed, my friend, though not without difficulty." He finished his water, then set the glass down in front of him near the card of the Bostt. "Thankfully, it had a great aversion to the power of the light from my world. I was able to, perhaps similarly to your game, drain much of its life force."

Rob smiled so wide Tarin feared his face might rip in half. Tarin wished he felt as happy. He was thinking about how he had thrown the light that seemed to have just saved them across the floor—if he'd broken it, well, he wasn't sure what would have happened since Gil apparently used it against that UFO.

Gil's expression grew thoughtful and sad as he looked at him. Through labored breaths, Gil said, "I am sorry about earlier. I know it was extremely painful what happened to you, both what your dreams show you and what happened with your parents." He paused. "And I am sorry that I was not able to intervene directly. But I can tell you, the dark power you saw manifest tonight via that object in the sky is connected to all that now haunts you."

Tarin met Gil's eyes. Who was this man? And, was there some truth to what he was saying? Only hours before, he would have found all of this completely crazy. But now, after seeing the phial and the UFO, his whole worldview felt less certain. And he could no longer blame the alcohol.

Gil picked up a card that depicted a knight approaching a dilapidated stone tower next to a body of water.

"'Mizran's Tower,'" Rob whispered as he gazed at the card.

"Tarin," Gil said, "if you would permit me, I would like to share more about how I know you and of your life, both here—and elsewhere."

Tarin's friends all turned to him at once. He looked at them individually, absorbing their pleading expressions. Finally, he turned back to Gil. "Go ahead," he said. "I'm ready."

CHAPTER 4

Gil took a deep breath and leaned forward, still holding the card. "You do not remember me, but long ago, I was once very close to you—a mentor, you might say. Just after your eleventh birthday, I was forced to go on a journey. When I returned a year later, I found you had disappeared. I then spent endless days and nights exploring the light with the intent to find you, to return you home, where you belonged— and where you were greatly needed. In this exploration, I saw you had retreated from a battle and discovered a tower." He tapped the card. "After that, you were not seen again."

Tarin's face grew hot with emotion. He had no recollection of anything before he was twelve. And now Gil was telling him that he knew him during those invisible years? His mind swirled with confusion. He needed to try to ground himself. Maybe what Gil was saying was still just fantasy. His eyes darted over the card table. They fell onto a particular card. He picked it up.

"If that light really showed you my dreams, then you'd have known the tower I see is way taller than the one you're holding." He showed everyone his card, one called "Tower of the Door." "It looked more like this."

On the card was a tall white tower with sharp edges, shaped like an elongated cube. It appeared to be constructed of solid stone and metal. Its top was hidden from view but cast multiple beams of light onto the ground, one of which seemed to be blinding a passerby.

"Excellent find, Tarin. You are right. That is a much better depiction."

Tarin cursed and tossed the card back on the table. "What does any of this matter? These are all just dreams . . . they don't mean anything. And there's no way you used to know me."

Gil stared at him, his eyes kind but stern. "Tarin, I believe you have always known that this world is not your home and that your dreams are not just dreams."

"If they aren't dreams, then what are they?" Tarin asked, his voice tense.

"They are memories, Tarin."

"Hold on, hold on," Josh interjected. "What are you suggesting, Gil? If Tarin's dreams are actually memories, that means he *was* actually in some sort of medieval battle. And that would mean he's like . . . he's like a time traveler or something." He groaned. "I can't believe I'm even saying that, but I did just see a real UFO. Still, this is all getting really weird really fast." He looked around at the others. "This is all pretty crazy, right? Are you all finding this hard to accept?"

"You know what I'm having trouble accepting?" Rob added, looking at Gil. "How you got onto the roof of the house without a ladder."

Josh threw his hands in the air. "*That's* what you're interested in? Are you serious?"

Gil set down the card of Mizran's Tower and said, "I had to climb up using one of the bushes next to your house. It was not as easy as I had hoped, but I had to get into a higher position to cast away the dark craft before it positioned itself for an assault." He looked around the room. "Do any of you happen to know where my . . . what did you call it . . . coffee has gone?"

Tarin instinctually took the mug that was now next to him on the armrest of the couch and handed it to Gil, even as he was furiously processing what Gil was saying.

"This gives me strange energy," Gil said. He turned to Josh. "I understand why you are disheartened and confused. Much happened tonight that is very contrary to what you are accustomed to. I will share more, but may I drink for a moment first? I am still winded from my battle."

"Go ahead." Josh sighed. "Maybe I'll grab a quick shower while you finish—and pop a few extra anxiety meds. It might help me calm down a bit."

"Good idea," Allen agreed, "and I'll get a fresh batch of coffee brewing in case we need more later." He went to the kitchen.

Rob followed and said, "Is any of that leftover pizza still in the fridge?"

Tarin and Gil were left alone. Gil looked around, then whispered to Tarin, "You and your friends are in great danger."

"Danger?" Tarin asked, barely managing to avoid yelling the question. "So not only are my dreams apparently real, there's danger involved?"

"When I came to this world weeks ago from the tower, after finally breaking a seal at its top that had blocked the door to this world for many years, I awoke near a lake set between mesas and an arid landscape."

"You keep mentioning some other world. What do you mean by that?"

"I mean exactly that. You and I are not from this earth. We are from another world. Most in the region you come from call it Arvalast."

Tarin rubbed his hand over his face and moaned, "Do they now?"

Gil's brows lowered. "Do you wish me to continue?" he asked.

Tarin whispered a curse. "Go ahead, I suppose."

"Very well," Gil said. "After I broke through the seal, a malevolent force greeted me, one I now presume was behind the seal. It confronted me, and I quickly discovered terrible events to harm you were in motion and had been for many years."

Tarin's mind began to swim. "Malevolent force? What? Why would anyone be after me? I'm . . . I'm nobody," he stuttered.

Gil's voice grew stern. "Do you still not believe what I have told you or what your dreams have shown you? You are not of this world. You are of *my* world. And all from my world bring entities of darkness great power."

"Entities of darkness? What are you even talking about?"

"I understand you have forgotten about such things," Gil said, "but unfortunately, they have not forgotten about you." He paused and looked out the window. "Though why it had an interest in the woman who seemed to have no connection to you or our world remains a mystery to me," he said, as if to himself.

"Hang on," Tarin said, "are you talking about the person you mentioned to me earlier when we were walking here? What happened to her?"

Gil continued to stare at the window. "When I first arrived in Philip last night, she was in the final moments of her life, and a curse was upon her." His eyes grew sad. "She died alone, her soul in a near-hopeless state." He looked up. "I did all I could for her as they attempted to take her away. And now I must work to ensure they do not take you or your friends."

"Take us where?"

"To places I would prefer not to speak of."

At that moment, Rob came back into the room, chewing on a leftover slice of pizza. Tarin turned toward Rob and said as calmly as he could muster, "That looks good. Could you grab me a slice too?"

"Sure thing," Rob said and walked back into the kitchen.

Tarin felt dizzy. He thought he might faint but managed to compose himself. "That evil entity you're speaking of, are you saying it sent that UFO to kill that woman? Then it followed you here to attack my friends and me? You led it here?"

"You must understand, I had to come here because your fate is very much tied to the fate of my world, of our world, and even of this world. Pieces were already in place that would soon manifest as a new and magnified stage in your pain." He noticed Tarin's quaking hands and placed his hands on them. "But I will protect you and your friends if you will allow me. That evil may have hastened its plans, but I do not yet believe it understands what has just come into this world to hinder it." He paused. "Will you let me?"

Tarin studied the earnestness in Gil's face. Slowly, he pulled his hands away from Gil's and stared blankly forward. In less than three hours, he'd seen a magical light, run from a UFO, and discovered Gil knew more about him than anyone else other than his friends and could prove it through his strange phial. Gil could also recount details of Tarin's dreams—or memories—more than any stranger should be able to guess.

Still staring ahead, Tarin said, "I can't believe I'm saying this, but if there actually is a chance that some evil thing is out to get me and my friends, then I don't think I have much of a choice but to play it safe and let you help us."

Gil smiled. "I understand this all must feel terribly strange, but thank you for your trust."

Rob walked back in with another slice of pizza. Allen followed, appearing flush. He offered Gil a fresh pour of coffee, which Gil gladly accepted. A few moments later, Josh returned from the shower, looking more relaxed. "You caffeinated enough to tell us more about yourself?" he asked Gil.

Gil shot a knowing glance at Tarin and said, "I am ready."

Though Gil didn't share with the others as much as he'd shared with Tarin, he told them about how he'd arrived in where he learned was a land called Utah, then awakened to the presence of some mysterious evil. However, he said nothing of that evil's intent to harm them, despite their prodding to learn more about it. He then detailed his journey from Utah to South Dakota. He'd been startled by what he'd learned were cars and tried to avoid the roads where they seemed to congregate. He shared how he'd eaten off the land and drank from springs for multiple weeks as he traversed a range of mountains. On the other side, he found a stable of horses and bonded with one that, for many days, carried him more speedily across flatter lands. As he drew closer to Philip, he'd set the horse free and traveled the remaining distance by foot.

"And how did you know the way here?" Rob asked at one point.

Gil touched the side of his hip, and Rob said, "Ohhhh, that's right."

"Okay," Josh said, "you've caught us up on your time since coming to Earth, but you still haven't told us where you come from?" He looked at Tarin. "And apparently where Tarin comes from too."

"Yeah," Rob said, "what's it called? Is it another planet somewhere in our universe? Is it where that UFO came from too?"

"I'm not certain about the origin of the UFO, as you call it, but I fear it does tie back to the evil I encountered when coming to this world. As for the world I came from, it is called Arvalast: It is a world much like your own, though, as I have now seen, significantly less technologically advanced, at least in some ways. For example, we do not have hanging water dispensers for bathing."

Before Gil could continue, flashing lights appeared beyond the living room blinds, followed by headlights pulling into the driveway.

"Uh oh," Josh said. "I wonder if that's the cops. Maybe someone called in about that UFO and the lights on our roof."

"It wouldn't surprise me," Allen said, "it was like a fireworks show out there but without the explosive sounds. Just that awful humming."

Moments later, there was a knock at the door, and Allen got up to answer it. A female police officer stood outside. She held a flashlight in one hand. Her other hand rested at her waist over tan pants. She was older than Tarin and his friends but still young, probably early thirties.

"Allen!" she said with a wide smile. She seemed to notice the crowded living room. She took off her wide-brimmed hat, revealing a dirty blond ponytail underneath, before turning her attention back to Allen. "Got a few calls from around here about an hour ago. It all sounded pretty goofy, but after I finished some paperwork, I decided I'd head over just in case to check things out and make sure you were okay."

"Thanks, Liz," Allen said sheepishly. "That's kind of you. What were the calls about?"

She looked over Allen's shoulders and said, "You've got a bit of a party going on here tonight." With a teasing smirk, she turned back to Allen. "Didn't think to invite me?"

"Well, um, it was game night, and I didn't think . . ." he stuttered.

"No worries," she said, "you're right. Not a big fan of that game of yours, but back to why I'm here. A few folks reported some bright flashing lights in the area, and one of your neighbors claimed they saw someone on your roof and . . . a big cigar-shaped craft in the sky." She rolled her eyes and said to the room. "Now, none of you guys saw a big UFO earlier tonight, did you?"

Rob opened his mouth to speak, but Josh kicked him under his chair.

"We've just been playing our game all night," Allen said, holding his hand out toward the living room, "with Tarin and his friend from out of town, Gil."

Gil waved at her and smiled.

"Well, now, glad to hear it," she said. She leaned in and whispered to Allen, "So that Gil guy, he's Tarin's friend, huh? Is he all right? I got a few locals calling in about him because he was dressed like a weirdo or something." She shot a glance at Gil. "But he just looks like one of you harmless nerds."

"Come on," Allen said. "That's not nice. But yes, Gil's fine. You know how the people here get with anything out of the ordinary, and everyone is even more skittish because of the war. Gil's just a bit eccentric—likes to do a little cosplay, you know . . . like me and the guys do sometimes."

"Okay," she said, "that makes sense, I guess, but keep an eye on him." She looked into the room and put her hat back on. "Have a good night, fellas! And try not to get abducted by any aliens," she added with a wink.

The group chuckled, not without apprehension, as she walked back to her vehicle.

"That was awkward," Allen said, closing the door. He sat back down on the couch by Gil. "But I'm also relieved we weren't all going crazy. There really was something out there!"

"I think she likes you," Rob said with a smirk.

"And I think you like her too," Josh added.

"Shut up!" Allen threw a pillow at them.

"I sensed it as well," Gil said, "the exploratory blossoms of a beautiful energy working to understand the possibility of an eternal union."

"What?" said Allen, his face bright red.

"Cut him some slack," Tarin said, unable to hold back a smirk even in his melancholy state. "He's a bit unfamiliar with Earth culture."

"Yeah!" Rob agreed. "He's from Arvalast. They probably talk like that there."

"I take it I may have misspoken," Gil said. "If so, I apologize and wish you and your potential bride only the best."

Everyone but Allen snickered. With his face still bright red, Allen said, "So how are any of us going to get any sleep tonight after everything that's happened? Is it even safe for us to go to sleep with that UFO potentially prowling about? Should we set up some sort of shift to keep a lookout for it?"

Gil yawned. "You will have nothing to worry about tonight. I managed, I believe, to cast this UFO far from here."

"You believe you did, or you actually did?" said Josh.

"Indeed, you all should be able to have a restful night tonight," Gil said, "though I cannot guarantee what tomorrow will bring. And while we are speaking of a night's rest, you have already been extremely hospitable, but would you be so kind as to allow me to stay the night? I am tired, and the effects of that wonderful coffee have worn off. And the thought of finding a place to sleep in the fields outside of town is very unappealing at the moment."

"I think that would be a good idea," Tarin quickly added. "After all, if the UFO comes back, it seems like that light of yours would come in handy. And I think I'll crash here as well."

Rob snickered. "'Cause you're too scared to go back to your trailer?"

"Yes," said Tarin, "and I bet you'd be too if you were me."

"Absolutely," said Rob.

"No problem," Allen said, "I'll grab you and Gil some extra sheets and some pillows. Gil, you can stay on the couch. Tarin, I can throw a sleeping bag in my room for you if that works?"

"Perfect," Tarin said.

Rob began to clean up the cards. As he reached for the last one, that of the Bostt, he paused. "So you really don't think that UFO or any other weird stuff is going to come around tonight?" he said to Gil.

"You will be safe tonight," Gil said, "I will see to it."

Rob sighed. He picked up the Bostt card and added it to the box with the rest.

At the same time, Allen walked back into the room with some pillows and sheets. "Let me know if you need anything else," he said.

Gil gladly accepted the bedding. "This is far better than I have had since coming here. Thank you."

Tarin and his friends headed to their respective rooms. On his way, Tarin turned out a final hallway light. As he did, he heard a faint sound, like a glass being set on a table. A gentle flicker of light danced along the hallway walls. Tarin entered the bedroom and closed the door behind him save for a small crack.

CHAPTER 5

A woman lay in a meadow. Her tattered white gown was strewn across the grass and barely visible in the darkness of the night. A breeze wafted across her face and ruffled her long brown hair as it lay splayed on the dewy ground beneath her. She stirred, and her green eyes fluttered open. Slowly, she became aware of her surroundings. Fully encompassing the edge of the meadow were tall trees, grand and imposing. Their gnarled branches stretched out as if guarding the grassy opening beneath them against any who dared to trespass into their abode. Deep green leaves rustled in the wind. The sound created a sense of whispering among the trees. It seemed as if they were discussing the stranger and what to do with her.

The woman managed to pull herself to her feet. She looked up into the moonless night, then turned around, seemingly confused. The whispers in the trees gave way to another sound, one far more ominous: a hissing. She frantically scanned the tree line, searching for the sound. Then, just within the forest only fifty yards from her, she saw the faint silhouette of an upright figure, possibly a person, broad-shouldered and standing slightly hunched over. It appeared to be both cloaked and hooded and weaved from side to side as if studying her.

The wind grew still. Many moments passed. She feared to move. Then, she heard the same hiss, louder this time. To her horror, she saw that it came from the figure in the woods. It took a slow step forward out of the trees and into the meadow. The starlight shone through a gap in the overcast night sky long enough for her to see that its garb was red. Beneath its hood, she saw the sharp edges of teeth protruding from a mouth that was not human but that of some sort of scaly beast.

The starlight again disappeared behind the clouds. The monster charged her.

She turned and fled toward the other end of the woods, but the creature traveled at twice her speed. With long, thick claws at the end of its scaly hands, it reached out as it approached her.

There was a blinding flash of light. The woman stumbled and fell to the ground. She toppled through the grass and saw the beast cover its face, hissing wildly as if in great pain. She came to a stop near the end of the forest and looked up to see two other figures. They were human—one a woman, the other a man. Both held what looked like containers of brilliant light. With her remaining energy, she crawled toward them and held out her hand. The woman reached down and clasped it. She pulled her to her feet, and the man yelled, "Hurry, come with us!"

Tarin sat up in a cold sweat. He panted and looked around the room. He half expected to see tall trees surrounding him or perhaps some terrifying, red-cloaked monster peeking through the still partially opened bedroom doorway. But all he saw was Allen's bed to his left and a small window to his right. The first signs of morning light glimmered through the old grey curtains that covered it.

He rubbed his face. "That was new," he said quietly, his voice raspy with sleep. He reached for a glass of water on the sill and noticed his hands were trembling. He'd had many dreams of that same forest but never of the meadow, the red-cloaked beast, or the woman in the white gown. Her face had a simple beauty he struggled to erase from his memory.

"Sleep well?" Allen asked, sitting up in his bed with a yawn.

"I did until just now," Tarin said. He took another sip of water. "I had another dream, but this one was different and very strange."

"You mean it wasn't about the battle?" Allen said, now very alert.

"No, it wasn't. There wasn't that odd music, or that . . . awful terror whenever I see the gallows. But it was still ominous."

Tarin shared the details of this new dream as Allen got up and made his bed. "Wait a minute," Allen said. "The light you saw—was it the same as Gil's?"

"I don't know," Tarin said. "But maybe. I wonder if my subconscious mind is getting things confused and merging all the stuff that happened with Gil last night with my usual dreams . . . or memories."

Allen stared at him. "Are you starting to believe Gil's story?"

Tarin ran his hand over his face and moaned. "I don't know, Allen. Everything going on is just so weird. I'm not sure what to think."

"What about the woman?" Allen said, his voice growing more excited. "Was she anyone you've seen before? Why would she be in the dream?"

Tarin wondered if it had to do with the woman Gil had told him about, the one who died. Could that story have somehow made its way into his dreams? Gil hadn't shared that detail with his friends last night, presumably so as not to scare them. So he shrugged and said, "I'm not sure."

Bacon and eggs sizzled on the stove as Tarin and Allen made their way to the kitchen. Josh was tending the skillet, always the early bird among the group. Gil sat at the small table near a kitchen window overlooking Allen's tiny backyard. He had a cup of coffee in his hands and a wide smile on his face. He still wore the same sloppy clothes he'd had on last night. "I may never return to Arvalast," he said, "unless I can somehow bring the magic of coffee with me."

Josh flipped the bacon on the skillet with a pair of tongs. "Don't you have coffee beans in Arvalast?"

Gil took another sip from a mug with a picture of all five faces of Mount Rushmore on it. "If we do, we have not yet discovered how to turn them into this beverage. We do steep various plants to create a similar type of aromatic drink, but nothing compares to this drink's perfect bitter flavor and energy-inducing qualities."

"I think you mean tea," Allen said, taking a seat next to Gil. "And I agree, coffee is superior."

"I prefer tea," Rob said, walking into the room, bleary-eyed. He adjusted his glasses. "Coffee gives me a headache."

Josh tossed some bacon onto a plate and walked to the table. He set the plate in the center and said, "You'll like this too, Gil. Try it."

Gil took a piece of bacon, sniffed it, then ate it. He moaned and said, "Delicious. Though, this we do have in Arvalast. But it has been a long time since I have had any."

Josh returned to the stove. "So, how did everyone sleep?" he said, dishing up the eggs and bringing them to the table as well.

"I had nightmares all night," Rob said. "But at least I didn't get taken by aliens."

"I slept fine," Josh said, joining the group at the table. "Overall a dreamless night."

Allen said, "Me as well." He looked at Tarin, who put his head down and stuffed some eggs in his mouth.

"And what about you, Tarin," Josh asked. "Any dreams?"

"The usual," Tarin muttered, not wanting to share about the woman and the light to avoid his friends asking more questions. Not until, at least, he could find out more from Gil about his apparent plan to keep them all safe.

The group finished breakfast, and Gil said to Allen, "I have been meaning to ask you: I believe you took my clothing to wash last night, and though I am truly grateful for the loan of these garments of yours, I would very much like to have my own clothing back if they are ready."

"Well," Allen said, "about that. I think we need to have a talk. You see, townsfolk apparently have been taken aback by your outfit, and I think it's best if you keep a low profile while you're here in Philip.

Would you be open to going into Wall, a nearby town? We could buy you a few more normal-looking outfits to wear."

Gil's face briefly grew downcast, before he forced a smile. "You are wise to suggest this. It is time for me to establish a more consistent appearance with the culture here. I will accept your request." He stood up. "When shall we go?"

"Once we tidy up the kitchen, we can head out," Allen said. At Tarin's recommendation, they decided they would all go.

The sun shone brightly that morning, and the air was crisp and cool. Everything seemed so welcoming and safe. It was hard to believe that it was only last night that the UFO had come . . . and Tarin was told he was from another world.

Allen's small blue car was parked on the other side of the street. Its windows reflected the sunshine and the large tree above it. A few children were playing in a nearby yard, throwing leaves up into the air and running around in circles. Farther down the street, Old Bill stood on the sidewalk, looking into the sky with binoculars.

"So," Gil said, "it is at last time for me to enter one of those horrendous transport machines. I will admit, I am not eager, but I trust it will be safe."

"Not as safe as flying," Rob said.

"Flying?" asked Gil, his eyes wide. "Can this machine also fly?"

Allen laughed. "I wish I could afford a sky car. But my consulting gig doesn't bring in enough on top of my universal basic income for anything luxurious. Plus, sky cars are only legal in the bigger cities. It would be mostly useless this side of South Dakota."

Gil still eyed the car nervously.

"Don't worry about it," said Josh. He patted Gil's shoulder. "It'll be fine, I promise."

Gil was the tallest and a guest, so they agreed he would get the front passenger seat. Allen would drive. The others squeezed into the back. Allen pushed a button on the dashboard, and a small holographic image appeared above it, indicating the current battery charge, speed, and car's location on a map. Gil tried to touch it, and his hand passed through. "I have seen something like this before," Gil said, "when at your local pub. What is it?"

"It's a hologram display," Allen said as he started the car forward. "Been around for about ten or so years now."

"Even more interesting than the hanging water dispensers, aren't they, Gil?" Rob said with a laugh from the back seat.

"Indeed," Gil whispered. "Indeed they are." The car sped up. Gil took in a deep breath, and put both hands on the dashboard. But after a few minutes, he relaxed his arms and stared out his window, a small smile on his face as he observed the passing scenery.

They drove for about thirty minutes when a large statue of a dinosaur rose over the horizon. Gil pointed and said, "What a remarkable creature! Both great and impressive like the legendary beasts of Arvalast. Do they live here in this world?"

"Not anymore," Allen said. "They went extinct long, long ago."

"You have dinosaurs in Arvalast?" Rob asked.

"We have large creatures similar in size," Gil said, "but none that look like this dinosaur of your world."

Tarin and Josh looked at each other with raised eyebrows while Rob smiled widely. Allen merged onto Interstate 90 for the final few minutes of the drive, and Gil yelled, "Watch out! There are many other transport devices here!"

"It's fine," Allen said. "There are rules about driving that'll keep us from hitting each other. And the car is programmed to keep us out of trouble, even if I or one of the other drivers makes a mistake."

Gil settled down, then leaned forward to look out the front window. "Is that the town of Wall?" he asked, pointing ahead.

"Yep," Allen responded. "And soon you'll have your first taste of Wall Drug, one of the most famous places in all of South Dakota. Believe it or not, it started out as just a modest store, but clever advertising for ice water and cheap coffee along hundreds of miles of interstate in both directions brought in a lot of business until it grew into this sprawling complex. I don't think the advertising has even changed for over a century."

"Wish it didn't attract so many tourists," Josh sighed.

"I love it!" Rob said. "Makes this area more lively, and it's the best place to buy anything and everything."

They drove into Wall and into a large parking area. There were massive strip malls, each with a Western flair, on either side. Allen found a parking spot and plugged in his car. The group headed into the store. Gil marveled at the various Western mannequins lining the interior halls. Eventually, they made their way to a gift shop with clothing.

"I'll go find you some essentials," Allen said as he headed to an aisle with socks and underwear. "The rest of you help Gil find some stuff that'll help him blend in better."

Gil followed Tarin, Josh, and Rob through aisle after aisle as they handed him an assortment of jeans and shirts. "How do I know if these articles of clothing will fit me?" Gil asked. Josh pointed to a door on the far side of the aisle. "You'll go in there and try them on."

Not long after, Gil was dressed in jeans and a flannel and staring into a mirror. "I like these," he said. He peered around at some of the other customers milling about. "And I now look like most of the other men I have seen. Though some are wearing wide-brimmed hats. Is that something I should acquire as well?"

"Yes it is!" Rob said. He hurried down a nearby aisle and returned with a cowboy hat. "You'll look awesome in this." He handed it to Gil, who carefully put it on.

Gil looked into the mirror and smiled. "I approve."

Moments later, Allen returned with a handful of socks and underwear. "So, now to the matter of how we're going to pay for all this stuff. Do you guys mind splitting the cost across our monthly universal basic income allotments?"

"That's fine," Josh said. He took out a wallet and removed a thin, silver card. "Rob and I also have a good bit in savings from our supplemental income working at the grocery store."

"Yeah," Rob added, "happy to help. After all, you charge us almost nothing to stay at your place. It's the least we can do."

"You know I'm limited to a range I can charge by the Lattice," Allen mumbled, "but thanks." He turned to Tarin. "What about you, any spare funds?"

"I might be able to chip in a little, but I'm close to zero for the month. And I only have enough left in my supplemental savings for essentials."

"You mean your stash of illegal cash?" Josh said with a smirk. "And beer's not an essential."

"Speak for yourself," Tarin said.

The group paid for the clothing then trooped into another gift shop where Rob wanted to buy more LOB cards, but just inside the doorway, Allen stopped. "Liz is here," he said, pointing into the store.

Sure enough, Liz stood near the register in her police uniform, talking to a very tall man dressed in a black leather jacket and a white collared shirt. Beneath the jacket were equally dark pants, and above his slick brown hair rested blue tinted sunglasses. The man was towering over her, arms crossed.

"Let's find another shop," Allen said. He started to leave.

Tarin held out his hand. "No. Let's wait until they're done talking and see what's going on. That guy looks suspicious, and Liz looks a bit nervous." With everything he was still processing about Gil, among other things, a story about a new weirdo in the area, especially one not connected to his past, might be a nice change of pace.

Gil leaned in close to Tarin. "You have good perception. I also sense something is not well here."

Tarin's optimism faded. Gil was proving to be a consistent source of foreboding. But as Tarin continued to watch the animated conversation between Liz and the stranger, his curiosity remained. He might as well still see what was going on.

They all waited a few minutes until the man in the leather jacket nodded and began heading toward them. Tarin and his friends started looking at items on the shelves in an attempt to appear inconspicuous. After the man walked by, Tarin said, "Come on," and started toward Liz. She was writing something in a small notebook, looking frazzled.

"Hello, Liz!" Tarin said as they approached.

She looked up, her eyes briefly indicating surprise, then smiled. "Tarin! Great to see you again." She glanced at the others, her stare lingering slightly longer on Allen's red face. "So you all decided to take a little field trip, huh?"

"We needed to get Gil some new clothes," Rob said, holding up a plastic bag filled with the merchandise they'd bought for Gil.

"Glad to hear." She laughed and looked at Gil. "Now maybe I'll stop getting calls about people dressed like pirates."

"So," Tarin said, "saw you talking to that guy in the leather jacket. Don't usually see a lot of leather around here outside of the Sturgis motorcycle rallies. You able to tell us anything about him?"

Liz rolled her eyes. "Ever the inquisitive one, aren't you, Tarin? You know I can't tell you everything about police business."

"But you can tell a friend something under the table, can't you?" he responded. "It's not like you haven't before. Remember last week at Old Cotton's when you told me about one of John's farmhands caught breaking into that . . ."

"Shut up!" she said in a loud whisper. "You're going to get me in trouble."

Allen cleared his throat and shuffled on his feet. "Come on, Tarin. We really shouldn't be trying to force her to tell us stuff she can't." He smiled at Liz, then turned to the others as he held out his hand toward the exit. "Let's go, guys."

Tarin shot him an angry glance and said, "But don't you want to know more too? You seemed interested enough when Gil came into town dressed weird. Why aren't you interested in this guy who's dressed like some sort of secret agent or something?"

"Well," Allen said, "I am, but . . ."

Liz looked at Allen with a half smile, then turned back to Tarin. "Fine, let me finish this report quickly, and then I'll meet you at the restaurant here in this building in about fifteen minutes. Honestly, it might help me to talk this through a bit. Things have been getting odd since last night after all those UFO calls, and now I'm dealing with these guys in leather jackets asking a bunch of questions."

"We'll see you in fifteen," Tarin said, then turned to his friends. "Let's go."

It was working. This little quest was distracting him from the previous evening's events, and the dream of the girl. However, as his mind lingered on an image of her gentle face, he realized her memory brought intrigue rather than pain.

They left the store and walked down a hall to the restaurant. The atmosphere was warm and inviting, albeit busy. The rustic décor gave it an old-world charm. They placed their orders at the front counter, found a table in the corner, and sat down.

Not long after, their number was called, and Josh and Allen went to fetch their food. Upon returning, Gil stared down at his burger and fries. Slowly, he lifted a fry to his mouth, then closed his eyes. "This potato, it is incredible."

"Here," Rob said and squirted some ketchup on his plate. "Try it with this."

Gil picked up another fry and added the ketchup. He popped it into his mouth and then smiled at the group as he chewed. "What an unbelievable infusion of tomato and salt," he said. "This cuisine is remarkable!"

Tarin began to laugh with the others—which he found to be a nice surprise—when he noticed a flutter in his stomach as if something in the room was just a little . . . off. He scanned the area, unsure what he was looking for but still needing to look. Finally, his eyes settled on three individuals sitting in another corner of the restaurant behind a group of people. Once he saw them, he wondered why he hadn't noticed them before because of their strange attire. Tarin studied their faces, then gasped.

Two of them were dressed like Gil when he'd first met him, and the other, a woman, was in a white and weathered gown—the same woman from his dream. She looked to be shaking, and one of the others, also a woman, was attempting to comfort her. She offered the first woman a cup, which she took and drank from. A few moments later, with the cup still at her lips, the first woman glanced in Tarin's direction. For a brief moment, their eyes met. The woman's eyes were deep, green, and full of both surprise and curiosity. Tarin's heart beat hard in his chest. He felt a sudden urge to go to her—to try to comfort her.

"Tarin," a voice said.

Tarin started and lurched back in his seat.

"Are you okay?"

Tarin realized it was just Allen. He glanced around, looking for the three people he'd seen in the corner earlier, but now all he saw was a family of five sitting at a table against the wall, where a dad was trying to calm down a crying toddler in a high chair while the mother frantically worked to pile fries in front of the other two young children as they greedily stuffed them into their faces.

"Yeah," Tarin said. "Sorry, just . . . zoned out for a second." He tried to process what had just happened. It was like, for a moment, a dream had merged with reality in that one corner of the room.

What is going on with me?

Allen stared at him, and Tarin could tell he sensed something strange had just happened. But Allen didn't press the issue. Instead, his face turned red as his eyes moved to the restaurant entrance. Liz was walking toward them. She grabbed an empty seat from the neighboring table and maneuvered it into position between Allen and Gil. She sat down, removed her wide-brimmed police hat, placed it on her lap, and leaned forward. "Well, boys, I'm hungry. What did you order me?"

"Um," Allen said, looking down at his half-eaten burger. "I'm full if you'd like the rest."

Without hesitation, she pulled Allen's tray over, dipped a fry in some ketchup, and put it in her mouth. "Thanks, Allen," she said as she chewed.

He smiled nervously and nodded. "Sure thing."

"So," she said, then took a bite of the burger, "I've had a strange day." She looked over at Tarin. "What's wrong with you? You look like you've seen a ghost."

Tarin took a sip of soda to cover his surprise. "Don't know what you're talking about. I'm fine."

"Okay then," she said. "But you might want to try to get some more sun. You look pale."

"Noted," Tarin said, taking another deep sip of his soda. He coughed as it went down the wrong tube.

Gil took a break from eating his fries. His eyes darted back and forth between Tarin and Liz as if waiting for them to continue.

"Enough about me," Tarin finally sputtered. "I'd like to hear more about that man in the black jacket you were talking to earlier. He didn't look like a biker. He seemed more formal—clean-cut, maybe even government-like. What's he doing in town?"

"He is government," she said, taking another bite of Allen's burger. "And for what he's doing, he's looking for aliens."

"Wait," Josh said, "seriously?"

Tarin was relieved the attention was off of him. But aliens? He rubbed his temples. *Why not.* He was already dealing with new worlds, magic lights, and UFOs.

Liz reached into a pocket of her police vest and pulled out several photographs. "I'm exaggerating a bit, but he was interested in any UFO sightings in the area. Must have gotten to the higher-ups that folks in town were calling in about something last night. He gave me these." She tossed the pictures onto the table. "They asked if anyone had reported seeing anything similar. He told me to give him a call if I did, that they were of government interest and should be treated as a security threat. He had me write down his number and his name."

"What was he doing here in Wall?" Allen asked as he picked up one of the pictures. "And why did you meet him here instead of in Philip?"

"I got a call from one of the store owners here who's a friend of mine," she said. "She told me there was an odd man dressed like a fancy biker asking folks a bunch of questions. She wanted me to come out and just get a sense of what he might be up to. This is out of my jurisdiction, but I figured I'd come out anyway since she's my friend and seemed pretty nervous. I found the guy talking to some tourists in the store you saw me in, so I just played the role of a local cop and asked some questions."

Gil picked up one of the pictures while the others did the same. "Did you see any other men similar to the man you spoke to?" he asked.

"No," she said, "but my friend told me she heard from people in Rapid City that a bunch of similarly dressed folks are staying in a few of the local hotels, and there're rumors they're canvasing all the local towns in white vans asking people related questions." She tapped the photo Allen was looking at. "So what do you make of that?"

"It looks like a blurry orb in the night sky," he said. "Maybe it's just a star or planet."

"According to them, it's something else," Liz said. "What about you, Tarin? What's on yours?"

Tarin studied the photo. It was a picture of a woman walking along a sidewalk on what looked to be a small town's main street. The woman had dark hair and glasses. She wore jeans and a blue jacket and was otherwise unassuming. But over her shoulder was a glowing orb. "I see an orb in this photo as well, but this one's definitely not a star." He squinted. "Also, that place she's in looks familiar."

"Mine has a bona fide UFO on it!" Rob exclaimed. He held out the picture. "Looks like a flying saucer! Is this real?"

Tarin and the others glanced up. Sure enough, the picture contained a silhouette of a stereotypical flying saucer hovering above a small mountain in broad daylight. The saucer was too distant to make out any features besides its shape, and, at first glance, it looked like it fit the scene rather than having been added.

"Fake," Josh said, then held up a photo he was looking at. "Just like this one that looks like a white tic tac in a blue sky. These government guys must be a bunch of idiots. All these pictures look like the fake crap you see all the time in tabloids."

"But what if they're real, like the one we saw last night?" Rob said. Tarin, Allen, and Josh all turned to him. Josh rolled his eyes and let his breath out in a huff. Allen shook his head. Gil just looked at Rob blankly but Liz narrowed her eyes and smiled.

"So, Rob," she said. "You fellows did see something last night, just like the other folks in town?"

"Well, I uh," Rob stuttered. He looked at the others.

Josh groaned and replied. "Yeah, we did." He tossed his photo onto the table and crossed his arms. "But as you can imagine, we didn't want to look like a bunch of crazies when you came knocking at the door. And, for your information, what we saw didn't look like any of these pictures."

"You should've told me," Liz said. "First off, I already think you're all a bunch of crazies, so it wouldn't have changed my opinion even a little. Secondly, I really could've used some more credible information. Most of what I was getting from townsfolk was hysteria with little to no useful information. Flashing lights, humming sounds, things like that. If you guys had told me about it, I would have been able to dig into it a bit more."

"Why would you treat our word any differently than the townsfolk?" Allen asked.

She looked at him, and her face softened. "Because I trust you guys," she said. "You help out at community events, you're generally pretty nice, and you stay away from town gossip." She looked at Tarin. "Well, most of you." She shook her head and sighed. "Anyway, can you please tell me what you saw? Seems like with these government folks snooping around and you all actually seeing something, I might actually have a real case on my hands."

Tarin and the others all traded looks. Josh shrugged. "Might as well," he said.

Ten minutes later, Liz leaned back in her chair and put her hands behind her head. "Not what I was expecting to hear."

Gil had told her about the UFO attack while managing to avoid the topic of his origin, his claims about Tarin being from another world, and the phial.

"So," Liz said to Gil, "you scared it away with magic words somehow while Allen was puking in the living room and the others were laying low?"

Allen slid lower into his chair as Gil replied, "Yes, I have had some experience with things of this nature."

Liz tilted her head. "You like a paranormal researcher or something? Is that why you came to town dressed so weird?"

Gil and Tarin quickly glanced at each other before Gil turned back to Liz and said, "I am, let us say, familiar with what you call paranormal things and events."

"So what's your take on what you saw?" she said. "It seems like it must be dangerous if it was scaring so many people and causing poor Allen to be sick. Do you think I should be concerned?"

"Yes," Gil said. "We all should be. That thing was evil."

"Oookay then," she said. "And what do you make of these photos and of the government people asking about UFOs?"

"I have not formed a strong opinion of them yet. Though the man you spoke with earlier, I fear I did not have a good sense of him. Yet I do not know why."

"Well, if it makes you feel better," she said, "he gave me the creeps too."

"What's that?" Rob said, pointing to the back of the picture Tarin was holding.

Tarin turned the picture around, and indeed, there was writing on the back. He read it, and his eyes grew wide. "It can't be," he whispered.

Josh snatched the picture from Tarin from across the table, turned it around, and read, "East Fairfield, Ohio. September, Year One of the

Great Peace." His eyes also grew wide. "Tarin, doesn't that line up with when you moved to East Fairfield with your adoptive parents?"

Before Tarin could answer, Gil reached out and said, "May I see the photo?"

Josh handed it to him.

He studied it for what felt like many moments until he finally whispered, "Iris."

All eyes turned to Gil, and Rob asked, "Who's Iris?"

Liz went stiff in her seat and said, "Uh oh." She started snatching up the pictures on the table. "Quick," she said in a harsh whisper, "give them all back to me now!"

Tarin looked up. Near the front of the restaurant, he saw the same man in the leather jacket from earlier. Almost instantly, the man's dark eyes locked with his own. Tarin tried to break away from the gaze but found himself unable. He had become paralyzed, transfixed. He tried to speak, to scream, but nothing came out. He could see his friends notice something was wrong with him, but he couldn't hear anything they were saying.

The man smiled, and his eyes began to change—morphing slowly into pools of yellow liquid. These took the form of his pupils, turning them into yellow slits. Tarin grew dizzy and felt himself fall from his chair and collapse onto the floor. Eye contact was broken. The strange power the man had over him snapped. Tarin blinked and sat up.

He looked around, but all he saw was a sort of haze that had consumed the room. Through it, he could see silhouettes he assumed were his friends surrounding him. But they seemed to grow more distant with every passing moment, fading into the mist until Tarin was alone in the fog.

Slowly, he became aware of music. It sounded like the organ on a carousel. The haze was lifting, and he realized he was lying on a sidewalk. Surrounding him were scores of people filling what looked like the main street of a small town, not all that different from Philip's. Only the street had been transformed into a fair, with concession stands and gaming booths lining one side of the closed-off street. Various small rides filled other open spaces in parking lots, including a carousel behind him.

Immediately he recognized his old hometown of East Fairfield, Ohio. People passing by did not seem to notice him, though no one bumped into him, almost as if he was protected by a hidden forcefield.

He stood up, and the scents of hot dogs, cinnamon rolls, and all manner of fair food launched him back in time to the day he'd first experienced East Fairfield's annual street fair. Though future fairs would gradually lose their luster and charm as his home life took a turn for the worse, this first fair, which was coupled with the celebration of the first year of the Great Peace, had been a formative event in his life. He had new parents who, after fostering him, had decided they wanted to adopt him even though he was a young teenager. And unlike when he'd seen his parents in Gil's phial, he now felt a sense of happiness as he recalled how they'd seemed to truly love him, particularly his new mother.

He caught sight of a figure leaning against the corner of a nearby bank, and the feelings of nostalgia pouring over him ceased. The man wore Western attire, including cowboy boots and a leather cattleman hat, which made him stand out starkly from the rest of the crowd dressed in the usual midwestern attire of jeans or cargo shorts and any manner of short-sleeved and sleeveless shirts. The man was smoking a cigarette. But what was most striking about him was that he was the only one who seemed to notice Tarin's presence. In fact, he was staring directly at him.

CHAPTER 6

The man briefly averted his gaze from Tarin. He took a deep draw from his cigarette, blew a plume of smoke into the air, then tossed the butt onto the ground. With one booted foot, he snuffed out the final smoking embers on the sidewalk. He tilted his hat down lower over his forehead and slowly walked toward Tarin.

Tarin felt a wave of terror wash over him. He tried to turn to run, but his feet seemed locked in place, as if the intent of his mind was disconnected from the muscles in his body. The man continued to approach. Tarin grimaced as he struggled against the unseen power holding him still until, with a great force of will, he managed to turn around and take one step forward. He stopped. The same man now approached from that direction. It was then Tarin realized this had to be some sort of dream. He began slapping his face and yelling, "Wake up! Wake up, Tarin!" But nothing happened. He was trapped.

The man continued toward him slowly but with purpose and determination. Tarin grunted against the force holding him in place and managed one step back. He took notice of the man's long grey hair, pulled into a ponytail behind his hat. The man quickened his pace.

"This little light of mine," the man said in a raspy, rugged voice. His lips were set in a thin line, like an animal stalking its prey before pouncing. He didn't look at anyone else at the fair or even acknowledge their presence; instead, he stayed focused on his mission, and that looked to be Tarin. "I'm going to let it shine," he continued, almost mockingly.

"Who are you?" Tarin said, his voice quaking. He clenched his fists and managed to back up a little farther toward the carousel filled with kids squealing in delight and blissfully unaware of the standoff happening in front of them.

The man came closer. "This little light of mine . . ."

"Why are you saying that?" Tarin yelled.

The man's lips twisted into a sinister smile. "I'm going to let it shine."

"What do you want from me?" Tarin yelled. "Why am I here?"

The man took the final few steps toward Tarin. "This little light of mine"—his voice meandered into an ominous-sounding song—"I'm going to let it shine." He brought his face inches from Tarin's and finally said, "let it shine . . . let it shine . . . let . . . it . . . shine."

Tarin could smell smoke on his breath, and he turned away in disgust.

"Hello, Tarin," the man said. "Been a while."

Tarin's breathing grew faster. His heart rate increased. "I . . . I don't know you."

"Oh," the man said, tilting his head slightly to the left. His deep green eyes were locked on Tarin's forehead, just above his eyes. "Pity," he said. "I certainly know you." He spun around, took a few steps back, lit another cigarette, and turned back to Tarin. "Want one?"

Tarin slowly shook his head. "No, thank you, I don't smoke."

"Suit yourself," the man said. He put the cigarette in his mouth, pulled in a few deep breaths, and blew out a cloud of smoke. He opened his arms. "You recognize this place, though, right?" He breathed in deeply through his nose. "I love that fair food smell! Don't you, boy?"

Tarin nodded.

"Why so quiet?" the man said, his smile fading. "Cat got your tongue?"

"I'm . . . I'm just not sure what's going on," Tarin stuttered. "I'm not sure how I got here."

The man's smile returned, and Tarin noticed he had perfect white teeth behind an otherwise aging and careworn face.

"Got here?" the man asked. He walked back to Tarin and tapped him on the chest. "Here is everywhere," he said. "And this here in particular, it will always be in there," he continued, with his hand on Tarin's heart. "I made sure of that."

"What do you mean?" Tarin asked. "This . . . this is my old hometown where I lived with my parents. It's just a dream."

"Dream?" the man said with annoyance. "Dream, reality, here, there, what's the difference?" He shook his head and looked down at his boots. While still staring at the ground, he said, "You ever wonder what finally happened to your dear sweet mama after she left?" He looked back up at Tarin and returned his eyes to a place fixated just above Tarin's forehead.

Tarin felt his chest tighten. Briefly, he recalled his mother's smiling face, her long red hair that she always kept tied back in a ponytail, and the ball cap she'd always wear when going out. She was athletic—a runner—which had led Tarin to become a runner too. For a moment, fond memories of spending weekends going on runs through town and having long conversations with her filled his mind. He recalled the city park and the small lake they'd often include in their route. On sunny days, the lake always sparkled and reflected the blue sky, a backdrop to the manicured trees and gardens surrounding the body of water as they'd run by. Being in this place, dream or not, brought him back to those first couple of years of the Great Peace, living with his adoptive mom and dad, a man he was at first happy to call father, until things had started to change. Until his mother had started to change.

The man took another draw from his cigarette. "Despite everything, you loved her dearly," he said as smoke poured out of his mouth at Tarin. "It was hard to see her break down, wasn't it? But when she ran away, why didn't you go after her?"

"Stop," Tarin said. His throat tightened, not only because of the smoke but because he did not want to revisit memories he'd spent so many years working to repress. "There was nothing I could have done."

"Really?"

Coward. The accusation from his dreams was back, and it was strong. The man kept staring at his forehead.

"Please stop," Tarin pleaded. "I don't want to go there."

The man lifted his free hand and placed it on Tarin's shoulder. Tarin tried to pull away but, again, found himself unable to move.

"But that's where you keep getting things wrong, boy," the man said. "There . . . is . . . here." He pulled back and said quickly, "But what's not here yet is the knowledge of the fate you abandoned your dear mama to, and you better believe I was there!" With his free hand, he took his hat off and placed it over his heart, revealing his full head of pulled-back grey hair. With the other, he lifted his cigarette toward his mouth. "Join me," he whispered in a snarl. He put the cigarette in his mouth, drew in a deep breath, and blew it out in the direction of the carousel.

The smoke turned from white to black. It spread out and began to block the scene behind it. The sounds of the merry organ and the gleeful children began to fade as the edges of the cloud appeared, almost like hands tearing a portion of this already strange reality apart to reveal yet another reality. But as it emerged, Tarin could see that this one was dark and rainy, a stark contrast to the blue skies and puffy white clouds hovering above where Tarin stood.

The portal continued to expand until it almost covered Tarin's entire field of vision in that direction. He felt the wet and chilly night air blow from the opening. He shivered.

He could now see what looked like a road. This was confirmed a moment later when a car came driving along it from just beyond the edge of the rift. It stopped abruptly. Two men got out of the front of the car. The man from the passenger seat hurried over to the nearest back seat car door and flung it open. The driver joined him and reached into the car. He pulled out a frail woman. She was barefoot and wearing just a tank top and jeans.

Tarin couldn't see their faces because of the darkness of the night and the rain. They dragged the woman out to the front of the car. In the headlights, she looked up, and Tarin recognized the face of his mother, though it had aged far beyond what he remembered from the last time he'd seen her. It was an unnatural aging he'd seen in others who had met with hard lives of pain and hopelessness, one that, for his mother, had begun while they were still together but had clearly become far worse afterward.

"Stop this," Tarin said as he tried to turn away from the scene. "Stop it now! I don't want to see this!"

In Tarin's peripheral vision, he saw the man shake his head left and right. "It's too late now," he said. "And you always suspected this is how things ended, though I sense you still had some hope of something turning out different. But hope deferred makes the heart ill, Tarin. I'm healing that for you. Keep watching."

Tears started to stream down Tarin's face, "No, Mom, no." He watched as she tried to force herself past the men and get back into the car. But the men began pushing and shoving her toward the ditch on the side of the road. "Sorry, Chrissy," the driver said. "You served us well, but you're past your prime, and it's time to part ways."

"Let me back in!" she screamed. "You can't do this to me!"

"Can't do that, girl," the other man said. He pulled out a syringe and injected her with something. "This will help things go faster." With that, he shoved her into the ditch, and she collapsed into its muddy bottom. She lifted her head back up and screamed, "Come back! Take me back! You can't do this!"

The men ignored her, got back into the car, and drove away.

Tarin watched as his broken mother lay in the ditch for what felt like an eternity. Though he tried to break free to help her, he was locked in place, held captive by whatever force or magic governed this hideous world he was now trapped inside. He saw his mother look up at the sky as large raindrops pelted her face. And in that face, he saw the final light of hope go out as she realized this was, in fact, her end. A few moments later, she began to convulse as whatever terrible toxin those men had injected her with took effect.

"Mom!" he screamed. But she didn't hear him. He struggled and pulled against the invisible force holding him still. He looked over to the man, who stood silently, watching, his face devoid of expression, his eyes still unwilling to meet Tarin's. "Let me go to her!" he said. "Let me help her!"

The man said nothing.

Tarin turned back to his mother. "Mom! I love you. I love you! I'm sorry I didn't help you! I'm sorry I can't help you now. I'm trying, but I can't!" He tugged and pulled, but his feet stayed firmly in place.

Finally, she stopped quaking and fell still. Her face plummeted into the ditch, and her frail and broken body lay there, rain pelting it, washing away the mud but not the sorrows and agony within. No one was there to help her. She had died alone and utterly destroyed.

Tarin began to sob, then paused, as he saw what appeared to be dark shadows crawling out of her. One after another, smoky tendrils like fingers came out of her back, head, and legs. As they emerged, they appeared as thin silhouettes of humanoid figures, darker than even the backdrop of the night behind them. Tarin counted three, then four, then ten. One looked his way, and Tarin shuddered at the sight of two hideous yellow eyes meeting his own. All of them finally lifted themselves from her lifeless body and stood side by side on the road, staring down at her, waiting.

A pale light appeared in the center of his mother's back. A moment later, a different silhouette emerged, this one in the shape of a woman. Long flowing hair glowed behind it, and as it stepped out from his mother's body, Tarin saw two small orbs where eyes would have been, glowing slightly brighter than the rest of the figure. The ghostly woman spotted him. A soft voice said, "Tarin?"

"Mom!" Tarin screamed. He struggled and finally, using all his might, broke free from whatever was holding him in place. He rushed toward the rip between realities and held out his arms. "I'm coming!"

But just before he made it to the opening, the ten smoky creatures lunged for the pale glowing essence of his mother and grabbed her.

She screamed and struggled. "Tarin!" she called again, this time with urgency. He reached the gate, but as he made contact with it, he was struck by what felt like electricity and thrown back to where he'd been standing earlier.

"Let her go!" he screamed and stood back up. He again lunged for the gate and again was thrown back. "Leave her alone!"

He watched in horror as the creatures completely enveloped his mother and another portal, this one red, opened up above the roadway where the car had just been. He heard hissing and snarling and the muffled sound of his mother screaming. He lunged for the opening. This time, he was about to fall through. But it was too late. The creatures had pulled his mother into and through the portal, and as Tarin landed in the same muddy ditch his mother had just been in, the portal closed. All became still except for the rain pelting against Tarin's tear-stained face.

"Mom!" Tarin screamed one more time. "I'm sorry! I'm so sorry!" He collapsed into the ground and wept. Time became meaningless as he hunched over and buried his face in his hands. Never had he felt so much pain. Never had he experienced such hopeless agony. Vaguely, he became aware of the rhythmic thump, splash, thump, splash of boots on wet pavement. He looked up, and there was the man. His hat was back on his head, his cigarette back in his mouth.

"You know," the man said. "This all happened because of you."

"What do you mean?" Tarin asked.

"What I mean is," the man said in a soft voice, "she was just a simple midwestern girl, living the simple midwestern life. Then you had to come along. You just had to come along and . . . let's say . . . screw everything up for her. Then, when she left, you didn't even go after her."

Guilt coursed through Tarin's body as he slumped forward. "Why?" he said.

"Why what?"

"Why didn't I go after her?"

A terrible melody began to play in his mind.

Coward.

Tarin slammed his fist onto the ground.

Coward.

Tarin lurched his head back and screamed. "Why am I here?"

The man took a few steps forward, reached down for Tarin, and pulled his limp body up as if he weighed nothing. He held Tarin in front of him and, with both hands on Tarin's shoulders, said, "Look at me."

Tarin tried to lift his head but couldn't.

"Look at me, boy!" the man screamed. The man grabbed Tarin's hair and pulled his head back. For the first time, the man's eyes met Tarin's. And as they did, the green surrounding his dark pupils gradually gave way to yellow slits. "You're here . . . for me," he said, thrusting Tarin back into the street, where he crumpled onto the pavement.

"Who are you?" Tarin sputtered. He felt blood dripping from his mouth where he must have hit the pavement.

The man took a deep breath and repositioned his hat back on his head. "My name?" he mused. "There are more than a few I've acquired over the years. But let me pick something sweet, something simple, something that will allow you to comprehend what I am at the most basic level. His eyes flashed as he offered a mocking bow. "I am Maximus."

"Maximus?" Tarin managed to say as his voice quaked.

"That's what I said!" the man called Maximus snarled through clenched teeth. "Is that not easy enough for you?" He rubbed his hand over his smooth chin and forced a smile. "Means 'greatest,' which I feel suits me well, don't you think?"

Maximus reached for a pouch hanging from the side of his hip. "Feel free to call me that, at least for the next few moments. After that, it won't much matter." He pulled a phial out of the pouch. It looked a lot like Gil's phial, but this one glowed crimson, and as it did, Tarin felt a pull from within his body, as if some energy within him he'd never noticed before was being drawn out of him toward the light.

Tarin's right arm began to reach for the glass against his will. Then, from the corner of his eye, he saw something move in the murky ceiling above him— an object, but he could not determine its shape. Beneath it, a small opening in the sky began to appear, similar to the one that had consumed his mother, but this one had a deep green hue. He felt a competing pull of his energy in that direction as his left arm reached for it.

"Edin-Lirum, curse them," Maximus muttered. "They won't take this from me." He began to approach Tarin.

The phial's light grew brighter. Its beams burned Tarin's eyes. Tarin screamed and tried in vain to cover them when he saw something just beyond Maximus. It was a figure of a person, and it was running fast toward them from farther down the street. Maximus heard the footsteps and spun around. He was too late. The figure shoved him to the side, rushed to Tarin, knelt next to him, and placed one hand on his back. With the other, the stranger lifted a phial of light, this one glowing pure white, as Gil's had. "Get back from him!" the stranger ordered. It was the voice of a woman.

Maximus steadied himself. He put his crimson light back under his waistcoat and smiled. "Well, well, well. If it's not Tarin's little protector. Iris, am I right?"

"Let him be!" the woman yelled. Tarin tried to look up. But in the dark night, and feeling quite dizzy from hitting his head on the ground, he couldn't make out her features. All he could see was the light glowing in the darkness.

Maximus approached them, his boots splashing against the wet pavement.

"I said get back!" the woman said. She pulled Tarin closer to her and whispered. "Don't worry. I got you."

"Oh, do you now?" Maximus said. He stopped just in front of Tarin and the woman. "You've got him like you had him years ago when you failed to save his mother?"

Tarin wiped some blood from his still-bleeding mouth. In the light of Iris's phial, he was able to make out her features and suddenly recognized her. She was the woman from the picture he'd seen earlier that day—if, in fact, this was that same day. He was so disoriented he was no longer sure if the world he'd come from was real or if this place was actually real, let alone how much time had passed since he'd been at the restaurant in Wall. Still, he managed to sputter, "Iris?"

"Iris indeed!" Maximus said. He turned to her and continued, "Had a bit of a preference now, didn't you?" He returned his gaze to Tarin. "Liked your father a bit better," he said with a wink. His face fell into a frown. "She's not all that dissimilar to the other who just came to this world . . . the man—the man with power." His lips curled into a sinister half-smile. "Be mindful of who you trust . . . Tarin. The agenda of some, even those who at first seem trustworthy, extends beyond the obvious."

"What's he saying?" Tarin asked. "Is he talking about . . . Gil?"

Iris didn't respond but instead shouted at Maximus, "Leave him alone!"

Maximus licked his lips and let them slowly curl into a broad smile. "If you say so." With that, he turned his eyes to Iris's light. With a quick puff, he blew it out.

CHAPTER 7

A woman lay in a bed in the darkness of a small room of a log cabin. Her breaths came quickly in troubled gasps. The thick quilts on her bed were tossed about. Her face glistened with sweat, and strands of her brown hair lay matted to her forehead. She sprang to a sitting position and screamed, "Let them be!"

She looked around the room. No one was there. She wiped the wet hair from her face and stared blankly at the wall, breathing heavily. A moment later, a curtain in a doorframe leading to the room opened, and another woman looked through. She appeared to be slightly older than the first woman, with dark black hair that hung loosely across her shoulders. She wore a simple nightdress and carried a lantern in one hand and a phial that gently glistened with white light in the other. She stepped into the room and said, "I heard you scream. Is everything well?"

The light from the phial glowed ever so slightly brighter than that of the lantern, and as it shed the darkness from the room, the terror in the first woman's face appeared to melt away. She closed her eyes, took a deep breath, and said, "I saw the man again." She opened her eyes and pointed toward the other woman. "The one I saw earlier today, from within your phial." New tears glistened from the corners of her eyes. "He is in great danger."

∘ ∘ ◇ ∘ ∘

Tarin groggily awoke to a sterile, white room that smelled of antiseptic and the faint odor of sweat. His head felt heavy, and his eyes were sluggish. He tried to take in his new environment. Slowly, he realized he was lying on a hospital bed, surrounded by beeping machines and blinking lights.

In the corner of the room, he saw a figure standing near a window covered by white blinds. At first, he expected to see one of the women he'd just observed in the log cabin in what had felt like yet another dream—or, perhaps, a dream within a dream. But he quickly realized this was not the case. Rather, in the corner stood a tall man dressed in a black leather jacket whose dark-eyed gaze was fixed on Tarin. A few moments passed, and then the man said, "Glad to see you're awake."

Confused, Tarin lay in silence for some time, unable to speak. Was he back in South Dakota, or was he in another strange, dreamlike location? On his left side, he noticed a wire snaking its way around his bed, connected to monitors displaying various readings indicating he must be injured or ill. "Am I back home?" Tarin asked.

The man approached the bed and looked down at Tarin. Now that Tarin could see his face clearly, he realized his dark eyes were, in fact, a deep shade of blue. Hadn't he seen this man before somewhere? His memory continued to strengthen. He felt his chest tighten. He'd seen this man before, at Wall Drug, before that terrible nightmare—or whatever it was. He recalled how the man's eyes had morphed into yellow slits before he'd found himself surrounded in that strange fog.

He looked at the door and considered ripping off the wires connected to his body and running out of the room for help. The nearby monitors started beeping as his readings apparently passed some preset threshold. The man walked over to them and pushed a blinking red button. The beeping stopped.

"Calm down, Tarin," the man said. "I'm not going to hurt you." He shook his head at the monitors. "Such primitive equipment," he muttered. "Seems even the Lattice hasn't figured out how to distribute all things equally." He turned to Tarin. "But I suppose outside the densest cities, investing in medical smart rooms, or even healing pods, isn't worth the cost." He shrugged. "But who am I to doubt our algorithmic overlord?"

Tarin glanced back at the door, then returned to look at the man. "Who are you?" he asked. "Where are my friends, and where am I?"

"Your friends," the man said, "are in the waiting room and, by now, hopefully getting a well-deserved bite to eat."

"So I'm in South Dakota," Tarin said, feeling a sense of hope and potential relief that this was, in fact, reality. Perhaps his recent experience had just been a sort of amalgamation of his dreams and recent odd adventures combined into a nightmarish, subconscious soup.

The man sat down in a chair near Tarin's bed and looked at the monitors. "You are," the man said. "This is the local hospital in Philip, South Dakota. After you collapsed at the restaurant, you fell into a violent seizure, which your friends told me had never happened to you before. Your friends rushed you here, and because of the nature of your collapse, a sudden-onset seizure, I had to insist I follow them and you here."

His voice grew lower and more serious. "I've seen others succumb to these unexplained seizures in my time here . . . two in Rapid City, one in Sturgis, more across Deadwood and Spearfish, even a few across the border into Wyoming."

He patted the bed and continued. "Your friends have been terribly worried about you, understandably. You were out for about four hours with dangerously high blood pressure and fast pulse. Your numbers have improved tremendously over this last hour. But unfortunately, I could not let them into the room until I cleared a few things." He pulled out a badge. "I work for a government agency called MJ12-2 and am leading an investigation into both the seizure phenomenon and some other highly unusual events that have been reported locally."

Though the man seemed far less intimidating now than he had earlier in Wall, Tarin still felt distrust. "What other events?" Tarin asked.

The man's smile faded. "Well . . . now, Tarin. I think you already have a pretty good clue about that." He stood back up and walked to the window. He opened the blinds, and a red glow from what appeared to be the evening sky shone through the glass. "I'm investigating unidentified aerial phenomenon in the area." He turned back to Tarin. "Much like the ones you saw in the pictures your police officer friend showed you, though I would have much preferred she'd been a little less flippant about sharing those so quickly and seemingly with anyone."

"Why?" Tarin asked. "They were just pictures."

"True," the man said, "and also true I didn't explicitly say they were classified, which they were not, or I would not have given them to her. But I did ask for discretion as she helped with our investigation." He rubbed his clean-shaven face and sighed. "Just don't want to create a panic among the locals. You know what I mean? Folks here are, how do I say this, a bit conspiratorial and skittish."

"I'm sure it helps a lot to ease their concerns with you dressed like that," Tarin said.

The man chuckled. "Ah, a bit of sarcasm." He walked back to the bed. "I think that means you're probably feeling better enough that I no longer need to monitor you. I've also run some tests while you were asleep, and you should be back to normal soon."

"What do you mean?" Tarin said. "Medical tests? Are you also a doctor?"

"No."

"Then what are you?"

"I already told you. I'm an agent within MJ12-2."

"But what is that?"

The man said nothing for a few moments. Then his voice dropped an octave and he replied with a grin, "Sorry, that's classified."

Tarin's monitors started beeping. "What about the others? The ones you said had seizures like me? What happened to them?" he asked. "Are they okay?"

The man glanced at the monitors and reached for a remote on a small, rollable shelf next to Tarin's bed. Tarin hadn't noticed before, but a small, primitive, flatscreen TV hung on the room's far wall. It was on, but the volume had been down. The man clicked the remote a few times, and the volume increased.

A woman news reporter from a popular network, one he'd now seen many times over the last year, stood in front of a backdrop of what looked like a ruined European town.

"Another day, another bombing," she said. "This comes on the heels of President Silverton's pledge to visit the war zone later this week in hopes of brokering a peace deal between the New Alliance and the Peacekeeper Nations. But leaders within the Alliance continue to threaten that any attempt to hinder their advances deeper into Peacekeeper territories they claim to be liberating will only force them to answer with greater force. Right now, the world waits and wonders, would Incognito and the Alliance risk the use of nuclear weapons and potential mutual annihilation to further its mission? President Silverton hopes to bring a steady hand to this ever more dangerous situation."

The man clicked the remote and turned off the TV. "It's a bit unnerving, the threat of nuclear war," the man said. "Wouldn't you say? At least, for those of us awake, aware, and with the potential to either be affected by this danger," he moved his eyes to meet Tarin's, "or play a part in its eventual conclusion."

Tarin didn't reply, but the beeping in the room grew faster.

"To return to your question earlier about the others who shared similar experiences to what you suffered today," the man continued, "the good news is, they're still sleeping." He grinned. "And they probably will be for quite a while."

Tarin thought back to his nightmare. Were the others suffering the same way as he did, with their own terrible nightmares? "How is that good news?" he asked.

"Because they lack the capacity to worry about the same issues you and I must contend with," the man said with a gesture at the TV, "even as they unwittingly play a part." He stood up and walked to the door. "You might want to call in your nurse. Your heart rate seems to be spiking." He started toward the exit but paused and said, "I'll be around if you happen to see anything else unusual in the skies. I took the liberty of adding my number to your phone. It's in your contacts, under 'Chief.'"

With that, the man finally left. The sounds of his footsteps echoed down the hall until, at last, they grew too distant to hear.

A moment later, Tarin heard another set of footsteps approaching, these ones lighter. A nurse entered the room, and Tarin immediately recognized her as the woman he'd seen at Old Cotton's the night before—the one who'd paid for his last beer.

"Well, look who's finally awake," she said with a smile. "And looks like I finally don't have to contend with your government friend anymore, either." She walked over to Tarin's monitors, pushed some buttons, and the beeping stopped. "That guy was really getting on my nerves, with all his 'knock first before coming in' nonsense, even when I needed to check your vitals." She walked to Tarin's bed. "And his friends outside were even worse. I've never seen anything so ridiculous. Telling us how we could and couldn't care for you, even when your heart rate and blood pressure kept spiking. Though, thankfully, you never went into critical territory. Speaking of which, try to take a few deep breaths. You're running a bit high even now."

Tarin nodded and breathed in deeply. He let it out and repeated the exercise a few more times. Finally, he said, "I remember you. Your name's Samantha, right?"

The woman smiled and attended to an IV drip beside Tarin's bed. "That's right. And you're Tarin," she added with a smile. "I was going to joke that all your drinking finally caught up with you, but I just looked at your blood results, and there's nothing there indicating any problems."

"It's nice to meet you," Tarin said. "So, do you know what happened to me?"

"Your friends said you blacked out at Wall Drug. Sounds like you fell off your chair and had a seizure. Liz rushed you here. I understand you know her. She thought you might be having an epileptic episode. But by the time you got here, your seizure had ended. Your vitals weren't great, but nothing was critical. Then those government folks, who'd followed Liz and your friends here, once they confirmed you were stable, told us they needed to monitor the situation and run some tests. Liz and your friends argued with them, but apparently, they had some legitimate government right to do that. I've never heard of such a thing. But I wasn't in a position to do much other than make sure you weren't hitting any dangerous numbers." She shrugged. "Otherwise, I was to 'knock' and come in to help."

She pulled out a notebook. As she did, something fell out, but before Tarin could let her know, she said. "So, do you have any history of epilepsy or any other neurological disorder that might have led to this?"

"None that I'm aware of," he said. "Well, other than that, I do have memory loss of anything before I was twelve."

Samantha jotted down some notes and then looked up. "You have amnesia? Have you been to a doctor about that before? I couldn't pull up any prior medical records for you."

"I haven't been to a doctor since I was in my early teens," Tarin said, "shortly before I was adopted. My new parents didn't bring me in for anything routine, and I was generally pretty healthy, otherwise."

"You didn't even go in for a sore throat or flu or anything?" she asked quizzically.

"With how good over-the-counter meds are, why bother?"

She raised an eyebrow and shook her head. "Alrighty, then. To each their own, I guess. But, no prior seizures, right?"

"Correct, at least as far as I know," Tarin said.

She scribbled some more in her notebook and said, "Got it." She tucked the notebook back into a waist pocket in her scrubs. "So how about I let your friends know you're ready for a visit? That is, if you feel well enough for some company?" She lifted her head toward the monitors and said with a smile, "Looks like you got yourself calmed down. Nice job with the breathing exercises."

"Thanks," Tarin said. "And yeah, I'd like that."

"Okay then." She headed toward the door. "I'll go fetch them for you. They'll be glad to finally see you. They've been bouncing around, scared to death, and asking a million questions all afternoon. Hit the call button on your remote if you need anything in the meantime." With that, she left the room.

Five minutes later, Tarin heard fast steps and excited voices coming down the hall. A moment later, Allen, Josh, and Rob, but not Gil, all burst into the room, carrying balloons, a teddy bear, and even a bouquet of flowers. "Tarin!" Allen said and ran over to him. He clasped Tarin's hand, bent down, and gave him a hug. "Thank you for not dying!"

Rob and Josh rushed over, and Rob shoved the teddy bear next to Tarin's head. He tussled Tarin's hair and said, "Don't you ever do that to us again!"

"Yeah," said Josh. He set the flowers on the rollable shelf beside the bed and tied the balloons to the bedframe. "You had us scared to death!" He sat down at the foot of Tarin's bed. "So what happened to you back at Wall? Do you remember anything?"

Tarin thought back to his dream, vision, or whatever that strange journey back to his hometown had been. He looked at his friends and wondered if he should burden them with it. They were already worried about him, and beyond that, he was not in the mood to recount the horrors of what had apparently been only the last few hours. So he said only, "I'm not sure. I just saw that man in the leather jacket back in Wall while we were eating. You know, the government guy that was here earlier, the same one Liz was talking to at Wall Drug, and I blacked out."

"I knew that guy was evil!" Rob said and punched the teddy bear.

"Not the bear's fault," Josh said.

"Sorry," Rob said, "I'm just so angry at those idiots from . . . what did they call themselves?"

"MJ12-2," Tarin responded.

"How did you know that?" Josh asked.

Tarin gestured toward the open door to the hallway. "Because 'Chief MJ12-2' told me."

Josh chuckled, "Ah, so boss man calls himself Chief, does he?"

During the conversation, Allen remained quiet, staring blankly at the window on the other side of the room. "MJ12," he whispered. "I swear I've heard of that before." But before he could continue, Gil, dressed in his new jeans and a plaid shirt from Wall Drug and still wearing a cowboy hat, walked into the room.

For a moment, Tarin nearly screamed as an image of Maximus, who had been dressed similarly, flashed through his mind. Gil's kind, broad smile quickly washed away that comparison. But, it did not wash away the memory of something the phantom had seemingly suggested: that Gil's motives were not obvious. What had Maximus—assuming he was even real—meant? Tarin hoped it didn't matter and that Maximus was just some terrible continuation of his now broadening landscape of dreams. But as he recalled his mother's eyes as they looked at him one last time, he feared the worst. As Gil approached the bed, still smiling, Tarin decided that for now, while he was still so confused about his recent experience, he'd be wary about what he shared—even with Gil.

Gil now stood over the bed. "Tarin!" he exclaimed and, like Allen had, grabbed Tarin's hand and held it between his own. "I am so happy to see you awake and looking ever so much better."

"Gil's been busy trying to contact his friends to come help us out with all this weird government agency and UFO stuff," Rob said. He leaned down and whispered into Tarin's ear. "He's using his phial of light like a phone. I swear I saw him outside whispering to it."

"Rob," Josh said. "We can all hear you. Even your whispers are loud."

Rob looked around sheepishly, then peered at Gil.

"Not to worry, my friend," Gil said. "The methods of Arvalast will feel odd in this world. I understand your wonderment about them. And you are right. I have finally managed to contact others from my world, and they have agreed to come and assist. They will be arriving by what they called planes the morning after tomorrow." He sighed sadly. "These planes sound similar to those hideous car transports you people use—specifically, the ones you say can travel in the air."

"Glad to hear you managed to convince them to come," Allen said, still looking pensive. "Things are getting a bit out of hand, and I don't feel good about those MJ12-2 government folks." He met Tarin's eyes. "Gil thinks they are trouble as well."

"Indeed," Gil said. He looked at Tarin. "And I am sorry I was not in a position to keep them from holding you in isolation. I feared interference would make things more problematic, and at this time, I do not have the cultural wherewithal and, what I understand now, the legal right to have interfered with their demands without consequence to myself that would have further limited my ability to help you in the future."

"They threatened to put Gil in jail if he kept insisting to join you in the hospital room," Rob said. "So we advised him to leave the matter be for now, since you were stable, until we learned more."

"It's okay," Tarin said to Gil. "Things turned out fine."

But as Gil maintained eye contact with Tarin, Tarin could see in Gil's expression that he understood there must be more to the story than what Tarin was revealing. Tarin turned away.

"What's this?" Josh said, picking up a piece of paper from the floor.

"Oh," Tarin said, happy at the change in subject. "The nurse, Samantha, dropped that earlier." He reached down for the monitor by his bed. "I'll give her a ring to pick it up, and I also want to ask when I can be released. I feel fine, so I want to get out of here as soon as possible."

"Looks like it's an obituary," Josh said. He stared at the paper for a few moments. "She looks so young. Can't be older than any of us."

Allen snatched it from Josh's hand and added, "Yeah, looks very young." He began to read.

"Abigail Yoder, a resident of Philip, South Dakota, passed away after an illness at the age of thirty-one. Abigail had a passion for life, and perhaps more than anything else, she was a lover of books and nature. She spent most of her time enjoying the beauty of the South Dakotan plains, Black Hills, and Badlands. She was born in Cashton, Wisconsin, to Ezra and Rachel Yoder and leaves behind siblings Mary and Ezekiel. Prior to moving to Philip, she lived in Pittsburgh, Pennsylvania, where she studied at the University of Pittsburgh, receiving a degree in English. She will be dearly missed by her friends and family."

Tarin reached out his hand. "Let me see that," he said. Allen handed the obituary to him, and on it, he saw a woman. She had the face of a country girl, simple, devoid of makeup, both quaint and beautiful, with long brown hair draped over her shoulders. As he stared into the green eyes in the photo, and they looked back at him, seeming almost lifelike, his monitors started beeping. It was the girl from his dreams.

CHAPTER 8

As Tarin continued to stare dumbfounded at the obituary photo, Samantha's voice came through the monitor. "Be right over."

Quickly, he handed the obituary back to Allen and leaned back in his bed.

"You okay?" Allen asked.

"Yeah," Tarin replied. "Just had a dizzy spell for a second." He looked up at his friends. "Don't tell the nurse. I want to get out of here as soon as I can." He breathed a few times deeply and the monitors stopped beeping.

Gil was trying to catch Tarin's eye. Tarin noticed but ignored it.

Samantha came in and said, "Good news, Tarin. Since everything has come back clear, you can go home this evening. But you should get a checkup in a week." She handed Tarin a thin tablet. "You'll need to sign a few things here, and I've added a list of doctors you can see to your Lattice Health account, which now has some actual data tied to it. It looks like you've never signed in, but once you do, from your phone or any other connected devices, you'll have access to all the info." She patted his arm. "I know you don't seem to be the type to go to doctors, but please, consider a follow-up. Seizures aren't anything to be taken lightly. You should also consider getting health tracker glasses, or the implants, assuming the trials continue showing good results. Both catch a lot of stuff early and overall keep a good history of health."

"I love my glasses," Rob said. "Help me keep my blood sugar under control. Never getting the implants though. Creeps me out."

"Sure," Tarin said and took the tablet. "I'll consider my options." He signed the electronic forms and handed the tablet back to her.

Samantha proceeded to unhook Tarin from the monitors and disconnect his IV. Allen left to fetch Tarin his clothes—he was currently in a hospital gown—and Josh, Rob, and Gil left to wait for Tarin in the waiting room.

"You've got a good group of friends," Samantha said as she finished disconnecting Tarin from the tubes and wires. She lifted his bed to a sitting position. "One more test. Let's make sure you can stand up." She took his hand and helped him to his feet. He managed to stand without issue and she smiled. "Well, looks like you're good to go. I'll be out by the front desk if you have any questions before heading out."

Tarin nodded, then remembered something. "Wait. You left this here." He held out the obituary.

She looked down at it, and her face grew sad. She took it and said, "Thanks. It must have fallen out from my notebook."

"Was she the same woman you mentioned at Old Cotton's?" Tarin asked. "The one you were caring for?"

"She was," Samantha said. "Abigail was a great girl. Didn't get out much. Not sure if you ever met her in town. Maybe at the grocery store or post office?"

"No. I'd never seen her around."

Samantha stared at the paper. "She had so many dreams, but her head was in the clouds. I'm sure she would have pursued some of them more if she hadn't fallen so ill so fast. I feel so badly for her."

"If I may ask," Tarin said, "what did she die from?"

Samantha looked up at him. "We never could diagnose her illness, despite having many experts analyze it. It seemed she just began shutting down without cause. She had occasional seizures as well. Another reason I strongly suggest you see a doctor soon, just to be safe." She brushed a tear from her cheek. "Anyway, her funeral is in two days. She wanted a burial, probably because of her Amish upbringing. I guess they don't often cremate. But her family isn't coming, sadly. I guess there was some trouble there between her and them. I don't think they were too happy about some of her life choices."

She handed the obituary back to Tarin. "If you think about it, feel free to come on out. The address to the church is on there. I know you didn't know her, but it would help make the ceremony feel a bit less lonely. Since she had so few connections, just hoping . . . you know, to try to make it as nice as I can."

Tarin fixed his eyes on the photo again. Those deep green eyes stared back. They seemed so alive, despite being but a conglomeration of pixels on a piece of paper from a now deceased woman he'd never met.

Samantha left the room. Fifteen minutes later, Allen returned, Tarin dressed, and they met with the others in the waiting room. Another fifteen minutes after that, they were back at Allen's house, resting in the living room and waiting for a pizza order to arrive as the final orange rays of sunset filled the living room with a pleasant sense of calm.

Allen received a call from Liz. She'd been dispatched to check on a report from a local rancher but wanted to hear how Tarin was doing. She was delighted to hear he was well, and Allen would have been delighted to have continued to talk to her, but the pizza came, so he said goodbye. Soon the group was in the kitchen digging into the food. Of course, it was Gil's first time having pizza, and to no surprise to the group, he vehemently expressed his approval of what he called a "masterful culinary creation."

"You know what we need to do?" Rob said, stuffing his mouth with a large slice. "We should teach Gil how to play LOB."

"We do need a break from all the craziness of the last twenty-four hours," Josh said. "Gil, what do you think? Want to learn how to play?"

Gil glanced over at Tarin. Tarin continued to sense Gil knew something was wrong. Part of Tarin wanted to share everything, to release the burden of confusion pushing down on his chest. But he just couldn't shake the ominous words from Maximus about Gil's motives. Yes, Gil seemed very trustworthy. Yes, he'd seemingly saved him from the UFO. But Gil's presence, and his phial of light, had also resurrected a terrible aspect of his past, one he'd worked so hard to repress. It had also added a potentially new element to his past—his origin from another world.

Beyond his new concerns about Gil, Tarin additionally needed to understand who this Iris woman was that saved him, and the overall link between all of this and the woman in the cabin, whose face he found was consuming his mind more and more since reading the obituary. He needed more time to gain some distance from the events since Wall Drug to process things. Then, maybe, he'd be ready to talk things over with Gil, or his friends.

"I think a game would be a good idea," Tarin said.

They finished eating and spent the next two hours teaching Gil the nuances of LOB. He was slowly drawn into the strategy and frequently drew parallels with various cards to elements from Arvalast. Eventually, even Tarin found himself able to let go of some of the built-up anxiety and focus on the strategy of the game, which he had become quite talented at from years of playing with his friends at weekly game nights.

After an hour, Gil dropped a card called "Healing Elixir." Its image featured a mystical, arcane-looking glass container filled with a glowing orange and blue liquid.

"Nice move!" Rob said. "That will reduce the potency of the virus card draining your beasts each round."

"You're doing really well," Josh added. "You might actually win this game."

Tarin stared at the card, the shape and style of the glass container reminded him of something else. As he continued to fixate on it, the blue and orange seemed to transform into a deep crimson until he finally tore his eyes away, got up, and said, "Be right back. Going to grab another slice of pizza."

"That sounds like a good idea," Gil said and stood. "I will join you."

"Bring whatever's left when you come back," Rob hollered at them as they went to the kitchen.

Once alone, Gil leaned toward Tarin's ear and whispered, "You do not need to tell me anything, but I know you have encountered something that disturbed you. I wanted to say I am available to discuss if you so choose."

Tarin stood over the half-full pizza box on the counter. Two other boxes lay empty on the floor near a trash container. He stared down at the box on the counter, unwilling to make eye contact with Gil. Tarin picked up a slice of pizza and, as he did, noticed his hands were trembling. Quickly, he handed another slice to Gil, grabbed the pizza box, and walked back into the living room.

"You know what?" Allen said as he reached for a pizza slice before Tarin could set the box down on the coffee table. "I have a suggestion. Sounds like we have a whole day before Gil's friends get here. Rob and Josh don't work tomorrow, my consulting job is flexible, and Tarin, you only work at the farm Thursday through Sunday, so why don't we take a bit of a tour of the area tomorrow? You know, show Gil some of the sights—like Mount Rushmore and some of the attractions in the Black Hills. Would be good for us to get out and have a bit of a normal adventure."

"As long as the outing doesn't end up like the one in Wall," Rob said.

"Yeah, let's try to avoid any 'government business,'" Josh added, making air quotes with his fingers. "But otherwise, I like that idea. Would be good to get out. Would be good for you too, Gil. We can better acquaint you with some landmarks of the good old United States of America and maybe share a bit of history with you. You did say you were interested in assimilating more into the local culture."

"I would like that very much," Gil said. He picked up his cowboy hat, which had been perched behind him on the couch, and put it on his head. "And now I should attract less attention to myself with these new clothes."

"Looking good," Allen said. He gestured to his own sporadically stubbled face. "You got a good beard situation that's working nicely with the hat. The rest of us would look a bit less classy with it, but it works on you."

"I think his original outfit was good too," Rob said.

"Not saying it wasn't," Allen agreed. "But it would only make sense at a comicon. The cowboy outfit works better for modern South Dakota. But on a different topic, I've been thinking a lot about those government folks, the men in the leather jackets, that Tarin said called themselves MJ12-2. I finally remembered why I thought that name sounded so familiar."

Tarin and the others turned their full attention to Allen. "Do tell," Josh said.

"Well, about five or so years ago, I went down a UFO rabbit hole. It happened as I got to talking with Old Bill about all his conspiracies. I remember him telling me about a government agency rumored to have existed long ago, back in the 1980s."

"That was over a hundred years ago," Rob said.

"I know," Allen said. "I heard that back in the late twentieth century, and again about thirty years later, UFOs were a big deal. There were lots of anecdotal sightings and significant media interest. But that group, in the 1980s, I remember now that they were called MJ-12, which stood for Majestic Twelve. I'd need to talk to Bill to remember all the details, but from what I recall, they were an alleged secret society made up of the world's most powerful figures, including government officials and military leaders. I think they were founded in the 1940s by President Truman, who was dealing with a lot of interest in Roswell, New Mexico. It was the location of one of the most famous UFO sightings."

"I think I remember it was actually a UFO crash," Josh said.

Everyone now turned to look at him. He shrugged. "It's a small town. I've gone down the rabbit hole with Old Bill a bit too. We all have."

Rob nodded in agreement. Gil continued to listen intently while Tarin remained silent and pensive.

"Anyway," Allen continued, "the group is believed to be highly secretive and to have access to technologies that are far beyond anything known—military or private. They're also thought to be in charge of covering up evidence of the existence of extraterrestrial life on Earth. I even heard MJ-12 served as a global governing body, keeping watch over the nations of the world while working toward some hidden agenda only they're aware of."

The room went silent, other than the sound of Rob chewing on a piece of pizza.

"Can you eat more quietly?" Josh huffed at him.

"Sorry," Rob said. "I always chew loudly when I'm intrigued."

"Thank you for sharing this information," Gil said to Allen. "Do I understand you believe this MJ12-2 group could be a sort of continuation of that previous organization? Assuming, as you stated, the rumors of their existence bear some truth."

"I do indeed," Allen said. "And with what's going on with the war in Europe, and now UFOs here in our backyard, it wouldn't surprise me one bit that if a covert government organization did exist, it might want to pay us a visit."

"But don't you think it would arouse a lot of suspicions by overtly using that name?" Josh said. "I mean, it's basically like wearing a sign saying, 'We're a UFO organization with lots of secrets and power.'"

"You would think that," Allen added, "and they would know we would think that too. So . . . maybe they want us to think that?"

"But why?" Josh said.

"I don't know!" Allen said in frustration. "To create confusion and misdirection? Like, they want people to think they are tracking otherworldly stuff because maybe they are actually doing something else, like trying to manipulate the earth by more conventional means. Beats me, but whatever the case, they're acting pretty weird, like when they wouldn't let us go visit Tarin earlier, and how they're looking to talk to people who've seen UFOs around here."

Tarin recalled how the chief had told him about other locals having similar seizures to his own. Was there some psychological component to all of this, and were Tarin and those falling ill just part of some sort of government-related mind game created by MJ12-2?

He sat silently—thinking. Maybe he should just open up to Gil and his friends and share more about his encounter with Maximus and what he saw happen to his mother. But as he considered it, he felt the pressure of tears begin to build up behind his eyes. What if it wasn't a mind game? What if everything in the nightmare was real? If it was, he continued to be uncertain if he could trust Gil, and he didn't want to add additional burden to his friends.

He blinked twice and made his decision. For now, this would remain his problem.

"I need to go to bed," he finally said, feigning a yawn. "I've had a long day. Hopefully, I can get a good night's sleep so I'm rested up for our field trip tomorrow."

"So are we going to the Black Hills?" Rob asked.

"Yeah," Tarin said. "I agree with Allen. It'll be good to try to step away from the crazy events of the last two days and try to have a normal day. And I promise I'll do my best not to have any seizures," he said, managing to force a smile.

"You know what else would be fun?" Josh said. "If we stopped by Gaka's house. He lives in Custer, close to Mount Rushmore and the Crazy Horse monument. In fact, he works at the Crazy Horse museum in the mornings, but I bet he'd be happy to have us over in the afternoon. He might even make us dinner." He looked at Gil. "You haven't eaten Earth food until you've tried his Wohanpi."

"Then there is no doubt we should pay Gaka a visit," Gil said with delight.

Josh and Rob both laughed. "He's not your Gaka," Rob said. "That is the Lakota word for grandfather. I'm sure he wouldn't mind you calling him that, but he usually goes by Michael."

"I see," Gil said. "Thank you for the clarification. Then I would be quite excited to pay Michael a visit and expand upon my knowledge of Earth cuisine while I wait for my counterparts to arrive."

"I think we could tell Gaka about the last two days as well," Josh added. "He's very open-minded and knowledgeable about things of a more paranormal nature. He might have some insights into what we've been going through." Josh turned to Tarin. "Sound good to you too?" he asked.

Although Tarin usually loved an excuse to visit his friends' Gaka, Tarin felt reluctant. Michael had an uncanny ability to almost see through a person and articulate their current mood or state of spirit, as he liked to say. And at the moment, Tarin's spirit was in a bit of turmoil. Michael might be able to pierce his facade. But maybe that wouldn't be a bad thing? Michael was disconnected from everything that had happened the last day. He might actually be a good person to open up to. "Sure," he finally said, "sounds like fun." He stood up. "Going to grab a quick shower before I go to bed. Can I crash in your room again tonight?" he asked Allen.

"Figured on it," Allen said. "Sleeping bag's still in there." He started picking up some of the trash and paper plates and asked the others, "After I tidy up a bit, want to play more LOB?"

"Let's do it!" Rob said. Josh and Gil agreed as well.

"Oh, and Tarin," Allen said, "we picked up some clothes at your trailer while you were at the hospital just in case you were going to be there for a while. They're in a bag in the car. Sorry, I forgot to bring them in earlier."

"No problem," Tarin said. "And thanks."

Tarin fetched the clothes from the car. Before he returned to the house, he took a nervous glance into the now dark sky.

No UFOs.

He hurried back into the house, and after a quick shower, he went to bed. That night, at long last, he had no dreams.

The next morning, the group rushed to eat breakfast, opting for only cereal rather than cooking something. They then piled into Allen's car to begin their journey toward Rapid City and the Black Hills. Allen introduced Gil to country music, which, for the most part, Gil claimed to be satisfactory, though he found the consistent themes of broken relationships interwoven with the upbeat tempo puzzling.

"Why does the music not fit with the narrative?" he asked, receiving little in the way of a satisfactory answer from the group. But he seemed to accept this as a nuance to Earth culture and spent most of his time staring out the window of the car and marveling at the sights. "The landscape from this vantage point looks even more fascinating while moving at this speed," he said. "Although not fully dissimilar from riding a horse, my ability to fully appreciate the view from the side as opposed to maintaining a forward focus offers an incredible perspective."

"More like riding a horse when driving," Allen said, his eyes fixed on a semitruck in front of him as he prepared to pass.

"Why don't you turn on self-driving?" Josh asked.

"Boring," replied Allen.

"Just wait," Josh said. "I bet it's the next thing the Lattice is going to regulate."

It took more than an hour to reach Rapid City, the largest nearby town. It rested directly against the Black Hills, which stood out in stark contrast to the otherwise flat plains, rolling hills, and badlands of the rest of the region.

As they drove through the city, the sun shone brightly, glinting off of the cars passing by. Traffic was rarely heavy in Rapid City despite its lack of skylanes. Although it was sizeable from the perspective of the rest of the nearby towns, it was not so compared to many other, much bigger cities across the country and didn't require the additional tier of travel to mitigate congestion.

Allen navigated Interstate 90 into the city's eastern side, which blanketed the mostly flat prairie with scattered auto dealerships, small stores, and some strip malls until they entered a denser area filled with, primarily, hotels, restaurants, and big-box stores frequented by the many tourists. In the distance, the majestic Black Hills reached up toward the sky, where the South Dakotan plains finally gave way and submitted to their watchful stare.

They merged off the interstate and made their way to Route 16, which led directly into the Black Hills. Allen called out different establishments and told stories of the area while they drove through town and toward their first stop of the day, Mount Rushmore.

At one point, Josh pointed out the window and yelled, "Is that one of the MJ12-2 guys?" Indeed, a man dressed very similarly to the MJ12-2 chief who'd monitored Tarin at the hospital stood on the sidewalk near a coffee shop, listening to someone waving their hands and pointing in the sky.

"Just ignore it," Tarin said, a lump forming in his throat. He still didn't know if MJ12-2 was the cause of his nightmare and encounter with Maximus. And he wasn't eager to test the possibility through a direct encounter, surprise or otherwise. "Drive, Allen. Fast."

Another thing to run from.

Allen obliged without a word, and soon they reached the southern end of the city. The markings of the town gave way to a steady incline that, over the course of only a few miles, provided a sweeping view of the city behind them while the pine-tree-covered mountains grew ever taller in front of them.

Gil continued to marvel at the landscape. "It reminds me of the Great Forest of my world," he said. "Not completely dissimilar from the western end of that forest where there are also rising hills and mountains."

Though Tarin stayed silent, he, too, felt this drive was bringing him back to the forest backdrop of his dreams. Still, he had never let that deter him from a visit to the area. Though these hills carried with them a whisper of foreboding tethered to the shame he felt from his actions in his dreams, their music of beauty and adventure was much louder.

Over the next half an hour, Allen navigated the small car along a winding road surrounded by steep walls of pines as they traversed well-trodden corridors between the mountains. Soon they passed through

Keystone, the self-described "Gateway to Mount Rushmore." It was a picturesque town nestled in a valley hugged on both sides by hills. Its main road hosted old Western-style stores, saloons, and lodgings. When they reached the other side of town, they began a sharp ascent. After coming out of the canopy of trees, they were greeted with a sweeping vista on one side and Mount Rushmore on the other.

"There it is!" Allen said, pointing through the windshield at the large sculpture at the top of a mountain peak. "You can see all five presidents from here. From left to right, we have George Washington, Thomas Jefferson, Theodore Roosevelt, Abraham Lincoln, and finally, Feleti Kama, who, after over a hundred years of no new additions, was added for her role in leading the world into the Great Peace."

CHAPTER 9

The holographic projection at the front of the small theater in the Mount Rushmore Museum went dark, and the hourly showing of President Feleti Kama's famous speech to usher in the Great Peace ended as quickly as it had begun.

Tarin, Josh, Rob, Allen, and Gil were preparing to get up to leave their position at the front of the nearly empty theater when a soft voice began to speak from the back row.

"If only we'd realized," the male voice said in an Eastern Asian accent, "how hubristic a thought that a broken world could birth a righteous creation immune to the darkness indwelling us." They looked behind them. An old, balding man stood up, returned their gaze, and said, "We were fools," then walked out of the room.

The president's speech had brought Tarin back to fifteen years ago, though not quite like Gil's light had done. This time, it had been more nostalgic than painful. His mother was still sane then, and his father was still a man he respected. But as he'd watched the hologram of Feleti Kama speak in her trademark navy blue suit as her pearl earrings sparkled in the noonday sun, her message of hope and promises of peace and prosperity seemed so foreign—so naive.

Europe was at war.

Tarin pondered the president's closing remarks as he and the others got up to leave the theatre. At the same time, he took a fast peek around the room to make sure none of those MJ12-2 leather jackets were hiding in a corner, waiting to jump out and knock him back into some terrible nightmare.

"The Trinity Lattice with its self-created security apparatus is truly and completely self-contained," Kama had said, "rendering it immune from the same flaws that plague those with corruptible minds, which are rife with selfish ambitions and short-sightedness. It is not a singularity that is to be feared but a self-governing and self-correcting duality that, when coupled with humankind, creates a trinity that will open the gates to entirely new worlds of opportunity."

Tarin shook his head. *The Trinity Lattice*. Yeah, it was a clever title for Earth's AI administrator, but for the most part, the stupid thing seemed less like Earth's savior and more like an annoying parent who made it harder for him to drink away his pain.

"Why did that elderly gentleman speak of hubris?" Gil asked as Tarin and the others entered the museum's main hall. "Was he not inspired by this leader's message of hope and her new technological creation?"

"Unfortunately," Allen responded, "the Great Peace President Kama promised wasn't long-lived."

"That's an understatement," Josh said. "It took less than fifteen years to go from Great Peace to bracing for a possible global war."

They paused in front of a wide mural depicting the National Mall. Thousands of specks representing the unending crowds covered most of the mural, while a small figure in the distance stood on a great stage with barely visible outstretched hands.

"What happened to sully this grand opportunity your world had set before it?" Gil said. "What broke the system in place, this Trinity Lattice, to ensure the Great Peace would endure?"

Everyone stood silently for a few moments until Allen said, "There's a really nice trail just outside that leads to the base of Mount Rushmore where we can get good views of all the presidents. I'll tell you more as we walk."

Meanwhile, Tarin again scanned the area for any signs of men dressed in black jackets. Though there were a moderate number of tourists taking pictures and meandering along the stage in front of the mountain, none wore all black. Tarin let his shoulders relax, sighed, and followed Gil and the others down the concrete path.

Not far in the distance, the faces of the presidents greeted them, sculpted from the wall of one of the mighty peaks of the Black Hills. Their expressions radiated thoughtfulness as they peered into the plains beyond with stately gazes. But despite their direct connection to the country through the mountain, they seemed otherwise detached from the struggles of a world that they had, in large part, helped build. Their likenesses now looked out over an uncertain horizon.

Allen began sharing some history of the monument with Gil as they walked. The mountain grew taller and the presidents' features became crisper. They continued down the path until Rob pointed ahead and said, "Let's show Gil the outcropping where you can see George Washington through a crack in the rocks."

The group headed down a short staircase and into a small enclave of rocks where, on the far side, was a slit facing the mountain. Each of them took a quick peek in turn, and then Gil approached and looked through. "This is indeed a unique perspective to the first face upon the mountain," he said. He turned around and said to Allen, "You shared earlier that this man was your nation's first leader?"

"First president," Allen corrected. He shared more about the nation's founding as they continued along the wooded boardwalk that was the Presidential Trail. Tall pines surrounded them and rustled in the cool November breeze. The trail provided many viewing areas, which they took advantage of, and as they looked more closely at each president's face, Allen provided a short summary of their history and accomplishments.

Toward the end of the trail, they reached a final viewing platform. Beyond the pines in front of them, they looked up at the impressive figure of Feleti Kama. On her face was carved a faint smile, and her expression was the same one of grand optimism about the future she'd presented during her speech. As the only woman in the group, she was the prominent figure, carefully crafted to look as if her face was carved at the same time as the others, but also set upon the mountain in such a way that it was clear she was representing the future, her gaze active, while the others seemed more reflective.

"President Kama," Allen said, and held out his hand toward the sculpture. "Even though I was still a teenager at the time, everyone I knew was so excited when she won her second term with the largest victory margin of any president ever."

Allen shared that before her first term, she was a little-known media personality of Polynesian ancestry, but by her second term, she had become a legend because of her ability to eloquently navigate politics to bring people together and get things done. "But despite Kama's impressive victory and triumph with the Great Peace," Allen shared, "ten years after her time as president was over, and the Trinity Lattice had proven to be all that she claimed it would be, something strange began to happen. The Trinity Lattice disconnected one small nation in Europe from the rest of the global economic system. As a result, that nation's economy began to collapse, and its people began to go hungry as the Lattice also disrupted the nation's power systems. When world leaders queried the system to ask how its tactics to shut off this nation's connection to the rest of the world could possibly meet the requirements of the algorithm, which, as you saw in the video, was to maximize global prosperity and peace, it only replied that its charter was still active and this had to occur to maintain stability toward that charter."

"Seems contradictory," Gil said.

"That's what many others felt as well," said Allen. "And this is when things started to go really badly. I remember being in my early twenties and Rob and Josh's Gaka talking to us about the erosion of trust building among nations. Despite years of peace, two clear points of view began to form about what to do next. Some countries wanted to recommend the world find a way to shut down the Trinity Lattice altogether.

Others urged for patience. But within weeks, the countries in favor of shutting down Trinity found themselves in the same fate as the first country. Trinity decoupled them from the rest of the globe. This forced these disconnected countries to unify together and form the New Alliance. The remaining nations still thriving under the Trinity Lattice were dubbed the Peacekeeper Nations."

Allen took a seat on a nearby bench and looked back up at the face of President Kama. "Efforts were made by the Peacekeeper Nations to reconnect the New Alliance to the global systems, but Trinity sabotaged all attempts at this because it was fully integrated into and in control of all these systems, making it impossible to change them otherwise. So the New Alliance built an independent apparatus of trade that resurrected their economies to allow them to at least survive. After a few years, though they were far weaker than the Peacekeeper nations, they found their footing."

"Then *he* came," Rob said.

"Yeah," Allen said. "Three years ago, a new leader further unified the New Alliance, and he declared war on the Peacekeeper nations. Those nations had no choice but to defend themselves. At the same time, Trinity rescinded its lock on previously decommissioned nuclear weapons, which were said to have been fully dismantled during the Great Peace when Trinity had determined this was the needed path forward to ensure long-lasting stability on Earth. The Alliance, in control of its own nuclear weapons, followed suit."

"And what is a nuclear weapon?" Gil asked.

Allen's face grew somber, and he said, "It is an explosive device, a bomb, that can blow up most of a city and then poison the surrounding area for hundreds of miles with deadly radiation."

Rob added, "And there are lots and lots of these stockpiled bombs still around in missile silos, despite all the ones that could be fired from subs and planes being destroyed."

"In fact," Allen said, "there's even a decommissioned bomb in an underground bunker near Philip that the US just put back online."

"Can the Trinity Lattice choose to utilize these mighty weapons if it so wishes since it seems to have the capabilities to restrict their use?" Gil asked.

Allen shook his head. "The Trinity Lattice can control almost everything as it relates to the economy, and it has control of the electrical grid to manage overall power consumption, which is also how it can lock weapons such as nukes, but it was never set up to control any military device directly through offense. It's less clear what the capabilities within the Alliance are, though."

"Let's hope that's still true," Josh said. He had taken a seat on the wooden floor of the observation deck and was leaning back against the rails behind him.

"I'm fairly certain it is," Allen said. "As part of my consulting job, which is related to helping existing corporate systems navigate the nuances of the Lattice and its ever-evolving 'recommendations,' and also just for fun, I understand its history and capabilities very well."

"Nerd," Josh said with a sigh. "And if you could hurry up, I'm getting hungry and would like to head over to Crazy Horse next to see Gaka and convince him to let us come for dinner."

"I'm almost done," Allen said. He looked at Gil. "That brings us back to the state we're in now, with two rival groups of nations. One is convinced the Trinity Lattice is still the way of the future. The other, the New Alliance, now unified around a single leader, sees the Lattice as a threat that must be destroyed."

"Who is this leader of the New Alliance?" Gil said.

"No one knows," Allen replied. "He presents himself as an anonymous figure shrouded in darkness with his voice distorted. Honestly, it's not clear if he's even a man, but the general consensus is that he is. Most everyone calls him by his now global nickname: Incognito."

"And what has become of Feleti Kama? It seems her leadership would be very valuable for such a time as this."

Allen looked back up at Kama's face on the mountain, then said, "She disappeared from the public scene more than five years ago. No one knows where she's been since then."

Josh pointed back down the path from where they'd just been and said, "Take a look. I think we have some company."

Tarin felt his chest tighten as he and the others looked to where Josh was pointing. Just around a bend beyond some trees overhanging the boardwalk, a man dressed in a black jacket and pants stood talking to a small group of tourists. He carried a tablet and was writing and nodding his head as they spoke.

Tarin felt adrenaline surge into his limbs at the terrible thought of seeing Maximus again. "Hurry," he whispered as he started to run. He forced himself to slow to avoid creating a scene. Looking back at the others, he hissed, "Let's get out of here."

They followed him along the boardwalk and began descending a number of sets of stairs until they reached a concrete portion of the path and headed back uphill toward the parking lot. The forest at the base of the mountain still surrounded them, offering Tarin some sense of safety as it obscured him and his friends from any onlookers behind them on the boardwalk.

"Do you think he saw us?" Rob whispered to Tarin.

"I don't think so," Tarin said. "And let's keep it that way." He hastened his pace. The others followed suit until they climbed another long set of stairs that led to a break in the trees with the parking lot just beyond. They broke into a jog, but just as they did, a white van drove by slowly, and in the passenger window, Tarin saw yet another person in an MJ12-2 leather jacket staring at what looked like a map.

"There's more of them," Tarin whispered. "Hurry, let's get to the car fast."

They continued their jog toward Allen's car, visible a short distance away. Tarin watched the van pull up alongside the front entrance to the monument. The man in the passenger seat got out, followed by two other leather jackets who exited a side sliding door. Moments later, Tarin and his friends reached Allen's car and got in, and without a word, Allen started the car and made a hurried exit. Tarin turned and looked out the back window. As the MJ12-2 agents grew more distant, he slumped down into his seat and closed his eyes. This trip had been meant to create more of a sense of normalcy after the UFO encounter and incident at Wall, but thus far, it had done little to quell his anxiety. He hoped the next stop to Crazy Horse would be better.

CHAPTER 10

Allen drove slightly over the speed limit as he snaked through the mountainous roadways deeper into the Black Hills. "What do you think MJ12-2 were doing at Mount Rushmore?" he said, his eyes fixed on the road ahead.

"Looked like they were interrogating more people, probably about the UFOs," Josh said. "I'm glad they didn't seem to notice us or you, Tarin, since they seem to have a special interest in you."

An image of yellow-slitted eyes briefly flashed through Tarin's memory. "Yeah," he finally said, "glad we dodged them too."

Rob fidgeted and said, "You don't think they'll be at Crazy Horse, do you, guys? Maybe we should call Gaka and ask if we could meet him at his house after work."

"Gaka doesn't carry a personal phone," Josh said. "Remember? He's still convinced they give you radiation and only has a landline. Plus, reception is bad out here unless you pay for satellite coverage, which he won't, so he finds them useless."

"Can't we call him on his work phone?" Rob said.

"I don't know the number," Josh replied as the scenery around them opened up into the grassy fields that made up the central high portion of the Black Hills. Josh pointed out the window. A wooden sign marking the entrance to the Crazy Horse monument appeared in front of them. "We're here already. Let's just meet with him in person. If we see any leather jackets, we can leave and head over to his house and hope he doesn't stay late or run any errands after work."

Allen pulled into the small road leading to the monument. He stopped at an entrance booth, showed the guard a card, and continued driving between frosted meadows and pine trees until arriving at a large parking lot. He parked directly facing the Crazy Horse monument. It stood in the distance, depicting the Native American chief Crazy Horse pointing ahead while riding a great steed. It seemed to dwarf the sculptures of Mount Rushmore and was cut with such detail, from the warrior's wind-whipped hair to the fiery intensity carved into the face of his horse, it made one feel as if an actual living stone giant had emerged from the side of a mountain.

"Truly awe-inspiring," Gil said as he got out of the car and marveled at the sculpture. "Allen, please tell me more about this man's history."

"I will save that pleasure for Josh and Rob's Gaka," Allen said. "Let's go see if we can find him, and I'm sure he'd be happy to tell you more. He knows the history of Crazy Horse and the tribes of this area better than anyone else I know."

They approached the extensive museum and visitor center on the other end of the parking lot. They entered through one of the three large wooden doors and were greeted by a grand foyer full of Native American relics, tools, and weapons. On the walls hung pictures of individuals and families from the local tribes, complete with storyboards describing their history and more scenic images depicting various time periods of the region from long ago. Colorful tapestries blanketed portions of the available wall space, creating a sense of comfort as Josh led them through the atrium and into another large room that housed a teepee as well as lifelike mannequins dressed in traditional garb. The museum was not quite as densely packed as the more touristy Rushmore, and thus far, it was devoid of any MJ12-2.

"Gaka should be working at the gift shop," Josh said as they exited the room with the teepee and entered another large room, this one a bit busier than the others. Josh pointed toward a counter in the room's center. "There he is!"

An elderly Native American man stood behind a currency monitor at the Crazy Horse museum gift shop. Long, thick white hair rested upon his still-strong shoulders, and his bright eyes glistened as he merrily spoke to a customer. Though his face was weathered, its age did not hide an inner glow even while his bony fingers carefully wrapped a glass mug adorned with a picture of the monument before placing it in a brown paper bag. Rob waved at him and said, "Gaka! How're you doing?"

The older man's eyes lifted from his careful attention to the mug, and he smiled broadly as he saw Rob and the others. He waved, then held up a finger to indicate he'd be ready to chat in a moment.

"We'll be waiting over there when your shift is done!" Rob said, pointing to a table in the room just outside. Rob's exclamation was a bit loud for Tarin's liking, as it led others in the gift shop to look in their direction. But after a quick scan of the room, he didn't see any tall men in black leather jackets.

"Anyone up for a quick game?" Josh said, pulling out two decks of LOB cards. They all nodded and forgot about their worries for the next thirty minutes as they became lost in the game, except for Tarin.

With each passing second, he was growing more concerned about his encounter with Maximus. Even though the nightmare was now a day old, he had no better sense of whether it was real or just a government mind game. He also didn't know if it was connected in any way to his recurring dreams of the otherwordly battle or even his new visions of the woman who had died—Abigail. Looking at Michael from the corner of his eye, he ran through his mind how he might attempt to explain his situation to him if he got the chance. Meanwhile, as the card game continued, Tarin took a moment to observe Gil.

Gil carefully studied his cards, his focus palpable. From the first time Tarin had met him, despite Gil's odd attire and the bold assertion that he knew Tarin, Gil's sturdy yet kind face and innocent approach to conversation made him difficult not to trust. Yet it was Gil's coming that had quickly turned Tarin's otherwise peaceful life in Philip upside down. And as Gil, still dressed like a cowboy yet mercifully having set his hat aside, played a card while wearing a broad smile as the others groaned, Tarin continued to wonder: Was Gil really here to help them, or was he the reason Tarin had that encounter with Maximus? He didn't want to think it, but . . . could Maximus be that evil entity Gil had told him about?

"Well, hello there, boys!" a voice said with a slight Lakota accent. "To what do I owe the blessing of a visit from such a fine group as yourselves today? And with a guest, I see!"

Josh and Rob's Gaka had a voice that resonated with genuine happiness. Behind his twinkling, merry eyes, he also exuded an aura of wisdom that inspired a curiosity about what hidden pearls of insight one might draw from him.

Rob introduced his Gaka to Gil, and Gaka exclaimed he'd be happy for anyone in the group to call him Gaka or Michael. Gil politely opted to do the latter, which Tarin assumed was to respect the relationship between grandfather and grandchildren.

As they made small talk, Gil fairly easily convinced Michael to give him a brief account of Chief Crazy Horse's life and adventures. Gil marveled at the story about the Sioux warrior who was remembered for his leadership of Native American forces during the Great Sioux War and the Battle of the Little Bighorn.

"The stories of these lands continue to fascinate me," Gil said. "I continue to find so many parallels to the histories of my lands."

"And where are you from, Gil?" Michael asked, tilting his head to one side and glancing down at Gil's cowboy hat. "At first glance, I figured you to be local to South Dakota or maybe Wyoming."

"That's what we were going for!" Rob said, smiling. "I knew the cowboy hat was a good idea."

"Before we get into that," Josh quickly interrupted, "we wanted to ask you, have you seen any strange government folks around here today? They'd be wearing black leather jackets, possibly blue-tinted sunglasses."

"Can't say that I have," Michael said. Tarin breathed a sigh of relief. "Why do you ask?"

"They've just been a bit of a nuisance," Josh said, eyeing Tarin, "and we're trying to avoid them."

"Well," Michael said, "then I'm happy to say I've not seen anyone like that around here. But I do think I remember someone mentioning that some folks like that were here yesterday, asking people about UFOs or something of that nature." He smiled, "Now, you boys haven't got yourselves mixed up in anything like that have you?"

The group looked around at each other nervously, and Josh said, "Well, it's possible."

Michael met Josh's eyes for a few moments before he allowed his gaze to drift to the rest of the company one by one. "Hmm, seems we might have some things to talk about. Do you boys want to come over for dinner today? Would be happy to have some company."

"You read our minds!" Rob said and jumped up from his seat. "We wanted to introduce Gil to your cooking and maybe get your thoughts on, well, what we've just been talking about."

"Sounds like a treat," Michael said. "Let me get my jacket and we can be off."

Thirty minutes later, the sign for Custer appeared along the roadway ahead as Allen drove them into the small town nestled among once lush rolling hills before the cold had dulled the landscape into a muted green. Michael's one-bedroom brick house stood near the downtown center, surrounded by a few others of similar build. Shortly after Allen pulled along the curb to park, Michael pulled up behind them in his vintage purple petroleum-powered pickup truck, got out, and met them along the short walkway leading to his front door.

"I don't know how you young folk all drive those electric cars," he said, staring at Allen's car with dismay. "I'm so glad the Lattice never outlawed vintage petro cars, though dealing with all the permits is such a hassle. And now I hear there's even flying cars in some of the cities."

"There are," Allen said. "I tried one once in Chicago. It was pretty cool." He pointed to Gaka's truck. "How do you even find fuel for that thing? I haven't seen a gas station since I was a teenager."

"I have my ways," he said. He held out his hand toward the house. "Why don't we head in, and I'll get some dinner started for you all." He winked. "Then let's tell some stories."

An hour later, the group sat on benches at a wooden table. It smelled of cedar, and in its center rested a large black pot still steaming with the remainder of Michael's famous Wohanpi. It was a soup of potatoes, along with other vegetables, bits of bison, and seasonings that Michael added to give it a vibrant flavor. "There's a reason I'm still as healthy as I am," Michael said, "even at eighty-eight years old." He gestured toward the kettle. "There are many minerals and vitamins in that soup. Good for both mind and body." He glanced briefly at Tarin before lifting another spoonful to his mouth and turning his attention to Gil. "How do you like it?"

"I must say," Gil said, "this food reminds me far more of my home than anything I have eaten thus far. But the flavor of the pieces of meat is unique and truly a delight."

"Delicious as always!" Rob said, pushing his glasses closer to his face after they'd slipped down his nose. He lifted his soup bowl to his mouth and slurped up the last bit. He sighed. "So, if we're all about done here, why don't we fill you in on some of the adventures we've had the last two days." He looked around at the group and held out his hand toward Gil. "I think we can begin with our new friend. Gil, would you mind sharing a bit more about yourself? Like how you found yourself in Philip?"

Tarin watched as Gil glanced at Rob, raised an eyebrow, then turned to Michael. Tarin hoped Gil would start the storytelling. It would make it easier for him to talk to Michael about his nightmare if Gil broke the ice with his own story, though Tarin would also still have to find the opportunity and the courage to speak up when given the chance.

The compressor in the refrigerator in the kitchen turned on, and somewhere outside, a car drove by, but no one spoke. For what felt like many minutes, Gil and Michael stared at each other, seemingly locked in some sort of silent communication hidden from the others. Then, at last, Gil said, "As I told Tarin when I first met him, my path to this place is a bit unconventional, but I sense you are open to such things, so if you permit me, I will provide you details of my journey, and in part, my business in this place."

Tarin took in a deep breath and leaned forward. So far things were going well.

Michael did not speak. He lifted his spoon back to his mouth, took another sip of soup, then carefully set it down. "If you'd like to all join me in the living room," he said, "I'll start a fire in the fireplace, and we can hear what you have to say, Gil." He glanced back at Tarin briefly.

Tarin averted his gaze and took a sip from his glass of water.

A few minutes later, they all sat in Michael's living room: Gil and Michael in wooden rocking chairs near the fireplace, Josh in a plush chair in a corner, and the rest huddled onto a couch on the far side of the room. Michael pulled out a cigar, lit it, and took a few puffs. "So, Gil," he said, "tell me, what brings you to South Dakota?"

The firepit crackled, and the smoke from Michael's cigar filled the room with a sweet scent of tobacco mixed with the pleasant aroma of burning pine. Gil took a deep breath, closed his eyes, and began speaking. "It all began weeks ago when I found myself lying in an arid patch of land at sunset."

Everyone listened as Gil recounted his arrival in Utah, his travels through the mountains, and ultimately his arrival at Philip, where he met Tarin and his friends. However, he didn't mention the evil entity or the woman. Nor did he yet mention his place of origin, Arvalast. Tarin frowned in disappointment. Little Gil had said would make his own experiences easier to share with Michael if he got the chance.

The group took a short break while Michael fetched them all some cake before Gil continued. He told Michael about the encounter with the UFO and how he'd managed to drive it away, though he didn't share anything about his phial of light.

Michael took a few puffs from his cigar, then turned and stoked the fire, causing the room to brighten with a gentle, warm glow. Michael's shadow danced behind him as he leaned back in his rocking chair and said matter-of-factly, "I've seen similar objects to what you described flying around the mountains here, usually at night, when I'm taking a ride down Needles Highway or coming back from shopping in Rapid City. But I've also seen them when I worked out in the Uinta Basin in Utah when I was younger as a rancher. That area is well known for UFO sightings and paranormal activity. In particular, a location in Ute tribal lands next to a reservoir in Roosevelt, Utah." He took another puff from his cigar. "It's called the Sacred Basin, and it's filled with all sorts of legends, even those about Mistai and Skinwalkers."

Rob leaned in and said, "Skinwalker? Do you mean what we talk about in our stories? Malevolent witches and sorcerers capable of shapeshifting into animal form?"

"That's right," Michael said. "That particular reservoir was a hot spot for all sorts of crazy paranormal activity for hundreds of years. Poltergeists, UFOs . . . even what people claimed were interdimensional portals." His eyes were fixed on Gil. "Long ago, there were science experiments performed there and documentaries made. But about sixty years ago, a set of Hollywood folks went to the area to make a movie. They centered the operations around that reservoir—Bottle Hollow, if I remember right. It was there they stirred something up. Something they shouldn't have."

Michael took another pull from his cigar. "I remember it well because I was working nearby herding cattle the day it happened. Almost the entire onsite movie crew began having strange seizures. The local hospitals filled up fast. Those that survived told terrible stories of hallucinations, and those that didn't left a stark reminder that no one should ever again trouble the grounds of the Uinta Basin in any way that may seem disrespectful. No one with any sense goes into that place anymore, other than a stray cow. But if those cows don't come back, locals don't bother to go in to find them. That is, except for one crackpot I knew."

"And who was that?" Rob asked in almost a whisper.

Michael set his cigar onto an ashtray and said, "It was me."

"What?" Rob exclaimed. "Why did you go in there?"

"Well," Michael continued, "one of the cows I was tending went in there. I wasn't in great standing with the boss then, so I worried losing that cow would cost me my job. So I hopped the short barbwire fence surrounding most of the basin and went in looking for it. Good news is, I found the cow I was looking for." Michael paused. "But the bad news was, it was completely mutilated."

Rob lurched back onto the couch. Tarin and Josh had to lunge out of the way to avoid getting hit by his flailing arms. "Who'd do something like that?" Rob yelled. "Or was it an animal?"

"It wasn't an animal," Michael said. "That I'm certain of. There were precision cuts like someone was intentionally carving off pieces of it. All the blood was also drained, but none was spilled nearby. After seeing that, I didn't have to worry anymore about my boss being mad. I quit my job, left Utah for good, and returned home to the Black Hills. But for a long time after that, you might say I had strange dreams and night terrors. Eventually, they subsided, but not without a high cost to my mental health." He glanced at Tarin. "I wish that experience on no one."

Tarin felt sweat form on his hands and forehead. He met Michael's eyes for a few moments before turning away. His heart beat fast. Michael's story was uncannily similar to his experience, both the seizures the Hollywood crew had suffered and the horrible dreams. He glanced at Gil, whose hand had moved to his hip, where Tarin presumed his phial of light was hidden. As his mind began to race, he thought about how Gil had come from Utah. Could he have been close to this Sacred Basin area? As much as he still didn't want to believe it, could the evil entity Gil encountered somehow be connected to the region, to MJ12-2 . . . and to Maximus?

Tarin started as Gil broke the silence. "I would like to show you something," he said to Michael. Gil's hand reached beneath his shirt near his belt on one side. "I have not told you everything about myself," he looked around at the others, "nor have I shared all that I encountered when I first arrived in this world." His eyes landed on Tarin. Tarin knew Gil was about to show Michael his phial, and he remembered what he'd seen in it last time. Images of his mother and father flashed through his mind, then the muddy ditch . . . then the shadows—his mother screaming. He backed into the couch as terror consumed him—a familiar terror.

Coward, the music from his dreams accused. *You didn't help them, and you didn't help her. Weak! Pathetic! Coward!*

"I think it's time," Gil said. He pulled out his phial of light.

"Put it away!" Tarin screamed, jumping from the couch and causing Josh and Rob to pull away in surprise. "I don't want to see more! I can't see more!" He rushed from the living room and out through the front door. The evening had set in, and it was nearly completely dark out, save for the glow of a distant streetlight. Under the lone tree in Michael's front yard, he knelt and found himself quaking. That light—it was going to show him the things he did not want to see, things he was running from. Things about his past, about his dreams, about his parents. "Why's this happening to me?" he said as he rocked back and forth with his hands hugging his knees. "I'm losing my mind. I'm losing my mind."

"Tarin," a quiet voice said. Tarin darted his head up and saw Michael standing just outside the front door to his house. Michael slowly approached. His hand was outstretched like someone approaching a dog about to bite. "I've sensed something has been bothering you since I first saw you at Crazy Horse. Can I sit with you a moment?"

Michael's soothing voice calmed Tarin's nerves enough for him to say, "Yeah, go ahead." As Michael took a seat next to him, still smelling faintly of cigar smoke, Tarin felt the quaking in his body begin to subside, and in its place, a well of emotion began to build. "I'm . . . I'm sorry about that," he stuttered.

"About what, son?" Michael said.

"About my outburst," Tarin said. "I don't know what came over me."

Michael sat silently by Tarin. After a few moments, he picked up a small stick and began quietly scratching the surface of the earth with it. "You've nothing to apologize for," he said. "Your spirit is in a state of unrest. It is not your fault. Something has happened to you." He turned to Tarin. "Something has entered your mind that is bringing you terrible fear."

A picture of his mother seizing in a ditch passed through his memory, followed by Maximus's cruel smile, and he grimaced. "I saw something yesterday," he said. "I saw something terrible. I'm not sure if it was real, but . . . since then, I'm not sure what is real." He looked at Michael, and his eyes began to grow moist despite his best efforts to withhold tears. "I don't know what to do."

Michael met his gaze briefly, then began scratching at the dirt again. "These dreams—you mention they were terrible. What do you mean when you say 'terrible'?"

Tarin brushed aside a tear before it could slide down his cheek, and he said, "They are making me feel trapped and confused." He pointed toward the house. "I originally trusted Gil, but since my last dream, or more, a nightmare, I started to wonder, is he the cause of what's going on? I don't see how it could be possible, but it's him and his light that started all of this."

"What's leading you to think that?" Michael said.

Tarin's shoulders slightly lowered as he said, "I saw something in it when he first came to Allen's. Well, I saw someone . . . my parents."

"And how did that make you feel?" Michael asked.

Tarin watched as Michael scratched the dirt with the twig. "I felt . . . afraid."

Michael, still scratching the earth, said softly, "Why?"

"Because . . . because," Tarin stammered, "I didn't want to see them. I didn't want to remember." He recalled what Maximus had said about Gil's agenda and, for the first time, realized something. "I think I'm afraid Gil is trying to force me to remember."

Michael stopped scratching and looked up at Tarin. "May I tell you a story?"

Tarin nodded. He noticed he'd stopped quaking.

"Earlier this evening," Michael began, "I shared that after my experience at the Sacred Basin, I returned to this place but struggled for a long time with what I'll call nightmares. These plagued me multiple times a week, with no particular pattern other than they brought me tremendous fear, not only from their content but from the anxiety of wondering if I would have one that night. Over time, I grew ill from this fear and came to the point where I wondered if it was worth it to remain on this earth."

He began scratching the ground again. "Now, I'm a very spiritual man—it's part of my upbringing, but also something I've explored myself—and I've concluded I don't think things end here after we pass. I have many friends who think otherwise, and no one can prove it either way, but this is my belief. And part of the reason for this belief is that when I'd finally reached a point where I was most hopeless, something happened that changed my life."

"What was it?" Tarin asked.

"I had gone out for a drive on Needles Highway," Michael continued, "deep into the peaks of the Black Hills. I parked at a viewing area and approached the top of a high ledge. The sun was setting behind me, and an orange glow was spreading out before me in the distance. While I stared out at the vastness of the hills and plains beyond them, a car parked alongside mine. A man with thick red hair and a beard got out and approached me. I paid him little heed because I was deep in thought about what I would do to finally rid myself of my burden. But then he approached me and said, 'Michael, I'd like to help you if you'd permit me.'"

Michael laughed softly, then continued, "Obviously, I was a bit taken aback by his both knowing my name and volunteering to help me with something I presumed he knew nothing about. But because I was desperate, I simply said, 'At this point, I'll take any help you can offer.' He pulled out a small container of glistening light."

Tarin grew even more attentive, and his eyes widened.

"I stared into it," Michael continued, "and was drawn in by its beauty. But then, I saw images from my nightmares, the same things that tortured me night after night. 'What are you doing?' I yelled. 'Why are you showing me this?' I started to think I was actually back in one of my nightmares when he said, 'Are you willing to be free of this?' At this, I felt a sudden resolve in my mind, and I realized I was ready, and somehow, even though the light was showing me these images, it was also filling me with a strength I didn't realize I still had. So I stared hard into that little light. I stared really hard. And after what felt simultaneously like an eternity and a moment, the light flashed bright, then dimmed, and the man was gone. I went home and never had another nightmare."

Michael placed a hand on Tarin's shoulder. "When I saw your friend Gil today, it immediately brought me back to that time I'd met the man at the edge of that cliff. And when Gil showed us his light, I realized he was here to help someone, just like that man helped me. I don't understand how everything in this world works, or how everything works in the spirit realm, or whatever you might want to call it, assuming you even believe in it. But I've been around long enough to know the difference between good and evil." He stared deeply into Tarin's eyes. "Your friend Gil, he's good."

Tarin met Michael's gaze for a few moments, then turned away. "Then why am I so afraid of his light?"

"Perhaps," Michael said, "because you think you're not able, or ready, to face what's inside of it."

Again, the face of Tarin's mother passed before his mind's eye. He saw the smiling, healthy runner with red hair pulled back into a ponytail. But the picture quickly morphed into the haggard, defeated woman he'd seen in the ditch. "You're right. I'm not ready to face it," he whispered.

Michael patted Tarin's shoulder and then stood up. "By merely existing in a moment, you've proven yourself ready for it. Fear is but the lie that says otherwise." He held out his hand for Tarin, and hesitantly, Tarin grabbed it and allowed Michael to help him to his feet. "Now, why don't we head back inside and hear more about this Arvalast place your friend claims he's from?"

"Wait," Tarin said, "he told you about that?"

Michael laughed. "He caught me up on a few things before I came out." He stared up into the sky. "It's a big universe out there, Tarin. There's so much more than we know or understand. I'm getting old, so I think a lot about what's next for me after I finally leave this place." After a pause, Michael patted Tarin on the shoulder and began walking back toward the house as Tarin followed. "If your friend can give me some clues about what to expect, I'm more than happy to look through the window before I enter the house."

"So you believe that he's actually from this Arvalast place, whether it's a planet or another dimension of some kind?" Tarin said.

"Or something perhaps more spiritual," Michael said and entered the house.

Tarin stood just outside the door for a few moments, took in a deep breath, and finally followed him in.

Immediately, his friends all began talking at once, working hard to assure him they understood he'd been through a lot and not to worry that he'd had a bit of a breakdown. And though Tarin felt quite embarrassed about all the fuss regarding his outburst, their genuine empathy quickly brought him to a state of ease.

Gil, in particular, made a point of apologizing for so hastily taking out his light when he could tell Tarin was becoming uneasy as his story progressed. Tarin was grateful that Gil did not ask further questions about what led to that unease, though he continued to sense that Gil had some inclination as to the source. Tarin was also grateful that, for now, Gil had put the light away. He surmised that before Michael had come out, they had all agreed it would be prudent to avoid reescalating Tarin's anxieties until he could get a night's rest to settle his nerves.

But even in the absence of the light, they did discuss how it had been a strong deterrent against the UFO. Michael asked many questions about the encounter and even more about Arvalast, but Gil seemed hesitant to go into detail beyond sharing that he found the rumors of portals at the Sacred Basin quite interesting. He had passed through something similar from a tower in Arvalast to ultimately get to Earth. Though, despite Michael's keen interest in the details of the field Gil had woken in, he could not definitively tie it back to his memories of the Sacred Basin to verify any connection.

Eventually, the night grew longer, and Allen checked the time on his phone. "Oh, interesting," he said as his lips curled into a half smile.

"What is it?" Josh asked.

"Liz left me a message," Allen said.

"Aww, how sweet," Rob chortled.

"Leave Allen alone," Michael quietly scolded from his rocking chair next to the fireplace. "You are far too old to be acting like that, and what on earth is keeping you all from finding girlfriends, anyway?" he said, gesturing to Rob, Josh, and Tarin. "At least Allen appears to be making some progress. Maybe it's that game of yours you seem to love so much, Beast cards or whatever you call it. You all need to get out more."

Rob's face grew red, and he muttered, "It's called Legendarium of Beasts." But then the room's attention drifted to Allen as he held the phone against his ear.

"She says she found something today when she was investigating a situation at a nearby ranch," Allen said. He returned the phone to his pocket. "She said she'd like to talk to me about it since I'm already dealing with some other strange stuff. I'm guessing she's referring to our UFO situation."

"Just you?" Rob asked. "Why not all of us."

"Why do you think, you idiot?" Josh said, with a mischievous twinkle in his eye.

"Josh," Michael softly rebuked, "no derogatory words in my house, please."

"No, he's right. I deserved that," Rob said, then looked at Allen. "Good for you, buddy."

Allen smiled and glanced at Tarin. Tarin nodded at his friend approvingly. The poor guy had been pining away for Liz for nearly a year now, though he barely spoke of it other than on the rare occasion he'd had enough to drink at Old Cotton's.

"It's getting late," Allen said. "We should probably head out. We have an early day tomorrow to pick up Gil's friends." The others agreed, and on their way out, Michael whispered to Tarin, "You are braver than you realize; never forget that." The man's eyes sparkled with what Tarin knew was genuine care and honesty. Tarin nodded and offered a partial smile before following the others back to Allen's car.

As they drove back into the mountains, Tarin stared at the deep black sky from the car window, finding peace at the sight of the stars but still harboring an inner nervousness as to where this journey was ultimately going to take him. Michael had given him much to ponder, both about the light and about his fear of it. He glanced at Gil in the passenger seat. His cowboy hat was resting on his head as he, too, gazed pensively out the window, watching the deep shadows of the Black Hills drift into the distance. While they continued into the vast stillness of the flatlands toward Philip, Tarin heard Michael's earlier words whisper into his mind.

"Your friend Gil, he's good."

CHAPTER 11

"I can't believe I have to go to work today," Rob moaned as he stuffed some toast in his mouth. "Can't we call in sick or something?" he said to Josh.

The group of friends hurried around the kitchen, eating fast and otherwise getting ready for a busy day. "I'm the manager," Josh said, "I've got to go in. And I'm also *your* manager, and I need someone to unload the truck. So you're going in too!"

Rob huffed and stuffed the rest of his toast in his mouth. "Fine," he said with his mouth full. "But I'm going in protest!"

Allen had already arranged to drop off Tarin and Gil at the regional airport just east of Rapid City, where they'd meet the others Gil had contacted two days earlier to assist with the strange happenings in the area. From there, Tarin would rent a car to bring Gil and his friends, or what Tarin presumed were friends, back to Philip while Allen, who'd called off work for the next few days, went back to meet with Liz. Allen's car wasn't large enough to ferry the three additional people Gil had said to expect back to town anyway.

Though Tarin hadn't heard the specifics of what Gil told Allen and the others about why he wanted to bring in more aid, he assumed Gil had only told them what was necessary and didn't mention that they could be a target of some malevolent dark force—a force that Tarin, since talking with Michael, believed might be connected to, or could actually be, Maximus. However, the thought of that phantom actually being real, as opposed to a possible MJ12-2 trick of the mind, made everything going on feel even more ominous.

Tarin had recalled no dreams when he'd woken up in the morning and was feeling exceptionally rested. He even felt a tinge of curiosity at meeting others like Gil. So far, Gil had seemed like a lone anomaly, a singular otherworldly stranger sent to Earth to help against some mysterious foe—or perhaps drive Tarin to madness via his light. However, since Tarin's conversation with Michael, the doubt Maximus had sown about Gil's intent had significantly diminished. As Tarin watched Gil sip coffee and ask Josh and Rob about their duties working at the local grocery store, Tarin felt a shift in his thinking to consider that perhaps Gil was, in fact, telling the truth about his origins and his intent to help.

Allen, as he frantically worked to tidy the kitchen, bumped into Tarin. Allen had been hyper since first waking up. It was because of his meeting with Liz. Earlier, Allen had confided in Tarin that he felt torn between a sense of duty to actually help Liz with whatever she'd gathered the day before from the rancher and a feeling of concern that because she saw him as a worthy and trusted conversation partner to synthesize whatever information she had, he might not actually be able to help her and would look like a fool.

Tarin assured him he'd do fine and implored him to simply be himself and not worry. "That's what she needs right now," he told Allen. "A trusted friend who isn't going to freak out about the weird stuff going on and actually provide help. Do that first, and do that well, and maybe eventually you'll find yourself in a position to chat just about the two of you and not the otherworldly nonsense bringing us all together at the moment."

After finishing their quick breakfast, Josh and Rob bid the rest of them farewell and departed on foot to the grocery store located in downtown Philip. Soon after, Allen, Gil, and Tarin piled into Allen's car and started their journey to the airport.

An hour and a half later, they arrived. A plane zoomed overhead as it came in for a landing. It then slowed just behind the airport and hovered a moment before its wings retracted, and it lowered onto a segment of runway beyond view. Gil, dressed entirely in his Western outfit and now inseparable from his cowboy hat, pointed and shouted with childlike excitement, "Is that an air transport?"

"It's an airplane," Allen said, "and it's likely the one your friends are coming in on from Denver. Let me get you to the terminal." He checked his phone. "Then I've got to hurry back to Philip so I'm not late to meet Liz." Moments later, he pulled up along the terminal, looked back at Tarin, winked, and said, "See you a little later." Gil and Tarin got out of the car, and Allen sped away.

"Let's head in," Tarin said, holding his hand out to the sliding doors in front of them. "And if you'd like, I can get you a coffee while we wait."

"There is coffee here?" Gil said, his eyes wide.

"There's coffee almost everywhere," Tarin said.

Gil whispered, "I love Earth."

A short line of travelers was waiting to pass through security, but otherwise, the airport was not very busy. Tarin and Gil found a small table outside the security area at the lone coffee shop and sat down with drinks. They made light conversation for a few minutes until Gil's face grew somber, and he said, "I am truly sorry for frightening you last night. I felt it was time to share more with the others—what I had previously shared with you, about the entity I encountered when I first came to Utah and about the light and the power I had already seen it capable of even here on Earth."

Tarin didn't reply. He took another sip of his coffee and said, "So you were planning on telling them all about the danger they're in?"

"Do you not think it is time?" Gil said. "I had been hesitant until I knew for certain I had help coming, but now, I think it would be wise to reveal this to help them prepare." Gil kept his eyes locked on Tarin. "I sensed you were uneasy about me finally providing this information to your friends, but it was not until I displayed the light that I surmised there was more to it than that." He looked around the room, then leaned in close. "I know you have been concealing something that happened to you after your seizure, and I am now confident about what I have sensed since you first woke up at the hospital. Some darkness revealed itself to you, did it not?"

An image of Maximus flashed in Tarin's mind's eye. He saw the man's cruel face, his white teeth behind a malicious grin, and his terrible red light. He then looked at Gil. Gil's face was rugged behind his beard, but his expression was soft. Tarin thought back to what Michael had told him about Gil being good. He took in a deep breath. "I did see someone," he said. "But I haven't wanted to talk about it, and I still don't know how to talk about it. It was . . . horrible."

Gil sat silently a moment, studying Tarin's face. "I understand. I can only imagine what was shown to you and what was spoken to you. But I do know this—whatever is inflicting this pain, it is feasting on your unease." He lowered his eyes. "I have been under similar assault since coming here, both when I first arrived and met the entity and when I battled the UFO." His voice grew sterner, and he looked back up at Tarin. "It is not my place to pressure you to push back against this evil energy before you feel ready, but I would be unkind if I did not share this: there is no power beyond the very light you fear that is capable of defeating that which now torments you. It is also all that we have in this world that is able to protect your friends."

Gil must have seen Tarin's eyes flash with fear as he continued and said, "Yes, Tarin, they are all still in terrible danger. That is why we are here at this airport. That is why I have requested aid from more of my kind. But, we . . . will . . . not be able to win this battle alone." His voice softened. "Because in the end, this part of the battle is not ours. It is yours."

Tarin felt his heart race. Gil had been direct with him once before, at Allen's house after the engagement with the UFO, but never had he heard Gil speak with such authority and urgency. For a moment, Maximus's warning about Gil crawled back into his mind.

"Is that what you're trying to do?" Tarin asked, unable to mask the quaking in his voice. "Am I some sort of pawn in a larger game you're playing, where I need to . . . to win some sort of battle for you?" He remembered his recurring dream, and the four people he'd known were somehow significant to him in that place standing, heads covered, ready to be hung. Real or not, the pain of his failure to save them struck his heart like a bolt of lightning. "If that's your goal," Tarin continued, "then you've got the wrong guy. I'm a coward, Gil."

Gil continued to stare at him, unmoving, pensive. At the same time, Tarin thought back to his mother in the ditch, rain pelting against her muddy face. Running from the battle was only the first time he'd fled something he shouldn't have. He'd also run from the pain of seeing his mother slowly destroy herself and from the agony of watching his father break under a similar pain until the woman they'd both loved finally fled. But Tarin had not gone after her. He'd wanted to, but he'd seen no hope—or at least, no hope he'd had the will left to pursue. So instead, he fled too, leaving the shards of broken glass that had become his life lying scattered across the ground behind him.

"Even if this battle you're talking about is mine," Tarin said, "what can I do? I don't have a light like yours, and even if I did, I don't have the fortitude to wield it. Gil, if my friends' fate rests on my shoulders . . ." He couldn't bring himself to continue.

Gil's eyes pooled with empathy. "Tarin, I understand you do not fully realize who you actually are. But one thing I can tell you is—you are not a coward. The darkness will tell you otherwise, but please . . . please believe me when I say that you are brave, and despite an outward shyness, I remember when you were young, you were always one of the bravest people I had ever known." He smiled. "And you do have a weapon in this world that can help you, one that you . . . misplaced." He tapped the side of his belt and said, "You still have your light."

Tarin lifted his head as his eyes grew wide. "I have a light like yours?"

"Yes, Tarin," Gil said. "It's in East Fairfield, Ohio, with your father."

"My father!" Tarin yelled. But before he could continue, he heard a man yell from the direction of the gates, "Gildareth! How are you, old friend?"

"Gildareth?" Tarin replied, his eyes now so wide they almost hurt.

Gil smiled, winked, and stood up. "Ristun!" he yelled back and rushed to the man, embracing him in a great bear hug.

Ristun was a black man appearing to be in his mid-thirties with a crew cut and standing a few inches shorter than Gil. He wore jeans and a graphic t-shirt not that dissimilar to what Tarin might find one of his friends wearing on an average day. Ristun patted Gil's back enthusiastically and projected an energy so contagious that even Tarin was finding it hard not to smile despite his previously melancholy state.

"Dralo!" Gil shouted as another black man, looking a few years older than Ristun and a few inches taller than Gil, approached from behind Ristun. Gil released Ristun and held out his right hand to clasp Dralo's as he approached. Dralo was bald and wore a sweater over a collared shirt with tan, crisp khakis below that. Sunglasses rested on the top of his head, and though he smiled, his smile was one of polite joy at seeing a friend, far more subdued than his counterpart Ristun.

"It is good to see you after so long," Dralo said in a deep voice with an English accent, unlike Ristun, who spoke more like Tarin and his friends. "We have much to discuss," he continued, with a brief glance at Tarin. Tarin's heart stirred with a strange sense of nostalgia. But before he could ponder why, he saw her.

A woman appeared behind Dralo, slightly shorter than Ristun, with familiar black hair and glasses set against a round face adorned with the slightest hint of makeup. She wore jeans and a blue jacket and would have been otherwise unassuming if Tarin had not recognized her as the exact woman, nearly unchanged even down to the outfit she wore, he'd seen in the picture Liz had shared with him back at Wall Drug. She didn't look at Tarin, but he felt as if she was still studying him from the corner of her eye, even as she approached Gil with outstretched arms.

"I've missed you so much, friend," she said as Gil also threw out his arms and gave her a tight embrace.

Her voice, too, was familiar. Tarin's mind flashed back to the voice of the woman who'd saved him from Maximus in his vision days earlier.

"And I have missed you, Iris!" Gil said. He pulled away, looked at the others, and said, "It is so great to see you all!"

He held out his hand toward Tarin. "And this, my dear friends, is someone I am sure you all recognize!" He chuckled. "Though he is a tad more grown up and somewhat less gangly than the lad we lost from Arvalast. But I assure you, he is the same curious, thoughtful boy we once knew, though I must say, significantly less shy than I remember."

"Is that so?" Dralo said, turning his full attention to Tarin. His deep brown eyes studied Tarin, who still sat at the small round table.

Tarin was certain they could see the overwhelmed expression strewn across his face. There was so much information to digest. His mind began to race. So Gil was not Gil's full name? It was a nickname—for Gildareth?

In some ways, this made more sense to Tarin, as it seemed to fit better with what he'd imagine an Arvalastian name to be. Though he wondered, now that he was in the presence of more than one inhabitant of Arvalast, did they collectively call themselves Arvalastian? And they all somehow knew him? Other than that feeling of nostalgia, he had no recollection of them . . . except for Iris. But one thing at a time.

He had a light? And it was with his . . . father? He did recall that when he'd been adopted, he'd been given a small glass container by the youth center. They said it was all he had with him when he was dropped off—though by whom, he never found out. Waking up at the youth center was his first memory. At least what he used to think was his first memory. He found the glass unusual because it had no opening at its top, but it had never displayed any mystical qualities like Gil's phial. His mother had kept it on the mantle over the fireplace. But maybe it was, in fact, something more?

And then there was Iris.

Unlike the others who seemed at complete ease—or in Ristun's case, still very excited—she shuffled on her feet and tried to avoid looking at him, despite having an obvious interest in him, as evidenced by her many side glances. He was certain this was the same Iris in the picture Liz had shared before, as well as the woman who'd saved him in his vision.

Tarin nearly jumped from his seat when Ristun yelled, "I'm going to get us all some coffee real fast!" He hurried toward the cafe while maintaining a smile in Tarin's direction. "Then I'll catch up with you, Tarin!" He pointed at Gil and added, "I like that hat, by the way. Good look on you."

Gil tipped the cowboy hat and said, "Thank you. I was told it would help me blend in."

Ristun laughed and then started quickly talking to the young woman at the counter to place some orders.

"Please get me a tea," Dralo said to Ristun, who spun around in apparent disgust and said, "What? I thought you liked coffee?"

"It's been souring my stomach, so I'm cutting back," Dralo responded calmly.

"Souring your stomach?" Ristun protested as he turned back to the woman at the counter and said to her, "When all you have as an option for a hot beverage is tea for thousands of years, and you finally find a place with something different, you push through the pain!"

She nodded politely while looking quite confused, then started tapping in Ristun's orders.

"Can coffee sour one's stomach?" Gil asked Dralo nervously.

"It can if you drink it too frequently," Dralo said, "which I did for many years."

"Interesting," Gil mumbled, still looking slightly concerned, but then turned to face Tarin. "A problem for another day. Let us visit with our friend."

As Dralo and Gil approached the table, Iris remained behind and said, "I'll go wait for our bags at the luggage claim. I'll catch back up with you all shortly."

"Are you sure?" Dralo asked. "There're quite a few."

"I'll be fine," she responded.

Dralo shrugged and nodded, then sat next to Gil. Dralo held out his hand, "Pleased to see you again, Tarin. In particular, pleased to see you alive."

Hesitantly, Tarin took Dralo's hand and was given a firm handshake. "I take you have no memory of me?"

Tarin shook his head.

"And you have no memory of any of us?" he continued, "Gildareth, Ristun, and even Iris?"

Tarin nodded, though he felt somewhat dishonest since he *had* seen Iris. But as far as he knew, he did not know her.

"I thought you said he was no longer timid," Dralo said to Gil.

"Give him a little time," Gil said. "He has had a troubled few days."

"That's a monumental understatement," Tarin said, finally catching his voice.

Dralo arched a brow. "So you can speak?"

"Stop harassing the kid," Ristun said, then slid a chair next to Tarin and gave him a hard pat on the back. "Good to see you again, and all grown up! How's Earth been treating you?"

Before Tarin could attempt an answer, Ristun passed out drinks and continued, "Sorry we haven't been around. When we finally got here, we had to attend to some other urgent things. Plus, we knew Iris had your back."

At this, Tarin heard the sound of roller bags as Iris, pulling two large suitcases behind her and carrying a backpack over her shoulder, walked up to the table. "I wasn't able to get the last bag," she said. "I think it was yours, Ristun. You might want to get it before it gets stowed away."

Ristun stood up and said, "Take my seat." He pointed to a drink not yet distributed and said, "Got you a caramel latte."

"Thanks," she said. She rolled the suitcases over to the table, set the backpack next to the newly freed chair, and took a seat by Tarin while

Ristun rushed off to the baggage claim. With a sideways glance, she said, "Hello, Tarin. Happy to see you again."

Tarin said nothing for a few moments. Dralo and Gil watched with intent until Tarin finally replied, "Good to see you again too, Iris."

Dralo looked at Gil and then back at Tarin. "You remember Iris?" he said. "You just indicated you didn't know any of us."

"He saw her in a picture," Gil replied on Tarin's behalf, for which Tarin was grateful. "There are government agents in the area who had pictures of something they are looking for information about. Coincidentally, one of those pictures also captured Iris at Tarin's hometown many years ago."

Tarin discretely studied Iris's still-sideways glance. He replayed the voice he'd heard in the dream with Maximus—her voice. "If I may ask," he said, "where were you two days ago?"

For the first time, her deep blue eyes met his. Tarin saw a complex mix of emotions as she replied, "I was in Florida, where I received contact from Gildareth, who informed me of the danger this place is in. I then alerted Dralo and Ristun, who were elsewhere, and coordinated travel for us to all arrive here as quickly as possible." Her voice grew quieter. Tarin thought he saw the faintest sign of moisture in her eyes. "There is nothing that would keep me from helping you, Tarin, if there was help to be given."

The care in her gaze became so strong he grew uncomfortable and turned away. "Thank you for coming," he finally said. He was unsure what else to say. Though he longed to ask her if she had any recollection of already helping him during his encounter with Maximus, as with Gil, he still wasn't sure how to articulate the experience. And like with Gil, Maximus had said something about her too—that she . . . favored his father, whatever that had meant. Also, after now seeing Iris in person and in the nightmare, he believed it was even more likely that the vision wasn't just some MJ12-2 trick of the mind. But it still seemed the agents were connected to the vision—and to Maximus—somehow. All of this felt pretty insane, but as he considered the fact that he was surrounded by a group of people claiming quite believably to be from another world, he wasn't sure what actually was the threshold of insanity anymore.

The sound of Ristun's voice in the distance momentarily broke Tarin's introspection. It was not the happy tone he'd already attributed to the man but rather one of irritation. About a hundred feet away, beyond the coffee counter and toward the entrance to the baggage claim, Ristun stood arguing with a man in a black leather jacket. In one hand, Ristun held the handle of a roller bag. The other was waving about angrily and adding emphasis to an already heated discussion.

A lump formed in Tarin's throat, and without hesitation, he got up and said, "I need to go." He nearly tripped over his chair as he hurried toward the other end of the terminal toward the exit.

He could hear Gil urging him not to be concerned, that he and his friends would see to his safety, but Gil hadn't been able to protect him at Wall Drug the first time he'd encountered one of the MJ12-2 leather jackets, nor had he been able to assist at the hospital when Tarin was left alone with the chief. He would not risk falling into another seizure and potentially being transported back to Maximus's terrible lair if, in fact, MJ12-2 had the capability to send him there.

Tarin made it outside. He took a deep breath and rubbed his temples, then turned and rested against the terminal wall. It felt safe out here. The roadway in front of him was nearly empty except for two cars dropping off some travelers: one a couple, the other a woman with a child. He was beginning to feel more calm when he heard a voice behind him.

"Tarin, are you okay?"

He spun toward the voice. It was Iris. She stood just outside the sliding doors to the airport, her expression soft but uncertain. For a moment, he studied her. She truly seemed unaged and unchanged from the picture he'd seen of her, although it had been taken more than fifteen years earlier. She was very pretty, but in a simple way, seemingly curating her appearance to draw as little attention to herself as possible.

Her round glasses and the way she consistently peered nervously through them made him feel almost foolish at his inability to engage with her in a confident manner. Yet, finally calmed from his brief panic at seeing the man in the black leather jacket, he took in another deep breath and managed to say, "I'm fine. And . . . I'm sorry I've been acting so strangely around you. I've had a rough couple of days."

He held out his hand and walked toward her. She also took a step forward, clasped her hand with his, and, for the first time, offered him a smile coupled with a look of relief.

Tarin let go of her hand and pointed to the airport. "You think your friend Ristun will be all right in there? I've not had very good experiences with those guys in leather jackets. They are government agents who've been, let's say, harassing my friends and me the past couple of days."

"Ristun will be fine," Iris replied. "We are all very accustomed to dealing with them and their kind."

"Their kind?" Tarin said.

"Yes," she replied. "They are from an organization called MJ12-2. Dralo, Ristun, and I have been monitoring them and their involvement with individuals impacted by the phenomenon for many years. I believe you have had your own encounter with the phenomenon?"

"Phenomenon?" Tarin asked.

"In your case," Iris said, "the phenomenon was a UFO. At least that's what Gildareth told me."

"I'll need to get used to that name."

Iris looked at him with a quizzical expression. "What do you mean?"

"He told my friends and me his name was Gil. I had no idea his full name was Gildareth."

"Oh," she said. "But why would he do that?"

"My guess," Tarin said, "is he simplified his name even before meeting us because he might have shared his real name with someone, maybe on his journey here to find me, and they said it sounded odd. By the way, Iris is a reasonable Earth name, but Dralo and Ristun are a bit strange. Are they all your real names?"

Iris seemed to be growing more and more at ease as the conversation continued and said, "Upon arriving, I did discover my name was at least somewhat common on Earth, so I never felt compelled to change it as Gildareth apparently did. But Dralo and Ristun tend to be fairly stubborn. Even if they thought they were drawing attention to themselves, they wouldn't have cared. Of the remaining Glorions here on Earth in human form, they are the ones least concerned about revealing their true natures and identities. I think they've simply grown weary of the occasional absurdity of your kind to care anymore about what people think of them."

"So you all call yourselves Glorions?" Tarin said, quickly becoming fascinated. "What are Glorions?"

Her ease diminished as she looked nervously back toward the airport. "Gildareth hasn't shared all this with you yet?"

"No, he's told me much more than he's told my friends, but again, it's primarily relevant to his own experiences on Earth and some conjectures on how he got here from Arvalast as well as the danger he feels my friends and I are in." Tarin felt silly speaking about Arvalast as if it was just some other location like Africa or Asia, but in some ways, it was beginning to feel like a reasonable comparison.

"I should probably wait to share more once we all gather at your friend Allen's house," she said, "which is where I understand Gildareth wants us to go to organize a plan to aid you all in your situation. We can talk more about all things Arvalast then. By the way, weren't you planning to rent us a car to get there?"

"Oh, yes," Tarin said, slapping his forehead. "I completely forgot about that." He turned back toward the airport, but his legs felt stiff with unease.

"Don't worry," Iris said, apparently noticing his struggle to take that first step back toward the terminal. "You'll be safe from the agent. I'll see to that."

At this, Tarin paused. Iris had again alluded to what seemed an insatiable desire to make sure he was well protected, and the burning question

Tarin had been avoiding could no longer be contained. "Two days ago," he said softly, "I had a nightmare, or what I think was a nightmare. It happened after I locked eyes with one of those government guys. I know this probably sounds crazy, but . . ." He struggled to get the words out as Iris silently stared at him. He finally pushed through and said, "Did you somehow come and help me at the end of that nightmare?"

She fidgeted, and her hand touched the side of her hip in what looked to be a reflexive motion.

"No!" Tarin said.

She pulled her hand back in surprise.

"I'm sorry," he said and rubbed his hand over his face. "It's just you had a light in that nightmare." He glanced down at her waist. "And you helped me with it. But since then, the light, or at least Gil's light, brings me back to dark places. And I just can't go there." He pushed back a swell of emotion. "I'm sorry . . . I just can't."

Iris's expression mirrored his, her face tightening with emotion. Her hand drifted farther from her waist, and she said, "I understand, and I'm sorry." Tarin saw what looked to be a flash of fearful remembrance pass across her eyes. "The entity in your nightmare," she continued in a whisper, "is a creature I am familiar with." She paused. "And yes, I was there with you when you met it."

Before Tarin could respond, a bright flash of light sparked behind the nearby glass sliding doors. He yelled and turned away. The doors opened. Three men in black leather jackets came rushing out of the airport and into the parking lot.

Iris held out her hand, shielding Tarin as the men rushed by while at the same time backing both of them up along the concrete walkway running alongside the terminal. Seconds later, Ristun came walking out holding a light very similar to Gil's. It was glowing bright enough to easily see in the full daylight.

Tarin shielded his eyes.

"Yeah, you better run!" Ristun yelled after them as they hurried toward a white van. "We're here now, and we're coming for you. No more games! I didn't come all the way from Cleveland to let you mess around, especially with Tarin!" He glowered at the fleeing men for a few moments longer until he finally noticed Iris and Tarin. "Oh!" he said. "Hi, Tarin." He quickly hid his light under his shirt and nodded back toward the doors. "You better get in there and rent us that car. I think folks in there are still trying to figure out what that light was. Hopefully, Dralo managed to convince security it was just a power surge. But that little chase isn't going to do a whole lot to help his case."

Just as he finished his sentence, Gil and Dralo ran out the doors, dragging or carrying all of the group's luggage. "We're in trouble," Dralo said.

"Uh oh," Ristun said. "Too late."

Tarin saw security guards running toward them through the glass door, and in the distance, he heard the faint wail of sirens. "What happened?" he asked. "I don't think I'm going to be able to rent a car if you're being chased down by police!"

"Astute observation," Dralo said.

"Cut him some slack," Ristun said, "I told him I thought we might have time."

Dralo groaned, then turned to Gil. "We're going to have to deal with this mess, and fast."

"I am still relatively new to Earth," Gil said. "What is the protocol in situations like this? Certainly, we cannot make ourselves known overtly to people of this world beyond what is absolutely necessary."

"What does he mean?" Tarin said to Iris, whose hand had returned to the side of her waist.

"Fight your kind in order to get out of here," she replied.

"Is that something you've done before?" Tarin asked.

"We avoid it as much as possible," she said, "but there are always exceptions. And you're important enough that we could make an exception."

Ahead of them, Ristun looked around frantically until his gaze fixed on the unmarked white van the leather jackets had fled to. He smiled and rushed toward it.

"Don't do it!" Dralo yelled after him, but it was too late. Ristun jumped in front of the van just as it began pulling out of its parking space and held out his hand. "Get out!" he yelled.

The van continued to drive forward. There was another brilliant flash of light, this one so bright Tarin fell to his knees and had to cover his eyes. He heard screaming as the doors of the van opened, and the three MJ12-2 men fell out. They writhed on the ground, furiously rubbing their eyes.

"Hurts, doesn't it, you yellow-eyed freaks?" Ristun yelled. He waved for the others. "Hurry up! Get over here." He pointed to the van. "I just rented us a vehicle." He sidestepped the previous occupants and jumped into the driver's seat.

"So compulsive," Dralo said with a sigh, "but effective." He ran over, threw his load of luggage in a still-open side door, and joined Ristun in the front passenger seat.

"Hurry," Iris said to Tarin, helping him to his feet. "We need to go."

As best as he could, Tarin ran with Iris to the van and got in. A few moments later, Gil jumped in as well, tossing in two roller bags and a backpack. They closed the side doors, and Ristun peeled out of the parking lot. He turned onto the road just outside the airport and headed toward Interstate 90. All the while, the sounds of sirens grew louder.

"Which direction, Tarin?" Ristun asked, peering at interstate on-ramp signs ahead.

"East," Tarin replied, remembering to buckle up. Iris and Gil, on either side of him in the middle row of the van, followed suit. "But you know there are security cameras at the airport," he continued, "and those guards clearly called the police, not to mention we just stole a van belonging to those government men. Aren't they going to come after us?"

"Don't worry about the agents for now," Ristun said. "They're in our jurisdiction. It's your people I'm worried about."

"You mean the cops?" Tarin said.

"Yeah," Ristun replied. He merged onto Interstate 90 East and started speeding down the road.

Tarin saw the odometer hit eighty, then ninety, then one hundred. He clutched the front of the seat in front of him as cars in the parallel lane zipped by so fast they almost appeared as if parked. "We're going to die," Tarin whispered.

"This is indeed somewhat fast," Gil said, also clutching the seat in front of him. "Ristun, if we perish in this escape, centuries, if not millennia, of efforts will be wasted."

Ristun looked out his rearview mirror. "Noted, but we've got to move quick, Gildareth. I can see some flashing lights now."

Dralo leaned forward and looked out the windshield ahead of them. "They're probably going to set up a blockade in front of us, too, if they haven't already. Somehow we have to get to Tarin's friends' house without getting caught, then take cover in town."

"I can probably get some help from the local police there!" Tarin said over the sound of the air rushing along the sides of the van. "If we can make it. I'm friends with the sheriff, Liz. I bet she'll cover for us since she's also involved in the same situation my friends and I are in. She's also no fan of MJ12-2."

"Perfect," Ristun said. "If we can ditch this van and get to town uncaught, we should be good."

An off-ramp appeared in front of them. "Take that!" Tarin yelled. "I have an idea."

CHAPTER 12

It smelled of old hay—very old hay. The hum of car tires along a nearby roadway echoed along the slatted walls of the empty barn—empty, that is, except for an unmarked white van parked at its center. The noise of the car faded into the distance. Tarin sighed, and his shoulders relaxed. There hadn't been the sound of a siren for more than an hour. Perhaps it was finally safe for him to contact Allen to pick them up. Though he doubted the local police were highly sophisticated, waiting too much longer did yield the slight risk of someone doing enough detective work to identify him from airport security footage and find them by tracking his phone. None of the others carried a phone, so he was the weakest link.

Tarin and company had managed to exit the highway before the police drew near enough to see where they were going or search drones could be deployed, mainly because of Ristun's manic driving and Tarin's quick thinking to take the exit that led to this abandoned barn. They'd managed to drive inside just as sirens had started to wail by from the direction of the interstate.

Dralo paced with his hand on his chin while Iris and Gil chatted quietly in the corner, occasionally glancing in Tarin's direction.

"This reminds me of the old days," Ristun said as he leaned against the van. "Remember, Dralo? Hiding out from agents and their indwellers, trying to avoid the fate of the ongoing purge of our kind."

"Please don't remind me," Dralo said. "Thankfully, you and I survived, with Iris and the rest of the remnant. Those times were terrible."

"It's going to get like that again," Ristun said, "if we can't help settle things here with Tarin and his friends. You see what's starting to happen across the world. It's like a powder keg on the brink of exploding." He spread out his hands and yelled, "Boom!"

"Shhh!" Dralo said. "You don't want us to get caught now, do you?"

"There's no one around," Ristun said. "Tarin's plan seems to have worked very well. Tarin, what did you say this place was again?"

Tarin shifted from his crossed-legged position to get more comfortable. Though he was curious about what Ristun meant regarding agent indwellers and the purge, he was more worried about safely getting back to Allen's. He decided to just answer Ristun's question rather than asking any of his own.

"Before I moved here, the building next door was a catering place, but it's been abandoned for a while. My friends and I sometimes come to the property to look at the stars and play games around a fire, or if the weather isn't great, we might play in this old barn. It adds to the ambiance of our game."

"Like a board game or something?" Ristun asked.

"It's a fantasy card game called Legendarium of Beasts."

"No way," Ristun said. "You all play that game? I love that game!"

"Yeah?" Tarin said, "It's a bit of an obsession, to be honest. If there's time between fighting agents, UFOs, or whatever you plan to do to help us, maybe you could join us for a round."

"Dralo," Ristun said, "I'm even more glad we came here."

Dralo stopped pacing and said, "Lovely. This is all I'm going to hear about until we complete this mission."

"So," Ristun said to Tarin, "why don't we go ahead and call these friends of yours, whichever one you said had the car—Allen, right? I think things seem pretty safe now. We're going to have to take the plunge and sneak our way into town sometime. Now's as good a time as any."

Tarin couldn't argue. He got out his phone, tapped the button to dial Allen, and waited. No answer. "That's unusual," Tarin said. "Allen always picks up for me unless he's in a meeting for work. Or . . ." He thought of Allen's meeting with Liz. There's no way they could still be talking, unless perhaps it had turned into a full-fledged date. But knowing Allen, that was unlikely.

"What's he doing that could be more important than answering for his best friend?" Dralo said as he continued pacing. He stopped. "Wait, are you both still best friends?"

"I suppose you could say that," Tarin said. "But what do you mean 'still'?"

Before Dralo could respond, Tarin's phone started humming, and he lifted it to his ear. The others all watched with great interest. "Allen?" Tarin said. An excited voice chattered on the other end. Tarin struggled to keep up until he finally said, "Hang on, hang on. So there are cattle mutilations? Here?" More chattering. "More UFO sightings as well?" Iris and Gil began walking closer to Tarin while Dralo and Ristun listened intently. "Okay, yeah, we can talk more about that later, but right now, we need your help."

Tarin hurriedly explained their situation and told Allen he needed to pick them up immediately. "I'll share more after you get here," he finally said after Allen agreed. He hung up.

"He'll be here in about thirty minutes. But"—he pointed to the luggage—"there won't be room for all that since the car trunk is tiny."

"But whatever will I wear!" Ristun said.

The others gave him annoyed looks.

"We can leave everything here and make a separate trip to pick it up later in the day," Tarin said. "And it's going to be a very tight squeeze. Allen's car isn't that big. So four of us will have to fit into the back seat. Gil, you can have the front again since you're, well, the biggest."

"I'm taller," said Dralo.

"But he's broader along the shoulders," Ristun said. "But it wasn't always that way. Earth has made us weak." He curled his arms to show off very average-looking biceps. "See what happened to us?" he said to Gil. "You've only just arrived. Don't worry. It'll fade."

"Speak for yourself," Dralo said. "I've maintained some of my muscle mass. And although I agree with you that Gil is still enjoying the lingering effects of Arvalast, for those of us who still frequent a gym, that strength is maintained. You just prioritize sloth."

Ristun let his arms fall back to his side. "Gaming, my friend, is not sloth. And as you know, those I interface with are heavily into games and, by proxy, heavily into the Lattice. I must fit in."

"Do you mean the Trinity Lattice?" Tarin asked.

"What other Lattice is there of any relevance?" Ristun said.

"But what do a bunch of gamers have to do with the Trinity Lattice?" Tarin asked.

"Many of them were part of the training program for it years ago," Ristun said. "So they know it well."

"Well, you can keep obsessing over technology," Dralo said, "while Iris and I keep the darkness hunting us at bay."

"I beg your pardon," Ristun said. "I fight the darkness too, just in a different way."

As Tarin tried to make sense of the conversation, the sound of a distant siren began to draw closer. Tarin looked at the others, who all stood still until the sound faded into the distance. "Perhaps it was unrelated to us," Iris whispered.

"Regardless," Dralo said quietly, "the sooner we get into Philip and set up base at Allen's, the better. If we hide here much longer, we'll get caught eventually."

Thankfully, Allen was on time, exactly thirty minutes from when his call with Tarin ended. A few minutes before he pulled into the dirt driveway leading to the barn, he called Tarin, so he knew it was him. Tarin then opened the barn door, and as Allen drove in, Dralo grimaced and said with a groan, "That is indeed a small car. Someone, please share—why can't one of us stay behind with the luggage and be picked up later during the second trip?"

"Because," Tarin said, "we don't want to risk any of you getting caught here before we can get into town. You'll all be safer at Allen's house. And if they do track me somehow through my phone, they'd look for me at my trailer first. I have a security system in place there, so I'll know. Plus, we can probably get a lot of help from Liz once we're in Philip. Probably best for Allen to come back to get the bags after he drops us off since he wasn't involved with the airport mishap."

"No mishap," Ristun argued. "That was all very intentional."

"Please be quiet," Dralo said. He straightened his collar and continued, "If we must squeeze, then we shall squeeze."

A few seconds later, Allen got out of the car and stood dumbfounded in the presence of Gil and his new team.

Ristun looked him up and down. "All grown up too, I see. Just like Tarin."

"Huh?" Allen said, peering at Tarin nervously, then back at Ristun. "Do I know you?"

Ristun paused a moment, then smirked. "Forget it," he replied and pointed to Allen's car. "Mind if I drive?"

"Seriously?" Dralo said.

"I can't squeeze in the back! I have a pinched nerve in my neck from playing too many video games! Plus, as you saw earlier, I'm a fantastic driver, so if there's any lingering trouble on the roadways, I'll get us out of it." He held out his hands. "Keys, please."

Allen glanced at Tarin. Tarin shrugged and Allen handed over the keys.

"Get in, folks!" Ristun said as he ran to the driver's side door. "Let's get to home base before anyone or anything tags us out!"

Seeing little use in debating with Ristun, the group made their way to the car. Gil got in the front seat next to Ristun, and the others did their best to fit into the back. Poor Dralo's head touched the ceiling, forcing him to sit very hunched over, while Iris crunched her shoulders next to him, followed by Allen. Before getting in, Tarin opened the barn door for Ristun to drive through, then closed it behind them. He managed to fill the remaining gap in the back seat with great effort.

"So anyone going to tell me why I needed to pick you up at a barn rather than you all renting a car like we'd planned?" Allen asked.

"It's a long story," Tarin said. "But I'll fill you in on the way." Allen gave Ristun directions, and they were off.

Over the next thirty minutes, Tarin caught Allen up on all the events since he'd dropped him and Gil off at the airport. By the time Ristun parked in front of Allen's house and those in the back seat fell out with many a moan and groan, everyone was quite relieved to at last be at their destination without more interference.

Allen stretched his arms out and worked to rub a kink out of his shoulder. "Guess I'll head back now to get your luggage. Josh and Rob won't be back for another couple of hours. After that, I can fill you all in on what I've learned today. For now, make yourselves at home. Tarin, there are some leftovers in the fridge if anyone's hungry. If I'm not back in an hour and a half, please come looking for me."

"We don't have a car, remember? But I'll call Liz if you get into trouble."

Allen smiled.

"Now, don't get any ideas!" Tarin said.

"I won't," he said, then leaned closer to Tarin, "I had a really good time talking to Liz. But a lot of it was a bizarre conversation, and I mean bizarre."

"I'm not surprised, and hurry up. We need to all get together and figure out what Gil and his"—he paused and watched as Gil's counterparts stretched and took in their surroundings—"team is thinking we should do next."

Allen nodded and was soon driving away in the direction they'd come.

As Tarin let everyone into Allen's house and did his best to disperse what drinks and food he could find to the now very hungry and thirsty travelers, Ristun noticed a deck of LOB cards on the table in front of the couch. He tenderly picked them up, smelled them, and sighed. "I do hope we can find an opportunity to play," he said.

The others stared at him, and Dralo said, "Don't you think we have more important things to do near-term?"

But Gil reached out and said, "I will play a quick game while we wait if you would like. I rather enjoy the game."

Ristun handed him some cards and said, "I always tell everyone you're my favorite friend. Tarin! You said you play. Care to join us?"

"Sure," Tarin said. "Might as well. We have some time to kill." He looked at Iris, "You play?"

Iris fidgeted with her glasses and said, "I've played a few times quite a while ago, but if you don't mind, I'll pass for now."

"No worries. Dralo, you want to play?"

Dralo drew a deep breath and let it out slowly, rubbing his hand over his bald head. "Fine." He turned to Ristun. "But don't yell at me if I happen to beat you."

"Why, I'd never do that," Ristun said in feigned surprise.

Both Iris and Tarin chuckled simultaneously. They briefly met eyes, and Iris turned away quickly, focusing instead on a picture of a landscape hanging on Allen's wall.

Tarin couldn't figure out why she continued to seem so uncomfortable around him. Though, his own awkwardness had likely not helped with that. Neither of them had made an excellent first impression on the other when they'd first met. And there was that thing Maximus had said after she'd saved him in his nightmare, or whatever that was.

Had a bit of a preference now, didn't you? Maximus had said to her. *Liked your father a bit better.*

Tarin hadn't wanted to revisit that memory, but as Iris continued acting strangely, he struggled to push it aside. She continued to avoid his stare, even as her hands were wringing on her lap.

Over the next hour, the group got lost in the game. To Tarin, the dangers outside and the anxiety within felt more distant and irrelevant as he allowed his mind to wander into another world of pretend magic and predictable strategy. Of course, it wasn't entirely lost on him that he was playing this game with people who actually were from another world tied to his own through some magic he did not understand.

Iris watched from the other side of the room, calmer than before. Tarin assumed her change in demeanor was because she was in no danger of being his focus while he attempted to counter attacks on his beasts from Ristun and the others. Their skills were on par with those of his friends—even Gil, despite him being new to the game.

Their merriment was finally disturbed by the abrupt entrance of Josh and Rob. Upon seeing the newcomers, they immediately went into a frenzy of introductions and questions until Tarin managed to calm them down and tell them they needed to wait for Allen to return before discussing more. Of course, joining in with the game was the only other reasonable way to pass the time, so Josh and Rob grabbed some cards.

Ristun was vehemently complaining about Dralo dropping a virus card on his strongest beast when Tarin heard the soft sound of a car door closing. A moment later, Allen walked into the room. He carried a backpack and held one roller bag. "The rest is in the car," he said. "Josh, Rob, can you help me bring it in?" He then peered around the room and said, "I didn't think through where everyone would sleep."

"We're flexible," Ristun said, "don't worry about it. I'll sleep in the kitchen if I have to." He got up and began helping the others bring in the bags until, at last, they all were sitting in the living room together. Allen had to bring in all the chairs from the kitchen table to accommodate them, but despite the small size of his house and living room, they all had space to sit comfortably. No one spoke for a few moments until Ristun said, "So, I think we have a lot to discuss. Who's going to kick things off?"

"Well, I have some good news," Allen said. "I called Liz while driving to pick up your luggage. I filled her in on the details about your little adventure. She said she did get a call earlier about a stolen white van and a commotion at the airport and said she'd keep a lookout. But now that she knows you're all hiding out here, she said she'd deflect any questions coming in about your little escape and not to worry. He paused a moment. "She did ask that I eventually get her more details, you know, about the light that caused the commotion."

Ristun smirked. "Happy to help with that whenever I get a chance to meet her."

Allen raised an eyebrow, then continued. "Anyway, she doubts whoever is looking for you will be a bother as long as you stay in Philip. But you all should keep a low profile just to be safe. Now that that's out of the way, do you all want me to start with what I learned from her earlier?"

Dralo held out his hand. "Before you do, first, thank you, Allen, for explaining our situation to your police officer friend. I'm pleased we have one less thing to be concerned about. But before you tell us about your conversations today, Gil, are all present aware of the events leading to your coming here and what we are here to do?"

Gil looked around the room, then at Tarin. "Some, but not all," he said.

Tarin knew Gil was silently asking permission to finally share about the evil entity he'd encountered at the ranch, the one threatening to harm his friends in order to, in turn, harm Tarin and draw energy from him.

Tarin knew that once Gil shared this danger with them, his friends would no longer be naive to the full scope of their plight nor enjoy the naivety he only wished he had. He also feared that this entity would somehow be confirmed to be Maximus. But he was doing his friends no favors by not telling them the truth about their predicament. And now Gil's counterparts were here to help.

He nodded to Gil, and Gil nodded back, even as Tarin suppressed a growing knot in his stomach.

"There is more to the story of my coming to Philip than I have yet shared with you, Allen, Josh, and Rob," Gil said. "But it is now time."

The room grew utterly silent, except for the click and soft hiss of the furnace turning on from the basement.

CHAPTER 13

A cold wind blew across Gildareth's bearded face as he pushed himself to his knees. Just beyond a deep blue lake, he could see mesas under an orange sky. Whether it was sunset or sunrise, he couldn't tell. He had no idea how much time had passed since he'd finally broken the seal on the tower and stepped through a portal from his world before losing consciousness. But he knew he was no longer in the Great Northern Forest of Arvalast.

His legs strained beneath him, but he managed to stand. This place either had a stronger gravitational pull or the power he once had in Arvalast did not travel with him here. He brushed dirt and dust from his cloak and closed his eyes, reaching out to both explore his surroundings and search for a being of a good heart to assist him in orientation. He only saw the blackness behind his eyelids.

He opened his eyes, again greeted by the lake and surrounding arid landscape. Fulfilling his goal would be more challenging than he'd initially anticipated. Like his strength, his ability to sense and see the struggles and triumphs within those connected to the light had, apparently, not traveled with him.

But what of his light?

He reached for his waist and pulled a glass phial from a small pouch attached to his belt just under his cloak. It shimmered softly with a faint glow strong enough to be visible in what he now realized were the waning daylight hours of this world. Relieved, he put it back and began walking. Since he could not find help by the usual means, he would have to explore. He found his legs to quickly regain strength as he pressed forward and gained speed. Now moving at a jog, he began to wonder: perhaps he still had some of the capabilities he once carried in Arvalast after all. He approached a large rock about his height, sprinted, and jumped. He rammed into its side and slid back to the ground. He rubbed his chest, which had taken the brunt of the force. No, he was undoubtedly weaker here.

There was a rustle in some brush across from a nearby ditch. Gildareth trained his attention on it and rested his hand on the clasp holding his phial of light. He thought he saw some fur within the thickets and shrubbery and searched for movement. Suddenly, a massive hairy creature, perhaps a wolf, but appearing twice the size, darted from the undergrowth and ran at great speed into the fields beyond until it disappeared into some higher grasses.

"Strange," he whispered, then started walking again, around the rock this time, toward what looked like a road. Then he heard a voice. He wasn't sure whether it was in his mind or audible, but it carried a menacing tone. "Trespasser," it slowly whispered in an eerie hiss.

"Who is there?" Gildareth said. He scanned the area for the source of the voice. "Reveal yourself!"

"You seek the one . . . you lost?" the voice said, again in a whispering hiss.

A faint humming began somewhere in the distance. It seemed to come from the sky, but nothing was visible except some fleeting red-hued clouds as the sun descended over the mesas. The hum grew louder. Gildareth heard a ringing in his ears, and his head ached. "Who is there?" he yelled again.

"How did you arrive?" the voice said in a more humanlike tone, this time seemingly directly into his mind.

"Through a door," Gil answered, "from the tower amidst the ruins of Undertree."

"You come from Arvalast? Do you bear . . . the light?"

Gildareth did not respond, even as his fingers wrapped around the cool glass of his phial.

The humming became unbearable, replaced by a cacophony of intense dissonances, like a hundred orchestras simultaneously playing a different piece and conflicting across a broad range of incongruent keys.

"Stop!" Gildareth shouted into the sky. He pulled out his light and thrust it upward. "Show yourself!"

Immediately the sound receded, and Gildareth fell to his knees. The pain in his head subsided, and he could think again. He heard footsteps. From where the wolflike creature had fled, about fifty yards away, stood the silhouette of a man. It was now too dark to make out any distinct features, but Gildareth could tell he was wearing a brimmed hat, boots, and a long waistcoat. He seemed to be smoking because an orange ember flared briefly where his mouth would have been, followed by a wisp of vapor that shimmered in the final rays of the setting sun.

The man began walking toward him. "Nice light," he said in an unfamiliar accent. Gildareth realized he was still clutching the phial tightly in his right hand. Its glow lit up the area around him with an intensity similar to the full moon.

"Again, I ask you," Gildareth said, "who are you?"

"Perhaps I should be asking you that question first since you're the guest knocking at the door of the master's house." The man was now about twenty yards away. He held out his arms. "These lands are all mine. And those within serve me and my purposes. You are trespassing here, as many others also did before I sealed the gate in the sky above this basin years ago. But it seems you might have gone and kicked it in for some reason." The man paused. There was another glow near his mouth, followed by a billowing plume of smoke that surrounded his head. "You must be somewhat stronger than the others. You come for the boy too?"

Gildareth stood and held his light out in front of him. "I am here seeking a boy, or perhaps a man, since it has been many years since I lost him from where I came."

"Thought so," the man replied and continued his walk toward Gildareth, the underbrush crunching beneath what Gildareth now saw as brown leather boots with pointed toes. "The others did as well, though most of them are dead now. You see, the boy you seek, he's been quite helpful to me, and I don't really feel like giving him up, if you know what I mean."

"I do not," Gildareth said.

"Then let me show you." The man lifted a glass container not dissimilar to Gildareth's, but this one glowed crimson.

Immediately, pain shot through Gildareth's head—a pounding, unbearable ache. He fell back down to his knees and looked up. In the red light of the phial, he saw the man's beardless face. Pure white teeth spread inside a broad smile. The man's green eyes seemed to burn with delight at Gildareth's pain.

A haze covered Gildareth's field of vision, and he saw a young man writhing on the ground. Darkness billowed from his body like the smoke from a chimney as silhouettes of other people around him screamed in torture. Shadowy figures swirled around the humanlike shapes, pulling at their limbs, casting them to the ground, and then pulling them back up only to throw them back down again. Some shadows entered the silhouettes, leading them to turn against each other and beat one another as other smoky entities swirled around them in what appeared to be manic excitement. These reached into the fighting figures' heads, leading them to wail into the sky as they continued beating each other.

The young man in the center of the chaos remained on his knees, holding his ears and shaking violently.

"Enough!" Gildareth ordered, and there was a flash of light. The shadowy beasts convulsed in unison and cried out in pain. For a moment, Gildareth could see all the humanlike silhouettes' proper form. Two, in particular, caught his attention. One was a woman lying on her back after being thrown down by one of the shadows as it seemingly pulled energy from her heart. The other was the man in the center, whose face he could never forget, though it had aged since the last time he'd seen it. A moment later, the vision lifted, and the mist around him fled as he regained control of his mind.

Only a few yards from him, Gildareth saw the man from before. He was lying on his back and groaning. The man struggled a moment to get back to his feet. As he did, he reached for the red phial of light from a nearby patch of weeds and put it back under his cloak.

"You're not like the others," the man whispered. He brushed the dirt off his clothing and stood to his full height, about the same as Gildareth's. The humming from before returned, along with a similar pain Gildareth felt in his head. The man knelt into the tall grass, and moments later, Gildareth heard the same growl he'd heard before. The humming's intensity grew until Gildareth was forced to hold his ears. Then it was gone.

A swirl of breeze enveloped him, and he sensed he was utterly alone. Night had fully set in, and other than the now gentle glow of his light, all was pitch black. He turned his attention back to the phantom dream. He needed to know more about the two people his attention had been drawn to: the woman he did not recognize and the man that he did.

He held his light to his forehead and closed his eyes. As he had done countless times in Arvalast, he willed to know more. For a long time, nothing happened, and he began to lose hope. Then, a location flashed in his head. It was a small house, sitting alone in a wide field of green grass and rolling hills. A woman was inside, the woman he'd seen, and she was ill.

He noted the location and drew his focus higher up. He saw a town, and his mind's eye trained on a brick building in its center. He zoomed in, and within, the man he recognized was drinking with a small group of other young men.

"Tarin," he whispered. But where was he?

He pulled back until the town was visible as a small patch within a great sea of green. A small mountain range was nearby, and then beyond that were empty and rugged lands, followed again by another mountain range, this one massive. He realized he was located near its western side.

He began to run east with all the strength he had. He would not have been able to see the man and the woman in the vision had they not been of intense interest to the entity. He had to get to them quickly. Tarin, the woman, and all the others he had seen in the vision were in imminent danger. Somewhere above him, he again heard humming, faint and ominous.

° ° ° ◇ ° ° °

All those in Allen's living room sat transfixed by Gildareth as he completed his story. He briefly recounted his visit to the woman's house, where he found he was too late, followed by his meeting with Allen, Josh, and Rob, who, after telling them what he knew about Tarin, had sent him to Old Cotton's. Finally, he shared with Tarin's friends the danger he believed they were all in and why.

Tarin, having now heard Gil's whole story, believed without a doubt that the dark entity Gil had faced was indeed Maximus. The similarities were too significant for any other reasoning to make sense. But this did not bring him any peace. Instead, the existence of Maximus was fully realized. His friends also now knew of this terrible danger, though unlike him, they had not yet had a direct encounter with it. But soon, they might.

Was he truly their only hope?

"Well, that wasn't what I'd call a nice bedtime story," Ristun said. "But no matter. Dralo, Iris, and I are here now, and we'll keep you all safe."

"How?" Rob said, staring blankly ahead. His breaths began to come out fast and swift. "That thing Gil met in Utah, it knows we're here."

His eyes darted back and forth as if he were reliving Gil's story himself.

"That humming Gil heard—that's also what we heard when the UFO attacked."

His breathing continued to quicken.

"That evil cowboy might already be here."

He looked around the room, now fully hyperventilating.

"We all need to get out of here. It already killed that woman Gil said he saw when he arrived in town. Now it's coming for Tarin. It's coming for all of us! We need to hide!"

Josh reached over and put his hand on Rob's shoulder. "Calm down. Things will be okay."

"How do you know that?" Rob yelled. "I was fine with the UFO. I was fine with Gil's light. But I had no idea it was all connected to some . . . wicked wizard living out in Utah! That thing was a skinwalker! It had to be. You heard how it transformed from a wolf to a human and back again. No one can fight a skinwalker! We're cursed. It's coming for us!"

Ristun leaned forward and rested his hand on Rob's other shoulder. "My friends and I have dealt with things like this before. I won't tell you there isn't any danger, but we know how to fight it. We'll take care of you."

Ristun's eyes searched the LOB cards still strewn on the table next to them. He reached for one and picked it up. "Think of my friends and me like shelter cards. For instance, this card, 'Cave of Solace.'" The card depicted a shield of light at the front of a cave deflecting a swirling beam of dark energy outside. "We know how to deflect the darkness in this world and keep safe those within our protection."

"Ristun is right," Dralo said. "Our kind has been fighting such evil for many millennia now, and though I will not minimize the power of our enemies, with courage and by maintaining our wits, we are the stronger force."

The calming words and Ristun's tactic of using Rob's precious game to distract him from his fear seemed to work. Rob's breathing steadied, and he regained control of himself. "I'm sorry," he said. "You're right."

He managed a soft laugh. "I mean, I should be thrilled, right? It's like all the fantasy stuff I love just became real. I have forces of good in my living room and forces of darkness outside for us to battle. This should be fun, right?"

"I wouldn't necessarily say fun," Dralo said, "but with all struggle comes growth, and that is something to be excited about."

"Let's go a bit lighter on the philosophy there, Dralo," Ristun said.

"Why?"

"Just not very helpful at the moment."

Allen started squirming on the couch and rubbing his knees with his hands. "So, about what Liz and I talked about—not sure you're really going to want to hear it, Rob, since you're already a bit stressed out. Maybe we can call it a night and talk more in the morning."

Ristun turned to Rob, "Why don't you and I grab a snack in the kitchen? I think you could use a break from all the storytelling, and I want to learn a bit more about the strategy you used earlier to beat me. I mean, the three beasts I chose were set up perfectly with key defenses. How'd you do it?"

Rob's attention darted back and forth between Allen and Ristun as beads of sweat formed on his forehead. Finally, he sighed, stood up, and said, "Grab the cards and I'll show you."

"Fantastic!" said Ristun. He scooped up the cards and followed Rob into the kitchen, where they began loudly bantering about various strategies and tactics of the game. The rest of them turned their attention back to Allen.

"Well then," Allen said. "Where do I begin?"

"How about with the cattle mutilations you earlier mentioned to Tarin on the phone," Dralo said.

"Glad we had Rob leave," Josh muttered.

Tarin braced himself. He wasn't entirely sure if he had much mental fortitude left to deal with Allen's story if it turned too dark too fast. But after already running out of a room twice out of fear, he decided to try to pull through this time without drama.

152

"Maybe I should start from the beginning," Allen said. "Would be best if you all had full context. I promise it won't take long to get to the mutilations."

"Get ready," Josh addressed the room, "Allen's known to be a bit long-winded as a storyteller."

"I rather enjoy Allen's stories," Gil said in Allen's defense, "like at Mount Rushmore."

"Please don't encourage him," moaned Josh. "But go ahead, Allen, tell it how you'd like."

"Thank you," Allen said flatly. "So after I left the airport, I drove to the police station and met with Liz. She said she'd had quite a night and morning and suggested we grab lunch at Old Cotton's. She also wanted a beer. She was pretty worked up, which wasn't something I'd ever seen before. When we got to the bar, she wanted to sit in the far corner, away from everyone else. After we got some burgers and drinks, she told me that the night before, while we were at Gaka's, she'd gone out to investigate a call. A rancher, John, said one of his cows had died, but not in a normal way. When she got there, John was acting really nervous. He took her out to one of the pastures, and sure enough, there was a dead cow. But it had its lips removed and its udders. Other parts too. It all seemed to have been done very surgically. But the weirdest thing of all: there was no blood and not a trace of anything that might have done it."

Allen paused. No one said anything, but all remained attentive. "The rancher also said that about ten minutes before he found the cow, he'd seen a strange object in the sky."

"Was it similar to what we saw here?" Gil asked.

"No," Allen replied, "it was different, more like a conventional saucer you often hear about when talking about aliens. In fact, it looked a lot like the saucer in one of the pictures Liz shared with us at Wall Drug."

"This is not good," Dralo said.

"The cow or the saucer?" Josh asked. "Both seem pretty bad to me."

"The combination in particular," Dralo continued. "My hope was this was potentially just a demented prank, which tends to be true in

153

the majority of such cases I've investigated during my time on Earth. But I always suspected some of the animal mutilations were tied to something, shall I say, unsavory happening beyond the planes of the physical. I have my thoughts on what they could be, based on some tales I've heard. We often see them in connection with appearances of agents, strange sicknesses, and generally paranormal events."

"Agents?" Josh asked.

"It's what they call the men in the black leather jackets from MJ12-2," Tarin responded.

"Oh," Josh said. "Got it."

"They have many names," Dralo continued. "And they are always harbingers of bad tidings, just like the mutilations, which almost always lead to some . . . event."

"What do you mean, an 'event'?" Josh asked.

Dralo glanced at Iris. "Should I tell them?" he asked.

Iris sat still in her chair, staring blankly at the wall on the other side of the room. Tarin noticed a strain in her face as if some terrible memory was replaying in the back of her mind. "Tarin," she finally said, "without your light, we may be able to stave off the evil descending on this place for a time. But eventually"—she paused, looked at Gil, then turned her gaze to Tarin—"I won't be able to protect you. And you will not be able to fulfill your destiny."

Tarin felt the pressure of her full being pleading with him to listen to her, to understand. His mouth went dry, and his body stiffened. He remembered Gil had indicated something similar at the airport, though less forcefully—that Tarin had a light and that this was his battle. But so much had happened after that conversation he'd had little time to process what it could actually mean. Still, over the last three days, and in particular after his encounter with Maximus, a dread had grown in his heart that if his friends were indeed in danger because of him, then he was, in fact, the only one who could help them. But the light, and what it seemed to want to show him—was it really the only path to victory?

A strange and familiar melody began playing in the recesses of his mind. He closed his eyes and saw himself standing on a brick roadway, watching a man prepare to pull a lever that would send four people— four friends—to a swift death by hanging. The music asked him, *"Who are you, just a boy, to lead a war against the darkness?"* For just a moment, he and that boy in his dreams became one, and he felt the abject terror of a child facing an undefeatable monster pierce his heart.

He opened his eyes, and could both see and feel the stares within Allen's living room. It reminded him of the stares of the battalion in his dream as they'd waited for him to again demonstrate a strange power, one he sometimes felt in his dreams, one that had brought them that far. But within the jaws of that hopeless situation, all strength had left him, and he'd run. The voice of the music moved from casting doubt to throwing accusations.

Coward.

As that terror within his young self inside the dream filled his adult body, he felt his mind starting to break. Losing his wits again would do no one any good, not him, and not his friends. He managed to stand despite the quivering muscles in his legs. He'd been terrified to go back to his trailer alone. But now, being alone was all he wanted. He needed to get away, even if just for a little while, until he could calm himself and think through what to do next.

He thought he heard voices urging him to stay, but their words fell into his mind like meaningless noise. For a third time, he was going to run from the light, and he was okay with that. There'd be a beer for him back at his trailer, maybe two. And a bottle of gin. Soon, all would be better.

CHAPTER 14

Tarin woke up. His head ached. His body ached. Where was he? Everything was blurry. He was on a couch. Some sunlight peeped through a crack between worn curtains hanging against the window across from him. Something smelled bad. His breath? He must not have brushed his teeth before falling asleep. He looked down at his phone. He'd missed some calls. He'd missed a lot of texts. That was fine. It had been days since he'd been alone, and he needed a break. Still, he might have *breaked* a bit too hard last night. A few days without drinking, mostly because of the distractions caused by all the strange events going on, followed by a binge, was not sitting well with him.

He managed to pull himself into a sitting position and eventually made his way to the kitchen, where he poured a glass of water. He drank it down greedily, then filled another. He gulped that down too. Then he headed to the bathroom to shower.

In the small mirror over the sink, he stared at his thin abdomen. He'd always been skinny, but he looked more gaunt than usual. And he was hungry—maybe some breakfast would help. He combed his hair, got dressed, and returned to the couch with a bowl of cereal. He turned on the old TV—he could never afford a hologram projector, other than the clock in the mirror, because he spent most of his extra money on alcohol. A reporter standing in what looked like a bombed village appeared. He quickly turned off the TV and groaned. "My whole world's become a hellhole," he muttered. "Inside and out."

He lazily lifted a spoonful of cereal into his mouth. Some milk dripped down the sides of his lips as he stared blankly at the slit in the curtains. They were somewhere out there: Gil, his friends, and the others. They were obviously worried about him but, mercifully, had not followed him back last night. Allen knew him well enough to know when he really needed some space. Tarin had been worried he'd have dreams, but last night's alcohol apparently was enough to hold them off—including the new one with the woman. What was her name again? He fished around in his jeans pocket and felt a piece of paper. Pulling it out, he saw her, the girl in his dreams. He began to read. *Abigail Yoder, a resident of Philip, South Dakota, passed away after an illness at the age of thirty-one. Abigail had a passion for life, and perhaps more than anything else, she was a lover of books and nature.*

He paused, poring over Abigail's picture. "So you were a bookworm," he said. He found her to be very pretty, even if a tad plain, but somehow that made her seem more approachable. He thought of himself and his friends as all a bit on the plain side as well, and he took pride in their above-average averageness. He marveled how the face in the picture matched exactly what he'd seen in his dreams, despite his dreams coming first. The deep green eyes, the long brown hair. He paused, internalizing how truly odd this was. He was seeing a dead girl in his mind's eye as if she was not dead at all. And she had seen him. "What's happening to me?" he whispered. His eyes drifted lower on the page. Her funeral was today at the little Lutheran church on the south side of town. It was barely a five-minute walk from where he lived. He checked the time. The service would be in an hour.

"So what happened to you, Abigail?" he mused. He recalled what Gil had told him—that he'd seen a woman when he first arrived, just before she'd died, and that the UFO that attacked him and his friends was also at her house. She was ill, but it hadn't been a natural illness, according to Gil. Was it possible Abigail was that woman, and she was somehow connected to everything going on—the UFOs, the agents, the strange illnesses even he had fallen victim to just two days prior? He hadn't had any seizures or other ill effects since then, at least not physical side effects, but why had he been spared while it seemed others were still suffering—or worse? His mind drifted back to the events of the last few days and, eventually, the light.

What was he going to do about the light?

Though he feared it, it was not because he didn't think it was benevolent. By now, he was convinced Gil had good intentions and would not be wielding something fundamentally evil. Still, it reminded him he'd not pursued his mother after she left, knowing she needed help but not knowing how to give it. Having so little memory of his life before meeting her, she was the stabilizing rock that had lifted him from a state of confusion into what was, for a time, the loving shelter of family.

For most of his teenage years, he'd been happy, largely because of her. He'd made a good life living in the small Ohio town. He'd developed a modest, close-knit circle of friends, worked at a local fast-food restaurant, enjoyed the fantastic, crisp autumn evenings, and endured the long, dark winters by a warm fireplace, entertained by both video and board games. East Fairfield had become home, and a happy home at that. Then, it had all changed. It had only taken a month for the depression to grip his mother, then the panic attacks, the voices, the screaming, the . . .

"No!" he shouted. Even just thinking about the light brought him back to those memories, to when the horror had reached a critical mass. It had broken him. It had broken his father. It had broken his friendships, including that with a young woman, a girl in his circle of friends he had come to love. No one wanted to be around that madness. Not her, and not even him.

"Chelsy," he whispered.

He noticed his breathing quickening. He managed to calm himself. Again, he looked at the obituary. Maybe he should go to the funeral. It would be a distraction, if nothing else. He studied the green eyes in the photo. They brought him an odd comfort, one that he'd not felt in a very long time. That was a feeling he wanted to chase, and chasing something, rather than running from it, felt good. He would go to the funeral. But did he have anything to wear?

He rummaged through his dresser and found a polo shirt and some khakis. The khakis were wrinkly. Should he iron them? It would be disrespectful not to, he thought. It took him fifteen minutes to find the iron and another ten to iron the pants and then get dressed. He looked at himself in the mirror. Other than the bags under his eyes, he decided he looked fine. He grabbed a jacket, stepped outside, and instinctively looked into the sky. No UFOs. He looked around the area. No one was wearing black leather jackets.

The walk to the church was pleasant. Not many people were out since it was getting colder. A couple of cars passed by on the side streets he walked along. He waved at the occupants, as by now, most faces were familiar in Philip. Then he saw the small white church ahead. It was a building he'd seen countless times while on walks through town, but never inside. The building itself was made of fading white bricks, with several tall windows. A thin sidewalk led to the front facade and toward large wooden doors that served as the main entrance. A few cars were parked along the road in front of it and a few more in the small lot to its side. He took a deep breath and allowed his feet to carry him closer to the church doors. It was time to bring the strange encounters with the woman from his dreams closer to the realm of reality. He pulled open the doors and stepped inside.

Soft organ music filled the little sanctuary, creating an air of reverence. A handful of people mingled near the flower-adorned open casket in front of the pulpit on the other end of the room. Tarin tilted his head in that direction. He was nervous yet eager to see Abigail for the first time outside the scope of a dream, vision, or photograph, but the people in front of the casket were blocking his view. A moment later, one of them turned to him, smiled, and waved. It was Samantha from the hospital. She wore a black dress, and he could see slightly smeared mascara under her eyes where moist tears still glistened.

She approached him, held out her arms, and gave him a hug. "Thank you so much for coming." She stepped back and looked toward the casket. "I was worried barely anyone would show up, but we've had a few folks in and out for calling hours. I think more will show up soon for the service itself." She handed him a program. "It will start in a few minutes, but you're welcome to pay your respects in the meantime." Again, she smiled. "So nice of you to come." The door opened, and an elderly couple entered. Samantha pulled out two more programs and went to greet them. Tarin turned his attention to the casket and began to walk down the aisle.

A hushed silence settled over the room as Tarin moved forward. The casket lay atop a platform draped in black velvet. The flowers adorning the casket added a splash of color to an otherwise somber scene. The few people previously blocking his view finished paying their last respects and moved to the side. Tarin took the final few steps toward the pulpit, stopped directly in front of the casket, breathed in deeply, and looked down.

There she lay. Beneath her closed eyelids, he imagined the soft green eyes he'd become so familiar with. He wished they would open. He wished he could look into them in this reality, just like in the other, whatever it was. "Hello, Abigail," he finally whispered. For a brief moment, he felt awkward speaking, then realized it was customary to speak when paying last respects. The rest of the church surrounding him seemed to disappear as his full attention focused on the woman in the casket. "What happened to you?" he said. "And why have you been in my dreams?"

He continued to look at her, becoming lost in the memories of seeing her first in the meadow, then at a wooden cottage. Locks of chestnut hair framed her pale yet still pretty face. Her lips were set in a calm yet strangely sad expression if one could be sorrowful after death. "What made you so sad?" he whispered. Certainly, being ill with the looming threat of death so young would fill anyone with grief, but the lingering expression on her face hinted at something more.

He thought back to when he'd overheard Samantha talking about Abigail's passing shortly before Gil had first stepped into his life. She had longed for a simple country life and a nice man, he recalled. Perhaps her expression now told the story of a search never concluded and a life whose deepest desire was never fulfilled.

Tarin thought back to the one time he'd felt love—for Chelsy. It was a young, naive love that seemed so rare. He recalled getting lost in simple fantasies of a chance meeting or the suspense as he wondered if she'd offer him her hand while they walked at the park and discussed the melodrama of small-town life. These were the things that had made his heart race, even while many peers seemed to prefer far faster movement toward deeper romance. That was simply not his way. And maybe that was why his love had not been anchored when the storm came. Perhaps that was why she'd withdrawn when he finally opened up his soul and told her what was happening to him, his mother—his family.

He now guarded his heart carefully. No woman, he'd decided, would ever again have such sway over his emotions. Even so, he now found himself resting his hand on the lip of the casket. "I'm sorry you never found anyone," he said. "I'm not sure what would be worse, honestly. Never having the chance to have felt love, or having felt it, only to be rejected."

He permitted his imagination to drift. Would he and Abigail have been friends had they ever met? Would she have been willing to join him and his friends in playing games? Probably not. She was Amish. He didn't think they were into fantasy games, although she'd left the community, so maybe she would have.

Wait, what was he doing? This was ridiculous. None of this mattered. She was dead. There was no chance for a friendship. Though, since seeing her in his dreams, he'd felt an odd longing to meet her because, like him, she seemed to be somehow linked to two worlds, even as a mysterious boundary currently separated them, only broken by . . . he recalled something Abigail said in one of the dreams. She'd seen him through a phial of light during their meeting at Wall Drug.

And prior to that, the light had somehow been involved in his other chance meetings with her. His mind raced. The first time he'd seen her, Gil's light had been visible through the crack he'd left in Allen's door. And the final time, it was in the presence of Iris's light as she fought back Maximus.

"You sure you didn't know her?" a woman's voice said to his side. He nearly jolted. Samantha stood next to him and a small line had formed behind him. He felt his face grow warm with embarrassment as Samantha placed her hand on the small of his back and began gently leading him away from the casket.

"She would have liked you," she said as he followed her guidance and made way for the other attendees to pay their last respects. "The service is about to begin. Will you be staying for it?" Tarin nodded, then took a seat in an empty pew a few rows from the back of the sanctuary. He watched as the people in the remaining line viewed the casket, then moved to their own pews. A minister stood from near the front of the sanctuary, approached a lectern at the foot of the casket, and said, "Let us pray."

Tarin's mind swirled as the ceremony commenced. He considered the light and its connection to Abigail. For the first time, he felt conflicted about the mysterious relic from Arvalast. While it still brought him significant unease as a window to his darkest memories, it now also presented a curiosity he could no longer repress. But his thinking was cut short by the soft creak of the church doors opening, followed by footsteps. While he was still transfixed, staring in the direction of the lectern, he heard the recent arrivals slide into his pew.

He muttered an internal curse. Why did they have to sit here? He wanted to be alone. But his annoyance was quickly replaced by concern when, out of his peripheral vision, he saw multiple tall men take a seat, dressed fully in black. For a moment, he felt hope because, after all, it was a funeral. Many were dressed in black. He turned his head very slightly so he could get a better view. His concern was realized. The three men sitting next to him stared blankly ahead, and all wore black leather jackets over collared white shirts with blue-tinted sunglasses on their heads. One of them he recognized well.

The man discretely slid closer to Tarin. Tarin considered running but was too embarrassed to disrupt the service and was also blocked from the exit by the agents.

"Good to see you again," the MJ12-2 chief said, his tone both amused and ominous.

Tarin closed his eyes and said nothing. Sweat beaded on his forehead.

"Have you been feeling better?"

Still, Tarin said nothing.

The man sighed and said, "If you're worried my men and I are here to hurt you or, perhaps, take you somewhere you'd rather not go, you can rest your mind. We are here only to observe."

Something about the man's statement and the tone in his voice made Tarin feel slightly less terrified. His heart still pounded in his chest, but he managed to slowly open his eyes. He hoped they wouldn't be met with other eyes—those with yellow slits. They were not, as the chief and his men looked onward toward the casket.

"Pity about the girl," the chief said, as he lifted the pair of sunglasses off his head. "She was less lucky than you." He began cleaning the glasses with a handkerchief from a jacket pocket. "Did you know her?"

"No," Tarin found himself able to reply.

The man put the handkerchief back in his pocket and slid the sunglasses on. He turned his head to face Tarin through a now mostly hidden gaze. Behind the blue screen, his pupils appeared black. "Then why are you here?"

Tarin felt his mouth go dry. "Why are you wearing sunglasses inside?"

"Because I told you I wasn't here to cause you any alarm, and I find they reduce the chance of an unwanted disruption," he said quietly as a few heads turned in their direction.

"What do you mean?" Tarin whispered back, somewhat relieved others had noticed the men sitting with him, though he wasn't sure what they could do to help if needed.

The chief ignored Tarin and gestured toward the pulpit. "I saw this woman at the hospital when I first arrived in Philip. Her illness was similar to yours, one I'd seen before, many times. I was not expecting her to wake. She surprised me. She even managed to go home, but the illness went with her. Eventually, its grip on her body tightened, taking away all that she loved, even her ability to read, because her fingers could not hold a book or turn its pages."

Despite Tarin's continued unease in the presence of the MJ12-2 agents, his heart also ached at the thought of Abigail trying in vain to distract herself from her terrible situation with a favorite story, only to be halted by something fully outside of her control. "Was there anything that could have been done?" he asked. "I survived—have others? Is there a cure?"

"There is no cure. Though I've seen, in rare cases, recoveries with minimal lingering consequences. But more frequently, I see . . . poorer outcomes. I did find it curious, the unusual strength this woman possessed. That's why we're here. We've learned it's always good to, let's say, check up on those with unusual cases, whether they live or die, just to account for any possible lingering anomalies." The man turned back to Tarin. "Funny. It seems today we do have an anomaly because . . . you're here. Are you certain you didn't know her?"

Tarin's pulse quickened as he realized they were suspicious of him. Were they aware of his dreams of Abigail? He decided to tell a half-truth. "I'm just acquaintances with someone who knew her. I've never actually met her before."

The man seemed to process Tarin's statement. "Intriguing," he finally said. "But if you do run into anything strange related to the girl or find out anything that links her to the phenomenon we discussed earlier, you have my number." He appeared to look as if he was about to stand up, then paused. "Oh, and by the way, the people you met at the airport: I'd suggest you break ties with them. Interfering with government business is not likely to serve you well." He noticed an unfastened button on his collared shirt and fastened it. "One more word of advice: be wary of those you care about." He smiled. "Love can be dangerous, especially for someone like you." He finally stood, and the two others followed suit. Together they made a fast and quiet exit.

Organ music began to play, and Tarin realized the pastor had finished the eulogy. All attendees began standing and slowly drifting out of the church. Samantha, the pastor, and what Tarin assumed to be deacons or elders began to attend to the casket and remove the flower displays. Tarin remained frozen in the pew. His mind flashed back to his friends, all of whom had been with him in the hospital. What if his friends were taken by the same nightmare that had consumed him? What if they met with Maximus or some other phantom whose singular mission was to break their spirit until they finally wasted away like Abigail? He imagined his friends, their hands shaking, unable to lift even a Legendarium of Beasts card, much as Abigail had lost her ability to turn the page of a book. Had Maximus sickened him so that if or when his friends met a similar fate, he'd know their suffering even better?

The casket closed.

In his mind, he heard the voice of Iris. "Without your light, we may be able to stave off the evil descending on this place for a time. But eventually . . . I won't be able to protect you."

It was clear MJ12-2 were aware of Iris, Dralo, and Ristun from the chief's ominous threat. Without the veil of secrecy, would the Arvalastians be able to fend off whatever evil was stalking his friends, even for a time? But what did it matter? Assuming Iris was right, his friends' ultimate fate was in his unsteady and cowardly hands. But as the melody from the memory of his recurring dream always reminded him, he was not ready for such a quest.

His mind raced. Still, he needed a path forward. He needed an idea. He couldn't just let fate play out as he had with his mother, nor flee as he had in the battle in his dreams. He clenched his eyes shut as both terrible memories filled his imagination. There was no way around it. To help his friends, he would have to at least, in part, suffer the pain of his past again. But then, why was that pain so agonizing?

He opened his eyes. It had been partly because he hadn't tried. It had been because he'd run. Now, he had a choice—would he run from the battle for his friends too?

An idea formed. Perhaps, just perhaps, he could try something different this time. Instead of running, maybe he could at least take one step toward his fear. Certainly, that was achievable, and if needed, if the pain became overwhelming, he could allow himself to fail once more, but at least this time with the dignity of knowing he'd given it a try.

He rose to his feet, glanced at the casket one last time, and left the church. It wouldn't be easy, but he would do his best to protect his friends from Abigail's fate, regardless of if he succeeded or failed. He would return to East Fairfield and see if he could find the courage to reclaim his lost light. And if he could, if he could manage such an impossible feat, he'd return and save his friends. But he knew he wouldn't be able to do this alone. He'd need help.

He rushed back to his trailer, filled a suitcase, and headed toward Allen's house.

CHAPTER 15

As Tarin approached Allen's house, he saw Liz's police truck parked outside. Why was she there? Had they called her out of concern for him? That would be humiliating. But maybe she was there for something else. Perhaps there'd been another event, a UFO or cattle mutilation. Strange how that felt more comforting than it being about him. Regardless, he just wanted to hurry up, share his plan, and move on to the next step before he could change his mind. He stiffened his jaw and continued on.

"Tarin," a voice said. Tarin spun around and saw Gil approaching from Allen's backyard. He must have sensed Tarin's unease because he held up his hands and said, "I was just outside getting some fresh air. I apologize if I startled you."

"I want to go to Ohio," Tarin said.

"What?"

"I want to go back to Ohio and see if I can find my light." As he said *light*, a picture of Maximus standing behind his friends as they unwittingly played a game of LOB flashed in his mind. He shook it off and continued. "I'm not sure how I'm going to pull it off, but"—he pointed at the house—"I have to try. For them."

Gil's arms hung loosely at his side. Tarin could not make out his emotion. Eventually, the silence grew too uncomfortable, and he said,

"I'd like you to go with me, if you would. I'm . . . I'm actually pretty anxious about this, and I might need some help."

Gil smiled. "Of course, Tarin, I would have it no other way if this is your desire. But what changed your mind?" A look of curiosity replaced his smile. "What is motivating you to face such a deep fear?"

Tarin considered this for a moment. Indeed, he was terrified for his friends, but he was also terrified for himself. He didn't think he could live with himself any longer if he ran again from an opportunity to help those he most cared for . . . those he loved. Was he motivated by a sense of concern for his friends or a sense of concern for himself? Or was it also because of his recent encounter with Abigail?

"You do not have to answer," Gil said, his face reassuring. "I was only curious. This road will be challenging, as I know you are already aware. But I will help you on your journey." He looked at the sky. "I have begun to feel a growing sense of urgency. I have not told your friends, but last night, I sensed a familiar energy, one I last encountered when on the roof of this house beneath the UFO—that of the entity. I notified Dralo, Ristun, and Iris, and together, I believe we managed to deter it from returning, but its strength is gaining. Liz also shared with us that there have been more sightings of UFOs across the area, though primarily dissimilar to the object we saw here. Still, we must convene about your decision." He held his hand out toward the house. "Are you ready to share with the others?"

"I am," said Tarin.

"Then let us hold council."

Tarin was relieved when upon entering the house, he was met with only smiles and no questions. Still, he could see the concern on Allen's face as Allen handed him a cup of coffee and a plate of scrambled eggs. Tarin gratefully took them and sat down on the couch next to Rob, who was busy writing something down on a piece of paper. "I'm putting some strategy notes down for Ristun," he said. "I think I have a new best friend—no offense to you guys."

"None taken," Tarin replied and spooned some eggs into his mouth. He could hear Josh in the kitchen talking to what sounded like Dralo and Liz. "Speaking of Ristun, where is he? And Iris?" Tarin asked.

"They were outside with me," Gil said as he, too, received a cup of coffee from Allen. He sat down across from the couch. "Shall I go fetch them?"

Allen looked intrigued and said, "Are we about to have a meeting or something?"

"Yes," Tarin said.

Allen nodded. "I'll tell the folks in the kitchen. And I need some ginger ale. I had an upset stomach most of the night." Tarin noticed his hand against his abdomen as he left. Meanwhile, Gil went outside to inform the others. Rob continued to write, but Tarin could tell he was now studying him through the corner of his eyes.

Tarin took a few moments to gulp down the rest of his eggs and sipped his coffee as the others gathered in the small living room. Some found seats. Some stood. Josh and Allen sat on the floor near the front door. Liz took a seat in between Tarin and Rob and patted Tarin's back as she sat down. "Glad to see you," she said. "It's been a weird couple of days, and I was worried when I heard you went home by yourself." Her voice trailed into a whisper. "Ristun showed me his magical glass jar. I get why it makes you nervous, but I just want to say, I'm all in on this now, and I'm going to do anything I can to help." She smiled. "You still feeling better since the hospital?"

Hearing that Liz was now fully integrated into their strange new club made Tarin somehow feel more hopeful. "I'm feeling better physically," Tarin said, "though I'm still going through a lot mentally, to be honest."

"You and me both," Liz said. "But we'll get things figured out."

The room fell silent, and all eyes turned to him. Though he knew everyone in the room, even if only fairly recently in terms of Gil and his party, being the center of attention made him nervous. It was bad enough on a normal day, but knowing what he wanted to share, it felt even more stressful. Regardless, he decided to keep pressing on while he still had the determination to do so.

"I've decided to go back to Ohio and find my light."

Allen jumped up and said, "Tarin, you don't have to do that!"

This was not the reaction Tarin had expected. "Yes, I do have to. Don't you remember what Gil told us? You are all in danger from the entity he saw when he first arrived . . . and . . . I've seen it too."

"You saw it?" Josh yelled. "When? How?"

"When I was unconscious after I collapsed at Wall Drug, I had another . . . dream. And the same man Gil described meeting in Utah, he met me."

"And what happened?" Rob now asked, almost falling off his seat.

"I . . . I saw something, something I don't want to talk about."

The room fell silent until Iris whispered, "Your mother."

Tarin looked at Iris in horror. "Why are you telling everyone that? You saw what happened." He grew angry. "You saw what he did to her!"

Iris's eyes were sad but stern. "I'm telling you because if you cannot even hear someone make mention of her without running from the memory, you'll have no chance to regain your light. I'm trying to help you, to protect you. You must be able to allow that memory some agency within your mind, or there isn't any hope."

"Iris," Gil said softly but with intent. "We cannot rush this."

She frowned at Gil. "I have known the pain of Tarin's suffering more than anyone else, more than any of you can truly know. And I know the minds of our enemies as they also have consumed my own. We must act fast." She looked at Tarin, her eyes quivering with urgency. "Please, Tarin, I know how hard this must be, but if you are unable to look into the darkness, if you are unable to face your deepest pain, you will not be able to reclaim your light, no matter how strong your resolve to do so."

Tarin met her gaze. Though still angry, he sensed something in her, something he couldn't help but wonder at. She cared for him—deeply cared for him. But why? He felt the tension in his face release as he thought back to how Iris had pushed past Maximus and shielded him from the crimson light. But as he recalled that memory, he also remembered something else, something that Maximus had said. His anger returned. "Why did Maximus say you favored my father over my mother?" he asked coldly. "No one who actually knew me, or cared for me, would ever have befriended my father."

Iris's eyes passed through him as some terrible memory seemed to flood into her own mind. He tried to hold onto his anger. But within the pools of agony behind her glasses, he saw his own reflection. He couldn't stand it any longer. "Forget it," he said. "I'm sorry. I know you're only trying to help." He forced himself away from her empty stare and looked around the room. "I agree things are urgent. And yes, maybe I'm too weak for this job. I admit it. I've not exactly given you all reason to believe in me. But I have to do my best. I can't just sit here and let you all get hurt if there's something I can do about it."

"But what if Iris is right?" Allen yelled. "What if you can't face your fear? What if you run, just like at the battle? I don't want to see you go through anything like that again!"

"Wait!" Liz interrupted. "What?" She had so far been sitting quietly—tense but attentive. "What battle? What are you talking about, Allen?"

Tarin, too, looked at Allen. He felt his blood drain from his face. "Yeah," he said. His throat tightened. "What are you talking about? You're acting like you were there."

Allen briefly met eyes with Dralo and Ristun, who offered knowing looks. Allen nodded, then turned to Tarin. "I was there. I was there when it happened. I was there when they took our village. I was there when they killed the governor, his wife, and his family. I was there when all that we had fought so hard to defend was stripped away. And I was there when you ran away. But I followed you. You were and still are my best friend, and I couldn't see you get hurt. There's nothing you can do to stop whatever is going on right now." He turned to Gil, "You know I'm right. Tarin is in no place to face what's out there. I'm still trying to figure it out myself, but I know it's been after him since we first arrived. And it's still after him now."

"Okay, okay," Josh said, standing up and waving his hands around. "Everyone, just stop a second. What is going on here? Allen, are you saying *you're* from this Arvalast place too?"

"I am," Allen said.

"And his name is actually Sarky," Dralo corrected. "I still have no idea why you changed it."

"Because Sarky is a stupid Earth name!" Ristun retorted, slapping Dralo on the shoulder. "Unlike ours."

"One thing at a time!" Josh yelled. "So Allen, or Sarky, or whatever you're called, why didn't you tell me and Rob any of this? We've known you for years, and you just sit there with this secret and don't say anything!"

"Would you really have believed me?" Allen yelled. "Until Gil came and showed us his light, and you saw the UFO, and we've been talking about cattle mutilations and government agents, all of this would have sounded completely crazy!"

"It still does!" Josh said.

"Exactly!" Allen yelled back. "Don't you think that just maybe I've been struggling with what to do about this secret . . . since . . . since I got here, always knowing there was really no good way to explain it, and wondering what it would do . . . what it would do if . . . the dreams . . . Tarin knew . . ."

Allen's voice trailed off as he met eyes with Tarin. Tarin found himself unable to speak. Instead, he frantically searched his memories, trying to find clues he'd missed as to Allen's origin. But his thoughts were interrupted when Rob said, "So wait a minute. When Gil first arrived, why did you have us play that little game between him and Tarin? Didn't you know Gil from Arvalast? Couldn't you have just had him explain everything to us then?"

"Yes," Allen answered, regaining his voice. "But I didn't immediately recognize Gil when we met him in town. It had been years since I'd seen him, and I had no idea how he could have gotten here. But after talking to him," he looked at Gil, "I thought he might be who I remembered. And if so, I thought he might be able to help Tarin with his dreams . . . and his past, where I never was able to." He paused. "And Gil might also finally create the opportunity for me to eventually share where I was from after all of this was . . . normalized."

Josh rubbed his hand over his face, "Normalized? All of this is never going to feel *normal*."

"In Allen's defense," Gil said, "I did not initially recognize him, either." He turned to Allen. "You have grown so much, and your hair is longer than I recalled. You also now have a beard."

"Debatable about the beard," Ristun said. "More like scruff. And I recognized him immediately. Don't know what's wrong with the rest of you people."

"Someone's going to need to help me out here," Liz interrupted, shaking her head. Her face was flushed, and her mouth hung open. "So, you folks from out of town all told me earlier you were from this Arvalast place, or planet, or whatever, then corroborated it with those magical lights of yours. I know it took me a minute, but I was willing to accept that. But now I'm hearing Allen, er, or Sarky, and Tarin are both from that place too?" She rubbed her temples and then looked at Allen. "Am I getting this right?"

"I'm sorry, Liz," Allen said. "There's so much I've wanted to tell you ever since we first met."

"You mean when I pulled you over for speeding?"

Allen looked rather ashamed. "Yeah, that's right."

She smiled. "Still the best ticket I ever gave out."

His face brightened.

"And it's fine, as long as you catch me up later." She sighed and muttered, "Things have already been getting so weird the last couple of days. What's a bit more strangeness going to matter?" She turned to Gil. "So the things that are happening here, the UFOs, the agents, the cattle mutilations, all this is related to where you're all from?"

"Likely," Gil said.

"And we can't let Tarin go charging out to deal with all of this on his own," Allen argued. "Gil, since you came here, it's like a hornet's nest got stirred up. We can't throw Tarin out in front of it all."

Tarin heard little of what had just been said. He felt woozy. How could Allen have somehow concealed who he was for so long and never told him? Still, in part, it made sense. He had always had a stronger connection with Allen than he'd had with anyone else except his mother. They had gone to school together in East Fairfield, both having moved there at a similar time after he'd been adopted. Allen had been fostered by a family living on the other side of town. When Allen moved away to another foster family during their senior year, Tarin had been devastated. But they'd stayed in contact. That's what had ultimately brought him to Philip. After Tarin's mother had left, it seemed to be the most natural and safe place to find solace. And he'd been right. At least up until now.

"Wait," Rob said. "I have an idea. So Tarin needs his light from Arvalast to somehow help us all out. But if Allen is from Arvalast too, don't you have a light? Can't you use yours to do the same thing?"

Ristun chuckled.

"This is serious," Dralo scolded.

"I know," Ristun said, then turned to Allen. "You want to tell them, or do you want me to?"

Allen frowned and looked to the ground. "I dropped it in the forest when I was chasing after Tarin in Arvalast."

The room went quiet for a few moments as Allen's face turned a shade of red. Finally, Rob broke the silence. "I have another question. How come you remember being from Arvalast, but Tarin doesn't?"

"I'm not sure," Allen said, "but I think it's because my light in Arvalast maintains a connection with me and somehow bridges the gap between memories of both worlds. Because Tarin's is on Earth, he doesn't have the same bridge." He looked at Gil. "And you and Iris, Ristun, and Dralo never lost memories despite maintaining your lights because you aren't human and are more intrinsically connected to the light by nature."

"You are correct," Gil replied. "Glorions, as a separate race from humans, have a nuanced connection to the light beyond that of humans. Though, in physical form, there are few obvious differences between the races, especially, as I have noticed, on Earth."

"I guess that makes sense," Rob said, "Glorions are kind of like elves from fantasy books. Similar to humans, but a bit more . . . interesting, and maybe . . . powerful?"

"Heh," Ristun said, "You got it bud."

"But, regarding the light, why is it so important Tarin gets his back? Gil, you have a light. Can't you use that to stop whatever is out there trying to hurt us?"

"We have lights as well," Dralo interjected. "They are very powerful against the shadows, but we cannot be in all places at once. Tarin needs his light, so he, too, has a defense against the darkness. Without his light, Tarin continues to be vulnerable, making all those close to him even more vulnerable."

Tarin managed to pull himself from the shock of Allen's revelation and return to the problem at hand. "He's right," Tarin said. "That thing I saw in my nightmare wants to hurt me. And he knows that hurting you, my friends . . . will hurt me more than anything else. Allen—you, Rob, and Josh, you're my family. I have to do what I can to keep you safe."

"You want to think that," Allen said solemnly. "But you know there's a part of you that's just scared of living with yourself if anything happens to us. And you know what, I have the same fear if I let something happen to you! Why do you think I never told you your dreams were real but was ok letting Gil tell you? I didn't want the guilt of hurting you directly. I didn't want you to know those idiots in the battalion really did call you a coward after all you did for them." He stood, opened the front door, and stormed outside, allowing the door to slam behind him.

Ristun let out a little whistle. "This is certainly a dramatic bunch."

"Ristun," Dralo scolded.

"Sorry," Ristun muttered, "just saying."

The room remained quiet for what seemed like a few minutes until Josh broke the silence. "So, there's no other way for us to fight off whatever this evil is other than Tarin getting his light back? No one else can fix this, not any of us, not even Gil?"

"It has to be Tarin," Iris said. Her face had transitioned from a state of sad reflection to determination. "He is the conduit through which the evil here finds a strength it's never seen before. It craves the energy from Tarin, and it won't rest until it feeds on every last drop it thinks it can absorb from him. That is why it has been tormenting him since his arrival. And that is why he needs to be able to defend against it directly. Time is short, and our enemy seems to be accelerating his plan."

"What do you mean, 'accelerating'?" Josh asked.

"Just last night, Gil, myself, Dralo, and Ristun felt something approaching. We feared it sensed Tarin was in a vulnerable state, so we acted quickly but not without great struggle. We managed to drive it away, but it is not far."

"Was it the UFO you fought off the first night you came?" Josh asked Gil.

Gil nodded. "I believe so. The negative force felt similar, and through similar means, we expelled it. It seems to be connected to the entity from Utah."

"Well," Liz said, "while you all keep figuring out this stuff with the evil entity and such, I'm going to go out and talk to Allen." She stood up. "By the way, I'm not magical, and I don't come from another world or anything, but I'm here to help however I can. I've already got the police off your backs after that airport incident. And I'm doing my best to figure out what's going on with those government agents. But when it comes to other worlds, UFOs, and magical lights, those are a bit beyond me, so I'll rely on you all to help me understand how I can help. For now, let me check on poor Allen." She turned to Tarin. "I think you should talk to him as well when you can. He really cares for you and almost can never shut up about you. Please do your best to understand his worries about all of this. They come from a good place."

Tarin closed his eyes and nodded. What Liz didn't know was how much anguish he was feeling at the moment about Allen. They'd spent countless hours discussing his dreams as Tarin agonized over what they meant, and Tarin had time and again confided in him about his insecurities about his amnesia, about how it made it hard for him to make friends, and hard for him to rationalize who he even was. Had Allen told him the truth, it would have helped Tarin make sense of his life—who he was, what he was, and where he'd come from.

But maybe Allen, as Allen had said, was fearful he'd break Tarin by telling him the truth. Maybe Allen was trying to protect him from the fact that he had run from his greatest fears when confronted by them at the battle. Had Allen told him who he really was, the dreams would no longer have been dreams. They would have been real, as they were now. But what hurt the most was that Allen seemed to also think that because Tarin had fled the battle, Tarin was truly not suited for this mission.

Gil's voice interrupted Tarin's musings as he said, "What would you like to do next, Tarin?"

Tarin opened his eyes. Regardless of what had happened at the battle, and regardless of Allen's lack of faith in him, he knew he still had to try to take that next step forward. "I want to get my light back," he said.

"And you think you are ready?"

"I . . . I'm not sure. But I have to try."

"Test him," Dralo said.

Iris stirred and shot Dralo a confused glance. "What do you mean?"

"Have him demonstrate that he has the courage to at least look at one of our lights. If he can do that, it will show he has found the strength to take the next step. If not, I would argue it would be better for us to all stay here so we can together protect him and his friends until he is ready."

"I disagree," Gil said. "Tarin must find his own path to the light. We should not force it upon him."

Ristun then lifted his hand. "But it would still be his choice, right?" Gildareth didn't reply.

Ristun turned to Tarin. "Do you think you could look at one of our lights just for a few seconds? If you can, that's a really good sign you might be ready for this journey. Then, you can hurry back to Ohio, do your best to find your light, and then show Earth what a bit of Arvalast can do in the hands of one of our own!"

"I like that." Rob suddenly retorted. "Tarin, I believe in you!"

"There we go!" Ristun said, slapping Rob on the back. "You got a bit of a fan club now. How about you, Josh? You rooting for Tarin too?"

Josh nodded, "I am." He looked at Tarin. "I believe in you, buddy."

At that moment, Allen and Liz came back in and stared at the group, most of whom were now on their feet looking at Tarin. Tarin met Allen's eyes, then turned to Gil. "Show me the light."

"And this is your choice?" Gil asked.

Before Tarin could answer, a flash lit up the corner of the room where Iris sat. "I'm sorry," she said as she held out a brilliant phial. "There's no other way."

"Wait!" said Gil. But it was too late.

Tarin lurched back as the light struck him. He tried to cover his eyes as Iris yelled, "Don't draw back! You can do it! Embrace it. Take what it has to show you."

Tarin saw two familiar figures begin to materialize in the phial, those he'd first seen in Gil's light. He knew who they were.

"No," he sputtered. "I can't do this again. I was wrong. I'm not ready!" He felt two strong hands rest on his shoulders. A voice came near to his ear and whispered, "You can do it. It is still your journey, but I will go with you this time." It was Gil's voice, and it came as a raindrop on an otherwise growing fire consuming his mind in the presence of the light and the image forming within. He embraced this calming sensation and forced himself to stay focused on the scene ahead. He watched as the hand of one figure pulled back and struck the other figure across its face. He grimaced but steeled his gaze, knowing what would happen next.

Over the next minutes, though they felt like hours, he watched as his father struck his mother, then his mother got up and pushed at his father, only to be hit again. It was a familiar scene, and one he'd for so long worked hard to repress. It had played out time and again after his mother began to lose her sanity, and his father had lost his ability to deal with her.

He thought he could feel his face growing wet, which he assumed was from his own tears. "Please make it stop," he sputtered. "Make it stop." Then, something happened. Something changed. He saw wispy shadows circling his parents while others ebbed and flowed in and out of them. Prior to each act of violence by either his mom or dad, the shadows would first lunge into one of them, causing them to shudder, convulse, then lash out against the other. A figure appeared behind this scene, a figure dressed in a leather jacket and a cattleman hat. A plume of smoke billowed from the figure's mouth, and green eyes lifted in Tarin's direction, not quite meeting his own.

"It's him!" Tarin shouted. "It's Maximus!" The scene disappeared, and he realized he'd fallen back into Gil, who was holding him up from falling on the floor.

"Who?" a voice that sounded like Josh's said.

"Maximus! The man from my dream. The entity that Gil saw when he first got here. He's what was behind my mom's insanity." He glanced at Iris. "And he was also influencing my dad." She said nothing. Her hand rested by her waist where she'd returned the light. Her own eyes were moist, and her face was full of pain.

Someone reached down and handed him a box of tissues. Tarin looked up. It was Allen, his expression stoic. "I believe in you," he said. "I'm sorry that I didn't before."

CHAPTER 16

Abigail awoke with a start. She'd had another dream, this time while taking an afternoon nap near a brook by the forest cottage. As she had after the other dreams or visions, she awoke to her heart racing and moisture beading on her forehead. She sat up, wiped strands of her brown hair from her face, and crawled over to the nearby creek. She looked down at her reflection in a small still pool on the side of the stream nearest her. She reached in, took some water in her hands, and washed her face. The far side of the creek babbled as it splashed against stones and roots that lined a muddy edge covered by old trees.

Her green eyes peered back at her from her reflection as her white gown shimmered in the glistening water. The dress had been cleaned since she'd first arrived, washed in this very spot, which acted as a sort of sink for the cottage. Now she wore a belt with the dress. It had been given to her by the cottage occupants to make it formfitting and allow her to avoid getting caught in thickets and branches as she traversed the surrounding woods. Additionally, the hem had been cut up to her knees to keep it from dragging in the grass. It was overall a comfortable outfit, which was good because other than a nightdress that had been loaned to her, it was all she had in this new place.

She thought of the man in her dreams. "Who are you?" she whispered to herself. This was now the third time she'd seen him, and as with the other two times, he appeared to be anxious and in some sort of danger. She heard a rustle behind her and turned around.

"Is everything all right?" a woman's voice said. "There were sounds like you were frightened."

"I saw him again," Abigail replied.

The woman took a seat next to her. She wore leather shoes, breeches down to her ankles, and a faded green blouse on which her long, slightly unkempt black hair flowed down to the middle of her back. She was slender but strong, a result of living independently in the forest, cutting firewood, and working with her husband to forage and hunt for their daily meals. "Tell me more," she said.

Abigail flicked a small beetle from the hem of her dress. "He was looking intently at something, something that seemed terribly unpleasant to him. He seemed so anguished." She paused. "I wish I could help him somehow."

There was the sound of boots crunching heavily against dried leaves and broken twigs as a male voice called out, "Ella! Abigail! Good news! I've got a couple of coneys for dinner."

"We will be right there, Jak!" Ella called back to her husband. She patted Abigail's knee. "Let's discuss more over dinner."

Tarin drove with Gil sitting next to him in the front passenger seat. Iris sat behind them, next to a large suitcase and some smaller luggage. She wore small earbuds, and Tarin thought he heard the faint sound of country music. Outside the windows, grassy plains and the occasional barn or farmhouse swept by as they drove along Interstate 90 East into the shadow of large puffy clouds and away from the setting sun.

The decision had been made earlier that day. Tarin, Gil, and Iris would go to Ohio on a mission to find his light. They would have to drive because after all the spending on Gil's clothes and extra food, there was little money left for airfare, and Gil wasn't in the Lattice database and would be unable to acquire a plane ticket. Dralo and Ristun would stay behind and guard Philip. Josh and Rob would do their best to continue their normal daily activities and go to work, though Allen had now formally taken time off from his consulting job because he was too nervous to focus. Tarin had told Howard he needed a week off, and thankfully he wasn't fired.

Tarin drove Allen's car. None of the others had any plans to leave Philip or, at most, the county. But if needed, Liz had her police truck, and though she admitted she shouldn't use it for anything outside of policing, she wasn't worried about making an "exception."

Having Liz involved brought Tarin comfort. He trusted her, and as county sheriff, she'd be able to monitor the situation on the ground, particularly as it pertained to MJ12-2. She'd also help keep Allen calm, who was still very stressed about Tarin leaving. Tarin had insisted Allen stay behind. Tarin knew the mission would be dangerous and didn't want Allen to inadvertently hinder him from doing whatever he needed to get his light back, as Allen had done when he'd originally protested Tarin's plan. Tarin also secretly hoped Allen would be safer apart from him than with him.

Dralo and Ristun should be able to handle any of the otherworldly aspects of things while Tarin, Gil, and Iris were away. Though everyone still had concerns about trouble from the airport incident, the risks seemed low. Liz had found out Ristun was the primary target of investigation for the disturbance, which made sense. He, after all, was responsible for terrifying everyone in the airport with his light and then stealing the van. Even if there was trouble, Tarin figured Ristun would be able to handle himself.

As they continued along the interstate, the golden hues of the setting sun cast a warm glow behind them and highlighted the gently rolling landscape and expansive grasslands in front of them. After a few hours of driving, they began to draw near the Minnesota border. Madison, Wisconsin, was their destination that night. If all went well, they'd be there by midnight and would stay at a hotel. The next morning, they'd finish the remaining eight hours to East Fairfield. It was on the northeast end of Ohio, only ten miles from the Pennsylvania border, and centered almost directly between Cleveland to the northwest and Pittsburgh to the southeast.

After another hour of driving, they decided to pull over at a rest stop to give the car a charge and grab a snack. Night had descended, and stars twinkled between dark clouds. There was a gentle breeze, and the cold air lacked any distinct scent. Tarin plugged in the car and headed toward the brick building on the other side of the parking lot. Far in the distance, he saw the first signs of wind farms. Each had hundreds of silent, waving sentinels that would fan the landscape in all directions. He watched the nearest windmill as its white blades shimmered in the rising moonlight. He found the motion to be soothing.

He and the others took advantage of the restrooms, and after Tarin had relieved himself, he approached a map hung behind glass next to a series of vending machines.

"Where are we?" Gil asked, returning from the restroom. Tarin pointed to a red dot on the western edge of the map of the state of Minnesota. Tarin had been navigating through the car's built-in navigation system but, when able, still liked to reference the large paper maps hung in most rest stops across the country. "Looks like we're near a town called Adrian. Still have a ways to go to get to Madison, but we're on track to be there by midnight." He looked around. "Where's Iris?"

"Perhaps the washroom?" Gil said.

Tarin nodded and continued to study the map. It put in perspective how vast each state truly was and gave him a chill of excitement any time the marker on the map highlighted how far he was from more populated areas, as it did now. Even though he realized a car afforded him the ability to quickly get back to civilization in any direction, having a vehicle was all that otherwise kept an excursion across the country from being far more treacherous. He still marveled at how Gil had managed to get from Utah to Philip on foot and horseback. He also envied such a journey.

They waited ten more minutes, and still, they didn't see Iris. "Maybe she's outside," Tarin said. He saw a door opposite those they'd entered through. From prior trips, he remembered it led to the open outdoor picnic area behind the building. "I'll go check out back."

"And I will see if she has returned to the car," Gil said.

Tarin walked out back and into the chill of the evening. He breathed in deeply. Though the final destination for this trip gave him no peace, being on the road momentarily compensated for that. He'd always loved road trips, and before things turned sour at home, he and his parents had taken one every summer for multiple years. His favorites had always been those that took them across the great plains. If happy memories could still exist, standing behind a rest stop at night and looking at the stars while in the middle of nowhere was one of them.

He thought he heard the sound of music nearby. His eyes searched for its source until he saw a lone tree standing near the corner of the building. Next to it, he saw Iris. She stared at the sky, no longer wearing earbuds but rather letting her music play directly from her glasses. He approached her and began to hear the lyrics. They were familiar to him, from an old country song about going through hell and pressing forward despite the fire, the demons, and the pain. He'd listened to it frequently after he'd fled East Fairfield. A strange mix of both happy and sad emotions filled him. He shook them off and continued toward Iris. She noticed him and tapped the side of her glasses. The music went silent, and she looked back up at the sky.

Tarin joined her by the tree. "Gil and I were wondering where you'd gone."

"Sorry if I held you up," she said. "I saw there was a door leading out here and decided to step outside and stretch. I needed to work out some kinks from being cramped up in the back of the car." She continued to look out over the distant horizon.

Tarin followed her gaze and, for a few moments, said nothing. Then, he began humming the same tune Iris had been playing before until he surprised himself by quietly singing its lyrics.

Iris turned to him. "You know the song?"

"I do," Tarin replied. "It became a sort of theme song for me after . . . well, you know. I felt like I'd fallen into hell, and sometimes, I'd get to the point where I wasn't sure I even wanted to go on." He quietly began singing the next line, not quite in tune, but close enough. Iris looked at him, her eyes reflective, sad.

He finished the song. "It would give me a little more hope in my darkest times," he said softly. "It took on even more meaning when I got to Philip. He looked back up at the sky. "I know it might sound weird, but Allen, Josh, Rob . . . they became my angels that got me through hell. They grounded me. And that stupid game we play, it grounded me too, or at least distracted me."

Iris smiled. Tarin wasn't sure what she was thinking, and he didn't really care. At the moment, outside, and having heard her listening to a familiar and comforting song, he was, for the first time in many days, feeling somewhat at peace. The gentle breeze, though cold, did not penetrate his jacket. Iris, in a denim jacket and a stocking cap, also seemed comfortable. Her dark hair fell just beneath the hat and slightly over her shoulders. Occasionally she'd wipe a bit of fog from her glasses. Over the next many moments, they silently listened to the periodic car or truck pass by on the interstate behind them.

Tarin took a deep and satisfying breath through his nose and looked back at Iris. There was a look of concern on her face. She pointed west in the direction they'd just traveled from. "What's that?"

Tarin looked up, and between two twinkling stars, he saw a small blue light. Unlike the stars, it did not twinkle, and also unlike the stars, it appeared to be slowly moving in their direction, with an occasional radical shift to the left or right. She lowered her hand. "We need to get back to Gil," she said.

"Maybe it's just a drone," Tarin said. The light moved closer, then made an almost instantaneous jump to the right, emerging far from its original location.

"Drones don't do that," Iris said.

"Yeah," Tarin agreed. "Let's get Gil." They began running back toward the building. Just before they reached the door, it opened, and Gil came sprinting out. He saw them and halted. "I take it you have seen it too?"

Iris nodded. "We need to get out of here. Maybe there's still time to outrun it."

"Not to be presumptuous," Tarin said, "but that looks way faster than a car. Wouldn't it make more sense for you to fight it off here?"

Gil strained his eyes toward the approaching blue dot. "Maybe Tarin is right. We could stand our ground and see if we can drive it away."

"Unfortunately," Iris said, "if that's what I think it is, our lights won't be a deterrent." She looked at Gil. "We need to get out of here."

"What do you mean?" Gil asked.

"I'll explain more after we're safe. Let's go!"

She ran back into the building. Tarin and Gil followed. They maneuvered past an elderly couple near the vending machines who stepped back, looking confused. Then they pushed past a red-haired, bearded man in plaid who'd just entered the building. He had to side-step them as they rushed by. "Excuse us," Gil said, as he and Iris maintained a steady forward focus as they hurried to the car. Soon they were back in the parking lot. Tarin jumped behind the steering wheel while Iris and Gil followed fast behind him. "Oh no," he said. "I forgot to unplug the car!"

"Hurry!" Iris said.

Tarin rushed out and put the power cord back on the terminal. He looked in the direction of the blue light. It was larger now, and he could see that it was not a single blue light but more of a saucer shape, with smaller blue lights around the outer edge. He cursed and got back into the car. "It looks just like some of the pictures Liz showed us!" He turned on the car, hit the accelerator, and peeled out onto the interstate.

Iris turned and looked behind them. "It's getting closer," she said. "It must be following us. Can you go faster?"

Tarin pressed hard on the accelerator, and the car sped up to ninety, then one hundred, then one hundred and ten miles per hour. "Do you think we can actually outrun it?" he yelled back to Iris.

"Not if they're hunting."

"Hunting?" Tarin shouted. "Hunting what? Us?"

"Not you—Glorions," she said.

A blue light flashed across the car windows. The car shuddered. Tarin screamed and slammed on the brakes. The sudden stop slung them against their seat belts. Outside the windshield, about a hundred feet in front of them, the object hovered above the currently empty roadway. A strange dizziness filled Tarin's mind as he watched blue lights rotate like a carousel around the craft's elongated middle. At the same time, he felt the hair on his arms stand on end—whether by some hidden electrical current or just out of fear, he wasn't sure. A moment later, a beam of light dropped down from beneath the craft. The car died, and its headlights went out. Tarin tried to turn it back on. "Come on, come on," he pleaded. Nothing. "It's like it's lost its charge," he said. "What do we do?"

Gil's hand went down toward his waist.

"Don't bother," Iris said. "They aren't affected by the light."

Gil turned to look at her. "What then do you advise? I am not familiar with all of the evils in this world. If not the light, what do we have as weapons?"

"Is there a gun in the car?" Iris asked.

"I don't think so," said Tarin, "but let me look." He reached over in front of Gil and opened the glove compartment. He pulled out old papers, some pens, and a map. "No gun," he said.

The light from the craft began slowly drifting in their direction.

"Then we need to run and hide," Iris said. She opened the door and sprinted toward a field just beyond the highway. Gil and Tarin looked at each other and followed suit. As Tarin ran, he noticed a windmill not far beyond them, rising high into the sky and emitting a gentle hum as its massive blades rotated. "Let's head for the windmill!" he yelled. "Maybe the UFO won't be able to fly close to it!"

"Good idea!" Iris yelled back. They fled in that direction. Tarin looked back. The light under the UFO had disappeared, and the craft slowly began following them. He could see some headlights farther up the highway approaching from both the east and west, but as they drew nearer to where Allen's car sat idle, the headlights flickered and went out. He realized that the UFO must somehow be disrupting their electronics as well.

The humming of the windmill grew louder. At one point, Tarin stumbled over a large rock. Gil helped him back up. Iris remained ahead, darting between shrubbery and jumping over small ditches that spread like cobwebs across the fallow field. Finally, they got close enough to the white mechanical giant to feel the movement of air beneath its swinging blades. Iris jumped onto the ground near its wide base and lay prostrate. She waved at them and, in a tense whisper, said, "Quick, over here!"

Gil and Tarin lunged forward and took up positions on the ground next to her. They all peered over the patches of dead grass in front of them. About a football field away, the UFO stopped. Perhaps their plan had worked. Had it been deterred by the massive rotating blades overhead? The craft seemed only as big as a small bus, so if it were struck, it would likely take significant damage. As if it were assessing the situation, the saucer's silver, edgeless body rocked one way, then the other. Finally, it began to silently descend toward the field.

One by one, the blue lights went out until the craft at last made contact with the ground. A masive windmill blade hummed as it passed over Tarin, Gil, and Iris. Then silence. Another blade passed over. Gil's and Iris's breaths came out fast but quiet. Something rustled in the grass. Tarin frantically scanned the ground ahead but saw nothing.

More rustling.

Then, Tarin saw it. Perhaps fifty feet away stood a small figure. It was the size of a child and silhouetted against the backdrop of the night sky. Its gangly, grey arms hung loosely at its sides. Its elongated head revealed black, bulbous eyes. They seemed to be scanning the area in front of it. Whether the creature was naked or wearing a skintight suit,

Tarin couldn't tell. Moments later, another appeared next to the first, then another, and yet three more. Soon Tarin counted six, then ten. His heart began to race.

"What are those things?" he hissed. "They look like . . ."

"Edin-Lirum," Iris whispered. "Though most on Earth call them Greys."

"Greys!" Tarin sputtered. "Like aliens?"

"Shhh!" Iris said.

The first creature slowly raised its arm, and Tarin heard a guttural clicking sound. The full group began walking toward them. "Run," Iris whispered. She stood and took out her light.

"No, Iris!" Gil yelled.

There was a brilliant flash. The Greys covered their eyes and stopped for a moment. More clicking sounds as they began to weave back and forth.

Iris searched the ground. She found an old piece of wood, perhaps left during the construction of the windmill. She picked it up and looked down at Tarin and Gil. "Gil, please, get Tarin to his light!" Gil stood and tried to reach out to stop her, but she escaped his grasp and raced toward the creatures.

Gil turned to Tarin with intensity in his eyes. "You must flee back to the car. I will help Iris and see if we cannot break whatever magic is keeping the car from running. If it starts, do not wait for us. If it does not, proceed on foot until you find help. We will find and join you if we can." He pulled out his light and raced after Iris.

He ran toward the creatures just as Iris reached the closest. She held the plank of wood high, then brought it down with a fierce swing. The Grey, just over half her height, fell sideways and collapsed. But the others immediately converged on her. She swung her weapon wildly, but even as she landed blow after blow, for every creature she knocked away, another got back up and pressed in. Gil joined the battle, lifting a blunt object he'd also found, and charged the Greys just as they began dragging Iris to the ground. With a few powerful swings, he threw many back until he reached Iris. He helped her to her feet, and together, they stood back to back and delivered blow after blow. But though the creatures would fall back after being hit, none stayed down for long.

Tarin stood and began backing against the windmill. He couldn't just let Gil and Iris fight what seemed to be a force too powerful for them. Their light seemed to be little more than a nuisance to this new enemy. But as the light danced within the battle, he realized he didn't feel any fear from it, which confused him. Was it because the current physical danger dwarfed the potential emotional pain the light usually drew out of him? There was no time to ponder this further. He had two choices: run to the car or see if he could help.

The battle continued as he played the different scenarios in his head. Both seemed futile. Helping would get him killed. But fleeing to the car would be useless if Gil couldn't figure out how to hinder whatever the UFO was doing to it. And looking for help? The other nearby cars were also affected, and if Gil and Iris lost the fight, the Greys would have an easy time finding and catching him. He was at a dead end.

He remembered something. He checked his pocket. Good. His phone was still there. He hadn't left it in the car. But would it work? He pulled it out. It was working! No time to understand why. He scrolled through his contacts until he found "Chief."

Something hit him from behind, and he fell forward onto his face. He spun around. A Grey stood over him. Its massive almond eyes stared down at him. Its tiny mouth opened and closed slowly. Was it breathing or trying to speak? Being this close, he could now see it was, in fact, wearing a dark grey skintight suit. And on its waist was a light belt and a holster with something that looked like a taser inside. Tarin shuffled backward to try to get away from it. But it followed him.

"You have no light," he heard a quiet voice say directly into his mind. *Was this thing telepathic?*

"Arvalastian," it continued as it walked forward, though again not audibly. Then he heard other voices join the first. "Arvalastian . . . Arvalastian . . . Arvalastian," they chanted. Abruptly, the voices stopped. The creature in front of him tilted its head as if confused. "No light," Tarin heard the collective think. For a long moment, the Grey stood, looking at him, silent and pensive, as if it were running the situation through some mental database to determine what to do next. Finally, it joined in with the collective and spoke one telepathic word.

"Kill."

"No," Tarin whispered. He managed to stand up and spin around. A short distance away, he saw Gil and Iris still fighting against what seemed to be a growing number of creatures. Both continued to swing their weapons wildly even as they were swarmed. Tarin remembered his phone. He tapped the contact. Then he got up and ran. Behind him, he heard his pursuer following closely.

"Tarin," a voice said on the other end. For the first time, Tarin felt relieved to hear the voice. "I'm under attack!" Tarin yelled. He looked back. The creature was catching up to him.

"Share more," the voice said.

"You said to call if I saw or heard anything about the phenomenon you and your team are investigating. I'm near a town in Minnesota called Adrian, and my friends and I are being attacked by grey aliens from a . . . from a metallic saucer, just like one of the ones in the pictures you shared with Liz!"

"Hold on," the voice said. A few moments later, it came back and said, "Hold the phone out." Tarin was preparing to obey when he saw a blue flash and felt his body go stiff. He convulsed as what felt like an electrical current coursed through his muscles. He fell onto his back, his arms and legs spread out across the ground.

The Grey stood over him. It held the device Tarin had seen earlier. Tarin managed to hold onto his phone. It was facing up. A moment later, it emitted a shrill sound. The Grey turned its attention to it. The phone now made a series of ticking noises, followed by another shrill sound. The creature leaned forward until its eyes were but inches from Tarin's phone. Then it took a step back, looked in the direction of the ongoing battle with Gil and Iris, and ran in that direction.

"Tarin," he heard a voice say. It came from the phone. He noticed he could now move his arm with effort. He brought the phone to his ear. "Tarin, are you there?"

"I'm here. I'm okay. The thing . . . it left after whatever you did."

"You're now safe," the voice said. "But there's nothing I can do for your friends."

"Wait!" Tarin said. "What do you mean? Why?" The phone went silent as the MJ12-2 chief hung up.

Tarin cursed and jumped to his feet. The sound of the battle had quieted. Two figures were being dragged toward the UFO. Two small phials lay glowing dimly in the grass where the battle had raged. Four creatures stood around them, staring down at the glistening glass and setting down something they pulled from what appeared to be a burlap sack. It looked like pieces of raw meat. More clicking, though now it was rhythmic, almost like a chant.

"No, no, no," Tarin frantically mumbled to himself. He searched the ground. There was nothing he could use as a weapon, and even if he found something, what could he realistically do? If Iris and Gil couldn't fend these things off, how could he? He cursed and pulled himself up to his knees. Maybe he could try anyway. Maybe if he distracted them, Iris and Gil would be able to break free. But what if it didn't work? Their mission was for him to retrieve his light. Should he try to get away and see if that was still possible?

As his mind raced, he noticed something in the sky. It was about as high off the ground as the top of the windmill, just above where the creatures stood next to the dropped phials. At first, it looked like a green star. Then it grew wider. It slowly opened up like a window in the sky. His eyes grew wide as he remembered. It looked exactly like the portal he'd seen in his dream as Maximus drew energy from him. Maximus had not been pleased when he'd seen it. What had he said again? He couldn't recall.

The portal opened to the size of a full moon. A strange and growing sense of power emanated from beyond it and filled Tarin with an increasing sense of unease. Strings of light began flowing from the fallen phials and toward the portal. At the same time, the Greys continued to drag Gil and Iris toward the saucer. Tarin could see them struggling, but without their lights and seemingly weakened from the Grey's taser-like weapon, they could not break free. The craft's blue lights came back on and began rotating slowly around its edge.

Tarin took one more look at the the tear in the sky, grimaced, then took a painful step toward the UFO. With a groan, he managed another step, then stopped. He felt weak, as if struck with a bad flu. "I can't," he whispered in defeat. But at least he'd taken a few steps toward the battle rather than fleeing. Though, because of the current state of his legs, fleeing was not an option.

He looked up. More strings of light curled and snaked toward the portal. His stomach tightened as he now felt like whatever was beyond it had somehow noticed him. Then, he saw what looked like two headlights approaching from the interstate. The sound of a loud engine soon followed. A vehicle turned off the interstate and started bouncing offroad toward the saucer. It had to be an old gas or diesel-powered car, Tarin realized. Otherwise, it would have been affected similarly to the electric vehicles.

As it drew closer, he saw it was actually a Jeep. The creatures noticed it too and started dragging Iris and Gil faster toward the craft. But they were too late. The Jeep careened past the saucer, spun around, and came to a halt. Someone jumped out. There was gunfire. Tarin covered his ears and watched two of the creatures nearest the Jeep fall to the ground. Whoever had the gun moved forward and continued to fire. One of the two creatures dragging Iris fell to the ground. Two more shots were fired. Both creatures holding Gil collapsed.

Gil managed to grab the foot of the final Grey still holding Iris and knocked it to the ground. Iris got up, and together they stumbled toward where their phials lay streaming light toward the portal.

The gunman continued firing toward the UFO as the surviving creatures fled toward it. More creatures fell to the ground. Finally, Gil and Iris reached for their lights, picked them up, and held them toward the portal. The strands of light, some of which had just begun entering the portal, retreated back toward their origin. Faster and faster, they returned to their source, and as they did, the portal slowly shrank—along with Tarin's unease—until the last strands of light returned to the phials. The portal snapped shut and disappeared.

The UFO lifted off the ground with whatever Greys had managed to get back inside. Its blue lights began swirling rapidly around it; it tilted to one side, and in an instant, the craft was gone. All grew still. The only noticeable sound was that of the windmill gently humming as its blades rotated overhead.

Tarin, feeling his strength returning after being hit by the Grey's weapon, ran toward Gil and Iris. They were about a hundred feet away and near the Jeep. He could hear them talking to the gunman but couldn't hear what they were saying.

When he got close enough to make out words, he thought he heard his name. He got a glimpse of their rescuer, whose face was slightly illuminated by the light of the phials. It was the red-bearded man in plaid from the rest stop. The man met his eyes, tipped his head as if saying hello, then got back into his Jeep. As quickly as he'd come, he bounded over the field and back onto the interstate and turned west in the direction of South Dakota. But in the back of the Jeep, Tarin saw another figure, smaller than the man and wearing a ball cap. He thought he heard a whisper in his mind, a sort of greeting, but he couldn't be sure. The Jeep disappeared along the highway, and Tarin turned his attention to where Gil and Iris stood.

He jogged toward them. As he grew closer, he saw Iris had a large gash on her hand and another cut on her face. Any exposed skin on Gil had cuts and bruises.

"Glad to see you are okay," Gil said wearily as Tarin finally reached them. Iris stepped toward Tarin and, to his surprise, embraced him.

"I thought you were lost," she said. Her voice seemed to be quivering. She let him go and stepped back. "I'm sorry I left you earlier. I thought it was the only hope for you to escape."

"Where are your glasses?" Tarin asked, noticing they were missing from her cut and dirty face. She reached up and searched for them. "I must have lost them in the fight." Tarin heard a faint sound, like music. They looked around until Gil reached down and picked something up.

"I think I have found them," he said. Sure enough, he held a pair of still-intact glasses in his hand as they played the same song Iris was listening to at the rest stop. He handed them to Iris. She wiped them on the hem of her sleeve and put them back on. She turned off the music.

The headlights from the cars previously stalled along the interstate came back on. He saw some people standing around them. They were pointing into the sky, and some were screaming. "We better get to the car fast before things start getting out of hand here," Tarin said.

When they reached the interstate, a man rushed to Tarin and grabbed him by his shoulder. "We saw what happened!" the man yelled. "What were those things you were fighting?"

Tarin pulled away as a nearby woman screamed, "It's the end of the world! The Alliance sent those things to attack us!" On the other side of the road, Tarin saw a family of five huddled around a car, holding hands, seemingly praying.

"Let's get out of here," Tarin said as he rushed toward Allen's car. The hum of the windmill diminished until he, Gil, and Iris, at last, managed to get inside the vehicle. It started, and Tarin navigated through a few remaining onlookers still staring into the sky from the center of the road before he passed through the commotion and was able to continue east.

CHAPTER 17

The smell of woodsmoke was thick in the air. The contents of a large iron kettle simmered over an open fire. The warmth from the cottage fireplace felt comforting. Abigail handed Jak a pouch of rosemary, which he took and sprinkled into the kettle. Its aroma filled the room, along with that of onion and other spices.

Jak carefully ladled the rich stew into three bowls, each with hearty chunks of rabbit meat swimming in a savory-smelling broth. He set the bowls on the hearth and sprinkled in freshly chopped herbs from a nearby plate. "Could you help me move them to the table?" he asked Abigail. She nodded, and together they carefully transferred the steaming bowls to the wooden table across from the fireplace.

Ella returned from fetching water from the creek. Together, the three of them settled down at the table and began to eat. "Ella tells me you saw the man again?" Jak said. His voice was youthful, though he appeared to be in his early forties while maintaining a strong, wiry frame. A few grey hairs decorated his otherwise black beard, and he showed some signs of a receding hairline.

"I did," Abigail said between spoonfuls of soup. She took a sip of water to ease the heat on her tongue. "He seemed very frightened."

"Remind me again what he looks like," Ella said as she sprinkled some salt into her stew.

"Sandy blond hair, probably thirty years old. He's somewhat thin, with very curious brown eyes."

Ella and Jak exchanged glances. "Has he spoken to you?" Jak said.

"He's not said anything to me, but he has noticed me."

"Abigail," Jak said, "since last we discussed, do you still have no memory of where you are from?"

"I don't," she said. "The night you found me is the first memory I have. Outside of that, everything feels like a dream. Somehow, I recall my name being Abigail, and in my memory, I see rolling grassy hills covered in wildflowers that I can see through a window in a small room. I also remember books. Many, many books along a great bookshelf. But I can't recall any of the titles."

"And you still have no memory of Arvalast, the Great Northern Forest, Lockspell, Northlake, or . . . Woodend?"

"No," she said. "I don't know of anything but this place, my name, and the books and window."

"Do you think she may have come from the lands beyond?" Ella asked Jak. "Could she have somehow entered where he left us?"

"I'm not certain," Jak said. The fireplace crackled behind him. "There is a tower," he said to Abigail, "that is said to house a door to another world. Years ago, we lost someone very dear to us to that tower, and since then, a friend of ours has been doing everything in his power to break a seal on its top and find a way to this other world. Weeks before we found you in the meadow, our friend shared with us that he thought he may have discovered a way past the barrier. We then heard nothing from him for many days and decided to go searching for him. That's when we found you."

Abigail had been just about to lift her spoon to her mouth but let it drop back into her bowl. "You think I may be from this other world?"

Ella and Jak sat silently, looking at her. Their shadows danced against the walls as the fire continued to burn brightly behind them. "I'm not sure," Jak said.

"You said you lost someone dear to the tower," Abigail continued. "May I ask who it was?

Ella turned and looked into the fire. "My brother."

Tarin, Gil, and Iris had driven another two hours through the southern reaches of Minnesota along Interstate 90. Iris found a first aid kit Allen had left in the back of his car, and she and Gil did their best to dress the majority of their open cuts with its contents. Their moans and grimaces made it clear both were still in quite a bit of pain. Tarin wasn't faring well either, though most of the lingering weakness from whatever device the Greys had used against him was finally beginning to diminish. Tarin suspected they had used the same device against Gil and Iris.

In the rearview mirror, Tarin saw Iris lift her earbuds to her ears and close her eyes. Next to him, Gil sat with his eyes closed and arms crossed over the cowboy hat on his lap.

Tarin wanted to ask them questions about the encounter with the Greys, such as what the creatures actually were and what they were doing with Iris's and Gil's lights. He also wanted to know the identity of the mysterious stranger in the Jeep who'd saved them. But he could tell Gil and Iris weren't feeling well from the encounter, and both now seemed to be sleeping. He decided, for now, he wouldn't bother them with questions. But he hoped when they got to the hotel, or at least after they'd had a good night's sleep, he'd be able to learn more.

Tarin saw a sign ahead for Rochester, Minnesota. He took the next exit, drove into the small city, and found a drugstore, where he parked. Iris and Gil stirred and opened their eyes.

"I'll go fetch some gauze and more cream for your injuries," Tarin said, "along with some pain medication. There's a restroom here as well."

Together, they hobbled into the store, doing their best to look inconspicuous. The single attendant glanced at them briefly, raised an eyebrow, but then went back to looking at her phone. About fifteen minutes later, they returned to the car without incident.

"The hotel I booked is only about three hours away," Tarin said. He checked the time. "Looks like we'll be there just before one in the morning." He handed them each a sandwich, a bag of chips, and a bottle of water. "I got these for you. Sorry, I know it's not much, but the hotel has breakfast included, so we can look forward to that in the morning."

"Will there be coffee and bacon?" Gil asked.

"Probably," Tarin said.

Gil leaned his head back against his seat, closed his eyes, and smiled.

Tarin wasn't feeling very hungry but had bought a protein smoothie for himself. He steered with one hand and drank with the other as he drove back toward the interstate. Traffic was minimal, and Tarin tested the speed limit while keeping a lookout for police.

Soon, they began the long descent toward the northern ends of the Mississippi River, which separated Minnesota from Wisconsin. Gil's eyes fluttered open, and he looked out his window as the vast body of water opened before them and shimmered in the lights of the high-way. They crossed over a bridge and drove beneath the welcome sign for Wisconsin.

"Not much farther," Tarin said with a yawn. Gil nodded, then again closed his eyes. The thought of a good night's rest sounded extremely pleasing to Tarin despite his ongoing curiosity about what had happened at the windmill. His eyes were growing heavy, and he still hadn't shaken the concern about another encounter with a UFO. For the full duration of the drive since the attack, he'd been periodically glancing at the sky any time a star seemed out of place, though the added vigilance hadn't done anything to alleviate his exhaustion.

At long last, the sign for the hotel he'd booked on the western edge of Madison emerged just beyond an upcoming exit. Tarin merged into the rightmost lane and, a few minutes later, pulled into the mostly empty parking lot. He plugged in the car, and while Gil and Iris began removing luggage from the back seat, he checked into the hotel, grabbed a baggage cart, and met them back in the parking lot.

They managed to fit everything onto the cart and rolled it toward the overhang above the hotel entrance. Once inside, the smell of chlorine greeted them. The pool was closed, but the snack bar to the side of the lobby desk was not. Tarin purchased a few candy bars, some crackers, and a few more bottles of water.

"Could you get me a beer?" Iris asked.

Tarin looked at her quizzically a moment, shrugged, and said, "I might as well grab one for me too. I should have enough alcohol credits since I haven't bought any in a few days. Gil, you want one too?"

"No, thank you," he said. "Just water for me."

Tarin led them to the nearby elevator, and they exited on the fifth floor. Tarin had reserved a suite with two queen beds and a pullout couch. Once in their room, Gil volunteered to take the couch, but Tarin insisted Gil and Iris should take the beds since they were the most injured. They agreed with many thanks, then, one by one, took turns washing up. Afterward, they met at the little round table in the kitchenette. Tarin fetched the beers he'd put in the minifridge and a bottle of water for Gil. It was now fifteen minutes until two in the morning.

"Not sure drinking so late is a good idea," Tarin said. He cracked the beer. "But it's been a rough day." Iris followed suit. Tarin lifted his can. "To another victory over another UFO," he said.

"Hear, hear," said Gil, raising his bottle of water and tapping it against Tarin's beer can.

"To a good drink and a good night's rest," Iris said and added her drink to the toast. For the next fifteen minutes, they found some relaxation over light conversation and the crackers. Tarin was considering taking advantage of the quiet moment while everyone was still awake to ask more about the battle with the Greys and the mysterious man who'd saved them when Gil said, "I fear I can no longer fight sleep. I am going to go to bed."

Tarin did his best to hold back a groan but ultimately agreed, along with Iris, that bed sounded like a good idea. Questions would have to wait for the morning. And with how late it already was, that wouldn't be long. Iris stood up from the table and tossed her beer can into a nearby wastebasket.

"I didn't realize people from Arvalast drank," Tarin said.

She smirked. "Oh, they drink. I doubt there's a world that exists without such a thing. But Glorions don't usually drink." She took off her glasses and set them on the table. "I acquired a taste for hops when I worked as a bartender for a short while."

"Where was that?" Tarin asked.

"A microbrewery in a small Ohio town." He could see memories flickering in her eyes. "Your town, actually." She walked toward her bed and, while passing, said, "Goodnight, Tarin."

Tarin considered this for a moment. She'd been a bartender in East Fairfield? He shook his head. "Continues to be full of surprises," he whispered. He opened the sofa, collapsed into it, and allowed the night to embrace him in what he hoped would be an uneventful sleep. At some point, he woke and thought he saw a light pass by behind the thick curtains on the far wall. Gil stirred and groaned, and before Tarin could think of it further, his pillow lured him back to sleep.

He awoke the next morning to the sounds of running water in the bathroom. He glanced toward the beds. Gil was sitting up on the edge of his bed, rubbing his shoulder. A moment later, Iris emerged from the bathroom, fully dressed and cleaned up well. "Let's get breakfast," she said.

Shortly thereafter, the trio stepped into the dining area just outside the hotel lobby. Spacious and mutedly furnished, the room was illuminated by the sunlight streaming through large windows. The inviting scent of freshly brewed coffee filled the room as they made their way to the breakfast buffet.

Tarin grabbed a plate and piled it high with breakfast casserole, then smothered it in hot sauce. He noticed a holographic projector in the corner of the room not that dissimilar to the one at Old Cotton's. Being displayed was a now familiar news report about the war. He shifted his gaze away, sat down at an empty table, and took a sip of hot coffee. Moments later, Iris and Gil joined him.

The atmosphere in the dining room was pleasingly tranquil, an oasis away from the events of the previous night and, aside from the news report, seemingly disconnected from the war on the other side of the world. Other guests conversed over their own cups of steaming coffee, and a couple of children scuttled about, asking when they could go swimming, as the projector now displayed an advertisement for a local restaurant. Then, the setting switched to a scene of the United States Capitol Building. An older man in the dining room walked over and tapped on a tablet hanging near the image. The volume grew louder.

"Mysterious lights and strange craft blanketed Washington, DC, last night," a male reporter said. The projection showed what appeared to be white cylinders with rounded ends flying over the Capitol Building, followed by another similar scene over the White House. "Residents across the city took video and pictures, and aircraft were scrambled to intercept. Upon engagement, the objects would disappear, then instantaneously reappear, sometimes miles away. Thus far, there have been no reports of injuries, but an already nervous nation is asking its leaders and President Silverton, who is expected to return from his trip to Europe later today, 'What has invaded our airspace?'"

"Aliens!" the children began to cry out. They started running around the dining room while their parents tried to hush them. The man by the hologram shook his head and muttered, "What's going on? War and now this?"

Gil took a sip of his coffee and glanced at Tarin.

"Well," Tarin said, "seems we're not the only ones dealing with them now. I'm not sure if I should be comforted or even more terrified." Maybe this was his chance to ask more about the Greys and what they were.

Iris stared at the projection as the images of the UFOs appeared back within the holographic display. "I don't recognize those," she whispered.

"Are you saying there are yet more entities on this earth beyond those we have already encountered?" Gil asked.

She continued to study the moving three-dimensional images. "When I first came to this place, I was fascinated by nature, in particular the rainforests. Over time, I learned that despite the countless creatures already discovered there, scientists would frequently uncover some new species of insect or variant of reptile yet to be cataloged. I believe that in the broader world, beyond Arvalast and beyond Earth, perhaps, there is similar diversity that may occasionally find its way to our current point of consciousness. It's possible that though we become aware of some of the more hidden aspects of this place, both for good and for ill, there may be others not yet discovered."

She lifted some eggs to her mouth, chewed, and swallowed. "I only hope the intent of whatever these may be is better than those we fought last night."

"Indeed," Gil said. "I still ache from the encounter."

"It could have been significantly worse," Iris said. "We were lucky."

Tarin could hold back no more. "What were those things?" he blurted. "And who was that man who saved you last night?" A few eyes in the room darted his way.

Iris took another bite of food, then said, "I told you, they're Edin-Lirum."

"So aliens? Like, what kids dress up as on Halloween?"

She shook her head. "Tarin, you of all people must certainly understand by now that, like I just shared, the universe is far more complex and diverse than most people realize."

"Yeah, but this feels different . . . more physical, whereas the light and Arvalast somehow feel more magical. So are these Edin-Lirum from a different world like you and Gil?"

"And like yourself?"

Tarin set his fork down and paused. "Sure," he said.

Iris looked at Gil, then back at Tarin. "We think they're from Arvalast, like us, but have been . . . changed by the darkness."

"Changed? How?"

She closed her eyes and sighed. "We can only speculate." She opened her eyes. "I'd rather not say more right now. Let's stay focused on getting your light back instead."

Tarin's mind raced. "If you don't want to talk more about the Edin-Lirum, can you at least tell me about that man that saved us? Who was he?"

"He is a Glorion, like me," Iris said. "But he has been on Earth far longer, battling the darkness endemic to this world."

"Endemic? What do you mean?"

"I mean that Maximus was not the first to darken this planet, though he is allied with it. There is a Shadow Prince that rules over the darkness upon Earth, and the Glorion you saw is one of the first to fight against it. He is also the one that found you when you came to Earth. It is because of him that both you and Sarky lived long enough to be hidden in Ohio, where I then eventually was sent to watch over you."

"And what's the Glorion's name?" Tarin asked.

"He is called Gabe," Iris said. "And he is one of the few friends of my kind I have left after the purge."

"You keep speaking of this 'purge,'" Tarin said, his mind racing as he processed all this new information. "Is it connected to what was happening to your lights as they were being absorbed into some"—he waved his hands around as he searched for the right words—"some green portal?" He paused. "I felt something . . . malevolent behind it."

Iris's face grew downcast. "Yes, it is connected." Before Tarin could ask more questions, she locked eyes with him and said. "My turn for a question. I'm curious. How did you escape the Greys after Gil and I lost our lights?"

Tarin wrung his hands together and looked away. "I . . . I contacted the chief agent."

"You mean from MJ12-2?" Iris said with surprise.

"Yes," Tarin said. "I didn't know what else to do."

She furrowed her brow. "Why would one of them save you? They are allied with the Greys."

Gil touched his hand to his bearded chin and rubbed it. "My assessment would be that these agents must desire that Tarin remain unharmed to fulfill some agenda of theirs, though I doubt it to be benevolent. And although Tarin meant no harm in calling the chief, the agent and his people are now aware of our journey east. This could put us in greater danger when we reach Ohio."

"Danger is ever present on Earth," Iris said solemnly, "Particularly for those of us connected to Arvalast. Tarin's call likely did little to change the amplitude of the threats facing us on this mission. All our enemies, by now, are well aware of our intent. It's as visible to them as the light is to us. But what they don't know is what Tarin will ultimately do." She faced Tarin. "The choices facing you, the places you must go: this is of great intrigue to them."

"As it is to us," Gil added. He smiled at Tarin. "And I have faith you will prevail."

Tarin appreciated Gil's confidence but was still concerned about his ability to find what he presumed was his own phial of light at his father's—likely the glass container he'd been given by the youth center—without having a full mental breakdown in the process. He knew what it might cause him to face, and even now, he still wasn't sure he would be able to face it. In addition, there was another barrier he'd have to overcome—seeing his father again after so many years. Unlike his mother, his father was not a painful memory within a terrible dream, but a painful memory that would be present, able to speak, fully physical, and potentially angry to see him again. And Tarin had no great positive feelings about the prospect of seeing him either.

He thought again about what Maximus had said about Iris favoring his father over his mother. What had he meant? When he'd brought it up with her earlier, it had impacted her deeply. He couldn't imagine it had been something of a romantic nature. Iris seemed somewhat disconnected from emotions of that type. She did have what seemed a strong affinity for Gil, as he'd seen with their embrace at the airport, but overall their relationship seemed platonic. And though her feelings for him were enigmatic, he did not at all sense they were romantic.

Tarin noticed his phone ringing. He lifted it up and looked at the screen. "It's Allen," he said. He answered. A loud voice blasted out of the phone. "Tarin! How's the road trip going?" He pulled the phone back from his ear and winced.

"It is Ristun!" Gil said. "Hello, my friend!"

"Not sure if he can hear you," Tarin said. He put the phone on speaker.

"I heard him!" Ristun said. "Iris there too?"

"Yes," said Tarin.

Iris's face brightened.

"Great! So, you all will never guess what happened here."

The trio looked at each other, then back at the phone. There was a long pause. It lingered and continued to linger until Gil finally said, "You are correct, Ristun. We do not have a guess."

"I thought not!" he replied. "So last night, there were ten living cows at a nearby ranch, having a fine time eating hay and chewing cud. Then, without warning . . . dead! Liz got a call around eleven at night from the same rancher she'd heard from before. The cows were mutilated, just like the others Liz has been investigating. Iris, you know what this means, don't you? We've not seen mutilations like this since the purge. Maybe one or two, but ten! I think the Edin-Lirum may be back and preparing for a hunt, just like they did during the purge."

Iris placed both hands around her coffee cup and leaned in toward the phone. "Ristun," she said. "The hunt has already begun."

CHAPTER 18

The police truck bounced along a dirt road. Dull fields blanketed a landscape lit up under an expansive blue sky. Cattle dotted the knolls. Some lazily looked up at the truck. Others stared mindlessly into the distance, chewing cud. Allen sat in the front passenger seat next to Liz, while Dralo and Ristun sat in the back seat. Allen had always found cows rather foolish. Lately, their otherwise simplistic existence seemed far more harrowing.

They approached a distant barn. It stood on an elevated section of pasture. On one side was a sharp drop-off. On the other was a dirt road leading to its entrance. Liz pulled onto that road. As they continued, Allen saw two men leaning against the barn and talking. The truck came to a stop. Allen got out. The others followed. He was surprised to recognize Old Bill talking to what he guessed was the ranch's owner. This man appeared elderly but firm, with grizzled facial features and a weathered cowboy hat. He wore tired leather boots along with dusty overalls. He saw Liz and waved. He and Bill began walking over to them.

Allen felt a small churn in his stomach. At the same time, he noticed the odor of rotting flesh. He placed his hand on his stomach. He'd felt fine on the way to the ranch, despite his heightened anxiety after hearing about the attack on Tarin, Iris, and Gil. He hoped the nausea was only due to that smell.

The rancher held out his hand. Liz took it in an earnest handshake. "Hi, John," she said. "So I hear we have more problems."

"Indeed!" He pointed to the barn. "Ten more, Liz. Ten! I don't know what's going on. And this time, it happened in the barn!"

Allen grimaced as he now understood the source of the odor.

"Was it like last time?" Liz asked. "Lips, ears . . . other parts, surgically removed, and no blood, no signs of struggle?"

"The same. And the barn was locked last night. And guess what? It was still locked when I found them this morning." His voice hushed. "By the way, you're not the only one taking a look at this. Some others came about two hours ago in a white, unmarked van. They were all dressed in black leather jackets, with dark blue sunglasses—really odd looking. They asked lots of questions, then demanded to see the cows. I let them in . . . wasn't sure what else to do. They wanted to know if you were involved. I told them I'd let you know and you were coming later. They took pictures and samples from the cows, then left."

"Can we see them?" Dralo asked, nodding his head in the direction of the barn.

"Sure," John said.

"I'd rather stay outside," Allen said.

"That's fine," Liz replied. She touched his shoulder. "Watch for those guys in black jackets and give us a holler if you see them." She and the others went into the barn, except for Bill.

Once no one was in earshot, Bill said, "Do you believe in aliens, Allen?"

"We've talked about this before," Allen said. "I'm very open-minded about them. I'm fairly certain there's much more to the universe than we see here."

Little did Bill know how much more. If only he could tell Bill about Arvalast. And what he'd just learned about the Greys from Dralo and Ristun. But that information, for now, would remain reserved for his closest friends.

Bill studied Allen, then lifted his hand toward the surrounding plains. "Since the first mutilation, John's let me put out security cameras over this whole area. And do you know what happened last night, around nine o'clock? The cameras facing the barn just died. Died, Allen! And I've heard of things like this before. Where folks have studied unidentified phenomena, like out in the Uintah Basin in Utah—all sorts of strange stuff happens to technology when trying to run experiments. Sensors go haywire. Cameras die. Nothing seems to work to capture anything definitively. Every now and then, someone catches a glowing orb on video or maybe gets a picture of a craft, but it's usually grainy. So all we have for sure is anecdotal evidence. And I'm telling you, the anecdotes have been coming in like a fire hose the last few days. Something's going on here, and I have a theory."

Allen noticed his stomach churning more than before. He looked at the barn. The door was slightly open, making the smell worse. But bad smells had never made him sick before. He thought back to the feeling he'd had when the UFO attacked shortly after Gil's arrival. He hadn't had an episode like that for over a decade, ever since he'd left Arvalast and come to Earth—ever since he'd been around . . . them.

"It's the war," Bill continued. "I think we're getting close to the end, and forces are moving to either push us toward it or pull us away. There's a battle going on, not just on the ground." He looked up at the sky and moved his head to and fro, pensive, his lips pursed. "I think there's a lot of them. Some of them are doing these mutilations. Some might be trying to help." He looked back at Allen. "I think some of them are involved with those government folks that have been all over the area." He paused a moment. "I might have heard you and your friends had your own encounter with those folks. What happened? I heard Tarin got sick and almost died. And who are these out-of-town friends of yours? Did Liz call them in to help?"

Allen was considering his answer when he saw something move on the far side of the old red barn. He trained his eyes in that direction. A cow's snout slowly emerged. Its dark, wet nostrils quivered as it took in a deep breath. Thick saliva dripped from its muzzle and down onto its chin. It took a step forward and began surveying its surroundings with wide eyes. Its ears twitched. Then it lumbered forward until its whole, square body was exposed. It turned in their direction and locked eyes with Allen. It had a knowing expression, unlike every other cow he'd ever seen, whose stares seemed devoid of thought. "Do you see that?" Allen said to Bill, pointing at the cow.

Bill turned around. "Yep, it's a cow. Must have gotten out of the pasture somehow. Lucky not to be like the ones in the barn."

"No, I mean, do you see its eyes?"

Bill squinted. "Yeah, what about them?" He paused. "Wait, something's wrong." He held out his hand in front of Allen. "Careful boy, I think that cow's got rabies. It looks sick." As if on cue, the cow began to walk toward them, not with a lumbering gait but methodically. Meanwhile, its eyes remained fixed on Allen.

Allen and Bill backed up. The cow kept approaching. Allen's nausea grew stronger. He doubled over and held his stomach.

"You okay?" Bill asked.

Allen looked back up at the cow. It was moving faster.

"John!" Bill shouted. He grabbed Allen's arm and helped him stumble toward the truck. Bill tried the handle. "Locked," he groaned. "John! Quick, get out here. I think we have a mad cow!"

The cow was close enough for Allen to see its pupils. "No," he whispered.

Yellow slits, wild and angry, flared at him. "Bill," he said. "You need to get the others. My friends, Dralo and Ristun, they'll be able to help," he sputtered, doing everything in his power not to throw up.

"Not going to leave you, boy," Bill said. He waved his hands at the cow. "Get out of here, you crazy beast!" It was only a car length away now. "John!" he yelled again. "We need help! Now!"

Finally, Allen couldn't hold it back anymore. He retched. A voice entered his mind. "Sarky," it hissed. The world around him seemed to slow and grow hazy. The cow began to shift and morph as its flesh became more like smoke. "Prepare," the voice continued. The remaining features of the cow slid away to reveal a wispy, faceless head. Only the yellow eyes gave it any sense of life.

"Prepare for what?" Allen responded as he clutched hard at his stomach.

"Feast," the voice said in a long, slow hiss. The yellow eyes flashed. A smoky tendril shot from the side of the amorphous head and reached for Allen. He lifted his hands to fend it off and heard someone shout.

There was a sound like water being thrown into a fire. The tendril dematerialized. A light flashed. Allen felt as if he were being ripped out of a dream. Bill stood over him. He had one hand on Allen's back and a stick in the other that he was waving at the cow. Dralo and Ristun stood in front of the cow. They held brightly glowing lights. The animal backed away, mooing manically. There was a gunshot. The cow shuddered. It turned its head toward the sound. Allen's stomach lurched as he felt its anger. "No!" he shouted. Liz stood behind the cow, holding out a gun.

The cow turned and charged her. She shot again. It stumbled to one side but regained its footing. "How's it doing that?" she yelled. She holstered her gun and ran to the other side of the hill. She approached the drop-off.

Dralo and Ristun followed. Their lights grew brighter as they shouted in some other language. Liz spun around at the edge of the cliff and faced her attacker. She bent her knees as it approached. Just before it reached her, she lunged out of the way. It tried to shift its weight, but its inertia carried it forward. It toppled over the edge. Allen heard the thud followed by a crunch as the massive animal plunged to what had to be a certain death. Dralo and Ristun stopped as Liz peered over the cliff. Suddenly, she was thrown back as if something had hit her. She began to seize. Allen screamed and tried to get up, but he was too sick to move.

"That's it," Ristun said. He looked at Dralo. "Let's end this." Dralo nodded, and they ran to Liz and knelt over her quaking body.

"Liz!" Allen frantically cried.

"Get him out of here!" Dralo shouted to Bill. "He's giving the beast more energy!" Bill turned and whispered to Allen, "Come on, let's go to the other side of the truck." Allen fought back, but as Liz continued to quake, he saw Dralo place his glowing phial over her forehead. At the same time, Ristun did the same to her chest. He realized his anguish was not helping. He gave in and allowed Bill to help him to the other side of the truck. He held his face in his hands and muttered through tears. "Please be okay. Please be okay."

Dralo and Ristun continued to speak words in another language. Minutes passed. He focused on their voices, trying to stay calm. Suddenly, his nausea disappeared. He lifted his head and jumped to his feet. Bill tried to hold him back but failed. Allen ran around the truck and saw Liz sitting up. Dralo and Ristun knelt beside her. Ristun's arm was around her shoulder. He was whispering something to her while Dralo continued to hold his light against her forehead. Dralo saw Allen. He lowered his light and waved for Allen to come over.

Allen rushed to Liz and collapsed in front of her. "Are you okay?" he said, unable to keep himself from pulling her into an embrace. Ristun and Dralo made room as she weakly wrapped her arms around him.

"So this is what Tarin went through," she said. She then sniffed a couple of times and frowned. "You smell bad."

He let her go. "Sorry, I uh, well, those things, they cause me some problems."

She managed a chuckle. "No matter. I'm just glad we're both okay." Her voice then dropped to a whisper. "But what I saw was terrible." She held out her hand. "Here, give me a little help." He reached out. She took his hand and allowed him to help her to her feet. She brushed some dirt off of her clothes, then looked around.

Dralo and Ristun were looking over the edge of the cliff. John stood at the barn doorway, staring out at them.

"What on earth was all of that?" he said. He took off his hat and rubbed his hand over his wavy grey hair. Then he walked over to Dralo and Ristun. He looked down and frowned. "I'm not sure how I'm going to keep going if I keep losing all these cows," he said.

"I'm sorry I had to shoot it," Liz said as she and Allen walked over. The cow lay mangled on a bed of rocks at the bottom of the drop-off. "I can see if the county can reimburse you for it."

"Liz," John said, "you just got attacked by what I can best describe as a possessed cow. I'd have shot it, too, if I'd had my gun with me." He sighed and muttered, "Still, I'm down twelve heads of cattle from whatever witchery is happening here." He looked at Dralo and Ristun. "You both exorcists or something like that? Did the church send you to see what's going on here? Is that why you were whispering over the bodies inside the barn with your magic jars and using them to blast away whatever devilry was going on out here?" He gestured toward the lights they still held in their hands, both of which now glowed just brightly enough to notice in the sunlight. "Is that holy water? Maybe I can have some. See if it keeps my cows safe."

"I think it reasonable for you to consider these as holy water," Dralo said, "though there are . . . shall I say, differences."

"Like ours is more useful," Ristun said.

Dralo offered Ristun a stern look. "You know we've seen artifacts of religion used to some effect here on Earth. Don't discount all the efforts of the people here to hold back evil."

"It wasn't the artifacts that granted mercy in those situations," Ristun said. "More like a Band-Aid when you need a tourniquet."

"That being said," Dralo interrupted, "we can offer you one thing." He turned to John. "Ristun and I can create a sort of seal around this place that may protect your cattle for a time, at least from what ailed the one that went mad. But there's little we can do about those that are mutilating them. These aren't deterred by our . . . efforts, so to speak."

"I'll take anything you can offer," John said. "But is there anything else I can do to stop the mutilations? I've only had one mad cow so far, but eleven others wound up like those in the barn."

"Well, there's one thing you could try," Ristun said, rubbing his chin.

"Anything," John said. "Just tell me."

An hour later, they were back in Liz's truck as she drove them away from the barn and toward Philip. Liz had mostly recovered, at least outwardly, though Allen felt she seemed quieter than usual. John was visible in the rearview mirror. He was driving a tractor with a large wagon toward the barn to dispose of the dead cows. He'd also called in all his farmhands, a group of about ten, and some friends and relatives to carry out Ristun's advice. Those who'd already arrived were either herding cattle toward a barracks adjacent to the barn or preparing to help dispose of the dead cows. "I hope the plan works for him," Allen said.

"It's the best chance he's got," Ristun said. "The Greys never kill in the open where they can be seen. They should be protected if they keep the cattle visible at all times and maintain a steady watch."

"What about the other ranchers around here?" Liz said. "Won't these Greys you keep talking about just move on to easier targets?"

"It depends on if, after this latest massacre, they've acquired what they've needed," Dralo said, "which is very likely. In addition, we learned long ago we cannot help everyone, and when we try, we help few or no one."

"Sometimes we need to trust others to pick up the slack where we can't," Ristun said. "My guess and hope is that John will notify as many other ranchers in the area as possible. He seems to be a good man. The idea will come naturally to him."

Liz turned out of the drive leading to the barn and back onto a county road. "We'll be back in Philip in about twenty minutes," she said. "My shift is over in an hour. A lot happened today, and you guys keep telling me about these grey aliens, and now there's something else that takes over minds, like mine and the cow's—though hopefully it found mine more intriguing. But I'd like to try to sort this all out. What do you all say we go to Old Cotton's and talk this over more? I also need to figure out what to do about these agents that keep coming around. I don't like that they went to John's before we got there. Maybe they have something to do with the crazy cow."

"It's not a maybe," Ristun said. "It's a fact."

"And that's exactly what I'm talking about!" Liz said. "You know things I don't, and as county sheriff, I need to know what's actually going on here. So what do you say?"

"Glorions don't drink," Dralo said.

"Well, with at least one exception," Ristun chuckled.

"Then have a soda or something," Liz argued.

"Do they have root beer?" Dralo asked.

"The best in South Dakota," Liz responded.

"Very well," he said. "I'm in."

Allen lifted his phone. "I'm going to call Josh and Rob to meet us there as well. We're all in this together, and I want them to know what's going on too." He pointed his thumb out the back window of the truck. Old Bill was in the bed, clinging to the sides as they bounced along the potholed roadway. "Can we have Bill join us? He saw everything that happened and went out of his way to help me when the cow attacked."

Ristun laughed and said, "Saved you from a cow." Dralo slapped his shoulder.

"Plus, he's been investigating this stuff for a long time and might have some interesting insight, at least on how it's shown up here in our area."

"Fine by me," Ristun said. "Not sure it makes a lot of sense to keep any more secrets with the people here. Things will just start getting stranger, so everyone needs to be ready."

"Makes sense to me too," Liz said. "But before Old Cotton's, I need to go back to the office to write up some paperwork and hand off my shift to my deputy, Jason. I'll drop you all off at Allen's first, though." She checked the clock on the dashboard. "Let's meet at Old Cotton's at four for happy hour."

They all agreed. Allen managed to connect with Josh to share the plan, and shortly after that, the tops of houses marking the northern end of Philip lifted over the grassy horizon. Liz turned onto Allen's road. Dralo, Ristun, and Bill got out and headed toward Allen's house. But before Allen got out of the car, Liz grabbed his arm.

"I need to tell you something," she said with urgency. "When that thing got into my head, I saw something. Silhouettes, a lot like what Gil told me he saw in a vision when he first got to Utah. I couldn't make out exactly who they were, but I know some were you, Josh, and Rob. A shadowy form started attacking you all. It zipped in and out of each of you. You all flailed around like you were being stung by a swarm of bees. Finally, one of you fell to the ground and stopped moving. The rest of you hovered over the fallen silhouette, like in despair. Then . . . I woke up." She leaned in close to Allen, and her voice quaked. "I'm petrified one of you is going to die."

"It was just a dream," Allen said as reassuringly as he could. "I know what these things are, and they do everything they can to scare people."

"But it sounded like what happened in Gil's story actually did happen, like that woman who died."

Allen wasn't sure what to say. Though what Liz saw might or might not happen, it was likely that the future presented was indeed the intent of the creature that had attacked her mind.

"Allen," Liz said. "I'm worried about all of you, but I'm really worried about you. If you're actually from this other world you all keep talking about, then it sounds like you're the biggest prize. And I know you and Tarin are super close, so if they want to hurt him . . . hurting you will damage him the most." She paused, glanced away momentarily, then again met his eyes. "I just wanted to warn you." Then, before he realized what was happening, she leaned in and kissed him. As her lips pulled away, she said, "Just keep being careful, okay?"

He watched as she placed one hand on the steering wheel and pointed at the car door with the other. "You can go now," she said. "I gotta get back to the office like I said. Now hurry on in with the others, and don't be late to Old Cotton's. We need to get all of this stuff figured out."

"Y—yeah," he stuttered. "Stuff figured out, right." He reached for the door handle, missed it, and laughed nervously. "Bye, Liz," he said as he finally found the door handle. He tripped upon exiting and nearly fell out of the truck.

"Bye," she said. But as he walked away, she yelled, "Hey, Allen, can you close the door?"

"Oh, yeah, right." He turned and shut it.

She waved at him and drove off back toward town. Despite all that had happened—the mutilations, the cow, his best friend heading off to face who knew what kind of danger, and whatever else was going on in the wider world—for that brief moment, Allen's world had shrunk to the tiny slab of sidewalk he now stood on. He smiled broadly, touched his mouth, and whispered, "Wow."

Upon entering his house, he saw Ristun standing at the living room window. Bill and Dralo sounded as if they were in the kitchen.

"Please tell me that wasn't your first kiss," Ristun said. One eyebrow was raised above crossed arms.

Allen could feel the blood pumping into his face. "Um, well, I've never really had a girlfriend before, so . . ."

Ristun shook his head. "Better late than never, I suppose." He walked over to Allen and put his hand on his shoulder. "Considering everything going on, hopefully that kiss isn't your last. Stay vigilant, my friend." He winked. "And just to say it, I'm happy for you. Now let's join the others and get a snack." He then smirked, "Maybe a nice juicy beef hamburger to commemorate the day."

Allen groaned and shook his head while they headed into the kitchen.

CHAPTER 19

Gil had never seen a skyscraper before. Driving through Chicago changed that. He flooded Tarin with questions as a jet-black tower rose in the distance, taller than many other grand buildings surrounding it. Tarin recognized the structure as Chicago Tower. Throughout its long history, it had taken many titles, including Sears, Willis, and others. But it was now a historic landmark, so there were unlikely to be further name changes in its future.

He was grateful Iris was with him because driving through Chicago on Interstate 90 and talking were incompatible experiences, at least for him. She managed to answer many of Gil's questions about the city, including why some of the cars were flying above them. She explained it was a skylane, and most of the biggest cities had them. Electric flying hybrid cars had grown popular in the last twenty years, though they were primarily used as taxis in densely populated areas to reduce congestion. Few other than the most wealthy could afford their own. And many didn't like them because they required fully automated drivers, which took the fun out of them. But it also improved the survival rate for occupants after many first-time pilots had met an early demise because of previously lax sky traffic rules.

Tarin's knuckles remained white as he guided the car through the city's heart, a journey through a forest of tall buildings and rivers of concrete in the company of others, all doing their best to get out in one piece. Ground traffic didn't have the same strict rules as sky traffic. Here, manual and automated driving could mix. Tarin had heard enough stories where this conglomeration of human and artificial intelligence had confused the self-driving feature enough to lead it to run traffic lights or swerve into oncoming traffic. So he never engaged it. Even on calm roads, he still liked to maintain control.

After Chicago, the drive grew easier as they passed through northern Indiana. It was flat, with forests and fields on either side of the highway and little to inspire Gil to ask questions. An occasional holographic billboard zipped by advertising good food or why one should join the Peacekeeper cause against the New Alliance. Another said something about, "Are you ready for the end?" Tarin ignored them. Instead, he imagined Lake Michigan, which he knew was nearby, rippling along Indiana's northwest corner. From his study of maps, he knew the body of water stretched hundreds of miles from south to north yet remained a smaller cousin to the mighty Lake Superior. That vast blue expanse proudly owned the title of the largest of the Great Lakes and separated the US from Canada in the upper Midwest.

The minutes passed by quickly, and he looked up. The big blue sign for Ohio grew more prominent as they approached. "Welcome to Ohio," he said as they passed it. He could hardly believe he was back. He'd never intended to come back.

He looked in his rearview mirror and watched the sun dip closer to the western horizon. Somewhere back there, his friends were biding their time, wondering, he was sure, if he'd be able to pull off this mission. In front of him, the sky was nearly cloudless. Because it was late in the year, there was little remaining summer construction to slow them. Hopefully the same would be true for any otherworldly blockers as well.

Two hours later, after taking a short break at a rest stop, they passed over the wide gap and a vast bridge at Cuyahoga Valley National Park. An ocean of bare trees spread beneath them as the promise of winter lulled them to sleep. Looking north, the tips of skyscrapers from the Cleveland skyline were visible in the distance. Their lights sparkled in the clear evening. "More skyscrapers," Gil said. "Will there be any more cities before we reach your town?"

"No," said Tarin. "We'll exit before reaching Youngstown. It's the last moderately sized city before Pennsylvania."

Growing up in the area, Tarin had learned that over a century earlier, Youngstown had been the epicenter of the rustbelt, a Midwest region along the Great Lakes that boomed in the twentieth century from the industrial revolution, hosting steel mills and auto manufacturers, but had faltered late in the twentieth century as it failed to pivot into the new technological era. But it experienced a renaissance when it became a haven to those wishing to escape more arid regions of the country. Water, it turned out, was a big deal, and the Great Lakes region had a ton of it.

Growth in the region exploded further during the Great Peace when hundreds of massive data centers were built, stretching from Pittsburgh to Detroit. Ohio's population doubled in less than twenty years, and Youngstown's tripled from sixty thousand to nearly two hundred thousand. East Fairfield had become a city during that time and grew from fifteen to thirty thousand as it assimilated a number of smaller towns until it became a prominent suburb of Youngstown. However, it maintained an old and quaint town center that remained essentially unchanged from its original host city. His mother had once told him what that city had been called, but he couldn't recall it.

They continued onward. A sign for Ohio State Route 11 appeared after another hour of driving. It would take them directly to East Fairfield and was the main highway connecting the data centers of northern West Virginia to the wineries of Geneva nestled against Lake Eerie in the north.

"We'll be there soon," Tarin said.

Not twenty minutes later, he saw the sign for East Fairfield. He felt his hands grow sweaty on the wheel. Years ago, he'd vowed never to return to this place, but fate had a different agenda. For the first time in ten years, he'd be back home.

Allen saw Old Cotton's up ahead. The brick building stood tired but proud in the orange light of the setting sun. It was five minutes before four. Allen's heart beat fast as he scanned the small parking area next to the building, then the streets on both sides. He didn't see Liz's truck. But she'd likely be there soon.

Earlier, Josh and Rob had returned from work eager to speculate more about the day's events and hear Ristun and Dralo's considerations of the root cause, including information about the suspected Greys' involvement with John's cattle. But Allen noticed them acting more distant around him. They were less talkative and occasionally whispered to each other while giving him side glances. He presumed it had to do with him hiding the fact he was from Arvalast all this time. He hoped they'd eventually understand. He hoped Tarin would understand too. They had not parted on the best terms. Still, Allen could tell Tarin's friendship with him had not changed despite the revelation about his origin and his own anxiety about Tarin returning to Ohio to find his light.

Behind him, he heard Bill bantering with the others. "And do you know what I'm thinking? I've heard a lot of folks say they've seen UFOs over by Bear Butte—you know, the lone mountain just north of Sturgis? I think something's going on up there. You boys ever been up that way?"

"Yeah," Josh said. "Our Gaka likes to hike at the surrounding park. We often join him. It's actually sacred grounds for the Lakota. We call it Matȟó Pahá or Bear Mountain."

"It's named after a great bear that fought off a monster," Rob added. "Legend has it that the bear killed the monster and then died of exhaustion, turning into the mountain. Gaka used to love to tell us that story when we were kids."

"You still ask him to tell it to you as an adult," Josh quipped.

"And why not?" Rob said. "It's a good story. And I'd be game for a giant bear's help about now."

"Maybe it could fight off demon cows," Josh snickered. Rob laughed too. Allen knew they were teasing him but said nothing. Bill had told them the whole story, mixed with a few embellishments, the moment they'd returned from work. To Allen's dismay, they found it more amusing than terrifying. But he knew that was only because they hadn't been there. Nor did they know what Liz had told him about her vision. Rob, at least, would have wet himself had he been there. However, Allen wasn't so sure about Josh. Little ever seemed to faze him.

"Good thing Ristun and Dralo were there to save everyone," Rob continued. He lifted an outstretched palm in Ristun and Dralo's direction for high fives.

Ristun enthusiastically provided one. Dralo did not.

"So, back to the topic of Bear Mountain," Bill interrupted. "Have you boys or your Gaka ever seen anything strange there, especially recently?"

"Not that he's mentioned," Josh said.

"Interesting. Well, the last few days, my phone's been lit up with calls from folks around there calling in sightings. They said they're seeing saucers, orbs, triangle crafts, the whole gambit of weird stuff." His voice lowered. "What if the things messing with the cows are up that way? You know, made it their base or something like that?"

"Hold on," Allen interrupted, lifting his hand over his eyes and squinting farther down the road. "Do you all see what I'm seeing?"

"I see a white van," Bill said. "Oh wait, isn't that what those government men have been driving?"

"Quick!" Allen said. They were only about fifty feet from the bar. "Let's get inside before they see us!"

They hurried toward Old Cotton's, doing their best not to arouse suspicion while they hastened their gait as the van drew closer. Thankfully, the van met with a stoplight farther down the street, and they got into the bar seemingly unnoticed. "I'll keep an eye out," Allen said. "He gestured to an open table in the far corner, "Why don't the rest of you claim us a spot?"

"What do we do if they come in here?" Rob asked nervously.

Allen glanced at Dralo and Ristun. Both offered reassuring nods. "We'll be fine regardless," Allen said. "Now hurry up and grab a table."

Allen held his breath. He couldn't see far enough down the road from his vantage point to see where the van had stopped at the stoplight. But, a few moments later, he watched it drive by. His clenched fists relaxed.

CHAPTER 20

After traveling a slightly winding road over rolling hills through a forested landscape, Tarin drove into the northern outskirts of East Fairfield just past six in the evening, or back in South Dakota, four in the afternoon. Just ahead, the sky began to glow a modest yellow with light pollution from the prevalent stores and businesses on that side of town. Soon the trees opened up, and the town appeared in front of them.

Nostalgia began to dance with Tarin's anxiety to create a strange cocktail of emotions as they passed fast-food joints and a local grocery store he'd frequented countless times. Little seemed to have changed since he'd left. Off to the left, near a gas station, a hotel stood taller than any nearby establishments and was where they'd be staying that night. His stomach growled.

"Do you all mind if we get a bite to eat before we check into the hotel?" he asked. "I don't think the hotel has a restaurant."

"I'd be in favor of that," Iris said, removing the earbuds she'd worn most of the way through Indiana and all the way through Ohio.

"Me also," Gil said.

"I know a good pizza spot if it's still open," Tarin said. "It's downtown. Should only take a few minutes to get there."

He drove them deeper into the small city. Well-maintained country-style homes lined both sides of the heavily treed main street until they saw a clock tower in the center of a circle that connected the main roads through town. The circle surrounding the clock was sometimes the fury of its residents because of the inconsistent way drivers utilized it. Some would barrel in without yielding. Others would yield for an eternity until the traffic behind them backed up and horns blared. It even seemed to confuse self-driving cars, though what didn't? But tonight, it was mercifully empty, and Tarin navigated it without a problem. On the other side, they found themselves in a quaint, small-town setting. Brick buildings lined both sides of the road, some connected, none more than two stories high. He parked on the side of the street and pointed ahead.

"Looks like it's still open," he said. "Let's go." He was relieved to see only one car parked along the street near the restaurant. Though he wasn't terribly concerned about running into anyone he'd used to know when living in town—it had been roughly ten years since he'd been there, and he doubted anyone would remember him because his social circle had been so small—he still wasn't eager to have to catch up with anyone.

As they got out of the car and crossed the street under the glow of lampposts, Tarin saw a parking lot nearby. He remembered it well, not only from growing up here but also from his nightmare. It was where the merry-go-round had been. It was also where the portal had opened . . . where he'd seen his mother. He shook away the memory. Hopefully, the restaurant still served beer. He needed a drink to get through this.

They found a booth inside and settled next to a window overlooking a well-lit alleyway beyond. The interior of the building was very red, giving it a retro feel. Tarin was reasonably sure nothing had changed since he'd last been there. The smell of pizza was thick in the air, almost like smoke, but he could also make out a faint hint of old wood common among the sometimes centuries-old buildings in many quaint downtowns across America.

A waitress approached the table. "Hi, folks!" she said. "Can I get you all some drinks? Water? Beer?"

"I'll have whatever local beer you have on tap," Tarin said, looking at the menu.

"Same for me," said Iris. Gil ordered his usual water. Tarin remembered the stuffed jalapeños being exceptionally good and tapped the menu.

"And I'll also get a side of these for the table." He looked up, and the blood rushed out of his face.

"Tarin?" the waitress said.

Tarin's heart started beating fast. He felt his mouth opening and closing, but no words came out.

"What are you doing back in town?" she continued. "Gosh, it's been years. How have you been?"

The smiling, blond-haired woman in front of him was secondary only to his father as the person he'd least like a surprise encounter with. Emotions he'd not expected to come so fast since getting into town overwhelmed him. "Hi, Chelsy," he said, but noticed his voice cracking. There was no way he was going to be able to carry on a sensible conversation with her, even in the realm of small talk. "Sorry," he said. He awkwardly slid out of the booth, careful to avoid bumping into Chelsy as he stood up. "I forgot something in the car."

He rushed outside, crossed the street, and got into the vehicle, slamming the door behind him. Hot tears welled in his eyes as he remembered the first time he'd seen the waitress at school when they were fourteen. They'd quickly become good friends. He stared blankly out the windshield as he thought of her, their many conversations . . . that last conversation.

His eyes moved down the street in front of him and toward distant railroad tracks. He pushed away the urge just to drive that way and keep going. But that would mean abandoning his mission—and his friends.

Allen's group huddled around an old wooden round table they'd claimed in the corner of the bar, nursing their drinks while they waited for Liz. The light smell of varnished wood blended with the lingering scent of yesterday's beer and cigarettes. There were only three other patrons that afternoon. They were locals, were elderly, and wore an assortment of jeans and plaid. One donned a worn-out cowboy hat. Dralo looked a bit out of place in his sweater over a collared shirt and perfectly shaven face. Ristun sat hunched over his drink while chatting with Josh and Rob about LOB. Bill, in between Josh and Rob, sat looking quite confused.

Allen heard the sound of the door opening and turned his head. There she was, wearing jeans and a green blouse. She'd also put on light makeup, which she didn't often wear. He wondered what that might mean. He wiped his hand over his hair, which he'd carefully combed before leaving the house, and scooted slightly over from the chair he'd strategically left open next to him.

Before Allen could say anything, Rob called out, "Over here, Liz!" and waved at her. She waved back and pointed to the bar. "Be right over!" Shortly afterward, she sat down with a tall IPA.

"What . . . a . . . day," she said. "And I have more great news for you if you can believe it." Her voice was sarcastic. "There are agents in town."

"We saw them," Allen said. His voice squeaked, and he cleared his throat. "They drove by in a van not long ago."

"They were at the police station before that," Liz said. "I caught them asking Jason questions before I turned my shift over to him. They wanted to know what we'd found at John's ranch."

Dralo stirred in his seat and set down his empty glass of root beer. "What did you tell them?"

"I only told them that we saw dead cows and suggested John keep a close eye on his herd until we figure out more. That seemed to appease them, and they drove off."

"So let's get right down to it," Josh said, taking a swig of his beer and bringing the glass to half full. "Who are those guys, those men from MJ12-2?"

"Or," Rob whispered, "what . . . are those guys?"

Dralo and Ristun exchanged glances. Bill took a slow sip of his bourbon while steadily staring at the pair from Arvalast.

Finally, Dralo took a deep breath and, in his thick, English accent, said, "I suppose, at this point, there's little I could say that would surprise any of you. You've already seen so much. It's time you all know what you're facing." He paused. "I need you to understand, Ristun and I don't know everything, nor do our counterparts who remain scattered across this land. We do have theories I believe are quite plausible. And these theories likely describe what we are dealing with in terms of both the agents and the Greys. Simply put, they are the embodiments of unique power structures of a very ancient origin, races originally, we suspect, from our land of Arvalast."

"I knew it," Rob said, slamming his glass on the table. "That's been what I was thinking all along too!"

"Then why didn't you say anything?" Josh asked.

"I didn't want to sound stupid if I was wrong," Rob said.

Bill chimed in. "Arvalast? You mean another planet?"

Dralo straightened his collar under his sweater and put his finger to his chin. "I would more readily liken it to what you might call a different dimension. Though with the vastness of the universe, dimensions and distant planets could be one and the same. As I said before, I'm not privy to all the secrets of the cosmos and am forced partly to speculate."

A boyish delight passed over Bill's face beneath his many wrinkles. "So all this time, there's been aliens. All the mockery, all the rolling eyes, and finally, vindication."

"Well," Ristun said, "if you believe what we're saying."

Bill nearly jumped from his seat. "Are you kidding? After what I saw you two do at the ranch today? It was magic! If you both say there are other worlds and aliens, then it's for sure!"

"Shhh," Allen said, noticing the barkeep shooting them a glance before turning up the background music. "Not everyone's seen what we've seen. Let's not make everyone think we're crazy."

Liz looked around too. "Yeah, until we get a handle on everything, we might not want to get folks riled up. I knew we were going to be talking about strange stuff and thought a drink would help me relax and process it better." She reached for her beer glass and took a gulp. "And it is, but let's just talk a little quieter for now."

Dralo nodded, then set both hands on the table and leaned forward. "Before I tell you more about the agents or the Greys, I think it is wise to reveal more about myself and Ristun."

Bill nodded furiously, his glass of bourbon set to his lips while some of its contents dripped down the side of his grey beard.

"We originate—just as we believe the agents and the Greys do— from Arvalast."

"You're aliens too?" Bill asked gleefully.

"In Arvalast," Dralo quickly replied, "we are known as Glorions. We are a race of great strength and wisdom, ambassadors of the light—heralds, you might say."

"Humility is also one of our strong suits," Ristun quipped.

Dralo ignored him and continued. "Until recently, our concerns have been with Arvalast, and though we knew other worlds existed, we did not actively seek involvement in them unless it was to support the affairs of Arvalast."

"That's not entirely accurate," Ristun interjected. "There have always been rumors of our kind stumbling into other worlds, sometimes intentionally, sometimes less so."

"Yes," Dralo said, "but as you noted, those have only been rumors."

"I've met some of our kind here that have told me otherwise." He took a swig of soda and burped. "But don't let me sidetrack you."

"Thank you," Dralo said with a slight frown. He turned back to the group. "Ristun, Iris, and I were part of a party that followed Tarin here after he was cast into a portal atop a tower after a terrible battle. During that battle, we hoped he'd be a catalyst for victory. Unfortunately, he did not fulfill that end."

"Poor kid just wasn't ready," Ristun said. "Too much pressure. We were wrong to put him in that position."

"We were not wrong to place our trust in him," Dralo interjected. "He'd had several victories before that. Remember Northlake?"

Ristun nodded, "I do. It was when we first realized how powerful he could be."

"And his power only grew after that," Dralo said, "despite being but an adolescent and outwardly very timid except when fighting the darkness. But something happened at Woodend that broke him."

"Do you know what it was?" Allen asked anxiously. "I saw it—when it happened. Tarin was so confident, but then, when we reached the town hall, and we saw . . . the situation, something changed. His face went ashen."

"We do not know," Dralo said, "But that is why we followed him here—because we knew something had interfered with his growing power and then had lured him from the battle and into the forest. Though by the time we finally managed to find out where he'd gone, and fight our way to the top of the tower and secure passage through the portal, there was no trace of Tarin—or you . . . Sarky."

"I'm never going to get used to that name," Liz said.

"You can keep calling me Allen," Allen hurriedly said. "I know Sarky is a stupid name."

"Maybe it'll grow on me. We'll see."

"Forgive me," Dralo said. "I'll use his Earth name to avoid confusion moving forward. But allow me to continue. After we came to Earth, we quickly met opposition. As I shared earlier, we soon realized that other kinds we had some familiarity with had already been on Earth before us, such as the Greys, perhaps for extended amounts of time. But they were not Arvalastian, at least not directly. Eventually, we realized they likely came here from somewhere else altogether."

"You mean somewhere other than Earth and Arvalast?" Rob asked, his glasses unable to conceal the excitement behind them. "I thought you said the Greys came from Arvalast?"

"I said they likely 'originated' from Arvalast," Dralo said. "Not came here directly. There is another world adjacent to Arvalast that, in the earliest of days, our peoples, of any race, could travel to. Its name, according to ancient documents in Arvalast called the *Annals of Illuminara*, is Shieth. Ages passed with our worlds remaining in harmony, but then something happened. A malice entered our land or, perhaps, finally chose to reveal itself if it had been present all along. Over time, we discovered this being gained strength through the connection with Shieth. Because of this, our world's leaders decreed the gateway to Shieth be forever sealed. This became the first mission of the Glorions. We assembled in a vast force, and though we met resistance from those who wished to maintain passage to Shieth, we eventually sealed the gate in the center of our world.

"I now move into the realm of speculation. In their isolation and anger at being locked out of Arvalast, I believe the races within Shieth changed—mutated, you might say—into spiteful forms of their previous selves. They became beings of Shieth, no longer beings of Arvalast. Over the millennia, some found their way to Earth, and here, they found great power and renewed purpose and eventually shaped the entirety of this planet's history. And as they manipulated the planet and the native souls of this world, they discovered that, through the darkness they created, they could reconnect to Arvalast and again feed the malignancy that had been dormant since their exile."

"How did you figure this out?" Allen asked. Though he was from Arvalast, this information was new to him. And though he'd heard of the *Annals of Illuminara*, he'd never read them.

"By seeing what the Greys did to the light from Glorions who fell victim to the purge," Ristun said solemnly. "Greys can open portals and send our light through them back to Arvalast. Those few Glorions able to escape such a hunt felt the presence of Arvalast beyond . . . and saw the shadow of a familiar evil feasting on the energy of our broken friends."

"Were you one of those that escaped?" Allen asked, his voice somber.

Ristun rubbed his hand through his short black hair, looking unusually downcast. "Yeah, and I lost a lot of good friends during the purge, very good friends. That's why I'm nervous about the cattle mutilations. They seem to happen in conjunction with their hunts. That's why Iris and Gil need to be extra careful now that we know they're actively being hunted."

"How long do you think the Greys have been here building these portals?" Rob asked, looking less gleeful than before.

"We're uncertain," Dralo said. "It could be decades, or it could be millennia. All we know is the seals between Earth, Arvalast, and Shieth are more porous than we ever realized, which is how the Greys likely got here. At this time, our worlds are connected, feeding off each other and supporting each other—they are symbiotic."

"Are there more worlds beyond those three?" Rob asked. "Or maybe I should say, dimensions?"

"There are," Ristun said before Dralo could answer. "Countless, but not all are as directly symbiotic as ours are, though every world is connected at least in some way. Wait until we tell you more about the harvests. But before we keep talking, I need to take a leak and get a pop refill. I'll be back in a minute." He stood up and headed to the restroom.

"I need another drink too," Josh said. "I don't think there's enough beer in this bar to help me process all this information." He noticed all the other empty glasses. "Anyone else want refills?"

Everyone nodded.

"Hang tight," he said. I'll put in the orders."

CHAPTER 21

Someone knocked on the car window, pulling Tarin from a steady stare at the accelerator beneath his shoe. He looked up and saw Iris. He hastily wiped his face to hide any stray tears and opened the window.

"Can I come in?" she asked.

"Hang on," he said and checked his appearance in the dim light of the rearview mirror. Maybe she wouldn't notice his still slightly damp cheeks. "I'll come out there."

He slid out of the car and stood next to her, his head hung low. "Sorry for the drama in there. What is this, like the hundredth time I've run away from something since you got here?"

"I don't recall that many," she said, offering a hint of a smile.

"Where's Gil?" Tarin asked.

"He's speaking with the waitress. She grew . . . concerned when you left."

"Yeah," Tarin said, "that all probably looked pretty strange."

"Would you like to talk about it?"

Tarin wasn't sure if he was in the mood to talk, but then again, what could it hurt? "Can we walk and talk?" he finally said. He felt that doing something would make it easier to keep his emotions under control.

"Sure," she said.

They began walking down the street toward railroad tracks. "So I'm guessing you're curious about that woman back at the restaurant?"

"I'm more curious about how you're doing," Iris replied softly. "But since the woman seems to have caused you some pain, then yes, I suppose I am curious about her too."

Tarin looked at Iris. She was avoiding eye contact and seemed a bit hesitant, like when they'd first met at the airport. He wasn't sure why, but that made him feel more comfortable as his emotions swirled. "Her name is Chelsy," he said, "and the reason I freaked out when I saw her was because I used to . . . have feelings for her."

A few moments passed until Iris asked, "Did she feel the same about you?"

Tarin felt a lump form in his throat as memories of his past friendship with Chelsy, and then eventually, something else, or at least something that seemed like something else, flooded his mind. "Honestly, Iris, I don't know." He felt more hot tears behind his eyes but managed to compose himself. "I had a lot of bad stuff going on the last time I saw her. I'd opened my heart up to her about . . . what was happening at home with my parents. But after I told her everything, she just walked away without a word, and I never heard anything from her after that."

Far in the distance, a train whistle sounded. "I don't know much about the kind of love you felt for Chelsy," Iris said. "But I've observed enough in others to know it's very powerful. Sometimes, I envy such feelings. Glorions can feel fierce friendship and loyalty, but we lack the capacity for the unifying love gifted to your kind, those based on romantic feelings. But all manifestations of love come with risks, such as a lack of reciprocation. Pain like that is little different than experiencing a death."

Tarin said nothing as they walked under the light of a lampost.

"Do you still love her?" Iris asked. "Is that why her presence hurt you so much?"

The train whistle blew again, closer this time. The tracks were, at most, fifty feet in front of them. The gates began to blink red and close. "Not in the same way," Tarin said as the thunder of thousands of pounds of steel approached. The engine whistle screamed, and the train sped by. Iris and Tarin stopped just in front of the tracks. Tarin counted ten cars, then twenty, and finally, at eighty, the last car whizzed by and slowly disappeared in the distance.

Iris stared forward into the dark roadway beyond, speechless, pensive. Finally, she said, "Why don't you return to the hotel and check in?" Tarin thought he noticed a tear on her cheek illuminated by the still blinking gate lights as they opened. "Gil and I will bring you back some food. I think you could use some time to settle in here."

"But if I take the car back to the hotel, how will you both get there?"

"We'll walk. It couldn't have been more than a mile from what I recall." She continued staring forward. "This will be hard, Tarin, being back in this place. But . . . you did it." She broke her forward stare and turned to face him. "You got here. You have more to do, but at least we're here to do it." Through her glasses, he was now confident her eyes were moist. "I'm sorry for what you felt at the restaurant with Chelsy. I've also felt love's trauma. The heartache haunts me to this day."

"I thought you said you couldn't have feelings like that," Tarin said softly. He could see the pain in her eyes and began feeling a deep empathy well up inside him.

"Love flows along many rivers, each with its own unique challenges." She forced a smile. "Now go back to the hotel and rest up. Gil and I will be there later."

Tarin watched her walk away for a few minutes, reflecting on what she said. What, or who, had broken her heart? Though he thought he might know. He put the thought aside and made his way back to the car. Moments later, he was heading back toward the hotel.

Allen watched as Dralo's knee bounced beneath the table, the Glorion's eyes eager with what Allen assumed was anticipation for everyone to settle in with their fresh drinks so he could continue storytelling. But just as Rob returned from the restroom and Dralo opened his mouth to continue, Bill raised his hand.

"Before you share more," Bill said, "I wanted to guess a bit at how those men in black leather jackets are tied into everything you're saying."

Dralo's cheeks drooped. He forced a tiny smile and said, "Please, guess away." He picked up his mug of root beer and took a long, slow sip as he stared at the table.

"I've been doing a lot of research since I was young, and I'm pretty sure I know what's happening. I admit, I've heard a lot more today than I've ever heard before, but so far, it still fits with my theories. For example, I've always thought the men you call agents—I've known about them for years—are not from here. Mind if I share my guesses as to their intent?"

Dralo took another sip of his root beer. "Proceed."

"So, all my life, there's been rumors about a secret group pulling the strings of all the governments in the world. Anyone we can see in leadership—a president, a prime minister, a chancellor—isn't really in charge of the big stuff. They only take care of day-to-day country affairs—basically middle management. When it comes to the big stuff—global trends that happen over decades, or major leaps in technology—these happen in the secret club at the top."

"Share some examples of this 'big stuff,'" Dralo said, his voice regaining some of its earlier energy.

"Well," said Bill, "I think it goes back to the rise of most, if not all, ancient civilizations. Any time you see people getting highly organized and taking control of huge areas, the top dogs are likely involved. Regarding specifics, I think the Sumerians and the Mayan civilizations are good examples of some of their first influence. They had complex civilizations and advancements in agriculture and architecture that are hard to believe would just spring out of nowhere. And there are patterns in those early civilizations indicating a common influence. Look at the pyramid-like structures found across the world. It started with Sumerian and Mayan ziggurats. Then, as everyone probably knows, the pyramids appeared in Egypt. These structures are all very similar in design despite the civilizations being oceans apart. He set his whiskey on the table and leaned toward Dralo. "Big stuff . . . like that."

"Leave it to Bill to make everything happening sound even weirder," Josh groaned.

"Shhh!" Rob hissed.

"You think that's weird?" Bill said to Josh. "What about all the commonalities in the old religions, like drawings, types of gods, and sacrifices?" Bill tapped his chin. "Come to think of it, those might have been to feed that evil thing you said is in Arvalast. But I digress. Looking later in history, there are lots of risings and fallings of big empires: Roman, Mongolian, British, and many more, which I think correlate to the top dogs manipulating things to keep control. Maybe when one civilization gets too big, it poses a threat to their power structure, so they find a way to, let's say, reset things and get their power back in a fresh new empire."

"Interesting theory," Dralo said. "But what's their ultimate agenda? What's their endgame?"

"I don't know exactly. It might just be for power and control. But after hearing your story, maybe it's also related to helping feed that darkness you say is in Arvalast—you know, by making sure our world is always a bit of a mess? In terms of what the agents actually are, some say they are a shape-shifting reptilian species from another planet. I often toyed with this idea, but I think it's unlikely. I do think they are a humanlike species not from here and that they 'blend in' and, for the most part, look just like us. And they get more visible and active when there's either another shift about to happen or something is getting a bit out of line that needs fixing."

"You're fairly astute in your observations and analysis," Dralo said.

"He is?" countered Josh.

"Yes, I think a large part of your theory is accurate, but there are some nuanced differences I hold that I'd like to share."

Bill lifted his glass into the air, hiccuped, and said, "And that's why I'm glad you're here. Please, enlighten me." He tilted his head back, finished the rest of his bourbon, then raised a furrowed brow at Josh. "Enlighten us all!"

"Hear, hear!" Rob replied, lifting his glass with Bill.

Ristun patted Dralo's back. "Well, aren't you the popular guy this afternoon? Don't see that very often."

"Content over charisma," Dralo said. He was smiling. It was the first time Allen had seen Dralo with what seemed a genuine smile since the Glorion had come to South Dakota.

The rest of the bar was beginning to fill up and grow noisier. Dralo raised his voice and continued. "Those of MJ12-2 are likely from Arvalast, or rather, Shieth, just like the Greys. The original Arvalastian people group we believe the agents mutated from are called the Utuka. They are noble, having tamed the northernmost Arvalastian sea to build a strong and peaceful civilization among the isles between the continents. But the heart of their earthly manifestation is one of power, of control, as you rightly deduced, Bill. They wish to rule humans and have found that they can best maintain control by governing from the shadows. But due to this, they must also govern with the shadows. And it is these, the shadows, that feast upon the despairs of the human race."

Most at the table leaned forward with hands or elbows on the table.

"In Arvalast," Dralo continued, "we call them Vulgheid, and we have discovered that somehow, a mutation of the malignant beings has at some point found their way to Earth and attached themselves to it like leeches. To achieve their goals, the agents have allied with these beings in a cruel pact that utilizes your species as livestock to feed, to milk, to kill, and to eat—not in body, but in soul. The shadows can also indwell the physical bodies of the beings of this planet and, to various degrees, control them."

Dralo turned to Allen. "That is what you saw happen earlier, with the cow." He focused on Liz. "And with you. When they enter, they torment the mind, sometimes overtaking it altogether. And if allowed to enter freely, they offer their host great power, though not without the host surrendering some, if not much, of its own will.

Many agents we have seen act as willing hosts for these shadows, giving those agents inhuman power and deeper influence on those around them."

"I see," Bill said. "So it's the combination of the MJ12-2 agents and the shadow creatures that run the world. And the alliance gives both groups what they want. The agents get to be in a position of power, and the shadows get the fuel for their survival."

"Correct," Dralo said. "And until around two decades ago, this partnership was fairly stable. But then, something happened that challenged that paradigm, something Ristun was, at least, indirectly involved in."

Ristun smiled and nodded. "I do like to be a troublemaker."

"What was it?" Bill asked.

"Artificial intelligence," Dralo replied. "For entities fully reliant on the manipulation of physical minds, which have a mystery and nuance not yet duplicated outside of those we call conscious—those with souls—there is no direct way to indwell and manipulate AI. Within a few short years, the power dynamic was crushed. AI, or shall I say the Trinity Lattice, was making the decisions. It was at the top. Now, the previous power structures are frantically working to regain control. Agents mobilized worldwide like bees whose hive was hit by a stick. Anyone who gets in the way will be stung, or purged in the case of Glorions."

"Even if that means risking tipping the scale to a harvest," Ristun said, then took a slow drink of his soda while his eyes darted one by one to everyone at the table.

"I think you've built enough suspense," Josh said. "Why don't you tell us what it is."

"Dralo," Ristun said, holding out his hand to his counterpart.

Dralo nodded and said, "A harvest represents the penultimate stage of a world. It cements its place as either one of light or one of darkness. I will not get into all the specifics, but if there is a dark harvest on Earth, which is the way the scale has been tipping for many decades, it would have terrible consequences for both this planet and for Arvalast. If there was a global catastrophe, such as a nuclear war, it would likely tip the scale." He paused. "My personal theory is that Shieth went through a dark harvest long ago, and that's why those there mutated toward the darkness, then . . . came here."

"Okay, okay," Liz said, holding her hands up. "As fascinating as this harvest stuff sounds, how is it relevant to what's going on right here, right now? Because that's my biggest concern. I've apparently got aliens from Arvalast partly controlled by shadow demons trying to retake the world. Why are they in Philip? And what can we do about it?" She blew a strand of her blond hair out of her face and leaned closer to Allen. "Boy, I'm glad I'm starting to get a bit drunk."

"We don't know," Dralo said.

She shot Dralo a stern glance. "What do you mean you don't know? You seem to know a lot of other stuff. Now let's get down to the practical. How do we keep everyone in my town, and in this room, safe?"

"All we know," Dralo continued, "is that Gil believes that Tarin is central to all of this, and what happens to him will ultimately affect all of us. And because of this group's connection with Tarin, you all are also in the crosshairs of the power structures trying to regain control of this world. To answer your question in part, we think Tarin is why the agents are in Philip. And Ristun and I are in Philip to watch, to help, and if needed, to fight to protect you all."

The group sat silent. Many hands held cups of various amounts of remaining beverage, though any with beer were more drained than those with sodas. Allen noticed the noisy ambient sound around him beginning to grow. It was later into happy hour, and the bar was nearly full.

Josh finally broke the silence at the table and looked at Allen. "And I thought *you* were the epitome of storytellers. Dralo and Bill got you beat."

Allen nodded. "Agreed." Even having come from Arvalast, he had never heard of other worlds before coming to Earth—Shieth or otherwise, which seemed in large part because he hadn't been exposed to the mysterious-sounding *Annals of Illuminara*. Coming to Earth had been quite the awakening for him, but now he was beginning to realize the greater universe and beyond was far more vast and complex than even his most recent expansion of horizon had suggested. Still, some of it was familiar—like the Vulgheid.

Allen noticed the previously boisterous, alcohol-strengthened banter in the bar had gone quieter. Though his back was to the door, Josh and Rob, on the other side of the table, faced it. Their expressions gave him a hard pause. Slowly, he turned around. Three men in black leather jackets, all with sunglasses lifted over their heads, stood in the entryway. They made their way to the bartender.

Tarin drove into the hotel parking lot and parked. After plugging the vehicle into the closest outlet, he pushed through the two rustic wooden doors at the lobby entrance and walked to the hotel counter. After checking into another suite similar to the one in Madison, he collapsed onto one of the two queen-sized beds and stared at the ceiling. Things were not going well. He'd not expected to see Chelsy. He'd assumed she'd likely have moved to a larger town and possibly started a family. He hadn't prepared for the strength of the emotions from an encounter with her. And if things had been that bad with her, how could he hope to maintain his composure when he went home and saw his father?

His father.

He'd have to get through his father to get to his light, or rather, the glass container he hoped was still at his old brick house located a block away from the park. How the glass object might connect to the light—that of Gil, and of Iris, and of Arvalast—he had no idea. And would the object still be on the mantle? Maybe his father had discarded it. These were risks he'd already discussed with Gil and Iris, but Gil had convinced him he was confident the phial, which is what Gil called it, was still in his father's home. Gil saw it through his own phial somehow. Tarin trusted his analysis, even if it was based on what was essentially magic.

An old clock ticked. Was it on the other wall? He didn't care. He continued to stare at the ceiling. His mind drifted back to the restaurant. Chelsy looked older, which made sense. He hadn't seen her for more than ten years. But even with a few more lines under her brown eyes, her face was still full of youthful energy. She'd changed her hair color too. It was blond now rather than auburn. It looked nice, he thought, but the butterflies he used to feel when seeing her had long died, and now, her image only brought him grief.

He turned around on the bed and put his face on the pillow. "How am I going to do this?" he said, the frustration in his voice muffled as he turned his attention to his father. There was no way he'd be able to keep his cool when he saw him. A memory of his father hitting his mother flitted by, and he winced. He hated him so much. The clock continued ticking. But he needed to get his light.

He forced himself to think of Allen, and of Rob, and of Josh. He'd likely not be here if not for them. And now he had a chance to protect them from whatever was working to devour the world. He rolled over and sat up.

The clock ticked again.

Maybe he should just do it now. Perhaps if he just went fast, he could stay composed and get this over with.

Tock went the clock.

If he waited, if he thought about it too much, he might not find the courage. He closed his eyes tightly and allowed the memories of his time in Philip, happy memories he never thought possible after he'd run from East Fairfield, to flood inside.

Tick tock. Tick tock. Tick tock.

He opened his eyes, grabbed the car keys, and walked to the door.

∘ ∘ ◇ ∘ ∘

"We need to get out of here," Allen whispered to Liz, who also had just noticed the newcomers.

"We don't need to go anywhere," she said. She downed the last bit of her IPA, stood up, and approached the bar.

Allen prepared to follow her when a strong hand pushed him back down into his seat. "Don't cause a scene." It was Dralo, and his hand rested firmly on Allen's shoulder.

"If he doesn't, I just might," Ristun said. His hands clenched into fists, and his eyes flared. "Just like at the airport."

"Don't," Dralo said. "If they were here to attack, we'd already have known. Let Liz investigate."

"One wrong move from them, though . . ." Ristun snarled.

Dralo interrupted, "Then you and I will take care of matters swiftly. But for now, patience."

Liz took up a position next to the tallest of the three, though none of them appeared to be the one Allen had seen at the hospital and at Wall Drug—the chief. She engaged with them in an animated but not hostile argument. The music in the bar continued to play, loud enough that Allen couldn't hear the conversation from where he was sitting. Everyone in the bar watched closely. A couple of grizzled regulars strategically took up positions near the agents. Allen wasn't surprised they were arousing suspicion among the locals. He'd even noticed a few folks previously taking note of his table with wary expressions. But Dralo and Ristun, despite being strangers, got a pass since Liz was with them.

Finally, the discussion ended. Liz held her hand toward the door, and the agents left. As they passed by, Allen's skin crawled, but his stomach remained still. He sighed in relief.

"What did they say?" Ristun said as Liz returned to her seat.

"They said I was under no circumstances to get involved in any more cattle mutilation reports. They claim they are related to a sickness that's been spreading in the area, and if I interfered anymore, they'd have to relieve me of my official duties."

"How could they do that?" Josh retorted. "You're the sheriff. Who do they think they are?"

"They're bigger than local governments," Bill said as his eyes flickered in the fluorescent light of the dimly lit room. "They can overrule anything they'd like."

CHAPTER 22

Abigail made her way through the lush forest, absorbing the natural beauty surrounding her. A nearby creek splashed and sparkled in the late afternoon sun as it meandered around rocks and fallen branches before it would eventually return to the cottage from where she came. As long as she stayed near it, she couldn't get lost. She continued walking, following the winding path up a small hill with tall trees lining either side of her. Finally, she reached the top and broke through the forest's leafy rooftop. In front of her was a majestic view of distant green mountains, though a few splashes of grey precipices extended above the tree line along the tallest peaks.

She stood unmoving for some time, the breeze upon her face, admiring every detail of the wide open landscape surrounding her. The mountains in the west descended into forested rolling hills that stretched to the horizon in all other directions. It was a sea of green, and she wondered what mysteries lay beneath the waves. Ella and Jak said towns and villages were sprinkled throughout this region, which was called the Great Northern Forest. She wondered, were any nearby? She longed to visit them, to explore more of this world she was in. But she'd been told it wasn't safe, and she must stay close to the cottage.

She thought back to the discussions they'd had the previous night about Ella's brother, Tarin, and a man called Gildareth, who'd gone to search for him after he'd vanished on a forgotten tower hidden somewhere within the mountains near the ruins of a city called Under-tree. In and around that city were evil beings, they said, who wandered the woods and now haunted the region after a battle in which the city of Woodend, somewhere on the forest's northern edge, had been over-thrown by a tyrant.

A strange sparkle to the west caught her attention. It emanated from a region of huge pines, perhaps a mile away, closer to the moun-tains. She squinted and focused in that direction. Had it just been her imagination? No, there it was again, like light shimmering through a prism. It flitted through the needly arms of the pines' lower branches, then danced upward. She considered returning to the cottage to inform Jak and Ella.

It shimmered again. Abigail glanced at the path behind her, which led to the creek, back to safety at the cottage, and then back toward the pine grove. It wasn't far, she thought. She looked around. Rocks the size of fists dotted the top of the hill. She pulled the lower portion of her dress up to make a broad pocket and filled it with as many of them as possible. Then she began descending the hill opposite the path and into the woods toward the source of the mysterious glow.

She cleared a small patch of ground of leaves and twigs about every twenty feet and placed a rock in the bare spot. As she walked, she did her best to kick away leaves and beat down undergrowth to form a vis-ible new trail. Every so often, she looked back to create a memory of the landscape for the return trip and verified she could see the track she was leaving in her wake.

After about fifteen minutes, she smelled the strong scent of pine as the maples and oaks gave way to conifers. The green giants rose above her, whispering in the gentle breeze as orange sunlight sparkled along the needle-covered ground. Again, she glanced back. Her trail was still visible. She placed down another stone and walked to the center of the grove.

Carefully, she studied the ground, slowly spinning, trying to catch any glimpse of what had caused that light. After many minutes of searching, she was beginning to give up hope when the branches above her shimmered. She spun around. A small glass phial was lying next to the mossy trunk of a fallen tree. Her mouth opened into a broad smile as she slowly approached it. Upon closer inspection, she could tell it was similar to the lights Ella and Jak carried. However, this one looked empty, whereas theirs always had at least a slight, steady glow.

She knelt and, with an outstretched finger, touched it. It sparkled. Startled, she hastily withdrew her hand. She watched it another moment, then reached down again. This time nothing happened. It was neither cool nor warm. She wrapped her fingers around it and lifted it.

Inside, she began to see a small swirl of light form. It grew wider and wider until the entire container was filled with its essence. Within the rotation, she thought she saw small figures take shape. She brought the phial closer to her face. Yes, there were figures there, people dressed in either black pants or skirts with light blue tops. A man, who was the tallest, wore a black hat and had a beard but no mustache. One was a young girl playing on the ground near the man while a more youthful boy dashed about, throwing what looked like hay into the air. Behind them, a quaint white house appeared. A woman stood in the doorway.

Abigail felt a rushing sensation in her head, like ocean waves crashing against the shore. She placed both hands on her forehead, with one still holding the phial. When the glass touched her, she felt like lightning had struck, and she became paralyzed. A brilliant light flashed before her eyes.

The pine grove turned into a stage where she saw herself as a child, growing up Amish in the state of Wisconsin. Time passed, and her childhood play morphed into more brooding teenage years. Even the love she felt for her little sister and brother, who brought her so much delight, was not enough to wash away the chains of a way of life she sensed was holding her back from her dreams.

She grew restless and got lost in the pages of countless books, wishing for a life outside her small farm and community where she could find romance and adventures like in her stories. The sun rose and set countless times until she saw her mother weeping and her father scowling. With a suitcase in hand, she left home to study in Pittsburgh as a young adult, hoping to become a writer or, perhaps, join a publishing firm.

Now she sat in a corner of a dark room, her head in her hands as she wept. Her plans had not gone well. She'd struggled to acclimate to city life. She was awkward, she'd been told, and made no close friends. Some men she'd thought could make her dreams of romance come true instead tried to exploit her naivety. As her heart broke time and again, she decided to return to the country. Perhaps the American West would be the sanctuary she now craved.

More days passed. She found a new home and a job that suited her far from the shadows of skyscrapers. She was smiling. She had a house and a garden. But still, she had no close friends, and her heart ached in the continued absence of love and the hope of romance. Then, darkness took her mind. Her body weakened. Her imagination grew consumed with the fears of dreams never realized. The sun rose and set, and months became years. She was very sick.

A man in a cloak and hood looked through her window as darkness in the sky approached to take her somewhere bad. The man lifted a light as she felt herself leaving her earthly body and being pulled toward a shadow. She felt a stretching as she was tugged between the competing forces until all went dark.

The smell of the forest filled her senses. Her eyes snapped open.

She was back in the pine grove. Tingles traversed her arms and legs as feeling returned to her body. But it came back so quickly that she could not stay balanced and fell to the ground. She lay on the forest floor in a bed of pine needles, and the phial she held dropped just beyond the reach of her hand. Her breathing hastened, and tears formed in her eyes. "I'm . . . I'm dead," she whispered.

She wasn't sure how she still had what seemed a physical body that breathed, that hurt, that felt, but she did—and the memory of where she'd come from was completely restored. Emotions previously hidden began to fill her heart. Her poor sister and brother, how she missed them. They'd been so close. She'd been almost a secondary mother to them, but she'd been unable to see them since moving from her community. Her father, or perhaps the community, had chosen to shun her when she'd shared her decision not to return. Even so, she still loved them both dearly.

She recalled standing at the front porch of their white farmhouse, suitcase in hand, waiting for her ride to Pittsburgh. The hurt in her parent's eyes had almost been enough to change her mind, but the allure of adventure had proven stronger. Now she wondered, if only she'd chosen differently, could she have found what she sought? But now, now she was . . . where? Neither heaven nor hell, it seemed.

The sunlight emerging from the gaps in the treetops cast a red hue around her. Evening approached. How long had she been in that trancelike state? It didn't matter. Dead or not, she had to get back to the cottage quickly. Nervously, she picked up the phial. It now glowed with a gentle, consistent white light similar to Jak and Ella's. She carefully placed it in a small pocket sewn into her dress and began to retrace her steps back to the hill.

Though it grew increasingly challenging to see her trail as the sun continued to set, she made it back to the base of the hill. On her way up, she heard a rustle behind her. She stopped. Was it a deer or perhaps a squirrel? A hiss made her heart grow still. Was it the same sound she'd heard in the meadow when she first came to this place? She began to turn around slowly. All was quiet. Somewhere, an owl hooted. She started backing up, hoping to reach the hill's summit and some lingering daylight before whatever was out there could use the cover of trees to find her.

Many moments passed as her feet quietly pressed against the ground. The trees grew thinner. She was almost there. Then, finally, she came out from under the leaves. She sighed. She was safe. But then, she heard another hiss. It was behind her. Slowly, she turned around. She screamed.

A figure stood hunched over in the center of the open area atop the hill. It wore a red cloak and hood and weaved slowly back and forth as it studied her. In the remaining sunlight, she could see yellow, jagged teeth beneath the hood, otherwise covering its face.

Somewhere in the distance, she heard a voice. "Abigail!" it yelled. She recognized it. It was Jak. Another voice called out. "Where are you?" It was Ella's. They were looking for her. But by the time they found her, it would be too late. She backed up a step. The creature leaned forward and let out a long, slow hiss. It dashed forward. She considered running, but there was no escape. She wondered, could someone die twice?

She felt something warm on her hand and remembered the phial. Why was it warm? There was no time to consider further. In an instant, the warmth spread up her arm and down into her legs. Finally, it rushed into her head. Hopeless fear gave way to a courage she'd never felt before. Almost instinctively, she pulled out the light and commanded, "*Edin Na Zu, Telal!*" Her voice was powerful, like nothing she'd heard herself speak before. Nor did she know what she'd said. The creature stopped as the light created a glowing orb around Abigail and expanded in its direction. Still feeling a strange power, she stepped forward and yelled, "*Barra!*"

The creature backed up a step. Or had it staggered? "Who . . . are . . . you?" it hissed.

She could hear Jak and Ella's voices growing closer. The creature looked in that direction, snarled, and darted away, disappearing into the forest's shadows. The rush of energy within Abigail subsided just as quickly as it had come. Her shoulders drooped, and she felt tired. The light's intensity returned to a faint glow as the orb around her contracted into the heart of the phial. Unsure what had just happened and concerned the creature might return, she ran toward Jak and Ella's voices as they continued calling out to her.

Soon she heard the babbling of the brook. Up ahead, she saw two other small lights bobbing as they approached. She held out her own.

"I'm here!" she yelled as it lit her path ahead of her. But then, a sudden sick feeling came over her, and she stumbled and almost fell. Her hand holding the phial felt as if it were being stung by bees. She let it go, and it fell to the ground. The once-white light flickered with a red hue. She backed away as the glow of red sent a wave of fear through her. Just as Jak and Ella reached her, an image of someone familiar flashed inside the glass container.

"Tarin," she whispered. He appeared to be walking down a roadway toward a small brick house. It was night.

The red flickering stopped, and the phial began to glow soft white again. Jak and Ella stared down at it, mouths agape. "Where did you find that?" Jak asked.

"In the woods. I'm sorry, I shouldn't have gone, but when I saw it from the hilltop . . . I . . . I . . ."

Ella pulled her into a hug. "We're just glad you're all right."

"Let's get back to the cottage," Jak said, "and quickly. It is not safe out here."

"Should I take the light?" Abigail said, pointing at it.

Jak paused momentarily, then said, "Yes, bring it." She reached down to pick it up, but it flashed a brilliant red and threw them all backward. They lifted themselves from the ground and heard a voice, sounding simultaneously close and distant, began to sing from the direction of where the light lay, still glowing red. "This little light of mine . . . I'm going to let it shine."

The lawn was thick in front of the brick house. Though this wasn't the nicest part of town, Tarin's old home stood out from its neighbors as the one least cared for. A broken gate hung open by the sidewalk, white paint peeling from its panels. A single porch light glowed dimly by the front door. A beat-up pickup truck sat parked in the cracked concrete driveway in front of the connected garage.

Tarin could hear music—country music—playing from inside, but he wasn't sure what song. This was it: his opportunity. He'd made it to the final destination of his quest. Well, almost. He still had to go into that house. He took a step forward and placed his hand on the gate. He opened it, careful not to knock it off its hinges. He stepped onto the overgrown walkway leading to the front door. The curtains were drawn on the living room window so Tarin couldn't see inside. It was just as well. He feared that if he saw his father, he might grow too emotional to continue, though he wasn't sure which emotions he would feel.

He kept walking, memories of helping his father tend the lawn and his mother plant a garden flitted through his mind even while, at the same time, he could almost hear her screaming and the thuds of her being hit. He'd left East Fairfield hating his father, but he did not hate every memory of him. After all, it was he who'd gifted Tarin the love for travel and the thrill of the road trip. Back then, his father had been happy and energetic, spending months planning and building anticipation for each new adventure he designed with the excitement of a child just before a holiday. It wasn't until his mother's mind faltered that the light in his dad's eyes transformed from a merry glow to an angry fire. And once that transformation was complete, Tarin never saw the happy version again. That man had perished along with his mother.

Somehow he'd managed to traverse the walkway, and now the door stood in front of him. The music was louder. There was a musty smell. He looked back toward the road. Would it be so bad just to go back, to hope that without his light, perhaps Gil and the others could still find a way to sort out whatever was going on and protect his friends? The temptation to turn and run grew strong.

No! He knew there was no hope without pressing forward. Before the urge to run climaxed, he spun around and knocked on the door. A weight dropped from his shoulders, and other than the music, all seemed still and quiet.

He waited. There was no answer. He knocked again. Still, no response. He grew concerned that his opportunity to get his light back would fail simply because he was unable to get into the house. He tried the doorknob. It was unlocked. With a deep breath, he turned it and pushed the door open.

A strong smell of beer and cigarettes penetrated his nostrils. To his left was a door with a window facing the connected garage, and to his right was an old stereo system belting out country tunes. Across the room a primitive flat-screen TV played news about the DC UFO sightings. But it was on mute. A recliner faced away from Tarin and toward the TV. A hand rested on a remote on the chair's armrest. And, to his dismay, the mantle on the fireplace beside the stereo was empty.

"Leave it on the porch," a gruff voice said, lazily lifting a hand. "I already paid."

"What?" Tarin said, confused.

"Leave . . . the pizza . . . on . . . the porch," the man said again. He changed the channel, this time to a newscast about the war.

Before Tarin could figure out how to respond, his father said, "Fine, you must want a tip, one second." He stood from his chair, groaned, and turned toward the door. Tarin felt a strange and unpleasant stillness capture the room as their eyes met. The remote fell from his father's hand. "Tarin?"

Tarin grimaced at his unkempt appearance. The man in front of him looked little like what he'd remembered. He'd once been well built, if not athletic. Now, he wore a tight white shirt over a gaunt body. The skin on his face gripped tightly to his cheekbones while his deep-set eyes looked Tarin up and down in confusion. "What . . . what are you doing here?"

Tarin found his voice and said, "I need something." He pointed to the fireplace. "There was a small glass container that used to be on the mantle. Tell me where it is so I can get on my way."

A look of sadness replaced his father's look of shock. "You mean you don't plan to stay?"

"Here?" Tarin said. The anger he'd been trying so hard to repress began to push toward the surface. He breathed in deeply and continued, "Where is the glass phial we kept on the mantle?"

His father took a step forward.

"Stay there!" Tarin yelled.

His father stopped, his eyes growing moist. "I . . . I can't believe it's really you," he said. "I never thought I'd see you again . . . after . . . after what happened."

Tarin's jaw tightened. "After what happened?" he snarled. "You mean, after you beat Mom up day after day for over a month?"

The TV in the background flashed images of destroyed buildings and crying children, but none of that mattered at the moment. Tarin glowered at his father, the skinny wretch. A few tears dripped down the man's unnaturally aged face. But they did nothing to quell Tarin's growing rage. Still, he knew he needed to stay composed. Unleashing fury would do little but delay his mission. And he was so close.

"Where is the phial?" he said again.

"The garage," his father said. "It's in the car." A small smile lifted from the corner of his mouth. "You know, the same one we used to take trips in." He paused and glanced downward. "All of us." He again met Tarin's eyes with a soft expression. "I kept it."

A brief flash of one of their road trips flitted into Tarin's memory. It lingered a moment until he looked into the nearby kitchen and saw a table. He recalled the sound of his mother's body being thrown into it. He glared at his father. Finally, he couldn't take it anymore. He rushed forward and grabbed the collar of his father's shirt. "Those memories died when you hit her!" he screamed. With his free hand, he pulled down a corner of his own shirt. There was a scar on his shoulder. "There's a memory for you! Remember giving me that?" He let go of his father and lifted his shirt, revealing his torso. "And how about that one! Remember that?"

Tarin's father stood hunched over, his shoulders sagged. New tears formed on his face. Slowly, he lifted both hands, palms facing inwards.

Tarin had not noticed before, but the backs of both hands were covered in scars. He lifted his shirt, and his torso was also cut, not just in one place but many. He leaned down and lifted a pants leg—more scars.

Tarin took a step back in shock. "Anger became a way of life for your mom and me," his father said. "And she always seemed to have a sharp object with her when she had a fit." His face dropped into a deep frown. "It's hard watching the woman you love lose her mind. It changes you. It eats away at your soul." He looked around the room. "This house, and hell, they became the same place."

Tarin's heart pounded. He stood silent for a moment. An overwhelming mix of emotions poured through him. Then, he felt a jolt. Was it in his head or in his heart? He couldn't tell. Also, was something humming? Suddenly, every memory of every strike he'd received or seen his mother endure flooded back into his memory. Rage crashed over him like a powerful wave, and he met his father's eyes with a fierce gaze. Feeling both in and out of control, he pulled back his arm and swung.

The sound of fist against bone rang through the room. His father staggered back, tripped over his chair, and collapsed by the TV. Tarin walked forward, throwing the chair between him and his father to the side. "Every scar, every cut, every bit of pain you got, you deserved!" he screamed. He pulled his foot back and kicked his father in the stomach.

His father groaned in pain and held out his hands. But it did nothing to stop the assault. Over and over, Tarin kicked him and screamed as years of pent-up tears rushed down his anguished face. With each kick, he saw his mother's countenance flash from the happy, gentle looks he remembered to the crazed expressions that dominated after her madness. He reached down and pulled his father's limp body to his feet. The man's mouth was bleeding, and he looked barely conscious. Tarin pulled his fist back, his teeth gritting in preparation for a final blow, when he saw a flash of red light from somewhere behind him. Before he could strike, his father sputtered in a faint voice. "I'm sorry I hit you. I'm sorry I hit her. I lost all hope. I broke . . . and destroyed everything around me."

Tarin saw him. An image of Maximus appeared in his mind's eye. His twisted smile was simultaneously ecstatic and cruel. Maximus's hand lifted and displayed a familiar glowing red phial. Its light began streaming toward Tarin. Tarin felt both an urge to run and to embrace it. He began to reach out. Somewhere, time passed, but Tarin's mind was no longer confined to time. He simply was. In this place, there was no mist and there was no haze. There was only emptiness.

Abigail shielded her eyes. The brilliance of the crimson light lit the woods as if the entire region was on fire. But there was no heat, only an apprehension that something was terribly wrong. She managed to pull herself to her feet and saw Jak and Ella nearby. She rushed to them and knelt down.

"Run back to the cottage!" Jak yelled as he and Ella stood up and pulled out their phials. Both shone but were like fireflies against a red sun. As he and Ella began to retreat, Abigail heard a humming. It sounded like the ominous drone of a million wasps.

A terror came over her. It felt as if, in the following moments, all things across all time might come crashing to their end. She turned to the phial she'd found. It continued to burn bright red, but as her eyes adjusted, she again saw someone within it. Immediately, she recognized Tarin's thin build and sandy blond hair.

Tarin was reaching out toward a hideous creature, a monster enveloped in shadow, a twisted figure in the form of a man composed of writhing, black, smoky tentacles. Its head was an empty void other than two piercing yellow eyes. They seemed to thirst for Tarin like a wild animal would its prey.

Somewhere behind her, she heard Jak and Ella screaming for her to join them, to escape from the red fire that seemed only to be growing stronger. But rather than fear, she again felt a strange power consume her body. Images of her family, both her parents and her siblings, filled her mind, along with all the love and pain connected to their memories. Then came sounds of the mockery she'd received while trying to understand city life and the empty promises of men who'd sought only to use her body for their pleasure, coupled with the agony she felt when she realized they weren't the princes she'd read about in her books. She then saw her sick and dying body, consumed by whatever strange disease had settled upon her. As she watched her sick form lie hopeless in bed, a rage grew in her. Yes, all these things had torn her down and brought her deep into the shadows. But all of this was a consequence of her thirst for adventure coupled with a fire inside of her to discover her ultimate destiny.

She brushed her brown hair out of her face, pulled her shoulders back, and stood up. She rushed to the light, and even as it blinded her, she grabbed it and pulled it to her face. With an intensity even more significant than that on the hill when facing the red-cloaked beast, she said, "*Edin Na Zu, Maskim Xul!*"

The next moment she was standing next to Tarin. Time slowed as he reached out for a glowing red tentacle mere inches from the tip of his fingers, but time flowed normally for her as she stared into the now confused eyes of the monster in front of her.

"Who are you?" it said in a long, guttural hiss, like a cacophony of dissonant music, an orchestra that had fallen into complete disarray without the steady guidance of a conductor.

Though she still felt a strong power within her, she was now unsure what to do next. So she simply answered, "I am Abigail Yoder, and you must go."

The beast laughed. Or was it hissing? Or coughing?

"I know you," it continued. "You were on Earth." A smoky finger pointed toward Tarin. "With him." She looked at Tarin. His eyes seemed filled with conflict and pain.

"Leave him alone!" she commanded.

Again, the beast laughed. "I remember when I saw you for the first time." Its voice became more humanlike as its form shifted, becoming more man and less beast. "Your spirit, it was so . . . innocent, but in such pain." It continued to morph. Soon it appeared as a man wearing a cattleman hat, leather jacket, jeans, and boots. "Yet there was a hope I saw in you that I found in few others that . . . enticed me. I liked that. You were sweet, like honey. Your love for your family, especially your siblings, was so beautifully . . . quaint. And your ability to still love your parents, despite their shunning you, was both confusing and delicious. I've always had, shall I say . . . a sweet tooth." He glanced at the boy. "He is the bread," he looked at her, "and you are the honey." He began approaching her.

Tarin remained frozen in time. His finger was still outstretched toward the tentacles of red light reaching out for him. Meanwhile, the man hastened his pace.

Abigail began to back up, but it was too late. The man stopped and stood directly in front of her. "I'm famished," he snarled, and grabbed her face in his cold hand. His mouth, full of perfect white teeth, opened wide. She felt energy being pulled from her as he started to morph back into the monster from earlier. For a brief moment, she thought that this was how it all would end, that there was, in fact, a death beyond death that led to hell. But then she heard a voice—or rather, the sound of music.

She saw herself on the lap of her father as a young girl. He was reading to her. It was where she'd first developed her love for books and thirst for adventure. The music shifted, and her heart began to dance to its rhythm. She smelled the sweet aroma of her mother cooking bread in the oven and heard the laughter of her dear siblings, Mary and Ezekiel, as they scurried around the house.

She then heard a gagging sound. The draining sensation ceased as energy rushed back into her body.

The creature before her had transformed back into a man. He was both quaking and gagging. He looked up at her, fear in his eyes. "How?" he said. Then his mouth curled into a horrified expression. "Wait. Where are you now, seed of Earth?"

PJ Dudek

"I'm here with you," she answered.

"No, where did you go after death?"

"To Arvalast," she replied.

The look of horror intensified. "Impossible." He looked away, then met her gaze. "Unless . . ."

As his eyes met hers, she again felt the power from before rising in her. Instinctively, she threw out her arms. Light exploded from her, and he reared his head into the air and screamed. She saw Tarin's hand fall limp to his side. The red tendrils shot back toward the man as he dissipated into a black and red wisp of smoke.

Her strange power withdrew in an instant. Tarin stood next to her in a trancelike state. She reached out for him, but before she could touch him, he disappeared. She was left alone in pure darkness. A few moments later, she smelled the scent of leaves and heard the sound of nearby water. She opened her eyes and found herself lying on the ground.

"Abigail!" Ella called out. "Can you hear me!"

"Yes," Abigail said with a groan. "What happened?"

"They attacked us," she heard Jak say. "But we fought them back." He was standing near the stream, holding up his phial of light and staring into the woods.

"What attacked us?" Abigail said, still adjusting to being back in the woods instead of whatever phantom world she'd just been in.

"Vulgheid," he said. "The shadows of the enemy." He turned to her. "Did you see Tarin? We heard you say his name."

"Yes," Abigail said. "I saw him. I also saw something else. It was terrible."

Jak walked over to them and held out his hand toward Abigail. She took it and allowed him to help her to her feet. It was then she noticed she was holding the phial she'd found. It glowed with a soft white light.

"Let's return to the cottage," he said, "and you can tell us what you saw."

o o o ✧ o o o

265

Tarin awoke with a start. After a moment, he heard the sound of country music and breathed in the scent of beer and tobacco. He noticed the flicker of a nearby TV and realized he was lying back in a recliner. Next to him, on a wooden kitchen chair, was his father. He handed Tarin a warm rag and a glass of water. "Doing better, bud?" he said. "You were out for a few minutes."

Tarin looked over. "What happened?"

"You fainted," his father said. His face was bruised, and both eyes were black. His lips were swollen and still bled. "I managed to get you into the chair after I picked it back up." He lifted an object that was resting on his lap: a small, dusty glass phial. "I did what you asked," he said. He held it out toward Tarin. "I went out to the garage and got it out of the car." He set it on Tarin's knee.

Tarin looked down at it. After days of battling to get here, he finally had his light back, although it wasn't a light, only an empty glass container. He reached down and touched it. It was neither warm nor cool and felt like any other glass object might, both smooth and hard. He was still confused about what had just happened and found himself simply asking, "Why did you move it from the mantle and put it in the car?"

"Because," his father said softly, "it was all I had left from the past that didn't make me feel pain." He focused on it, his eyes pooling with what seemed to be the essence of happy memories. "The only thing that's brought me any joy since you and your mother left was driving with this thing sitting by me in the front seat. Somehow, I felt as if you were there when I had this. And all the guilt I had, all the hatred I had for myself, all the rage, it would disappear, and I could go back to my happy place."

After a long silence, Tarin asked, "And what was that?"

His father smiled. "Going on drives with you and your mom."

Tarin stared into the object. Unlike the phials of Gil or Iris, this one did not begin to swirl with light or reveal any tangible scene. But his imagination filled the emptiness within it. He pictured his mom, her red hair blowing in the wind from the open passenger side window. Next to her, he saw his father, his face both rugged and youthful, his dark hair clean and his eyes wide with the thrill of what might lie over the next hill in front of them. Tarin could almost smell the scent of open fields and hear the sound of the engine purring. He sat up, took the phial, and said, "Let's go for a drive."

"What?" his father said, looking confused.

"I need to clear my head. Let's go out for a night drive."

He saw eagerness mixed with pain in his father's face. "Sure, I guess, if you're feeling up to it?"

"I am."

His father attempted to stand but fell back to his knees. "Sorry, you got me pretty good back there."

"Here," Tarin said, "let me help." He got up and carefully assisted his father to his feet. Then his father pulled keys from his pocket and tossed them to Tarin. "Do you mind driving? I've had a few."

The next hour, with windows open despite the cool night air, they drove across the rural farmlands west of East Fairfield in the old petroleum-based car that had years ago carried them in all directions across the country. Music played softly on the radio, familiar country music. The lights of the town disappeared behind them, replaced by twinkling stars, moonlight, and the occasional porch light from a farmhouse set back against the roadway. Neither of them spoke. Both just listened—to the wind, to the music, and to the echoes of the past, forever safe and unaware of the dark future that lay in wait around the next sunrise.

They drove for an hour until, as the gas meter began to read close to empty, Tarin slowly headed back into the driveway of his old home and parked just outside the garage next to the pickup truck. He retrieved the keys and handed them back to his father.

His father carefully took them. "I never thought I'd be given the treasure of a new happy memory in this life." The words came out trembling. "Thank you, son. I didn't deserve that."

Tarin looked at him—at the dark bruises, the swollen eyes. A car quietly passed behind them, its headlights briefly lighting his father's face even more, causing Tarin to turn away. His eyes landed on his own bloody fist. He grimaced, then got out of the car. With the empty glass still in his pocket, he walked away, a proper farewell trapped somewhere behind his lips. A steady stream of tears began to pour down his face. As they dripped onto the sidewalk below, he didn't notice the slight warmth growing in his pocket.

CHAPTER 23

The fireplace crackled and filled the room with the scent of cedar as it drove away the incoming chill of the night. Thick, rough-hewn logs encompassed the main room in the cabin. Abigail watched a few dimly lit candles cast wavy shadows on the walls. Jak sat in an old wooden rocking chair and smoked a pipe while Ella filled cups with water from a basin in an adjacent pantry. A few well-worn throw rugs covered parts of the slatted wooden floor.

Ella entered and offered Abigail a drink. She accepted it gratefully. For the last hour, they'd been discussing the events of that evening. Though wary of Abigail's light, which sat next to her on a small table still glowing softly, Jak and Ella agreed it was safe to keep in the house, despite the events from earlier. "It's not fully connected to anyone," Jak had said to Abigail. "It must be picking up the energies of different sources, though it now seems to have connected more fully to you."

Abigail pondered all that had happened, but mostly she was thinking of Tarin. Why was that creature attacking him? Was it one of the Vulgheid Jak had told her about that evening, or something else? Why did Tarin seem drawn to its power? And what was this strange energy that had now come over her twice and given her the ability to drive the creature away from Tarin? She could also now speak in some unknown new language, in what felt like an involuntary reaction. Part of her felt almost giddy about her newfound abilities. The other part was a mix of anxiety and confusion.

She'd told Ella and Jak everything: about her memory returning, about the world she'd left, and about Tarin. Jak was enthralled by her confirmation of another world beyond Arvalast. "I've believed it for so long, but now, having you here—remarkable," he'd said. He'd filled the room with the smell of tobacco as he'd puffed heavily, asking Abigail hundreds of questions. Ella had remained largely silent, her face full of anxiety. Finally, she interrupted Jak and said, "And what of Tarin? What of this . . . this thing that is pursuing him? How do we help him?"

Jak blew a plume of smoke into the air and said, "We could go to the tower, to the portal, and see if we can somehow bring him back from this other world?"

"But no one can go to the tower," Ella interjected. "Our enemies guard it. Even Gildareth struggled for years to finally reach it and break the seal. And now we don't even know what's become of him."

"It would be treacherous," Jak agreed, "but what other choice do we have?"

Ella ran her hand through her dark hair in frustration and sat down. "I don't know," she said.

Jak stood and began pacing. A moment later, he stopped and turned to Ella. "What if we signal for help? Going alone would be a fool's mission, but perhaps if we went in force, we'd have a chance to at least reach the tower."

Ella's eyes lifted and glistened in the firelight. "Do you think they'd come?"

"I'm not sure," Jak continued. "Besides, at our monthly gatherings for trade, we've not spoken of Tarin or Woodend's fall for many years."

Abigail leaned forward. "Do you mean to contact others like your-selves, people who live in the woods away from the tyrant in Woodend?"

"Yes," Jak said. "There are many of us scattered in this region south of the ruins of Undertree. Our presence generally deters our enemies from entering this area, either man or monster, though your encounters with the latter indicate they are growing bolder."

"Or that there's something larger at play," Ella said, "such as with Tarin."

"That's right," Jak said. "The Drilockk have a renewed energy, and now . . . we saw Vulgheid in the forest for the first time in a decade."

"What are Drilockk?" Abigail asked. Although Jak had already explained Vulgheid—shadowy entities that attacked both soul and mind—he'd not yet used the term Drilockk before. Though she had a guess as to what they might be.

"It is the name of the red-cloaked beasts you've now encountered twice," Ella answered. "They are a wicked race that has long plagued our world. After the tyrant's takeover of Woodend, they allied themselves with him, even as they were already allies with the Vulgheid lord."

"And now that both the Drilockk and the Vulgheid are on the move," Jak continued, "I'm concerned for the safety of all of us finding sanctuary in this region." He looked at Ella. "And that's why I think the others will come."

"How will we convince them to join us to go to the tower, though, to help Tarin?" Ella asked.

Jak took a deep puff of his pipe. "They will remember him," he said. "They know what Gildareth believed him to be."

"But what of the battle?" she said. "When Woodend fell, so did hope in Tarin."

"Not all lost hope," Jak replied.

Ella rubbed her temples and groaned. "Then let's get on with it. But if no one comes, I'm going to the tower even if I must go alone."

"You'll have at least me," Jak said.

"And me too!" Abigail said, jumping to her feet. As they looked at her, she blushed and sat back down.

"Seeing what you're apparently capable of," Jak said, "I actually think our odds improve significantly with you joining us." He turned to Ella. "Maybe we don't need the others after all," he winked.

Ella rolled her eyes. "Go get the horn."

"I was being quite serious," he said.

"Go . . . get . . . the horn," Ella repeated.

He got up and disappeared behind a curtain separating one of the two sleeping areas from the main room. There was the noise of shuffling and a couple of groans until he returned holding up what looked like an old ram's horn. "Found it!" he said.

Ella and Abigail followed him outside into the cold night air. An owl hooted somewhere in the distance. He went to the back of the cabin and returned with a stick ladder, which he set against the wall. He climbed to the roof, stood facing south, and blew three long blasts. They echoed through the trees and momentarily drowned out the babbling of the nearby stream.

"Could that alert the Drilockk, or the shadows, the Vulgheid, to where we are?" Abigail asked.

"The Drilockk already know we're here," Ella said, and the Vulgheid—a horn will not draw them."

"If the Drilockk know you're here, why don't they attack?"

"They fear our lights," Ella answered. "Beyond the glow, they also emit an invisible energy they hate. It's like a rancid odor to them. Though they are capable of attacking despite this, unless they're greatly provoked, we should be safe."

"But what of the ones that attacked me? The second time, I had a light?"

Ella turned to Abigail. "You'd entered their territory, which provoked them. But still, their actions do seem to be growing more erratic, just like Jak said."

The soft sound of yet another horn echoed from far in the distance, also blowing three times.

"We have a reply!" Jak yelled from the rooftop. He blew three more long blasts. A few moments later, there was another series of horn blasts coming from what sounded like a slightly different direction. Then three more, and three after that. Soon the whole area seemed to have woken up with a cacophony of responses.

"This," Ella whispered, "this might provoke them."

The glass doors slid open, and Tarin walked into the hotel. The dry November air had hidden his previous tears. He made his way to the elevator and was waiting as it beeped toward the ground floor when he heard someone say, "Complimentary cookies, if you're interested." It was the woman at the front desk. He realized he was hungry, and instead of walking into the elevator as its doors opened, he headed toward the voice. She looked to be in her early twenties and wore a collared shirt and a pin that read, "Esther." She watched him as he took three cookies.

"Thank you," he said.

"You aren't Tarin by any chance, are you?" she asked.

"I am."

"Some folks were looking for you earlier. A tall guy with a cowboy hat and a woman with brown hair and glasses."

"Where did they go?" he asked.

"They checked if you were in the room, then went out back." She pointed to a set of wooden doors on the other side of the hotel. "Out that way."

"How long ago?"

"A couple of hours."

Tarin pocketed the cookies. He noticed a warm sensation as his hand withdrew from his pocket but gave it no attention. He then went outside and scanned the parking area. There was no sign of Gil or Iris. He decided to circle the hotel but still didn't see them. Maybe they'd gone back into town. He walked to the car he'd left parked out front and unplugged it. He got in, double-checked it still had a reasonable charge, and drove toward the stoplight adjacent to the hotel.

He turned left and began slowly driving on Main Street toward downtown. He carefully scanned the sidewalks on both sides of the road but saw no one other than one late-night jogger. The town circle appeared in front of him. He drove to its other side and made his way to the railroad crossing he and Iris had stopped at earlier. Still no sign of Gil and Iris. There was only one other place he thought they might be, now that most establishments would otherwise be closed.

He returned to the circle and turned east toward the local brewery. It was still open. He parked next to about four other cars. The establishment was less a bar and more a retro-style arcade with drinking for adults and games for the kids. He and his father and mother used to go here once or twice a month when all was still well, and though he'd been too young to drink while he still lived in East Fairfield, he had fond memories of the games and food. After his mother's mind faltered, they'd stopped going, other than his father.

Inside the brewery, he heard the familiar sound of country music. The place seemed to have changed names since the last time he'd been here, but he didn't take note of it because he saw Iris sitting at the bar at the front counter, leaning over a tall glass of something dark amber. She was alone. Behind her, a few other drinkers sat at a table located in the large open seating area where long, communal tables with log benches ran parallel to each other, and next to them, arcade games beeped and buzzed.

Tarin approached Iris and sat down on the adjacent stool. The lone bartender came to take his order. Iris noticed Tarin but said nothing as he put in an order. The bartender poured him a tall drink, then went to check in on the table with the other guests.

"I thought you'd be here when we didn't find you at the hotel," Iris said. Her speech was slow, seemingly affected by the alcohol. Her hair, ordinarily straight and tidy, was slightly wavy and unkempt. Her glasses rested on the bar next to two empty beers. She had tired rings under her eyes.

"I went to my father," he said.

She turned to look at him. "What?"

"I went home and confronted my father."

"You went alone? But . . . how? After our talk earlier, I thought it might be days before you built up the courage to visit your old home." She paused. "How did the conversation go?" Her voice grew nervous. "Did you find the phial?"

Tarin's throat tightened at the memory of what he'd done. "There wasn't much conversation," he slowly said. He began instinctually to hide his still bloody hand within his pocket when, to his surprise, he touched warm glass. He realized it was his phial and hastily pulled it out. "I can't believe it," he said as he set the glass object on the table beside his beer. "There was nothing there when I first found it."

The phial glowed with an almost invisible but still-present white light. Iris, her hands shaking, reached for and put on her glasses. "You did it," she whispered. "I can hardly believe it, but you did it."

Tarin chuckled at his own surprise at seeing light in the glass container. He also marveled at how it wasn't bringing him any fear like most previous encounters with the light.

"I was hoping that with time," Iris said, "assuming you found your light, it might glow again, but . . ." she looked at him, spread out her arms, and pulled him into a tight hug. "I can hardly believe it!"

Despite the alcohol on her breath, he felt a surge of happy energy in her embrace, like hugging a dear friend or family member who'd just returned from a lengthy absence. It had been a long time since he'd felt such a feeling, not since the last time he'd hugged his mother, the day before she'd gone ill.

She let him go and continued to look at the phial. The bar music continued while a couple of other patrons entered, ordered drinks, and made their way to a table somewhere behind them. Iris's expression remained merry, almost carefree, but as an upbeat song changed to one more gloomy, her demeanor began to morph into one of concern. "When you went to retrieve your light, in the process, did you meet any resistance?"

"Do you mean from my father?" he asked.

"Either from your father"—she continued to watch his light glimmer—"or from another?"

Tarin remembered his dream, the red tendrils, and Maximus. "Yes," he said. "I saw *him* again."

Her eyes remained fixed on the phial. "How did you escape?"

He thought back. "I'm . . . I'm not sure," he finally said.

Iris sat still and pensive. After a moment, she took a swig of her beer, then, with a thud, slammed her glass on the table. "I can't believe I wasn't there to help you!" The bartender and other occupants glanced over. She ignored their stares. "How could I have been so foolish to leave you alone earlier tonight, to potentially risk you going back home by yourself to face that monster?"

Tarin leaned back in his stool at her sudden outburst. Was the alcohol affecting her? "How would you have known I'd go looking for my light tonight?" he said. "I even surprised myself."

She stared blankly ahead. Though physically still present in the bar, her mind seemed to have drifted elsewhere, somewhere that looked to be causing her pain. The feeling behind her expression seemed similar to how he often felt when he'd had encounters with images in Gil's light—or hers.

He set his hand next to hers but did not touch it. "I'm not the only one dealing with demons from the past, am I?" He glanced at his light, then at her. He remembered the song she'd been listening to at the rest stop in Minnesota. "What hell are you going through?"

She slowly pulled her hand away from his and met his eyes with a fierce gaze. "Everything you've gone through, everything that happened to your mother, the abuse from your . . . your father. All of that, it's my fault." Behind her glasses, moisture formed, but no tears fell. "I was sent to protect you," she continued, "but I failed."

Tarin felt electricity emanate from her, and at the same time, a swell of empathy rise in his own chest. "But did you fail?" he asked softly and pointed to the still glowing phial on the counter.

She took off her glasses, and her expression softened. "You've done amazingly, Tarin. I don't want to diminish this. But our enemy gained much power from my failures." A single tear slid down her face. "Years ago, when I came to this place to protect you, I quickly developed a deep regard and admiration for you. I could sense who you were, and I wanted to help you discover that within yourself. Much of my energy went into that cause." She stared at the counter for a few moments. "Until I found its focus drift toward another."

Tarin's heart began to beat faster. Though he wasn't sure he wanted to know Iris's full story, he knew it was time. "Iris," he said, "was it my father?"

Iris looked up at the bartender. His back was turned while he cleaned glasses in a sink on the other side of the bar. "I used to work here," she said. "Usually the night shifts. But occasionally, I worked afternoons and would see you and your parents. You'd play on the arcade or eat while they made conversation over a few drinks."

"I wonder why I didn't remember you," Tarin said.

"Memory is a fickle thing," she said with a faint laugh, "especially in your kind. But Glorions have a persistent memory, which has its uses, but also pains."

She took another drink before continuing. "Shortly after your adoption, I and others of my kind, though they were in a different form, stood guard over this town in order to protect you. We maintained great success in keeping you hidden from the darkness, though we knew it was searching for you. But in our success, I began to grow complacent . . . even restless." Her brows tightened. "I began watching the interactions between your mother and your father. I began to long for the bond they had for one another. Whether it was the touch of their hands or the mysterious force I sensed when they kissed, I marveled at a love I knew I would never have and could never have."

She met his eyes. "I also pondered the ever-deepening relationship between your mother and you. It was a beautiful bond, a melody that stirred my heart but, at the same time, brought me sadness. It was another love I was destined to never know."

Tarin saw her hand, the one on the counter next to her beer, clench into a fist. "A jealousy grew in me as my longing for what I could never have became stronger. But one evening, your father came and sat on the stool you sit in now. Other than light conversation when I took his drink order, he and I had never spoken in depth. But something was different that night. He appeared sad and, after a few drinks, shared with me that the bond between you and your mother was something he also longed for. Despite his efforts to find ways to deepen his relationship with you, he could tell you greatly favored her. That night, they'd fought after he'd shared his feelings with her. He'd left the house confused, dejected, and uncertain. An empathy filled me as I realized he also struggled with the inability to experience an impossible love."

"For the next number of months, I saw less of you and your mother but more of your father as he came here to drink night after night. I spent long hours listening to him as he shared his deepest feelings. I began to know him better than perhaps I knew myself. I didn't realize it at the time, but my loyalty was shifting as I became infatuated with our conversations. Though I still maintained a powerful internal bond with you, my primary focus became him."

Her face flashed with grief. Tarin felt his body grow stiff as he anticipated what she would say next.

"Rumors of strange illnesses filling the local hospital came and went. Farmers whispered about mysterious cattle deaths in the area. But I was too distracted to notice. One night, your mother entered the bar. She saw us talking and grew enraged. She and your father began to argue fiercely, and I realized the mistake I'd made. Then, I sensed it. A shadow was approaching the city. I felt the energy of the others of my kind ignite, then, quickly, falter. In my distraction, he had found your hiding place."

Her eyes darted to the doorway. "Moments later, he entered the bar, invisible to all others except for me. I did my best to intervene as he and his kind worked to latch onto your parents, but as he lifted his hand to drop a final curse, I had only the strength to protect one of them." She paused, then said, "I chose your father."

Tarin felt his own fists clench as his heart raced. She continued.

"The curse entered your mother, and the work of the enemy was complete. He left, but his shadow remained over this town, its tendrils deep inside your mother. I was too weakened to intervene further. Though I tried, all my efforts were in vain. Your father also broke, even without the direct influence of the darkness. There was nothing I could do for him. Night after night, I endured the pain of knowing in my spirit the abuse hidden behind the walls of your house but unable to help because my light had weakened due to the grief of my failure. I did alert the police to my suspicions, but your father always seemed to manage to hide what was happening. When your mother left, and then you also left, I lingered for a time, watching over your father, feeling guilt over what I had done, but finally, I could take no more of this place and departed."

Iris closed her eyes. Her cheeks now glistened with tears. Tarin could hear music and the sounds of conversations nearby, but they were muffled by the pain swirling in his mind.

"And that is why," she said quietly, "though you now have your light, I have still failed you . . . and for that, I am deeply sorry." She paused as if waiting for him to say something. A long silence followed. She lowered her head, and without another word, she stood up, tapped a metal card on a console embedded into the bar, and left.

Tarin sat for a moment, motionless. A faint light flickered from the counter. He looked down. His brows furrowed. He snatched up the phial and shoved it in his pocket. He paid for his beer with his own card, then turned and stormed out into the night. Rather than returning to the car, he walked back toward town. He returned to the location where he'd first seen Maximus in his nightmare, where the portal had opened and he'd watched his mother die. He lifted his fists into the air and screamed a curse, to who or to what, he didn't know, but as his voice reverberated through the empty downtown, he heard footsteps approaching.

Tarin spun around and saw a tall figure with a cowboy hat coming toward him. For a moment, this throat tightened, but then a streetlight revealed it was Gil. Dejected, confused, and defeated, Tarin approached him, dropped his head onto his chest, and wept.

Gil put his arms around Tarin. For many moments, they stood together. Then, far in the distance, a train whistle blew. "I have it," Tarin finally said, backing away from Gil. "I have my phial."

Gil did not immediately reply. The whistle blew again, closer this time, now accompanied by the rumble of metal against metal. Gil nodded and said, "Well done, my friend. Well done."

They returned to the car. Tarin silently drove them back to the hotel. When they arrived, Esther, who was still attending the front counter, called them over. "I was told to let you know that the other member of your party, Iris, booked another room."

"Did she give a reason?" Gil asked.

"No reason, but she did say she'd meet up with you in the morning."

Gil looked concerned, but Tarin was relieved. Once back in the hotel room, he collapsed into bed and allowed sleep to gift him a welcome reprieve from the unbearable truth of what had happened to his mother.

CHAPTER 24

Tarin awoke to the sound of a clock ticking. Daylight streamed through a small crack between the curtains covering the single window. He felt disoriented, but after a few moments of staring at the ceiling, he remembered. He'd seen his father. He'd found his light. And, he'd learned what had happened to his mother.

"Iris," he whispered, his voice both sad and angry. She could have saved his mother. She had the chance, but instead, she chose . . . his father. An image of Iris passed through his mind. Her eyes were full of tears as he revisited what she'd told him happened that night in the bar. Telling him had been hard for her, perhaps even agonizing. The tension in her voice had given that away.

As he continued to study the memory of her face and the quivering pain in her eyes, his anger merged with a different feeling, that of empathy. For years, Iris had been alone, quietly holding back a darkness seeking to find him—to hurt him. He could understand her need for a companion who understood her sadness at a lack of reciprocation for her love, someone she could talk to. But why did it have to be his father?

He sat up and looked over at the other bed. Gil was fast asleep. His beard had grown more and more ragged the last few days, and his sleeping face did not appear restful. Even in sleep, Gil seemed to be battling some darkness somewhere. But at least, at the moment, darkness didn't seem to be in the room with them.

After using the restroom and cleaning up, he shuffled through his suitcase to realize the only pants he had left were jogging pants. As he lifted them out and looked at them, his mind drifted back to happier times when he'd gone on runs with his mother. He continued to stare at the pants until an idea formed. He looked toward the window, then back at the pants.

Ten minutes later, he was running toward town. The air was cool but also invigorating. It was still early morning, and there was little traffic along the main road. He breathed in deeply, taking notice of familiar buildings and houses now more vivid in the daylight. A powerful nostalgia consumed him as the sun lit up his hometown. He didn't fight it. At an intersection, he made a left and, a few minutes later, saw a small lake surrounded by a sidewalk open up in front of him. It was the park, the one he'd frequented countless times while living in East Fairfield, sometimes to walk, sometimes to picnic, but mostly to run with his mother.

The roadway led him to the sidewalk surrounding the lake. It glimmered softly in the early morning sunlight, and reflections of the surrounding trees and pavilion danced on its surface. He briefly closed his eyes, and for just a moment, he captured a piece of a happy past and remembered a time before his soul had received its scars.

As he rounded a bend, he heard footsteps ahead. It was another runner, a woman with blond hair and a slim build, and she was approaching quickly. It wasn't unusual to see other runners at the park, but as he approached, he recognized her. It was Chelsy.

A lump formed in his throat, but he otherwise had no time to react. She was wearing earbuds similar to those Iris used and, at first, didn't notice him. But just before she passed by, her eyes met his, and a look of recognition formed on her face. He smiled and offered a polite nod, hoping she wouldn't stop so they could pass each other without any formal greeting, but instead, she stopped and said, "Tarin, I . . . um . . . hello."

Tarin knew there was nothing he could do. He stopped, awkwardly held out his hand as if for a handshake, and said, "Hi, Chelsy. Been a while."

She looked at his hand, appearing confused. He quickly put it down by his side and said, "How have you been?" They stood near a few large pines along that side of the lake. No one else seemed to be around. As he waited for her response, he noticed she was wearing a necklace with a glass or crystal heart locket. It hung just below her neck and was engraved with what looked to be the name of someone—*Amelia*.

"Why did you run away when you saw me at the restaurant?" she said. He could tell she was trying to make her voice sound playful, but it didn't cover the hurt she was trying to mask.

He looked at the ground and felt sweat form on the palms of his hands. "Because . . . I felt unwell." He knew that was only partially true.

"You seemed fine until you saw me," she prodded.

A dog barked somewhere in the distance. He felt a childish urge to just run by her and escape this terrible discomfort but resisted. He lifted his eyes to meet hers and said, "You're right."

She kept his gaze for what felt like a long time, but it seemed to pass through him. Somewhere behind those eyes, he knew she was replaying their past time together, first as friends, then as something on the boundaries of more than friends. Finally, she said, her voice sad, "Well, it was good seeing you again . . . nice day out, enjoy the rest of your run."

She began to maneuver past him. At first, he felt relieved. But then, fear gripped him. What if this was the last time he ever saw her? Did he really want to carry the burden of why she'd left him without a word those many years ago, despite their friendship and despite having poured his heart out to her about what was happening in his family? "Chelsy," he said. She stopped just as she was passing him.

"Yes, Tarin?"

He felt his heart beating against the walls of his chest. "I need to know. What happened between us just before I left town?"

She began to fidget with the hair she had pulled back into a pony-tail. "I . . . I got scared," she said, her voice cracking a little. "What you told me, about how you felt about me, about what was happening to you, it was so much, and I . . . I didn't know what to do. I did try so hard to work up the confidence to call you afterward, but . . . I was afraid you might bring up what was happening again, and though I wanted to help, I didn't know how. If I called the police or told anyone else, I was worried you might be angry. You told me you didn't want anyone else to know. I'm not even sure if you'd told Allen. But I wish now that I'd told someone—I was young though . . . and so scared and confused. And then, you left, and I had no idea where you'd gone."

Tarin felt burning behind his eyes and tried to hold back tears. All he'd wanted was for her to have said something, anything, when he first told her. He wasn't asking for her to help him, just to demonstrate care. How could she not know that? But he decided not to press the issue. He feared that if he did, it might just hurt more. Instead, he looked at the locket on her neck and said, "Who is Amelia?"

Chelsy looked down and took the locket in her hand. A tear dripped down onto it as her lips pursed into an expression of happiness mixed with pain. "She was my baby," she said.

Tarin suddenly realized the meaning of the necklace. A strong wave of emotion shifted through him as the sadness he felt for himself met with the horror of realizing that Chelsy had lost a child. Finally, he managed to say, "I'm so sorry."

A few more tears landed on her hand, the one holding the locket. "It's okay," she said. "It was a while ago." She looked up at him. "A couple of years after you left, I met someone and got pregnant. At first, we were happy and were even talking about getting married. But about twenty weeks into the pregnancy, I got ill." More tears dripped down her face, and she began choking up. "I'm sorry, Tarin. It's just so hard for me to talk about this. All the memories, sometimes they just come back as if I was there now."

"It's okay," Tarin said softly, still doing his best to hold back his own emotions. "If you can't talk about it, I understand."

"No, it's okay, just give me a second." She wiped her nose and eyes on the sleeve of her jacket. "Anyway, they said I'd have to deliver early, or both me and the baby would die. But she'd only have a ten percent chance of survival at twenty weeks, even with all the ongoing advancements in technology that even gave her that chance. There was really nothing I could do, so they took me in, and after a C-section, they did their best for twenty-four hours to help her, but her lungs were just too weak. They took me into the NICU and said it wouldn't be long." She paused a moment. "There was beeping, Tarin. This horrible beeping. They told me it meant her oxygen was too low and that they'd not been able to get it back up. She was starting to turn blue. They said I could hold her if I wanted before she passed. I agreed, and for the next few minutes, I held my baby Amelia and sang to her. I watched her chest heave as she tried so hard to breathe."

Chelsy clutched the locket tightly, her shoulders quaking. "But she finally couldn't fight anymore and went still." She wiped her eyes and nose on her jacket and looked back up at Tarin. "It was too much for Amelia's dad. He left me a month later." Her voice cracked again. "Sometimes I think to myself, was this some sort of punishment for me walking away from you when you needed me most?" She began to sob. "She was barely bigger than my hand, Tarin. I felt so bad for her. She tried so hard to live."

Tarin couldn't take it anymore. He stepped forward and pulled Chelsy into his arms. His own tears broke through, and he allowed them to fall. "Don't believe for one moment any of that was your fault," he said. He continued to hold her as she also wrapped her arms around him and buried her head in his chest.

"But you told me you were being hit by your dad," she cried. "You told me your mother had lost her mind, and you didn't know what to do. I was your friend, and I just walked away from you."

Tarin let go and took a step back. He looked deeply into her eyes. "I had no right to drag you into my mess. And I had no right to pressure you into being some sort of savior for me. And I'm sorry."

"But I was still your friend!" she said. "I should have said something. I should have done something, anything, to help you. But I just left you there. I ran."

Tarin managed a smile. "Well, if you didn't notice from earlier at the restaurant, I tend to be a bit of a runner myself."

Chelsy let out a soft chuckle and leaned back into Tarin. "I'm so happy to finally have gotten to see you again. I've missed you so much." As they held each other, Tarin began to feel warmth on his chest. It was a familiar sensation. He let go of Chelsy, and his eyes widened. The locket on her chest was glowing with a soft white light.

"Wait, how . . ." he whispered.

She looked down, and her own eyes widened. "What's going on?"

It was then he noticed something warm just above his waist, where he'd placed his phial in the front pocket of his jacket. He put his hand inside, and yes, the phial was very warm—not hot, just warm, more so than it had ever been before. He considered pulling it out of his pocket to inspect it but didn't want to startle Chelsy any more than she already was. But when he looked back up at her, she was smiling and holding the locket in her hand. It shone brighter than the morning sun, and the black letters that said "Amelia" were bold and clear in front of the light.

"It's a miracle," she said as new tears formed in her eyes. Tarin studied the little glass element. Somehow, his own light must have spread. But how? Was this even possible? It must be because the evidence was right in front of him. He let out a confused laugh. "I guess it is a miracle," he agreed.

"Amelia," Chelsy said. "Mommy's here. Mommy loves you. She brought the locket to her lips and kissed it. "You're my angel," she said. "I see you, my angel."

Tarin felt as if his whole body was becoming lighter. Watching Chelsy so happy, as if she was somehow actually reuniting with her daughter, was bringing him a joy he'd never felt before. He wasn't even aware that such happiness was possible. He allowed time to pass by freely, allowing his friend to experience this precious time—a moment, he felt, she so deserved after all she'd gone through. In some ways, he hoped, it would make amends for the actions on his part he now realized had brought her years of pain. And as he watched her, any remaining anger, confusion, and sadness from when she'd broken his heart was mended.

They parted ways with a renewed friendship, or perhaps, an even more real friendship than the one they'd had before. Neither finished their jog. After one final hug, Tarin simply began walking back to the hotel and Chelsy back toward the town where she lived. Chelsy's locket continued to glow. He had no idea what she was going to tell others if it continued to shine. But it didn't matter. She was happy, and that made him happy.

Things were different back at the hotel. Gil was sitting in the lobby, his body tense as he sipped coffee and watched a projection near a fireplace in the center of the room. "There's much happening today," he said as Tarin walked in. He pointed to the hologram.

A news reporter was standing in a field. Behind her was a fire surrounded by military vehicles. "The air force, we believe, has shot down a mysterious flying object over Memphis," she said. "All over the country, there have been similar reports. We don't have too many additional details, as the military is not allowing access to anyone, including reporters. We will provide more information as we have it." Three men dressed in black leather jackets rushed the reporter and stood between her and the camera. Tarin watched what looked to be an argument begin before the images disappeared and a block of text spun around, saying, "We'll be back in a moment."

Tarin looked around the lobby. "Where's Iris?"

Gil took another sip of his coffee. "I am uncertain. But we need to return to South Dakota quickly."

CHAPTER 25

Allen was making coffee in the kitchen, still thinking of yesterday's strange evening at Old Cotton's. Other than Bill, who'd stayed at the bar to gossip with other patrons, Allen and the others had returned to his house shortly after the encounter with MJ12-2.

Liz was growing increasingly concerned about the agent's involvement in Philip. Before she'd left Allen's, close to midnight, she'd warned them all to be careful and to try not to meddle until she could figure things out. She'd also told Allen he still owed her a date to tell her more about his apparent past life in Arvalast. He promised he'd set something up.

That night, Allen had had odd dreams: pictures of what looked like an Amish community. There was a girl, he recalled, and she was restless. He remembered other bits and pieces of scenes from what looked like a college or university, such as desks and brick buildings. He thought he'd seen images of a woman being ill. But his memory was all extremely hazy. He also was struggling to remember parts of his time in Arvalast. He recalled a tower and living in a great forest, but details were missing. Faces, he'd recalled, were now formless and empty. Names of familiar towns were disappearing. He hoped the coffee would help. It would be awkward when he eventually found time to tell Liz about his past life if he couldn't remember specifics.

He walked into the living room to see Dralo and Ristun leaning forward on the couch, intently watching a tiny holographic projection coming from a black metal box resting on the windowsill. The device had cost Allen a full month of supplemental income, but as someone who worked in technology, he'd felt he needed one. "They're getting shot down," Ristun said, pointing at the projection.

Josh and Rob entered the room wearing their work outfits and name tags. "What's getting shot down?" Josh asked.

"We're not entirely sure," Dralo said.

"UFOs?" asked Rob excitedly.

"It seems so," said Ristun. He held out his hand to Allen. "You get me coffee?" he said.

"Well, this one's mine, and I already drank from it."

"Don't care, need it."

Allen shrugged, handed it to him, and poured himself a fresh cup.

"So apparently, there's been major sightings the last couple of days," Ristun said. "Mainly over DC, but now all over the country. The news doesn't know what they are, and now agents are coming in to keep people from the wreckage."

Rob took a seat next to Ristun and also stared at the projection. "Yesterday, you said there's, well, grey aliens that make portals. Do you think those are what's getting shot down? Does our military have the technology to do that?"

"Where's Old Bill when you need him?" Josh said. "He'd have a theory on this."

"I got involved in working on a lot of interesting tech in Cleveland," Ristun said. "Was around some powerful minds who had some connections high up in government. I don't think your people have tech comparable to what I've seen the Greys or the agents have. Also, if one side had anything like that, it would quickly tip the scale of the war, either for the Peacekeepers or the New Alliance."

Dralo stood and began to pace. "I think this goes beyond the Earth war," he said. He pulled out his phial of light and stared at it. "I can sense a great unease outside the realm of the purely physical. Something is at play and is fast accelerating." He turned to the others. "Our enemy is growing increasingly uneasy."

"Do you mean the entity Gil met when first coming here?" Allen asked. "The one Tarin called Maximus?"

Dralo continued to focus on his light. "In part, and perhaps a significant part, but there's more I don't fully understand." He gestured to the TV. "These downings of unidentified aerial phenomena are puzzling me."

"Then let's figure out what's happening," Ristun said.

"And how do you propose we do that?" asked Dralo.

Ristun waved his hands toward the window. "Remember what Bill said last night? Something's going on at that mountain near here. What was it called again?"

"Bear Mountain," Rob said, his face lighting up.

"That's right," Ristun said, snapping his fingers and pointing at Rob. "Bill said he's heard rumors of strange stuff happening there related to UFOs. We should go there and see if we can find anything. Maybe we'd even uncover some clues as to what the agents are up to."

"And if we run into Greys?" Dralo said. "Let's not forget what Iris told us happened to her and Gil two nights ago."

"They were caught off guard," he said. He waved around the room. "We'll all go, and I bet you anything Liz will come too. He held out his hand in the form of a gun. "She can help with the physical." He tapped his waist where Allen knew his phial was hidden beneath his T-shirt. "And we'll handle anything else."

"If you want, I can call Liz now," Allen said.

"Do it," Ristun replied.

"And I'm calling off work," Josh said.

"Really?" Rob said. "But we don't have anyone to backfill us again today."

"Don't care," Josh said. "I'll just close the store."

"We'll get fired!"

Josh pointed outside. "UFOs are getting shot down across the country. There are people from another world in our house. And, apparently, there are aliens out at Bear Mountain. I don't particularly care at the moment about getting fired!"

Rob nodded. "Excellent points." He clapped his hands, and his glasses slid down his nose. "This is so exciting! Even better than LOB!"

Josh whispered a curse while Ristun went over and patted Rob's back. "That's the spirit, kid."

"Shhh," Allen hushed them as he held his phone to his ear. "I'm calling Liz." He ran his hand through his dark, stringy hair as his phone established the connection. One ring. Two rings . . .

"Talk to me, Allen," Liz's voice said on the other end of the line.

Even in the current situation, Allen felt lighter at the sound of her voice. Maybe eventually, he'd get that date, but other things were more important at the moment. After he explained their plan while she listened intently, she told him to give her a few minutes. He waited.

"She's talking to someone," he whispered to the others as they watched him with anxious expressions.

Finally, she came back on and said, "I needed to check that Jason can cover for me today. He can, but we have some other things going on I needed to make sure he can handle. I'll be over in about ten minutes." She hung up.

"Wait," Rob said. "I just realized something." He peered around the room as if he held some sinister secret. "Only four of us can fit in Liz's truck."

"Oh, brother," Josh groaned, shaking his head. "It's a pickup. Some of us can sit in the back."

"Ah, I forgot about that." Rob's nervous expression was washed away by one of embarrassment.

"It was a reasonable concern," Ristun retorted. Rob's face brightened.

Josh ignored the comment and took off his name tag. "I'm going to change out of my work clothes." He pointed to Allen. "By the way, you should bring your gun. Otherwise, Liz is the only one with a weapon." He turned to Dralo and Ristun. "I mean, a physical weapon."

Rob's face flipped back to nervousness. "Why would we need a gun?"

"If we do encounter Greys," Dralo said, "they are only minimally deterred by our lights. Josh is right. If you have weapons, we should bring them."

Allen nodded. He kept an old Smith & Wesson handgun locked in a safe in his room at all times as a security precaution and for occasional target practice. He also thought it looked very Western, which made him feel cool.

Josh held his hand to his chin. "But that still means we only have two weapons."

The group went silent until Ristun noticed Rob with his hand sheepishly raised.

"This isn't a classroom," Ristun quipped. "You're one of us. What do you have to say?"

Rob nodded and put his hand down. "So I'm not in love with the idea of bringing weapons, but if we have to, why don't we ask Bill to go with us? He knows the area well, and I know he has a shotgun he likes to hunt with."

"That's a great idea!" Ristun added. "See, you got a lot to add, buddy!"

Rob smiled.

A few minutes later, an extremely eager Bill stood outside the front door. He wore an old, tattered cowboy hat with jeans and his usual well-worn jacket. A shotgun was slung over his shoulder, and a cigarette hung loosely from his mouth.

Allen opened the door and pointed at Bill. "Not bringing that in here," Allen said.

"The gun?" Bill said.

"No, the cigarette. You know I don't allow smoking in here. The smell drives me crazy."

"Oops, sorry about that, lad, forgot." He spit out the cigarette and stamped it on the ground. At the same time, Allen heard the sounds of a vehicle approaching and looked up. Liz's police truck rounded the corner and headed toward the house. "She's here!" he yelled into the living room. He patted the side of his waist, feeling for the holster with the Smith & Wesson he'd left exposed outside his shirt. She pulled into the driveway, and he approached the passenger door and climbed in.

Liz wore dark sunglasses with her blond hair pulled back into a ponytail. She looked at him and said, "I see you brought something with you."

Allen looked down at his waist and shrugged. "Well, you know, not sure what we might run into up there."

"Do you know how to use it?"

He nodded as confidently as he could.

She chuckled. "Alrighty, I'll take your word for it."

The truck shook, and Allen looked out the side mirror. Dralo and Ristun had jumped into the bed. Both were wearing dark sunglasses and hats. Ristun wore a ball cap with a hoodie, while Dralo wore an English cap with his usual sweater.

"No worry about accidental outfit matching for those two today," Liz smirked. Meanwhile, Josh and Rob got into the back seat while Allen watched Ristun help Bill into the truck bed.

"You all good back there?" Liz yelled out the window. Ristun banged the side of the truck a few times and offered a thumbs-up.

"Well then," she said, touching the panel for drive. "Let's get going." She turned out of the driveway and soon reached the main road leading through downtown. They passed the grocery store, then Old Cotton's, but as they approached the hospital, Allen saw not one but two ambulances parked at the emergency room entrance. The parking lot was also full, which he'd never seen before.

"What's going on there?" he asked.

"That's what I had to talk to Jason about. We've been getting a ton of calls about people falling ill all over the area, a lot like what happened to Tarin at Wall Drug." Her voice grew softer. "And what happened to me. The hospitals in other towns and Rapid City are starting to fill up too, so they're bringing people anywhere there's been room."

"When did it start?" Allen asked.

"I've been hearing some reports of a similar illness for a few weeks now, but just last night, after I got back from your place, I started getting a *lot* of reports." She sighed. "Let's just say I didn't get much sleep last night."

They reached the other end of town. Just before they pulled onto the ramp to Interstate 90 to head west toward Rapid City and Bear Mountain, two familiar white vans passed by them on the other side of the highway.

"Uh oh," Josh said.

"Uh oh indeed," Liz said, looking at the vans in her side mirror as they headed back toward Philip. "That's all we need. They're probably heading to the hospital to monitor the sick folks. They told me when Tarin was there that their agency was tracking the illness as it spread around the area. I better warn Jason to keep an eye on them as well." As she merged onto Interstate 90 and radioed in, Allen watched the large statue of a green dinosaur that stood guard outside of Wall approach. His mind drifted back to their misadventure when they'd seen the first agent a few days ago, and Tarin had had his strange episode. He felt a wave of unease as they passed by the small town, and he hoped the people back at the hospital would all be okay.

As they continued the drive, passing by mostly open, fallow grasslands interrupted by the occasional ripple of hills and sandy cliffs representing the boundaries of the badlands to their south, he continued to notice his memory of Arvalast slipping. What once was vivid, like a memory of a childhood home or a particularly good vacation, now felt more like a distant dream. He knew his life in Arvalast had happened, but it continued to feel less real.

There was a loud bang and a flash from somewhere behind them. In the side mirror, back toward Philip, a fire burned, and a cloud of smoke rose into the air. Above the fire, three tiny objects were darting about.

"What was that?" Josh yelled, frantically staring out the back window. The sound of fighter jets erupted just above them as four of them blazed their way toward the incident. "They're sending planes from Ellsworth Air Force Base!" Josh yelled.

Liz quickly pulled over onto the shoulder and parked the truck. They all got out. Dralo, Ristun, and Bill stood in the truck bed, looking into the distance. The planes became specks in the distant sky as they approached the plume of smoke. A few flashes followed.

"They're shooting at the UFOs!" Josh said.

A moment later, the other objects darted straight upward at speeds no regular aircraft, even military, would be capable of.

"We've got to get back there!" Liz said. "Whatever crashed can't be more than ten miles from Philip."

Sirens began to approach. Allen looked up the interstate and saw flashing red and blue lights approaching, heading back east. Soon, five, then ten, then twenty police cars and multiple fire engines rushed by.

"Get back in the truck!" Liz yelled as she rushed to the driver's seat.

"But what about Bear Mountain?" Rob asked as they all began to follow her.

"Change of plans," Liz said.

The radio on the dashboard began emitting loud static. Three intense beeps followed. "This is an emergency broadcast," a robotic voice said. Dralo, Ristun, and Bill came over, and everyone huddled around the front of the car as Liz got in and turned the radio up louder. Allen joined her in the passenger seat. A deep and distorted voice began to speak, but he couldn't understand what it was saying.

"What's . . . what's going on?" Rob's voice cracked as he looked around frantically.

Ristun put his hand on his shoulder. "Don't worry, buddy. It'll be okay. Let's just listen."

The voice continued to speak, then finally, became clear. "Citizens of the Peacekeeper nations. Your president, Silverton, has informed the

New Alliance that he believes the objects flying with impunity over your airspace are an effort from the Alliance to stoke fear and escalate the war within your most powerful territories, specifically, the United States of America. While we maintain our options—all options—to ultimately deter the continuation of the failed experiment of the Trinity Lattice through our military exercise in Europe, I am here to inform your population that the events in your skies are not an aggression by the Alliance. Our cities, and our countryside, too, are experiencing this phenomenon, and we are investigating. Do not accuse. Do not escalate. And we shall also have no need to accuse. And we shall have no need to escalate. It is imperative for the greater good, which is the mantra of our New Alliance, that steady hands prevail. Over time, we will again find our peace, not a Great Peace, but a real peace. And the destination of peace is achieved from one of two paths . . . time—or a global reset." The voice paused for multiple seconds before adding, "Let us choose the former."

The radio returned to static. Liz turned it down and looked over at Allen. He felt sweat dripping down his face. "Was that who I think it was?" Liz said.

Allen stared at the now silent radio. "Incognito," he whispered.

Bill pointed into the sky and yelled, "Look! There they are! They're right above us!"

All of them looked up. At the height of the clouds, three triangular crafts dropped from the atmosphere and hovered over their location. They appeared to be about the size of a car and, after briefly stopping, started to drift west along the interstate. Three circular blue lights glowed below each point of the triangle, and a larger, brighter yellow light shone at the craft's bottom, centered among the other lights.

The sound of military jets returned and started growing louder. Allen turned to see the four aircraft from earlier fast approaching, coming back around to take another pass at their targets.

The center light in each triangular craft began to shine brighter as if in response to their pursuers. Seconds later, the lights flashed three times rapidly. The crafts shot away like bullets to the northwest.

"Where did they go?" Rob yelled. His voice was quaking. His whole body was quaking.

Bill slung the shotgun he'd been holding out in front of him back over his shoulder. "They're going back to the mountain," he said. "I've been telling you—I've been seeing UFOs head that way the last number of weeks!" He pointed into the sky and waved his hand frantically. "Either those triangles or ones that look like saucers, at least one that looks like a cigar, and even a few that looked like white propane tanks from back in the day!" He ran over to the driver-side door and looked at Liz. "We gotta go to the mountain." He pointed back down the interstate toward Philip. "There's gotta be a hundred cops already heading that way. They can take care of things. But they can't take care of the source of what's going on." He looked at Dralo and Ristun, then back at Liz. "But we can. We can figure out what's happening and maybe do something to stop it."

"I think he's right, Liz," Ristun added. "We can do little back there that isn't already being done," Just then, the sunlight reflected off something white farther up the road. Allen felt a familiar unease begin to grow in his stomach. He placed his hand over his belly as not one, but a full caravan of white, unmarked vans began passing by and heading toward the crash scene.

"They're going to cover it up," Rob said, still standing next to Ristun. "Just like they were doing at the other crashes."

Liz turned to Allen. She looked down at his hand on his stomach and then focused on his eyes. "It's them, isn't it?" she asked.

His nausea grew so intense that he thought he might throw up. The final van passed, and his nausea disappeared as quickly as it had come. He put his hands on his knees, took a few deep breaths, and said, "Yes, and it was a lot of them."

"A lot of what?" Josh asked.

"Vulgheid," Ristun growled.

Liz grabbed the radio receiver. "Jason," she said. "Do you copy?"

Static.

"Jason, I said do you copy."

No response.

"We gotta go back," she said, putting on her sunglasses.

"Liz!" Bill said. "I'm telling you, there's nothing we can do back there. Let's go to the source. Let's go to Bear Mountain!"

"Get in the back, Bill, or I'll leave you here. You're free to walk to the mountain if you want."

Bill prepared to argue as Dralo took his shoulder. "We'll get there when it's time," Dralo said. "Let's stay together for now."

Bill tipped his hat forward and muttered a curse. "Fine," he said, "I guess after what I saw back at the ranch with those cows, I better not get cocky."

After everyone was back in the truck, Liz shot back onto the interstate, found the first flat area she could turn around, and then flew back toward the east. "Jason," she said again into the receiver.

Still no response.

"Jason, answer the call!" She waited a moment, cursed, and flung the receiver on the floor. "I shouldn't have left him," she said.

Allen remained stoic. But he grew increasingly nervous as they headed in the direction of those white vans. He knew he'd be useless in any confrontation if he got sick again. He looked down at his gun. Even that wouldn't help if he were curled into a ball, vomiting.

Up ahead, he began to hear sirens. As they crested a small hill, he saw a swarm of police cars stopped and blocking traffic. Ahead of the police, at least five white vans were parked in a line just beyond a barrier of orange cones. What looked like fifteen MJ12-2 agents stood near the edge of the road with binoculars and radios. In the distance, the crash continued to burn. A group of agents busily unloaded ATVs from the backs of the vans and began driving off toward the billowing smoke. Liz slowed and parked next to the other police vehicles. She got out of the truck and approached the orange cones and a group of police officers.

A cop with a state trooper hat approached and held out his hand. "Can't go any farther," he said.

"I'm the county sheriff," Liz said, pulling out her badge.

The cop stood in front of her to block her. "This area is now under federal control," he said. He gestured back toward the agents. "MJ12-2 has taken command of the area until we can secure the crash scene."

Liz stepped forward until she was almost nose-to-nose with the other cop. "You're going to let me through now," she said in almost a snarl. "I can't contact my deputy back in Philip and need to verify the town's security."

"It's handled," the cop replied.

"By who?"

The cop stood silently. Though trying to maintain his composure, Allen saw beads of sweat building up on his forehead and cheeks. The man glanced back toward the white vans and agents, then turned to Liz and said quietly, "I don't like this any more than you, but there's nothing I can do about it. These idiots have been slowly taking control of all the local and state agencies over the last week, and they basically have jurisdiction over the whole west of South Dakota and most of Wyoming now. If you want to go over there and try to convince them to let you pass, I'll stand aside, but I'd strongly recommend against it." His eyes flashed with fear. "I've seen bad things happen to people who've tried to get in their way."

Liz's shoulders relaxed. "Understood," she said. She looked back at Allen and the others. "Stay here. I'm going to talk to them."

"Liz!" Allen said as he rushed forward and took her arm. "Please don't go! You heard what he said." He dropped his voice to a harsh whisper. "I don't want you to get attacked again, like earlier."

She smiled. "Just keep an eye on me. And if anything goes wrong, send in your friends with their lights." Before Allen could argue further, Liz marched toward the nearest group of agents.

Allen watched, feeling angry and frustrated. He was so useless. He wanted to help, to just push past the dozen or so officers and rush to go with Liz to confront the agents, but he knew if he did, and if there were any shadows in the vicinity, he'd just double over and not only look like a fool but put Liz in even more danger.

As he stood feeling sorry for himself, a strong hand grabbed his shoulder, and a confident voice said, "Your girlfriend's brave, but she's also stupid." Allen looked up. It was Ristun.

"She's going to need wingmen," Ristun continued, "and you kinda need a wingman too." He slid a cool glass object into Allen's hand and said, "Walk with me."

"What do you mean?" Allen said as the glass grew warmer.

Ristun turned around, took off his sunglasses, and said, "Me and you, we're going to make sure nothing bad happens to her, got it? Now get over here and stay close. And if you drop my light, I'll kill you."

Allen nodded and hurried over to Ristun.

"We're with her," Ristun said as they passed by the first cop who'd stopped Liz earlier. He nodded and said, "Go ahead."

Most of the agents had driven off in their ATVs by now, other than a few still standing on the shoulder as they set up some sort of antenna. A moment later, they caught up to Liz. "What are you doing here?" she barked.

"We're your wingmen," Allen said, immediately feeling like a fool the moment he said it.

"What?"

"Just do what you came to do," Ristun told Liz, "and pretend we're not here."

She groaned. "Fine, but please keep quiet and let me do the talking."

She continued toward the agents near the antenna with her badge held out. "Hey!" she yelled. "Who's in charge here?"

The agents turned and stared blankly through dark blue sunglasses at Liz. All but one went back to work with the antenna. He stood momentarily, seemingly sizing them up, and walked over to meet them. Allen braced for his stomach to lurch, but to his surprise and delight, he felt fine, other than what he perceived to be regular nervousness about their current situation. He clutched onto Ristun's light tighter.

"Get back behind the barrier," the agent said flatly.

"I need to get through," Liz said, moving in closer to the man. He stood a good foot above her.

"I said get back to the barrier."

"Look," Liz said. "I don't want to cause trouble. But I can't reach my deputy in Philip, so I'm going to go back into town and ensure everything is secure. I won't interfere with your search for whatever was downed over there," she said, pointing at the smoke.

The agent lifted a radio to his lips and said, "Chief, the county sheriff is here. Please advise."

Allen's throat tightened at the mention of Chief.

A voice crackled on the other end, though Allen couldn't understand what it was saying. The man in the black leather jacket listened for a moment, then turned the device in their direction.

"Can you hear me, Liz?" the voice on the other side said. Allen immediately recognized it as that of the agent who'd monitored Tarin at the hospital.

"Yeah," she said. "Now tell your goons to let us through if you don't want me to cause trouble."

The receiver was silent for a few moments. "You were told not to meddle," Chief finally said.

Liz took a step forward and grabbed the receiver from the agent. He didn't flinch.

"Let . . . me . . . through," she ordered.

Allen waited for the response as his palm covered the phial in sweat. Next to him, he saw Ristun's shoulders grow tense. Then, another voice came over the line, "Liz," it said, "Liz, is that you?"

"Jason? Yes, it is. What's going on?"

"Liz, you gotta listen to them. You can't come to the town. We're under quarantine. Everyone's getting sick. They're saying everyone needs to stay inside. And that thing that crashed, it was just a few miles outside of town. They're telling me it's got something to do with all of this. You need to go."

"Jason, I'm not just going to stand here and leave you to deal with all of this on your own. I'm going to come and help secure the town."

"Liz," the voice said pleadingly. "You . . . can't come."

Chief's voice returned and said, "I'll help you a bit more with your decision. You either go back the direction you came," his voice began to morph into an animal-like snarl, "or your deputy will experience one hundred times the pain you felt back at the ranch!"

The receiver went dead, and Liz reached for her gun. At that moment, the agent pulled off his sunglasses to reveal two blazing, yellow-slitted eyes. Allen felt the phial grow from warm to hot, and before he could react, Ristun snatched it from his hand and said, "*Seru!*"

The agent stumbled backward and put his sunglasses back on. The yellow pupils now appeared dark, almost normal. At the same moment, Allen's stomach lurched in pain, and he doubled over. "Back to the truck, now!" Ristun said.

He grabbed Allen by the hand as Liz fired a shot at the agent. The man stumbled backward a few feet, then fell to the ground. "Liz!" Ristun said. "Back to the truck, or I can't help you!"

She cursed and joined them. Allen then felt her arm under his shoulder as she also helped hurry him back in the other direction. He heard footsteps running after them as they drew farther from the white vans. "They're following!" Allen yelled, looking behind them.

"What did you think they would do after your girlfriend shot at them?" Ristun yelled. He still held his light in his free hand, trying to keep it focused on the agents.

As they approached the barricade, the cops stood blocking them, guns drawn. "Oh, come on!" Ristun yelled and stopped.

Then, the first cop stepped forward and said, "Go! We'll cover for you."

"What?" Liz said.

"Just go!" he ordered, then pointed his gun toward the agent. "Stand down!" he demanded. "Or we'll fire!"

Ristun and Liz looked at each other as Allen dry heaved and said, "I'd really like to get farther away if we could." Ristun slid his light back into his hand. Allen felt a jolt of energy and stood up straight.

"Let's go," Ristun said, and without asking any more questions, they rushed past the line of cops now defending them and toward a confused and nervous-looking Dralo, Bill, Josh, and Rob.

Josh rushed to meet them. "We heard a gunshot!" he yelled. "Then saw the cops mobilizing. What's happening?"

"Just get in the truck!" Liz said as she bolted toward the driver's seat. "We need to get to Bear Mountain!"

"Wait, what? You're changing plans again!"

"I'm having an indecisive day!" she yelled. "Now shut up and get in the vehicle!" She slid behind the wheel and worked to catch her breath as she put it in reverse and waited until everyone was back in. She turned around on the shoulder and crossed the grass barrier between the east- and westbound lanes. Allen saw a long line of cars backing up from the blockade where they'd been parked, then heard the pop, pop, pop of gunshots.

"Why'd they change their minds and decide to help us?" Allen asked Liz as she stared down the road in front of them.

"The agents must have unblocked the frequency back to Philip when they got Jason on the line. Any police scanner would have been able to hear what we heard." She pushed down harder on the accelerator, and the truck gained speed. "Now, the only way I can help Jason and Philip is to see if you guys were right about Bear Mountain."

The fields and rolling hills passed like a blur until they reached the outskirts of Rapid City. They flew through its northern end, Liz darting from lane to lane with her lights and siren on as she dodged traffic and maintained speed until Interstate 90 turned north around the Black Hills and toward Sturgis. Just before reaching Sturgis, as the noon November sun began to drop in the sky toward afternoon and grey clouds painted over the previously blue sky, Liz took an exit. The dull brown peak of Bear Mountain began rising in front of them.

CHAPTER 26

They'd already walked two hours through dense brush, then to a mostly overgrown path, then finally to a wider dirt trail. Jak walked out ahead of Ella and Abigail, carrying a knife and shouldering a bow.

Ella also carried a bow as she held her phial of light in her right hand. That night, she and Jak had each taken a three-hour shift to listen and watch for Drilockk. Much to their relief, the horn calls had led to no attack on the cabin, though Abigail still slept fitfully. Although she'd volunteered to take a shift keeping watch, Jak and Ella insisted she rest before their long walk at dawn. She thought they might also not have wanted to risk anything odd happening with her unpredictable new light.

Just before the sun rose, they began their journey. Jak had packed light loads with enough food and water to last about three days. He also noted they could hunt if needed, and there'd be plenty of water to gather from springs and creeks.

As they continued their journey, little could be heard except for their soft footfalls against the matted leaves on the otherwise dirt path.

"Are we going in the direction of the tower?" Abigail asked.

"Yes," said Ella. "Our meeting place at Kettle Falls is northwest of our cottage. From Kettle Falls, it is another three hours' journey to the tower."

"And Woodend? How close will it be when we reach the falls?"

"It is a full day's walk north."

Jak kicked a stick off the path as he continued ahead of them. "We sometimes hunt in this region," he said. "There are plentiful deer and bear, and it is rare to see any attack on travelers as we're still far from the primary forest roadway that we'd need to take to Woodend or any of the other forest towns and cities farther south. Other than that roadway, there are only trails like this scattered throughout the area."

"But attacks are not unheard of," Ella interjected. "Last year, we uncovered the body of one of our community, a young man who'd gone hunting alone not far from here. He had an arrow in his back and had been searched for valuables."

Abigail felt a tingle of fear as she glanced around, hoping not to catch sight of any enemy, whatever that enemy might be. But as they continued, and the trees around them began to grow thinner and shorter, nothing eventful happened.

After another thirty minutes of wordless travel, Jak stopped and peered into the brush to his right. "What is it?" Ella asked.

"One moment, he said, I think I see something interesting."

Ella sighed and looked at Abigail with her eyebrows raised. "Forgive him," she said, "he can be easily distracted."

Jak pushed through a short thicket and, a few minutes later, returned with an old, rusty axe. "A relic of when this place was a lumber camp," he said. "See how the trees are all young? Much of this area was forested. In my youth, I was a lumberjack. We'd travel from Woodend and harvest large swaths of timber for months, then, once depleted, we'd leave the area to regrow and find another quarry. Someone must have forgotten this." He smiled. "Now it's mine."

"But the handle is rotten," Ella said. And don't you already have three axes at home?"

"I do," Jak said, "and now I will have four."

They heard the crunching of footfalls behind them. Jak and Ella each pulled out their bows and stepped in front of Abigail.

"Stay behind us," Ella whispered.

Two figures wearing brown cloaks with hoods hanging behind their heads appeared from around a bend down the trail. One was a man with a predominantly grey beard below a thick head of slightly darker hair. Next to him stood a tall and sturdy woman, her silver hair draped along her shoulders as she carried a bow in one hand and a phial similar to Ella's in the other.

Jak and Ella lowered their bows. "Raulin! Rosie!" Jak said and rushed toward the newcomers.

A broad smile spread over Ella's face. She turned to Abigail. "Come," she said. "Come meet our friends."

Abigail felt a rush of excitement mixed with shyness. The man and the woman gave off a sense of regality, though Abigail couldn't tell if she perceived this because of the assumed wisdom from their years or because of how they stood, shoulders back, chins lifted, confident but not condescending. Either way, both were smiling, and they seemed friendly.

When Abigail grew close enough, the woman, whom Jak had called Rosie, looked at her. "And who is this lovely newcomer to our forest?"

"Her name is Abigail," Ella responded.

Rosie and the man, Raulin, bowed slightly.

"And where have you come from?" Raulin asked. "One of the forest towns, perhaps from the lands to the south, maybe Macalum?"

"Her skin is too light to be from the southern regions," Rosie said. "She must be from the forest or distant north."

Before Abigail could attempt an answer, Ella said, "She is from none of those places."

"Then where could she be from?" Raulin said. The lines under his eyes stretched as they gazed at Abigail with growing curiosity. "Wait," he said. He turned to Ella. "You aren't suggesting that . . ."

"I am," Ella replied. She pointed into the woods and said, "It's as the *Annals* have foretold that sometime in the future, others from distant worlds will be able to finally enter here. Just as it is said in times of old, those from Arvalast could journey beyond this land. We believe she is from the world that . . . that we think Tarin was lost to after Woodend fell."

"Shieth?" said Rosie.

"No," replied Ella. "At least, not that we believe. She calls her world Earth."

All stood silent for what felt to Abigail an uncomfortable amount of time. All of them were looking at her. She was starting to feel the urge to temporarily excuse herself into the forest to hide from their stares when Rosie said, "Dear, do you recall . . . how you got here?"

Abigail looked at Jak and Ella nervously, then said to Rosie. "In my world, I . . . I was ill." She hesitated, cleared her throat, and said, "I didn't get better. After that, my next memory, or perhaps my first memory, was waking up here in a meadow at night." She felt odd sharing this. Even here, it couldn't be normal for people to die and wake up in other worlds, but she desperately wanted to move the conversation forward and no longer be the center of attention. As she reflected on the strangeness of her situation, a vision of her little brother and sister filled her memory with such detail that it seemed they were actually bounding across the path just behind Rosie and Raulin.

She attempted to reach out to them when Raulin said, "I had always interpreted those stories as more legend than fact. But the *Annals* do indeed speak of movement between worlds."

Abigail's siblings seemed to disappear as if they were mist. Her heart sank.

"I think we are now seeing evidence these stories were not just legends," Jak said. "In addition, she's been seeing Tarin in places familiar to her from her world, such as a place called"—he turned to Abigail—"what did you call it again?"

"Wall Drug," she responded, remembering one of her first visions of Tarin, even as she peered longingly at the location where her siblings had disappeared.

"Yes," Jak said, "the Wall Drug trading post. And he appears to be in danger. Also, the Drilockk seem to have taken an interest in Abigail.

One attacked her the first night she arrived at the meadow northwest of our cottage. Ella and I were scouting the area after Gildareth's long absence and arrived just in time to drive it away from her. Then, yesterday, another came for her."

"We were also attacked by Vulgheid," Ella said. She pointed to Abigail's light. "She found this in the woods just before they came. It has some connection to her world and the evil there that is stalking Tarin. It shone crimson when the Vulgheid attacked, and Abigail saw Tarin next to a monster."

"The light shone crimson?" Rosie whispered. "Then we must be wary of this light. If it has some connection to the darkness, it could be dangerous."

Jak stepped forward and pointed at the pouch on Abigail's belt that held her phial. "She has since connected to it, or perhaps, it to her, and she has proven her ability to withstand any attacks from the darkness." His voice lowered. "She speaks the ancient tongue."

Raulin and Rosie stood silent and looked astonished. Abigail began to feel her cheeks grow hot. How she disliked being the center of attention. Rosie reached out her hand. "May I see it?" she said.

Abigail glanced down at her waist and said, "My light?"

"Yes, my dear, though we also call it an illumina, which is its proper name. But you may call it either."

Abigail pulled it from her pouch and slowly held it toward Rosie's outstretched hand. It felt warm and exuded an energy that almost seemed as if it were excited. As Rosie's hand wrapped around it, it shimmered more brightly. Rosie took in a fast breath as if she'd just jumped into cold water. Her eyes closed. "I see someone," she said. "It's a boy."

"Is it Tarin?" Ella said, moving closer.

"No," Rosie replied. She opened her eyes. "Where did you find this, Abigail?"

"In a pine grove toward the mountains from the hill near Jak and Ella's cottage."

"So you found it in the woods," Rosie said. She looked at Ella. "The boy I saw, his face, it looked like that of Sarky. It has, or had, a connection to him."

"Sarky!" Jak exclaimed. "We thought he'd been killed! We found his bloody and torn jacket after he ran after Tarin at the Battle of Woodend. Are you saying this could have been his illumina?"

"I am," said Rosie. "Though if he lives or not, I'm not certain."

"Who is Sarky?" Abigail interrupted.

"He was Tarin's closest friend," Jak answered. "We had thought that together, they might be the ones capable of driving the shadows from Woodend."

Raulin crossed his arms. "Jak, Ella," he said sternly, "when we heard your call, the three horn blasts, that was the signal indicating increased Drilockk aggression and the need to assemble to determine how to drive them back. But I sense the call may have had additional meaning."

Ella and Jak looked at each other. Then Ella pointed into the woods and said, "We want to go to the tower and see if we can bring Tarin back."

The forest sounds seemed to grow louder as Raulin and Rosie fell silent. Up to this point, the meeting had been friendly, despite the brief concern about her phial. But now, the atmosphere was different, like something had captured their breath. Finally, Rosie broke the silence. "No one goes to the tower. It is forbidden."

"Gildareth went," Jak interjected.

"Gildareth was a fool," Raulin said, his fists tightening. "Let's not forget who told the boys they were warriors, giving them false hope they could lead battalions of soldiers into battles. His trust in them was proven misguided at Woodend."

Rosie's face had grown sad.

"And where are the boys now?" Raulin continued. "Where is the 'Hope of the Forest'? Where is the 'Redemption of Arvalast'? Where are the warriors Gildareth claimed had finally emerged from the pages of the *Annals of Illuminara* to restore peace to the land?"

Ella pointed at Abigail. "Tarin, at least, is where she came from! And he is alive." She reached for and took Rosie's hands in hers. "Your husband did not die in vain. There's still hope." She pointed at Abigail's light. "We can bring Tarin back."

Rosie stood silently as a single tear slid down her cheek and dropped onto Ella's illumina. Abigail watched as it seemed to be absorbed into the gently glowing glass.

"The others will be angry you brought them to council for this," Rosie said. "They will believe, as we did, you intended to organize a resistance against the Drilockk."

"That's exactly what we're doing," Ella said, "and more. What good is it for us to simply drive them away when we could bring back Tarin and restore hope to the forest? Rosie, we could avenge your husband. And we can avenge the governor, his family, and all those the tyrant killed. We could take back Woodend!"

"The others won't have it!" Raulin said.

"Don't assume that!" Jak said, angry for the first time Abigail could remember outside of a confrontation with Drilockk or Vulgheid. "I speak to them when we trade. I sense a repressed anger in many, and all they need is hope. Now we have it." He placed his hand on Abigail's shoulder. "We have her."

Abigail hastily withdrew. She'd been growing increasingly anxious as she began to understand more about Tarin and what he'd been to these people. "I'm no one," she said.

"Not true!" Jak said. "You are from another world. You wield an illumina not your own, but it still claimed you. You've battled Drilockk and some beast inside the crimson light. And, somehow, you are connected to Tarin. You are here as a sign, for a reason." He spread out his arms toward the treetops above them. "You're here to restore hope to our forest and to our world."

"This is all . . . it's all a bit much," Abigail said. She noticed Rosie staring at her with a small smile on her face.

"Perhaps we should, at least, talk to the others," Rosie said to Raulin.

Raulin frowned. "You know they aren't going to entertain the idea of storming the tower."

"But they may," she said. "Her light, her aura, there's something different about it. Let's follow Jak's intuition on this. The next step, either toward the tower or back home, will be clear after we meet with the others."

Jak and Ella watched Raulin with eager expressions.

"Very well," Raulin said after a long pause. "Let's go to Kettle Falls and have our council." He put his hands on his waist. "But if the others are unwilling to go to the tower, we leave the matter be. Agreed?"

Ella looked as if she was about to argue when Jak quickly said, "Very well." He shot a knowing glance at Ella. Abigail knew what it meant. They would go to the tower regardless of what the rest of the company decided. But she now wondered, would she have the courage to join them? She put her light, or illumina, back into its pouch, allowing its warmth to bring her a momentary comfort as Jak said, "Let's be off!"

CHAPTER 27

In the rearview mirror, Tarin stared at the empty back seat and the backside of the "Welcome to Indiana" sign as it drifted into the distance. It had been four hours since they'd left East Fairfield that morning, and the noon sun now shimmered above the windshield. Tarin had argued with Gil that they should find Iris before they left town, but somehow, Gil knew she was gone and told Tarin to let the matter be. "She will be well," he'd said, "and time is of the essence. While you were still sleeping, I sensed something through my light, and I saw a vision of a growing shadow spreading like an outstretched hand toward the plains of South Dakota from the place I first arrived—the Sacred Basin, as your friend's grandfather called it."

"Is it Maximus?" Tarin had inquired.

"I am not certain."

Gil had earlier tried to contact Dralo and Ristun to learn more. But something was hindering the connection. And it wasn't just Gil's light that seemed to be malfunctioning. Tarin also couldn't contact Allen or anyone else in Philip on his phone.

At the hotel, they'd eaten a quick breakfast in the lobby before leaving. As they did, Tarin wondered if he would ever see his hometown again. The thought made him feel sad, which he found surprising. What could a place full of so many terrible memories offer him? But then again, this time, he was not running from pain—rather, he'd left behind a happy memory of one last drive with his father and a healed relationship with a friend.

Tarin put music on the radio as he drove into Indiana and prepared for the two hours of primarily mindless driving until Chicago. From there, they'd head north into Wisconsin, then back west to South Dakota. As the melodies played, Tarin allowed his thoughts to drift toward images of the family road trips he loved. Out of the corner of his eye, he saw Gil gently tapping the door to the beat of the music.

"Do you like it?" Tarin asked.

Gil continued tapping. "The music?"

"Yes."

"I will admit, I at first found the style of your earthly tunes somewhat jarring, more rhythm than melody, lacking nuance, and primarily a limited sequence of chords held together by a few threads of miscellaneous stringed instruments. But pushing aside this critique, I now find this music to have an odd sense of charm."

"I grew up on this stuff," Tarin said. "It's called country. I agree. There's not much to it. Lots of folks hate it. But I find it a nice distraction from my usual thoughts." He paused a moment. "Iris likes this music too."

Gil stopped tapping and looked at him. "I know," he said.

After a long pause, Tarin continued, "It's my fault she's gone. She opened up to me . . . about my mom. I think I knew, you know, that Iris was somehow involved. But hearing it from her directly . . . Gil, I know she could tell how angry I was, and when she walked away, even apologized . . . I didn't say anything."

"She had told me about her involvement with your parents," Gil said. "When we were at the barn after the incident at the airport. I knew it would be hard for you both, but I told her she should share it with you when she was ready. She was aware of the risks. But please know this, there is no distance, even between worlds, that would break a Glorion's loyalty to those to whom they choose to give it. She will always love you. It is embedded within her."

Tarin tightened his hands on the wheel, then relaxed them. "I hope I have the opportunity to speak to her again. It hurts Gil, that she . . . didn't protect my mother when she had the chance. But at the same time, I understand why she did what she did." Tarin's eyes narrowed. He saw the rain beating down on his mother's face just before she'd died. A figure stood over her, blowing a plume of smoke from his snarling mouth. In the end, it was not Iris but that monster who'd killed his mother. Tarin considered the phial in his pocket. At least now, perhaps, he had a weapon he could use against that beast.

They drove on until they reached a rest stop just outside of Chicago. "We better stop here in case we get stuck in traffic," Tarin said. He was also hungry and wanted a quick snack. At a vending machine, he started to hear a commotion behind him. A family was staring at their phones. What looked to be the mother repeated over and over, "What's going on?"

One of her three teenage daughters then said, "I think we should cancel our trip."

Tarin grabbed his candy bar from the vending machine as he saw Gil emerge from the restroom. Gil approached the family. "Is there something wrong?" he asked.

"Shhh," the mother said, turning up the volume on her phone. Now, Tarin could hear it too: an almost robotic voice, speaking stoically. "Our cities, and our countryside, too, are experiencing this phenomenon and we are investigating. Do not accuse. Do not escalate. And we shall also have no need to accuse. And we shall have no need to escalate." It followed with something about the "greater good" and a "real peace."

"That's Incognito!" one of the teenage girls yelled. "He's going to blow us up because of those UFOs! You know, the ones we've seen on the news? And I swear I saw one yesterday while we drove across Pennsylvania!"

"He's not going to blow us up," the father, who'd been quiet up to this time, said. "He was saying that as long as we don't accuse the Alliance of sending the UFOs, he's not going to retaliate."

"Silverton's an idiot!" the mother said. "You heard he's already accusing the Alliance of sending those things. He's going to get us all killed. We are not driving through Chicago! It will be one of the first places attacked if something happens."

"If there are nukes dropped, Mom, it won't matter where we are," one of the other three girls said matter-of-factly. "There's something called fallout. It'd be better for us to just die in the blast."

"Shut up, Fern, you nihilist!" the first girl said. "Mom, I don't want to go to Chicago either."

She and her mother then argued with the father as Fern glanced at Tarin. He'd not realized it, but at some point, he must have put his hand in his pocket, fidgeted with his light, then taken it out. It now hung loosely in his hand as its gentle light shimmered against the floor.

"What's that?" the girl asked without emotion.

Her mother looked over and let out a short scream. She grabbed her husband and one of her daughter's hands. "Let's go, now!" With that, they hurried past Tarin, each casting either angry, concerned, or in Fern's case, confused looks at him while careful to maintain a reasonable distance. They continued arguing their way to their car. "First UFOs and now magicians!" the mother said. "What's next?" The car door slammed.

Gil stood where he was, staring with approval at Tarin's phial. "I see you found not only your phial but also the light. And it does not appear to bring you any fear."

Tarin glanced down at it, then put it away. He shrugged and opened his candy bar. "I guess you're right. Though it seemed to scare them."

"They were already in a heightened state of anxiety from what they had just heard. It had little to do with your light. We should continue our journey. The darkness also knows you have found your light and will do anything to manipulate and hasten their agenda to limit any possible interference from you."

Tarin considered Gil's words. Although he knew he was apparently critical to his friends' safety, was Gil now implying there was even more at stake? He thought back to his dreams of the battle in Arvalast. Why had he been involved in it in the first place? He recalled his encounter with Maximus and then with the chief agent. Both had a keen interest in him. Why? And it wasn't just those with seemingly malevolent intent who'd taken notice of him. Iris had spent years watching over him. Dralo, Ristun, and Gil himself had also stressed his importance.

They returned to the car. Tarin was reaching for the button to turn it on when he paused. "Gil," he said. "Who am I, and what exactly are you expecting from me?"

Gil's eyes pooled with deep reflection. He then took out his light and held it in his hand. "If you are ready, I can show you."

Tarin's heart raced. Flashbacks to his dreams of the battle, the melody, the jeering, and the shame, poured through his mind. Is that what he would witness? But his resolve to learn more muted his anxieties. Before he could change his mind, he reached for and placed his hand on Gil's light.

Instantly, his mind went dark. After what felt like anywhere between minutes and hours, he saw a glow in the distance. It grew brighter. He focused on it. A crimson light shone in the center of what looked to be a grassy meadow surrounded by trees. It was night. The air was cool but not cold. There were voices. Many voices.

A woman screamed.

Tarin spun toward the sound and saw a girl with long black hair, probably in her late teens. She stood with her hands bound to a wooden pole on a pedestal in the meadow's center. A young, dark-haired man with a light beard stood next to her, his hands also bound. Like the girl, he appeared in his late teens or maybe early twenties. His arms were bare and full of lean muscle.

As the scene continued to come into focus, the crimson light cast an eerie glow across the otherwise dark grass. Tarin realized a hooded man was holding a shining red phial. He was near the captives on the pedestal, weaving back and forth and chanting in a language Tarin didn't recognize. As he did, Tarin stared at the girl. She looked so familiar. A name seemed to be trying to find its way into his memory, near the tip of his tongue, but couldn't break through. Was he in Arvalast? If so, this was not the battle he'd been expecting to see.

The captives struggled and tried to break their bonds. But they were made of thick rope. It would be no use. The hooded man called out. "Come and take your quarry, beast, from the unexplored lands!" The man threw back his hooded cloak and thrust his hands into the air. He had dark skin and was bald. His eyes flashed with both passion and terror. "Take them! Take them and trouble us no more!"

Other voices joined in. The vision continued to feel more like reality than a dream. Tarin saw a small crowd to his left standing huddled between the pedestal and the forest's edge. There were perhaps thirty people: men, women, and some children, all dressed in loose-fitting garments of muted browns and greys. Some clothes were tattered and others were more intact, but all indicated a lack of wealth.

"Take them! Take them!" they chanted in unison. The children frantically clung to the adults, staring into the sky and pointing.

"Will it come?" one of them cried. But no one answered.

"What are we going to do?" someone screamed from Tarin's side. He jolted and looked over. It was Allen! Or wait, was his name Sarky? He was far younger than he recalled from Earth, a place that was now feeling more like a dream as this reality continued to come into focus. He was still just a boy, perhaps twelve. Tarin realized something. He felt his face. No stubble. He looked at his arms and legs. They were short but still gangly.

Then, like lightning, his memory of this event returned. He turned to the crowd. They were the villagers of Northlake, a small forest town he and Sarky had been trying to help. A great animal, or more a monster, had been stalking their village and killing their people. Tarin had tried to convince them that with the light, his illumina, he now recalled, they might be able to hold it at bay until his friend Gildareth could come. But they were instead convinced by their chief, a man named Sayin, the man with the crimson light, that a sacrifice was the only way to appease the beast. The village had turned against Tarin and Sarky, but not just them. Tarin's sister and her friend Jak had also been trying to help. Because his sister and Jak were the right age for the sacrifice, Sayin claimed, they had been chosen, bound, and dragged to this place for the ceremony.

Despite all of this, Tarin found himself briefly staring in amazement at the girl with dark hair. He now remembered her name. Ella. She was his sister. Part of him felt elated. His memory of sadness on Earth from being without family hadn't completely faded, so this revelation was profound. But wait. She was tied to a pole and about to be devoured by some creature! How did this scene end? He couldn't recall. He began to panic.

"Ella!" he screamed. She looked over. As their eyes met, he could feel her love for him and her sadness as he realized she was beginning to accept her fate.

Sarky grabbed and shook his arm. "Do something!"

"I don't know what to do!" Tarin screamed as panic seized him. A long, slow roar swirled down into the meadow. Tarin frantically looked up into the starless sky as the villagers erupted into screams followed by more chants.

"Take them! Take them!"

"Help! Help us!" Tarin yelled frantically. To who or what, he didn't know. But he didn't know what else to do. "Help! Please!"

A figure emerged from the trees on the far side of the meadow, on the opposite side of the crowd. It was humanlike, glowing, and beautiful. It seemed to exist more as an essence than a physical being. Dark eyes opened in its shimmering face and looked at Tarin. At first, they seemed pleased, but then they narrowed and Tarin felt as if an arrow of hate had embedded itself in his chest. Tarin realized this newcomer was no savior. But it couldn't be the animal the villagers were trying to appease. Could it?

The man with the crimson light took notice and immediately fell flat on his face. "My lord!" he cried out. Tarin frantically looked around.

The crowd continued chanting as if they hadn't noticed the shining figure adjacent to them. But Sarky had. He was quaking, speechless, and staring at it. Then, he fell to his knees and started gagging. "It's one of them," he sputtered. "It's a Vulgheid, and a strong one!"

The figure moved slowly toward the center of the meadow. Tarin could now see glowing, kingly robes hanging from its shoulders and glimmering over diamond armor. Its face, though humanlike, shone so brightly that distinct features were impossible to make out, other than the two small dark abysses that made up its eyes. They seemed like bottomless pits of malice as they continued to stare at Tarin. It moved—or rather, floated—until it took up a position next to Sayin, who was still lying prostrate. The crimson light shook in Sayin's hand, making the meadow seem like it was amid an earthquake. Finally, the entity released its gaze from Tarin and touched Sayin's back. Sayin shrieked, dropped his light, and turned to one side, writhing as if in great pain.

The entity then began to change form. Its glow darkened, and its body altered to appear more like smoke. As it did, it leaned toward Sayin and began reaching its long, thin, wispy fingers toward his head. "I see the doubt in you," it said in a deep, hissing whisper. "This sacrifice pains you."

"Not true!" Sayin screamed. "It's not true! I do this with full confidence! I am following the decrees from the parchments you and your servants gave me!"

The entity snarled and stuck its hand deep into Sayin's head as if it were not solid. Sayin began to scream. It was horrible to listen to. Tarin covered his ears. But then there was a roar that even covered ears could not diminish. It sounded like a lion, deep and guttural but far more powerful.

"It's here!" someone in the crowd shouted.

"Take them! Take them!" the villagers erupted in unison. Ella and Jak furiously tried to break their bonds as they stared into the sky, searching frantically for the source of the roar.

The smoky entity lifted its hand from Sayin's limp figure and turned toward Tarin. Like a fog in the wind, it drifted along the ground until it stood directly in front of him and Sarky. Sarky, still on the ground and still clutching his stomach, vomited. All fell silent.

The shadow began to morph back into the glowing figure from earlier. Its infinite, deep black eyes looked at Tarin with rage. It was then Tarin noticed two yellow slits swimming inside. "So this is the boy Gildareth believes to be one of the warriors of prophecy." It reached its hand toward Tarin's head.

Tarin, now paralyzed with fear, realized his world was coming to an end. Slowly, the creature's hand slipped into Tarin's head, and though it pierced no bone or flesh, he felt as if his mind was being torn into pieces. Horrendous images filled his mind. A city was burning, and in the fire, three figures hung from nooses, though a fourth noose hung empty. Then he saw a series of tremendous explosions and mushroom clouds billowing into the air as the voices of a million terrified souls screamed and then fell silent. He felt his knees give out as he collapsed to the ground, but the beast did not release its grip. Tarin lost the will to live and silently pleaded for his soul to be taken from him.

But as his pain and hopelessness reached their climax, he heard music. Was it a violin? And a drum? He didn't know, but it gave him something to cling to besides the intense pain in his mind. Instinctively, he reached for his waist and wrapped his hand around a warm glass object. He pulled it out and pushed it against the figure's arm. Instantly, all his memories from Earth returned to him. "Gil!" he yelled. "Help me!"

The phantom ripped its arm from Tarin and shrieked in agony. Tarin stumbled back a few steps. A moment later, he heard a loud thud. Everyone, including the entity, looked over toward the trees at the far side of the meadow.

"It's here," a man in the crowd said. "No one move! Remember what the parchments say. Stay still. The beast will take the sacrifice and leave us and our town be."

A massive, hairy monster, like a bear the size of a house with batlike wings and the fangs of a tiger, lifted its enormous head into the air and roared.

"Bostt," Tarin whispered, remembering the creature on the card from Legendarium of Beasts. But before he could consider this more, the animal reached for a nearby tree, picked it up as if it were picking up a weed, and then threw it at the crowd. People scattered. But it struck many. They lay on the ground under its boughs, motionless.

The glowing entity still in front of Tarin looked at him. Fury blazed in its eyes. Again, it began morphing back to its shadow form. It rose a few inches from the ground and moved toward the Bostt. The villagers ran and screamed toward the edge of the forest, while a few tried to help those struck by the tree. But Tarin's focus was on the shadow. Finally, it reached the monster and disappeared inside of it.

The creature snorted, closed its eyes in what almost seemed a grimace, then weaved from side to side as if it might fall over. But before it fell, it steadied itself and opened its eyes. They were now glowing with a hideous yellow light. It began to beat its wings. A wind blew through the meadow. Tarin looked over at the pedestal. Ella's hair blew wildly, and some of the villagers were knocked from their feet. The beast's eyes darted toward the pole. It fell to all fours and began to run toward it, aided by the thrusts of its wings. Ella and Jak both screamed.

"No!" Tarin yelled and ran toward them.

His eyes met Ella's. A strange fury and power—something he'd never felt before—surged in him, starting near his heart, then coursing through his body and into his arms and legs. He lifted his illumina and stared directly into the yellow eyes of the monster. "Edin Na Zu Alla Xul!"

His light flashed with an intensity greater than lightning. It struck the monster and cast it back. The ground shuddered as it landed and lay on the grass. He heard the sound of a galloping horse as a figure holding a brilliant sword emerged from one side of the meadow and charged toward the beast.

All went dark. He felt a falling sensation. He screamed. A moment later, he landed back in the driver's seat of Allen's car. He swiveled his head back and forth frantically. "Where am I? What's going on?"

A hand touched him. A man was sitting next to him. Tarin rubbed his eyes. It was Gil.

"Did you see the battle?" Gil said slowly.

Tarin took a moment to catch his breath. "Yes," he finally sputtered, "but that wasn't the battle I remember." He frantically felt for the phial in his pocket. It was still there. He grabbed it and a wave of calm came over him as his heart rate slowed. "I've never seen this battle before. This one . . . this one I won."

"A warrior's journey is met with many battles," Gil said. Tarin noticed Gil's hand still held his own phial. "Some end in victory. Some end in defeat. Both make the warrior stronger."

Tarin rubbed his hand over his now sweaty hair. "Warrior?" Tarin said. He remembered what the entity in the vision had said. *So this is the boy Gildareth believes to be one of the warriors of prophecy.* "Do you think I'm some sort of chosen warrior?"

"I wouldn't use the word 'chosen,'" Gil said. "It is more that one is something, and one is not something, and I believe you *are* a warrior. That is why I came here. To find you . . . and to bring you back to Arvalast." Gil then grew tense. "Wait," he said, leaning forward toward the windshield. He pointed, "Do you see those?"

Tarin looked to where he was pointing, and in the sky, three triangular objects moved at incredible speed toward the west. Moments later, military jets followed in fast pursuit.

Tarin groaned. "Wonderful, now the UFOs are back. Can't I just process one thing at a time?"

Gil leaned back in his seat and looked at Tarin. "Perhaps you are only processing one thing at a time. These may be more linked to what you just saw than I originally thought." He looked at Tarin. "You have become deeply connected to both worlds, Earth and Arvalast. And the shadows from both, I believe, are realizing who you actually are. We must hurry back to South Dakota."

Tarin thought back to the danger his friends were in and nodded. Though he wanted more time to reflect on the events of the last . . . how long had it been? Ten minutes? An hour? He knew they needed to press on. Still, there was one thing he wanted to learn more about.

"I saw an entity," he said to Gil as he backed out of the parking space. "It felt similar to Maximus and gave me visions of terrible scenes from my dream of the battle, the one I lost. It also gave me images of events here, of mushroom clouds and people dying." He maneuvered onto the on-ramp leading back to the highway. "Are there more things like Maximus out there?"

Gil kept his eyes trained on the sky. "There are powerful manifestations of darkness in all worlds, Tarin. Each has its own specific intent for that world as well as an overwhelming desire to be master of all worlds. I believe Maximus to be that which believes itself to be greatest here, or wishes to be greatest. The entity you saw in Arvalast, in the vision, was chief among many vying for power there but was not the greatest."

"Who is the greatest in Arvalast?" Tarin asked, though he wasn't sure he wanted to know.

"I will not speak his true name, even here. But he is the master of all shadows across all worlds. He is the originator of the darkness, the first to break from the light. He is the dissonance within the melody and the chaos within the order. And he, my friend, is why I need you back in Arvalast."

Tarin sped up to match the flow of traffic. "So this whole time, your plan has been to have me get back to Arvalast to deal with some ulti-mate shadow leader to save the world?"

"No," Gil said. "To save all worlds."

"All worlds! How many are there?"

"Many."

"More than Earth and Arvalast?"

"Yes, many more."

"You've got to be kidding me."

Gil looked at Tarin and smiled. "Do not worry. You will not be doing it alone."

"What do you mean?"

"You shall have help. There are others tied to this destiny."

"Who are they?"

"I am not sure yet."

"When will you be sure?"

"Tarin," Gil said softly. "We are getting ahead of ourselves. More will make sense with time. But for now, this journey is as much mine as yours. And it is as much yours as all who live or have ever lived." He pointed to the radio. "Might I recommend we listen to some music?"

Tarin sighed and nodded. "Fine," he said and turned on the radio. "Oh, you failed to mention I also have a sister."

Gil nodded. "Yes, you do. And you will continue to learn more of your past with time. As I have consistently told you, you are not from this world. You are from Arvalast, and in Arvalast, you have a separate identity from what you have here. Many more lessons are yet to come. Though it does not minimize your life on Earth any more than your life on Earth minimizes your time on Arvalast. But because you have lived in both worlds, you are now linked to both. When you return to Arvalast, it will come into deeper focus, and that which is here will grow fainter. But both will always be central to who you ultimately are."

Tarin saw the first glimpses of the Chicago skyline rising in the distance. But as they approached, there was no usual growing pileup of vehicles trying to get to the city center. Instead, traffic backed up on the side leading out of the city, both the primary lanes and the skylanes. Tarin thought back to the family at the rest stop. Had Incognito's warning spooked more than just them? As they reached downtown and headed toward the other side of the city, brake lights appeared—lots of brake lights, both ahead and above.

"Uh oh," Tarin said. "This doesn't look good. We've caught up to people trying to get out of the city in this direction."

Gil peered out the window, holding his cowboy hat on his lap. "There is a growing fear spreading over the earth," he said, "and I believe it is by design."

Now at a near standstill, Tarin slapped the steering wheel and groaned. "We're going to be stuck in this for hours." He reached for the radio console and began changing stations until he landed on one that sounded like a news channel. Tarin listened.

"Much of Europe has entered a shelter-in-place situation as world leaders brace their nations for the growing threat of a nuclear attack from the New Alliance. Despite the assurance of their leader, Incognito, Silverton and the Peacekeeper nations are still wary of the incursions in their airspace. We have reports that at least ten of these objects, described as silver or mercury-colored saucers, have been brought down. There have also been numerous reports of other types of objects: dark triangles moving at impossible speeds as well as white flying cylinders. Many continue to ask: Are we experiencing an otherworldly invasion, or is this merely an advanced technology discovered by the New Alliance, taking their war effort to a new and dangerous level?"

Tarin peered up at the increasingly overcast sky, almost expecting to see some strange craft dart overhead.

"Do you think those saucers getting brought down are the Greys?" Tarin said. "Like the ones that attacked us? If so, that would be good, don't you think?"

Gil also watched the skies. "I am not sure," he said. "All I know is the great tension building across this world will draw many minds and many eyes. Different agendas are at play, I fear. Some for good, some for ill. Do not think that we are the only ones on a mission. You seek to protect your friends. I seek to return you to Arvalast. Others seek to control worlds. Other motivations are more subtle and mysterious."

The traffic started moving again, and Tarin inched forward as he considered Gil's words.

CHAPTER 28

I ris got off the plane and walked into the St. Petersburgh airport. The flight, as usual, had been calm, despite having to navigate thunderstorms spewing lightning and rain on final approach. Severe turbulence was a thing of the past. Planes equipped with AI pilots and a web of stabilizers along their exteriors could maneuver harmoniously through all but the most extreme weather conditions. Advancements in engine design allowed hybrid propulsion to provide near-supersonic speeds while utilizing minimal fuel. The only reason planes did not fly supersonic was due to regulations forced by the outcry of constant sonic booms decades earlier that were driving most of the population of Earth to near madness. Regardless, from when Iris left East Fairfield earlier that morning, it had taken her only an hour to get to the Pittsburgh airport and another hour and a half of flight time to get to Florida. It was not even noon yet.

She navigated through a flurry of travelers, purchased a coffee, and then walked to the ride pickup location just outside the terminal. At a kiosk near the road, she tapped in the address of her apartment and waited. A self-driving sky car pulled up. The door opened, and she got in the front seat.

"Welcome, Iris," an automated voice said. "It will be approximately thirty minutes to your destination. Would you care for a beverage?"

"Gin and tonic," she said as she tossed her now empty cup into a waste receptacle where the driver's seat would otherwise be. She heard a pouring sound, and in a few minutes, her drink rose from the dashboard in front of her. She grabbed it, took a gulp, and stared out the window as torrential rain began pelting the vehicle as it drove out of the airport and gradually lifted into the air. It easily bypassed the traffic below as it followed the same route as the highway in the direction of her apartment.

Though she liked the quaint nature of small-town life, she also enjoyed the simplicity of city life, which was governed by convenience and driven by the abundance of artificial intelligence and automation. And beyond the convenience, sometimes it was just nice not to interact with people, despite being surrounded by them. "Mute," she said. There was a beep, and she knew the car would say nothing more until they reached her apartment.

The wipers swished back and forth, not for the driver, but for the passenger. The car hummed along the skylane as it joined the river of other flying cars separated by strict algorithmic guardrails. Eventually, it descended until it carefully merged back onto the roadway and traded its hover technology for old-fashioned rubber tires against asphalt. A few minutes later, it slowed and parked along the curb next to one of a series of two-story apartments lining both sides of the road.

"Arrived," the car said. The passenger door opened, and Iris got out. She ran to the nearest apartment building as thunder rumbled around her. She stood in front of two glass doors and looked into an optical scanner. The doors opened and she hurried in. She climbed a set of stairs, went to the end of the hall, and looked into another scanner just outside a wooden door numbered 211. She heard a click, pushed the creaky door open, and entered her quaint one-bedroom apartment.

Somewhat drenched from the storm, she grabbed a change of clothes, took a quick shower, and then rummaged through the kitchen until she found a bag of chips in a cupboard. She tried one—stale. She didn't care. She sat on her couch, the only seating in her tiny living room, and put her feet on a coffee table. "Turn on TV," she said, and the small flatscreen attached to the opposite wall snapped to life. Though a relic from the past, she preferred the simplistic TV over the newer holographic display units now widely popular for both information and entertainment.

Immediately she was flooded with news about UFOs. They were here. They were there. Apparently, they were everywhere. She groaned.

"Greys," she muttered. "What are you little beasts up to?" A reporter stood on a highway surrounded by police vehicles and pointed at a plume of smoke rising into the air some distance from the road. Iris leaned forward. "Volume up," she said.

"Across the country," the reporter said, "multiple craft, described as saucers, have been brought down by what we presume have been our military jets. Additionally, there are reports of other objects, triangular in shape, also engaging with the saucers. Are we in the midst of some otherworldly battle? This is the question being asked of President Silverton, who has been mostly quiet on the subject."

Iris slowly popped a chip in her mouth and chewed. Bits fell onto her baggy blue t-shirt. "Agents," she whispered. She was all too familiar with their covert means of travel. However, although they'd been particularly active during Feleti Kama's presidential bid over a decade earlier, after they failed to stop Kama's victory, there had been no recent activity from the agents' triangle crafts—at least that she'd heard of. But why were they engaging with the Greys' saucers? They were allies, for the most part.

Lightning flashed outside Iris's window, and the power went out. Though it wouldn't be long before the grid self-corrected, she reached for the side of her waist, but her phial was not there. That's right. She'd left it in the bathroom by the sink before her shower. She stumbled to the bathroom, picked up her phial, and whispered, "Enir." Its previously faint glow grew brighter.

She was about to leave the room when she noticed herself in the mirror. Her hastily dried hair drooped along her shoulders. She'd not put on her glasses, and her eyes were red and puffy from being unable to sleep last night as she repeatedly replayed her conversation with Tarin. The pain in his eyes, or rather, horror, as he realized it was her fault his mother had met the fate she had, was something she'd never forget and something she knew she'd never be able to forgive herself for. But at least her mission was complete. Tarin had recovered his illumina, and he was with Gildareth, who should be able to protect him. By now, they were likely returning to South Dakota to fight whatever battle was next to save his friends, Arvalast, or whatever from . . . *him.*

Her jaw clenched as Maximus's image formed in her mind's eye, as if he were standing behind her in the mirror. He took a long pull from a cigarette, then blew a seemingly endless plume of smoke from his mouth.

She splashed water on her face and looked back up. The image was gone. She turned and went to the kitchen. A half-full bottle of wine sat near the fridge. She popped the cork, tossed another chip in her mouth, and walked to the sliding doors leading to a small balcony just outside her living room. More lightning flashed as she lifted the wine bottle to her lips and looked through the glass.

The electricity returned, and the TV came on. She took another long drink, swallowed, and returned to the couch. A panel of talking heads began discussing the UFOs and speculated about the New Alliance being involved.

"Next channel," she said. A reporter stood in a ruined town talking about the possibility of nuclear war. "Next channel." An old clip of Silverton shaking the hand of some frightened-looking world leader. "Next channel!" she yelled over and over. Each time, she saw tidings of a world in unrest, a world gripped in fear, a world teetering toward the edge of complete and utter madness. More and more crumbs of chips fell on her shirt until, with a screaming curse, she threw her remote at the TV and jumped to her feet.

She panted as she stood with her fists clenched. Somehow, the TV had not been damaged. Again, an image of Maximus came into her mind. His aged, wiry form stood over her. His black cattleman hat covered most of his face as he smiled a mocking grin of oddly perfect white teeth. She knew this was not his true form, if he even had one. He was a shapeless monster, a shadow, and had haunted her since she'd first come to Earth to find and protect Tarin after he'd been lost to Arvalast. But shortly after her arrival, he'd sealed the portal to stop other Glorions from coming through and began to engage with Tarin directly. In her constant struggle to keep Tarin safe from him and his legions, she'd soon learn more about her enemy.

He was not from Earth. He had come much later in its history but quickly integrated himself into the planet's nonphysical power structures. Unable to command the influence he wished within the realm of shadow, which was governed by a Prince more ancient to Earth, he allied himself with the physical power structures run by those in control of MJ12-2. And within this alliance, he grew in strength even as he aided their growing dominance over Earth's governments. She suspected his involvement in the Glorion purge, made possible by an organized and unified attack from shadows and Greys. From these many victories had come a glorified hubris.

Maximus . . . greatest. She shuddered at the arrogance of his self-proclaimed title. Would one so great have struggled so mightily against Feleti Kama's Great Peace? His power had come against something unknown and unexpected, an artificial intelligence devoid of usual fears and self-interest indelible to the human mind and soul. Thus far, he had not fared well against it, and his standing with the Shadow Prince on Earth and his allies had been waning. Though Maximus's new name revealed a renewed confidence, whether or not it was merited.

She felt a rage grow in her. Although her mission was ultimately successful, and Tarin's path unblocked to whatever end, hers was now irrelevant. She had hoped to fight alongside Tarin, to return to Arvalast, and eventually watch him grow into the warrior she believed him to be—and Gildareth believed him to be. But after her confession at the bar, it was clear to her she'd be more an unwanted distraction than a help.

Her fists clenched as she stared blankly at the TV. The wine bottle was nearly empty in her left hand. She ignored the lightheadedness moving through her skull and behind her eyes. She wished for a way to confront Maximus and cause him as much harm as he had caused her—and had caused Tarin. Even if it ended her life, the thought of being covered in his inky blood as she stood over him filled her with an unquenchable desire.

Thunder clapped. The electricity flickered but managed to stay on. Her eyes slowly drifted to her illumina, which she'd set on her coffee table. It grew brighter and started to flicker. Once, she thought it might have flashed a slight red hue, but she paid it no heed. She reached for it with her right hand and held it tight.

She knew at this moment she could not directly harm Maximus, but she could still punish him indirectly. With her illumina in one hand and the bottle of wine in the other, she walked to the glass sliding doors leading to the balcony and threw them open. She stepped out into the pouring rain and lifted her phial into the tempest. *"Peta Babkama Luruba Anaku!"* she screamed in the ancient language of both her world and of Earth.

Her phial flashed as bright as lightning, and in it, she saw them: hundreds of shadows clutching the walls of surrounding buildings or flying through the sky. They were like locusts, feasting not on wheat and grain but the energies of anger, of fear, and of hatred of their hosts. Their quarry was always plentiful, as the Earth was a garden forever ripe with the fruits they craved.

Yellow eyes flashed and turned toward her. She'd never invoked the ancient command of shadow-seeing coupled with a challenge. It was a death sentence without an army of Glorions. But death is what she now craved, as long as in the process she tore through the sinews of as many shadows as possible. Maximus would be aware and feel the pain of his legions' destruction. But even if all it amounted to was a punch in his hideous face, that would suffice. She had to hurt him, and this was the only way.

She lifted the wine bottle to her lips, guzzled the final few drops, and slammed the bottle to the ground. It shattered across the balcony. She stepped forward in bare feet and onto the glass shards. She embraced the sharp pain shooting up her heels and into her ankles and legs.

"Come and fight!" she screamed, holding her light into the sky.

A few shadows slid down the sides of the building and released their wispy fingers from the bricks before they detached and began drifting toward her like leaves in the wind. Others, higher in the sky and barely visible in the pouring rain, began to dive toward her at incredible speeds. She wiped water from her face and braced herself. This was not how she'd envisioned her end, but it would be rewarding, even if brief.

More shadows let go of the walls of the surrounding houses and apartments and joined the others moving toward her. She saw both a sense of excitement and a mix of confusion in their eyes. She doubted many Glorions, if any, had ever actively sought a battle like this. She closed her eyes and focused on the memory of Tarin as she'd told him about her failure to protect his mother. She thought about the look on the poor woman's face as the shadows consumed her. Power surged through her body, moving from her chest into her limbs. She stepped back with one foot, opened her eyes, and thrust her illumina forward.

Streaks of lightning shot from it. As they struck the closest shadows, each exploded into wisps of smoke and dissolved in the downpour. Iris looked up.

"*Edin Na Zu!*" she shouted as her light flashed. At least twenty diving shadows split into pieces as a clap of thunder echoed through the atmosphere. "Keep coming!" she screamed, knowing that any shadow she destroyed because of Maximus, even if that creature was not allied with Maximus, would infuriate the Shadow Prince on Earth. This would reduce Maximus's standing with the Prince and would be a blemish on Maximus's reputation—a punch in his horrid face.

With further incantations and among multiple flashes of light, she became one with the thunderstorm as she smote down more and more of her enemies. She now had their full attention. Others, previously hovering high in the sky or clinging to buildings, now joined the battle. She leaned over the railing, wiped saturated strands of hair out of her eyes, and cast more and more beams of light. The air filled with corpses of smoke.

But then, a diving shadow reached the balcony. Before Iris could lift her hand to defend herself, it struck her and knocked her backward into her living room. Almost instantly, it formed into the shape of a man, grew two strong arms, and straddled her as it held her to the ground. Other shadows swarmed in and grabbed her arms and legs as they helped hold her down, even as she thrashed and struggled. Soon her entire living room was full of them. She could see nothing but darkness and glowing yellow eyes. The first of them, the one straddling her, leaned forward until its formless face was mere inches from hers.

"Why did you summon us?" it hissed. Other hisses echoed the same question throughout the room. "Do you wish for death?" the first continued.

She spat in its face. "Tell your master to go to hell," she growled.

The creature said nothing as it stared at her through angry yellow eyes. Then, slowly, its face began to morph and take on flesh. Sandy blond hair grew from its scalp, and lips and a nose formed. She began to struggle as she realized what was happening.

"Stop!" she yelled. "Stop it!"

A moment later, she was looking at Tarin. His eyes registered shock and disbelief. "You killed my mother!" he yelled. "It's all your fault!"

She tried to look away but couldn't as shadows dived in and held her head still and her eyelids open.

"If it weren't for you, I'd never have lost my light in the first place because I would have never had to leave home! I would have had happiness, Iris. Happiness!"

She struggled but still couldn't move.

"You stole all joy from me!" Tarin screamed as tears fell from his face and dripped onto hers. "Why, Iris? For what? So you could get a taste of what romantic love might feel like?" His face then filled with malice. "Perhaps," his voice became a hiss, "that is what you still crave—Glorion."

"Just kill me!" she screamed. She grimaced and wished she could close her eyes. Grief coursed through her as she knew the words to be true. She had felt something with Tarin's father, something she'd never felt before, a connection different from that of loyalty. And though she was incapable of fully understanding or experiencing that love, she had felt as if she were touching its outermost shell in those conversations with him. She could not even imagine the power of such a force if fully realized. But it was that curiosity, that wonder, that had distracted her. It set the stage for Tarin, to whom she'd united herself in the bond of infinite loyalty, to lose his mother, whom he loved more than anyone else.

She stopped struggling and lay still. Rather than inflicting pain on Maximus, he had instead found a way to cut into her the deepest possible wound. This should not have surprised her; it was foolish to have summoned the shadows, but she was thinking through the lens of grief. Lyrics to a familiar song passed through her mind, lyrics about going through hell and still pressing forward, even as she felt the remaining energy within her being pulled from her body as the surrounding shadows drew in closer and feasted on her sorrow.

She wished she'd listened to the simple wisdom in those words. Instead, she'd confronted the devil and offered herself to him. As her energy drained, she knew that soon she'd find herself where so many other Glorions had gone before her during the great purge.

Or would she?

She had not been faithful to her calling. Perhaps, rather than being reunited with friends beyond the gates of Arvalast, she would find herself in hell, whatever that might be for her.

She saw lightning flash from somewhere beyond the darkness. She waited. Why was she not yet dead? More lightning flashed, followed by a chorus of hissing. The shadows around her withdrew in all directions. Some slammed against walls, others vaporized into smoke, and others fled to the now-visible balcony. Then she saw it. A small, shining orb dancing through the darkness, striking her enemies and stirring them up like a swarm of bees. Other orbs darted through the still-open glass doors and joined the dance. The room filled with hisses and smoke as if someone had just thrown a bucket of water over a smoldering fire. In moments, all but the shadow on top of her, still looking like Tarin, had been vanquished. It began to return to its original form as a man walked in from the balcony. He had red hair and a beard and was drenched with rain. He ran to Iris and thrust a glowing glass phial into the final shadow's head. Immediately, it exploded into a vapor. Behind the man walked a small figure wearing a ball cap, appearing like a gangly child.

Without a word, the man returned to the balcony and closed the glass doors. The smaller figure walked in and knelt next to Iris. She looked up at it. It was not a child but rather a Grey. It stared down at her through its oval black eyes, set within its long head. "You're drunk, Iris," it said directly into her mind. "Didn't anyone ever tell you not to summon legions of Vulgheid while intoxicated?"

"Ebe?" she said. Is that you? The creature held out his three-fingered hand, and she took it. He wrapped his long, spindly digits around her palm and helped her to her feet and onto the couch. Meanwhile, the red-haired man walked over. He picked up her illumina, which she'd dropped on the floor during the attack, and handed it back to her.

"Seems you've had a rough time since we saw you last," the man said in a deep Scottish accent.

"Let me get you some bandages," the Grey said, again without actual words. "Your feet are bleeding really badly." He scuttled off toward her bathroom.

"Gabe," Iris said. "What are you doing here?"

He looked back toward the balcony. "Ebe and I were monitoring a situation over Texas when we noticed a sudden movement of shadow in this direction. It became clear that something had stirred up the enemy.

So we fired up Ebe's craft and arrived as quickly as possible. I have no idea what you were trying to do, but you certainly made a ruckus. Thankfully for you, some of the Glorion remnant not in physical form got here sooner. I'm not sure you would have made it otherwise."

She looked down at the floor. "I wasn't trying to make it," she said.

Gabe walked into the room and sat down on the couch next to her. "Seems, despite that, it's not your time."

Ebe returned to the room with gauze in one hand and some ointment in the other.

"Prop up your feet on the coffee table," she heard him say in her mind. "Let's get you all fixed up."

CHAPTER 29

The journey to Kettle Falls continued another hour through a denser region of the forest where the path, now hardened clay with little overgrowth, nestled up against steep hillsides and switched back on itself multiple times as it gained altitude. Abigail felt the muscles in her legs burning with the hike, though she did not tire. Memories of her past life continued to deepen as she recalled how she'd become ill and lost the ability to bike into town or work in the garden. This gave her a deeper appreciation for the continued strength she felt even during the increasingly arduous hike.

The scent of mist began to mingle with the already persistent aroma of moss and leaves. Occasionally, a small lizard scurried across the path in front of Abigail, or the rustle of some animal captured her attention from either side of the woods. Vines grew in this region, slithering up the tallest trees and dangling down in front of them in a few areas. Here, Abigail realized Raulin had brought a sword she'd previously not seen because it was in a sheath behind his back. He cut through any vines blocking the path, allowing them unobstructed access as they continued onward. Behind her, Ella and Rosie whispered to each other. Abigail hoped it wasn't about her.

The thunder of water against rock echoed in the distance. The party rounded a bend on a shallow ledge, and Abigail saw the source. A tall waterfall with three separate streams tumbled from the top of a brown and rugged cliff face surrounded by trees into a vast, bowl-like basin below. Below the crashing waters, an old log from what must have been a massive tree extended from one side of the basin's outlet to an outcrop on the other. From there, a wide creek formed and flowed just below them. The log looked carved and flattened at its top to create a bridge on which two people now sat: a woman and a girl, both dressed similarly to Jak and Ella, with brown breeches and leather coats. Their booted feet dangled over the edge of the log and the basin where a pile of rocks and boulders created white water at the creek's start. It splashed and sprayed until it finally met with the unhindered flow just below where Abigail stood.

As they approached the waterfall, the woman and girl stood up and began to wave. On the other side of the bridge, a small group had set up a camp on the broad, flat outcrop. Two men, cloaked with their hoods hanging limply against their backs, stood cross-armed, talking to each other by a fire. Five others—three men and two women—were setting up a large, tentlike structure.

"Some are already here," Raulin said as the girl previously sitting on the bridge began to run in their direction. As she approached, Abigail couldn't help but notice she was about seven, the same age as her sister, Mary, when she'd left home, and even looked similar, with long, curly, auburn hair. Her mind again flashed back to her time on Earth, remembering Mary and Ezekiel playing in the fields just outside their white house. She'd been like a second mother to them, caring for them during the day while her mother engaged in household chores and her father worked in the fields. She was their outlet for fun in an otherwise busy life of duties and tasks.

"Daisy!" Rosie said and opened her arms.

"Gran!" the girl called and jumped into her embrace. "You came!"

"Of course, we've come," Rosie said. She looked up at the woman who'd also been sitting on the log and was following closely behind the child. "But why did your mother and father bring you here? Councils are no place for children."

"Because," the approaching woman said, "she has not seen her Gran in many months, and her mother insisted on coming."

"Maddie," Rosie said. She let go of Daisy and smiled. "I've missed you."

Maddie appeared to be similar in age to Abigail but with lighter hair. She hugged Rosie and said, "And I've missed you, Mother." Over Rosie's shoulder, Abigail noticed Maddie send her a glance before closing her eyes and giving her mother one last squeeze. She took a step back. "After we heard the horns, we thought it best to have the whole family journey together instead of me staying home with Daisy. We've seen increased signs of Drilockk activity—some close to our fishing hole, others near our cabin. They seem to be stirred by something." She focused on Jak. "I'm glad you called for a council. We had also considered it but weren't sure it was worth the urgency since there's been no direct aggression from them."

Maddie turned her attention to Abigail. "I do not believe I've met your guest."

"Ah, yes," Jak said. "Pardon my manners!" He proceeded to introduce Abigail in a very similar fashion as he had with Raulin and Rosie. Abigail again felt her face become flushed and her palms sweaty as he shared what sounded like embellishments, even though she knew they were not. As he spoke, Raulin, Rosie, and Ella excused themselves and crossed the bridge to join the two men on the other side of the falls, who continued to talk, now animatedly, by the fire.

Meanwhile, Maddie listened to Jak's story with serious focus. When he finished, Abigail sighed in relief. Perhaps this might be the last time she'd have to hear her story that day.

She noticed voices growing louder from the other side of the waterfall as Ella appeared to be arguing with one of the men by the fire. Jak took notice, too, and said, "Please excuse me." He started to trot toward the log bridge.

Maddie crossed her arms and looked Abigail up and down with furrowed brows. "I do not wish to sound skeptical, but Jak's been known to

. . . how can I say this politely . . . exaggerate in his storytelling. Is what he is saying true?"

Abigail chuckled nervously and shrugged. "He got it pretty much right," she replied.

"You're from another world!" the little girl, Daisy, chimed in from her mother's side. She'd been quiet up to this point, and Abigail had forgotten about her while anxiously waiting for Jak to finish his recap.

"I believe I am," Abigail said with a smile. She again saw her sister in the young girl's face, and her motherly instincts began to take over. She knelt to be at eye level with her. "I believe your name is Daisy, is that right?"

"Yes," the girl said as she clasped her hands together and swiveled right and left at her waist in evident delight at finally being noticed. "And you're Abigail."

"That's right," Abigail said. "I'm pleased to meet you." She held out her hand for a handshake.

Daisy giggled and looked up at her mother. "What's she doing?"

"I think she'd like you to take her hand," Maddie said.

Daisy nodded and stepped forward. Abigail took her small hand and offered a quick and gentle handshake. Daisy laughed some more. "You're funny," she said.

"This is how we say hello in my world," Abigail said. "It's called a handshake. How do you greet each other here?"

Daisy jumped forward and gave Abigail a big hug. Abigail now laughed and put her arms around the child. As she did, warmth flooded her heart as she recalled the many hugs she'd both given and received from her little siblings. How she was beginning to miss them.

Daisy stepped back and looked at Abigail quizzically. "Why do you look so sad?"

"Oh," Abigail said, standing back up. "I just miss my family."

"Where is your family?"

"They are back in my own world, I think."

"Can't you see them again?"

Abigail realized something she'd not yet considered. Her family, having broken all ties with her, likely had not immediately heard about her fate. They may not have even gone to her funeral—if anyone had. When ill and realizing she was short on time, Abigail had planned and paid for arrangements for a burial and had left all other money and belongings in a will, some to her parents to support their farm and the rest to her siblings. It wasn't much, but it would help them have a head start on whatever path they ultimately chose. Her heart sank as she thought about the pain they would feel when they learned of her passing. She wished she could be there with them and give them one last hug. She tried to fight the tears back but realized it would be a losing battle.

"Mother," Daisy said, "why is she crying?"

Maddie gently hushed her. "There is a small clearing just up the path on this side of the falls," she said to Abigail. "There is a willow in its center, with a few stumps we placed as seating for smaller group discussions during councils. Please feel free to use it for a little quiet if you'd like." She paused. "You have been through a lot, Abigail." Her face became downcast, similar to Rosie's when they'd discussed the battle at Woodend. "I, too, know sorrow. Sometimes it helps to be alone, under the trees, and simply allow it to wash over me." She took Daisy's hand and said, "Come, let's go to Gran and Papa."

Daisy followed her mother toward the bridge, watching Abigail over her shoulder with curious eyes.

Abigail waited a moment, feeling her tears grow hotter, then began walking as quickly as possible toward the path Maddie pointed out. She considered running but didn't want to draw attention to herself. Finally, she passed by the rocks on that side of the falls, and ahead of her, she saw the small opening in the trees where the sunlight broke through the forest canopy and onto a massive willow in the center of a small grove. No longer in possible eyesight of anyone else, she ran to it and, at the base of its trunk, fell to her knees.

She let the river of growing anguish break through. She knew the waterfall behind her would drown out the sound of her sobs and let

343

them flow freely. Up until hearing Jak share her story twice, her past life had still been more of a dream, but now, she remembered everything, and she mourned it. She mourned that she'd never see her siblings again. She mourned her failed attempt at city life. She mourned her lost ability, because of her illness, to do all that she loved: gardening, biking, and even reading. And most of all, she mourned that she'd died alone and without love.

Above her, the willow tree's slender branches rippled like the movement of water in a creek as the wind blew through its boughs. The rustling leaves created a peaceful ambiance as the sun illuminated the foliage and covered Abigail in a soft green glow. She listened to the whispers of the willow. It almost sounded as if it were speaking to her, or perhaps singing. She continued to listen, now with more intent. Her sobbing slowed, and her heart rate quickened. Was she actually hearing singing? She pressed her ear to the tree but heard nothing. She leaned back and, again, could hear the sound of not just singing but music. She began to look around.

"Hello?" she said. "Is someone there?"

She could definitely hear a piano and a guitar, the two instruments harmonizing above the gentle beat of a drum. As she listened, a soft flute joined in. The music seemed to emanate from her as if she had a radio in her pocket. She grew stiff. Wait, she did have something in her pocket, or rather, in the pouch by her waist.

The music continued, and the lyrics became clear enough she could make them out. A man's voice sang in a country accent about traversing a narrow, broken road and, after many trials, finally finding true love at the end.

The light was warm. She wrapped her fingers around it and closed her eyes. She remembered the song now. It was one of her favorites. She'd played it when first driving out west, her heart still aching from her trials and failures in the city as she wondered if her own broken road might lead her to something better.

The music continued. She lifted the light to eye level, then opened them. The light shone brightly but did not burn. She felt waves of emotion course through her body as the memories of dashed hopes of finding love crashed against her mind. She didn't want to feel pity for herself, but she couldn't help it.

As the music continued, the light within her phial began to swirl. She wiped her tears and narrowed her eyes. A figure started to form behind the glass. She brought the phial closer and stared into it in amazement. Tarin was on the other end! He was sitting in the front seat of a car with one hand on the steering wheel. His eyes were thoughtful, reflective, even sad. Was the music coming from his car radio? He looked as if he were being pulled out of the moment and into some hidden daydream.

"Tarin!" she yelled.

He jolted, and the car seemed to lurch. He got it back under control and yelled, "What was that?"

Apparently, he could hear her too, and quite well!

"Tarin," she said, softer this time. "I'm sorry. I didn't mean to scare you. It's me, it's . . ." She then realized he'd have no idea who she was. Though he'd seen her in at least one of her visions of him, they'd never met in person, as far as she recalled. "Tarin," she said again. "I . . . um . . ." She had no idea what to say next. Meanwhile, the song continued.

After a long moment, she heard Tarin say, "Abigail?"

She felt as if her heart might stop. He knew her? But how? It was then she noticed that her sweating palm had lost grip on her illumina, and before she could catch it, it landed in a soft patch of leaves by her feet as the melody carried on.

Another hour passed as Tarin and Gil continued their trek through Chicago until the traffic began to speed up and the countryside at last replaced the cityscape. The clouds were now thicker, and the sun had dropped lower into the sky behind them. Tarin turned on his headlights. "Mind if I play some more music?" he said as they passed the "Welcome to Wisconsin" sign.

"Please," Gil said.

Tarin flipped to one of his favorite stations and let his mind drift into a pleasant and empty space. He'd always loved Wisconsin, mainly because it was a welcome reprieve after surviving the usually stressful drive through Chicago, just like Indiana when traveling in the other direction. It also reminded him of the Ohio countryside, but one less touched by the ever-growing urban expanse of Pittsburgh, Cleveland, and Youngstown as the corridor for data centers fueling the heartbeat of global AI.

The evening settled in. A new song started on the radio. Tarin took notice. It was a song he had always found particularly beautiful when it had played before his mother had fallen ill. Afterward, he'd found himself changing the station when it came on. It hurt too badly because he couldn't relate to the lyrics. But now, as the soft sounds of piano filled the car, he reached down to turn up the volume and began tapping on the wheel.

Gil turned his attention to the radio and closed his eyes. "This song is different than most I have heard so far. I feel . . . a presence, a yearning."

Tarin felt it too. It was as if something else was there with them, some other soul, taking it in, allowing its own experience to amplify the themes within the lyrics. That's when Tarin heard it: a woman's voice. She called his name as if she was sitting just behind him. He jolted and swerved into the shoulder before regaining control.

Gil clutched wildly to the dashboard. "Steady!" he yelled.

The voice spoke again, softer this time. "Tarin, I . . . um . . ." It paused. He now recognized the voice. But it couldn't be. Could it?

Gil grabbed Tarin's shoulder. "Your light! Get out your light!"

Tarin fished in his pocket with his right hand while he held the steering wheel with his left. He retrieved the phial and lifted it up. Its light flickered along the dashboard as it swirled behind the glass. Not sure what else to say, he said the name of the person whose voice he thought he'd heard. "Abigail?"

The light flashed bright and nearly blinded him. Again he swerved. Gil groaned and said, "Perhaps it is best to pull over."

"Good idea!" Tarin yelled as he regained control and managed to maneuver the car onto the shoulder and put on his hazard lights. He lifted his phial closer to his face. It stopped flickering and now glowed gently. Within it, he saw a figure begin to materialize into the form of a woman in a white gown. She stood under a large willow tree, looking down at him.

The radio continued to play.

CHAPTER 30

The Jeep moved slowly toward the mountain, its tires crunching along the dirt road. Other than where the peak obscured the sky, the heavens had become an eerie grey, stretching out in all directions as a thick layer of clouds consumed it. The trees and shrubs around the road slept in the winter's chill. There were no birds or otherwise visible wildlife, despite this area usually being well populated by both. Allen looked behind him. Josh's face was stoic, and Rob's nervous. He couldn't make out the expressions of the rest of the party through the back window but saw them holding the edges of the truck bed as the vehicle bounced on the uneven road. Liz had both hands on the steering wheel. She still wore her sunglasses. Allen wondered when she would take them off. He'd barely be able to see if he were wearing any.

Allen heard movement in the back seat. "Why isn't there anyone here?" Rob said. He was fidgeting and peering out each window. "I was expecting we'd see at least something by now."

Josh pointed to a structure about a half mile in front of them near the mountain's base. "I think I see a pickup truck up by the education center in the parking area. There's at least someone here."

As they drew closer, Allen saw a rusty purple truck come into view.

"That's Gaka's truck!" Rob yelled, pointing between Allen and Liz through the windshield. "What's he doing here? We should have warned him the minute Bill told us he'd seen UFOs over here!"

If that was indeed Gaka's truck, Allen, too, was concerned. For the last few minutes, he'd felt a growing and familiar churn in his stomach. He hoped it was just his nerves.

"Even if it is Gaka," Josh said, "he knows what he's doing. He hikes here all the time."

"But not with aliens!"

"I'm not seeing any aliens," Josh answered, but Allen could hear the trepidation in his voice as Liz pulled in next to the purple truck and turned off the vehicle.

It was strangely quiet as they got out of the cab. There was no wind and not even the usual winter cries of crows.

Ristun jumped out of the truck bed and said, "I gotta pee, be right back." He jogged toward a nearby outhouse on the opposite side of the parking area.

"Doesn't look like the education center is open," Liz said, pointing at the modest, gabled brown building in front of them.

"It closes down in November," Bill said as he climbed out of the vehicle. He peered intently around the area. "That's what makes it a better hideout for aliens."

Liz put her hands on her hips. "I'm not seeing a whole lot of aliens at the moment."

"I doubt they'd be in plain sight," Bill said, though he was beginning to look a bit concerned himself. "We should scout the place out and get the lay of the land. I'm sure we'll find something."

"Then do what?" Josh asked with annoyance in his voice. "Do me and Rob throw some LOB cards at them and hope we have more hit points than the aliens?"

"Your Glorion friends seem pretty confident they can take care of things," Bill said, then he patted the gun slung on his shoulder. "And we're packing."

"So we shoot them?"

"Or your friends zap 'em with light."

Josh tilted his head back and moaned. "We're going to die."

"Do you think so?" Rob said to Josh.

Josh threw his hands into the air and moaned again.

Meanwhile, Ristun returned from the outhouse, coughing and muttering loudly to himself. "Those things are usually bad, but that one takes disgusting to a new level!" he said. "Anyone have a bottle of water?"

Liz, who'd been trying to contact Jason on the radio, paused and said, "One second." She fished a water bottle out of the truck and tossed it to Ristun.

He opened it and splashed some on his face. He then poured some in his hand, breathed it into his nostrils, and blew the contents onto the ground.

Josh winced. "Gross."

"You'd do it too if you made the mistake of taking a leak in that stink facility back there." He splashed some more water on his face and furiously rubbed his hands over his nose. "I'd highly suggest anyone needing to pee just go behind a tree or bush."

"Noted," Josh said as he excused himself and walked behind the education center.

"I know outhouses stink," Liz said, "but aren't you being a bit dramatic? Do your kind have a really sensitive sense of smell?"

"Nothing out of the ordinary as far as I know?" Ristun said.

"You do complain about my aftershave quite frequently," Dralo said.

"That's because you cover yourself in it like icing on a cake."

"Untrue," Dralo said.

"For what it's worth," Bill said after a brief silence, "I didn't notice it while I was sitting next to you in the truck."

"See," Dralo said.

Ristun glowered at him and slowly drank the remaining water in the plastic bottle. Then he noticed Rob, who'd walked over to the purple truck and put his hand on its hood.

"You doing all right?" Ristun asked him, his tone abruptly moving from irritated to soft.

"I'm really worried about Gaka," Rob said. He turned back to the others. "He shouldn't have come here. It's dangerous. I think we need to go look for him. Maybe he took the path up the mountain."

Ristun walked over to him and put his hand on his shoulder. "Well, good thing we're here," he said. "While we're looking to learn more about whatever has been messing with your town, if he's here, we'll find him and make sure he gets home safe. Sound like a plan?"

Rob smiled and nodded.

Meanwhile, Josh returned from behind the education center and said, "So, what are we doing next?"

"To start," Ristun said, pointing toward the peak, "we're going to head up the mountain to look for your grandfather."

"We'll get a good view of the area up there too," Bill added. "Maybe we'll find something."

"Do we really want to find something?" Josh mumbled.

"Sounds like you don't want to be here," Ristun said. "You seemed a lot more excited about coming here to see if we could get clues on what the agents were up to back at Allen's. Are you getting cold feet?"

"Maybe I am! And for good reason. We just saw a UFO get shot out of the sky and then got stopped at a police barricade. Do you all really think it's smart we're meddling in all of this? Maybe we should just get out of here. This whole area seems to be a hot spot for whatever is going on with the agents and the UFOs."

"But we need to find Gaka!" Rob argued.

"I'm not saying we don't look for Gaka! I'm just saying maybe we try to find him quickly, and then we all leave South Dakota and take him with us. Maybe we can go find Tarin in Ohio and hide there."

Ristun pointed to the sky and said, "Whatever is going on is happening everywhere. You couldn't even leave Earth to escape it at this point. Look, kid, I see what you're saying, but we need to start playing more offense if we're going to have any chance to influence things for the better. I've been around a long time. The darkness isn't great at pivoting when something doesn't go its way, so we need to mess things up for it and get it off its game."

"I suppose you can stay in the truck if you're nervous," Allen said to Josh, beginning to feel bad for his friend as he was clearly growing very distraught.

"Alone?" Josh said.

"I could leave my gun with you."

"I'd rather go with the rest of you. Seems there's not much of a better choice right now."

The group all stood silently for a moment looking at one another until Ristun slapped the side of Gaka's truck and said, "Well, then let's be off!"

Liz locked the police truck as the others started toward the trailhead sign on the side of the parking area nearest the mountain. When she was done, she jogged over to Allen, who'd just started to follow the group, and said, "What do you think about all of this? You feel anything?"

Allen looked toward the rocky mountain peak as its grassy walls stared down at him. His stomach continued to churn. "Yes," he said. "Something is going on here."

She put her hand on his shoulder and said, "Let's all stay close. I trust Ristun and Dralo. They were able to help us before at the ranch. I don't think they'd be leading us into something we can't handle, and at this point, I'm not sure if there's a better way to help Philip than seeing if we can learn more here. And, like Ristun said, we can try to throw a wrench into the plan of whatever is coming against our town—and world for that matter."

"Yeah, I agree," Allen said, trying to speak normally despite the pain in his stomach. He didn't want to admit it, but he was very worried about Liz, along with all his friends. He didn't want any of them to be hurt like she'd been at the ranch by the Vulgheid or whatever mutation the creatures had taken on Earth. And at the same time, he wondered how Tarin was faring on his own mission. Had he found his light?

They caught up to the others at the trailhead and together began hiking toward the mountain. Josh was near the back of the group. His shoulders were slumped, and he looked miserable. Allen positioned himself next to him and said, "You okay?"

"Not really," Josh said.

"What do you mean?"

"I just don't want to be here," Josh said. "Ever since the police barricade, I keep thinking more and more that we have no business getting involved with whatever's going on. We're just a bunch of dorks who got excited to feel part of something bigger. Now that we're in the middle of it, I know this is all a bad idea. I wish when we met Gil, we'd never sent him to find Tarin at Old Cotton's."

Allen considered putting his hand on his friend's shoulder but opted against it. Josh wasn't always one for physical forms of affection and less so when stressed. "I know how you feel," he said instead. "Everything's gotten so strange since Gil's arrival. I'm already missing the old days of playing Legendarium of Beasts and leading a nice and boring life."

"At least you have some experience with this stuff," Josh said, his tone drifting slowly from tension to reflection. "I mean, you're from Arvalast, isn't weird stuff like this normal?"

"It had its moments of chaos, but most days were pretty dull," he said. "Until I met Tarin."

"You met him in Arvalast, right? Not when you got to Earth?"

"Yeah, I met him just before things started going really bad where we lived, though some of the memories have been getting a bit hazy lately. I do recall we lived in a place called Woodend." He chuckled. "I was actually a bit of a bully. Tarin hated me."

"Seems you've mellowed in your old age," Josh said with a slight smirk. He paused momentarily, then said, "One thing I just can't figure out is how you've started a whole life here and lived a relatively normal existence knowing about Arvalast and, apparently, other worlds too."

Allen shrugged. "What else could I do? I could go mad, I suppose?"

"That's what I would have done."

"Come on," Allen said, finally feeling comfortable enough to put his hand on Josh's shoulder. He was relieved Josh didn't shove it away. "Give yourself more credit. You've handled things pretty well the last few days. I mean, learning about new worlds from Gil, finding out some of your friends are from that world, then dealing with UFOs, agents, and who knows what else . . . that's not something an average person could navigate without therapy."

"Who says I haven't contacted a therapist?"

Allen laughed. "Well, if we get through all of this, I'll do the same."

"What're you guys talking about?" Rob said, walking over.

Josh looked at Allen, sighed, then turned to Rob. "Arvalast and aliens."

"So, nothing new?" Rob said.

"No," Josh replied, then reached out and gave Rob a side hug. "Just rehashing all the crazy stuff that's happened over the last few days."

Rob leaned his head on Josh's shoulder and then said, "Do you think we're going to find Gaka and that he'll be okay?"

"I'm hoping so," Josh said. "I'm hoping so."

They continued walking on the mostly flat ground, surrounded in part by shrubs and short trees whose leaves were either brown or had fallen. Some branches contained cloth ribbons left by the local nations as part of their prayer tradition. Soon after, the trail grew steeper and began a series of switchbacks leading them higher up the mountain.

"Mathó Pahá," Bill said, breathing heavier with the incline. "I bet your Gaka comes here to pray. This place is very sacred to the local nations."

"He does," Rob said. "He says it gives him time to reflect and appreciate the depth of nature." He looked around. "Though it's not that pretty here this time of year."

A few wordless minutes passed by. Allen had been momentarily distracted by his conversation with Josh but was now beginning to feel sicker. If it got much worse, he worried he wouldn't be able to continue with the others. Dralo was nearby. Allen moved closer to him and whispered, "I'm not feeling very well."

Dralo looked down at him. "In what regard?"

"Like at the ranch, with the cow. There's something here."

"You are perceptive, Sarky," Dralo said quietly. He looked at Liz. "I mean Allen." She kept walking and didn't seem to have noticed Dralo using Allen's Arvalastian name. "Whatever serenity this place once had," Dralo continued, "seems to have been replaced by a much darker energy. I can sense it as well. They are watching us, and warily. However, I feel no aggression at the moment. I would draw out my light to help ease your pain, but I do not want to inadvertently excite them."

"I'm not sure I'll be able to go on given how I feel," Allen said. "I might have to stop here and let the rest of you go up."

Dralo looked down at him with concern. "That would be unwise. One moment, there might be something I can do to help." He placed his hand into his pocket, whispered something quietly, then removed his hand. "Take it," he said.

"Your hand?"

"Yes."

Allen reached out, and when their hands met, he instantly felt as if cool water had flown into his stomach and put out a fire of unease. "Thank you," Allen said as Dralo withdrew his hand.

"That should help for a time," Dralo said.

Feeling much better, Allen began to take in his surroundings. On either side of them, more cloth ribbons hung on the twigs and branches lining the trail. Bill and Liz walked at the front of the group, Liz with her hand next to her gun and Bill leaning forward into the incline, breathing heavily. Rob and Ristun followed closely behind them. Allen could hear them discussing elements of LOB. Josh followed next, with his hands in his pockets, looking less dejected than earlier. Dralo walked just ahead of Allen. In his somewhat formal attire of slacks and a sweater, Dralo seemed a bit out of place for a mountain hike. Though this wasn't exactly a hike; it was a mission, and all of them were a bit out of place, considering the circumstances.

Allen checked his stomach. He still felt good. Dralo's magic, or whatever it was, had been extremely effective. But he still sensed something was very wrong in this area. He looked out ahead at his friends. He was glad he was not alone. A deep sense of appreciation filled him as he considered their loyalty and understanding even as their entire world was rocked with revelations about where he'd come from while navigating earthly anxieties related to the war between the Peacekeepers and the New Alliance and now the onset of UFOs and MJ12-2 agents. Though he and his friends were from different worlds, the last few days' events had united them more profoundly, as the destinies of both Earth and Arvalast appeared to intersect.

As he considered Arvalast, it now felt so distant. Though he maintained some lingering vivid memories, others had dissipated into a dreamlike fog. He didn't doubt his life there. At this point, that would be harder than accepting it, but still, something had changed over the last few days that was puzzling, like the thread connecting his mind to both worlds had been mostly severed.

He looked back down the trail. They were over halfway up the mountain now, and he could see for miles to the south. The parking lot looked like a small grey square flecked with two dots where the trucks were parked, and beyond that, the blue waters of Bear Butte Lake rippled a mile from the base of the mountain. But then he noticed something strange. In the prairie grasses quilting the landscape was a series of circles, like indentations in the field. It almost looked like someone had taken their thumb and pressed it into the ground all along the mountain's base.

"Hey!" he called out to the others. "Come look at this!"

The others stopped and hurried back to him. Bill let out a whoop. "That's gotta be where the saucers were landing! He frantically scanned the horizon. "Wait, look over there," he said, pointing north from the depressions. "Do you all see that? It's a crop circle!"

Allen squinted and focused on the area. Sure enough, there was a geometric pattern in the ground, created by more circles and connected by an intricate series of lines.

"I bet that's some sort of map or guidepost for the aliens," Bill continued. "I knew we'd find something here!"

"I'd suggest you lower your voice," Dralo said. "If there are physical beings in the area, let's not draw them to us." He turned and pointed to the peak of the mountain, which was now only a few more switchbacks away. "Let's continue to the top and get a full view of the area."

"And see if Gaka's up there," Rob said.

"Yes," Dralo continued, "and see if we can find your grandfather." He started leading the rest of them back toward the peak. Allen watched as Ristun hurried to Dralo's side and whispered something into his ear. Dralo nodded, and both put their hands in their pockets and quickened their pace.

"They seem nervous," Liz said as she sidled up next to Allen. "Wanted to check on you again. How are you feeling?"

"I'm feeling better," Allen said, "but mostly because Dralo did something to help me."

"I wish I could say the same," she said. "I'm starting to feel my skin crawl all over, like at the worst part of a horror movie. I hope whatever we find, those two can handle it."

"Me too," Josh said, startling Allen and Liz. Both he and Rob had caught up to them and were walking just behind them.

"You two are cute together, by the way," Rob said.

"Hey, now!" Liz said, turning around. "What are you saying?"

"Come on," Josh joined in. "We're not stupid."

Liz smiled at them, then met Allen's eyes. He felt his heart flutter, an odd sensation considering all the bad stuff that was going on. Apparently, the seed of romance was oblivious to all that existed beyond its unifying essence. But he didn't have long to relish the brief happy moment. As they approached what appeared to be the final bend toward the peak of the mountain, he saw Ristun and Dralo turn around and hold out their hands.

"Stay there!" Dralo ordered. His other hand was in his pocket. Ristun darted around the bend. All went still. Then Allen heard it: a groan. It was from a voice he recognized.

"Gaka!" Rob screamed. He darted forward. Josh tried to hold him back, but it was no use. He reached Dralo, who grabbed him.

"Don't go up there!" Dralo commanded.

"Let me pass!" Rob screamed as he struggled against Dralo's tight grip. "He sounds hurt! Let me help him!" He struggled and thrashed some more, but Dralo's hold on him remained steady.

"Gaka! Gaka! It's me, Rob! Are you okay?"

Another groan followed. Rob burst into tears as Ristun came running down from the peak.

"We need to leave now," he said. It was the first time Allen could remember seeing him frightened.

"But what about Gaka?" Rob wailed.

"I'm sorry," Ristun said, "but it's too dangerous. I made a mistake suggesting we come here."

"What do you mean?"

"I mean . . ." Ristun hesitated as his voice fell to a harsh whisper. He pointed back from where he'd come. "He is here."

"Who?" Rob cried.

A loud humming sound began to vibrate through the mountain, so loud that all of them fell to their knees and held their ears. Allen looked up. Above them, a small section of clouds parted, and a cigar-shaped craft descended from the opening: the same one he'd seen on the night Gil arrived. But this time, Gil was not here.

"Get down the mountain, now!" Dralo ordered. He jumped up and rushed forward, frantically attempting to help the rest of them off the ground. No one budged as they continued to cover their ears.

"Can't you fight it off with your light?" Josh yelled. "That's what Gil did!"

Dralo looked into the sky. "If we draw out our lights now, we'll be flanked by hundreds of Vulgheid. With him here, we have no choice but to withdraw now!"

"No!" Rob screamed. He lurched to his feet and, with his hands still covering his ears, rushed past Dralo toward the top of the mountain.

"Stop!" yelled Dralo. But it was no use. Rob continued to run forward. Ristun tried to stop him, but the craft, as it descended, suddenly flashed a bright crimson. Ristun stumbled, but the flash had not deterred Rob. He sidestepped Ristun before he could regain his composure then disappeared around the final bend.

"Rob, no!" Ristun screamed.

At the same time, Bill yelled and pointed back down the mountain. "There are vans coming! White vans!"

Allen spun around. Sure enough, about ten white vans, followed by a cloud of dust, maneuvered off the dirt road and into the parking lot. Liz reached for her gun and pulled it out. She continued to wince from the painful humming even as she took aim at the craft above them. She fired. The sound was only slightly greater than that of the humming.

Bill jumped to his feet, pulled out his rifle, cocked it, and joined her. He fired a round. Then another.

"Stop!" Ristun yelled. "Don't waste your ammunition on that." He pointed toward the base of the mountain. "Save it for them!"

"What do we do about that thing then?" Liz yelled, pointing angrily at the cigar-shaped craft.

Ristun exchanged a glance with Dralo. "Looks like we don't have much of a choice," Ristun yelled. "We're going to need to confront him!"

"But we're going to get swarmed!" Dralo argued. "There's no way we can protect everyone."

Ristun groaned and looked around frantically. He rubbed his hand through his hair and said, "We're going to need to split up. You take Liz and Bill down the mountain. Keep them covered while they hold back the agents." He pointed at Liz. "Get a good position and hold them back."

"Got it," she said and cocked her gun.

"I'll see what I can do up here," Ristun continued. He looked at Allen and Josh. "You both come with me. Don't get more than a foot away from me, do you understand?" They both nodded.

A moment later, they heard a scream. It was Rob.

"What's happening to him?" Josh yelled. "We need to get to him now!"

"Go!" Ristun yelled to Dralo.

Dralo nodded and rushed down the mountain, followed closely by Bill. But before Liz joined them, she grabbed Allen's hand. "Don't forget about the nightmare I had at the ranch. Make sure you and your friends don't get yourselves killed." She let go and charged after Dralo.

Ristun took in a deep breath, whispered something inaudible, and then looked at Josh and Allen. "You both are going to need to do your best to keep calm and try not to let whatever you see freak you out. Fear feeds them. I know it's going to be hard, but if you have to, just close your eyes. Understand?"

"What's up there?" Josh said, visibly quaking.

"It's something with a hell of a lot more hit points than any of us have right now," Ristun said. He patted his pocket. "Best we can do is buy some time and hope. Now come on!"

He charged forward. Allen and Josh looked at each other and followed.

As they rounded the bend, a wave of pain came over Allen, and he lurched forward and grabbed his stomach. It felt as if he'd passed through a wall and into some room filled with pure malevolence. He felt a hand grab him and help him back up. It was Josh. With great effort, he managed to stumble forward, staying as close to Ristun as possible and allowing Josh to support him as they made their way to the peak.

A three-hundred-and-sixty-degree view greeted him. On a normal day, it would have been beautiful, despite the mostly grey landscape and thick clouds, but today, as the cigar-shaped craft hovered menacingly only a few hundred feet above them, it was as if he'd passed through the gate of hell itself. Josh supported Allen up a flight of stairs until they reached a wooden platform at the summit. On the far end was a bench, and on it, an elderly man lay on his back, seizing. Allen instantly recognized Gaka, though he looked ghostly, more like an animated corpse than a living man. On the ground next to him lay Rob. He was holding tightly to one of the old man's hands, and he, too, was seizing.

Next to Rob stood a hazy apparition, holding what appeared to be a crimson light over Rob's head. Slowly, the entity turned toward Allen. As if looking through a window between reality and a dream, Allen saw the figure of a tall, thin man wearing a cattleman hat. A cigarette hung limply from his lips. As the figure's formless eyes met Allen's, Allen felt his stomach lurch.

Unable to hold back, Allen vomited onto the wooden slats below. He heard Ristun yelling, "Close your eyes!" as a white light began to flash. Was it lightning? He couldn't tell.

The apparition in the hat—was it now a cowboy?—seemed to take notice, but only briefly. It trained his attention back to Allen and said, "You finally made it here, Arvalastian." He had a Western accent under a raspy voice. He smiled. His teeth seemed unnaturally white as his features became more clear. Through now crisp green eyes, he said, "Your friend here seems to have fallen ill with something. His grandpa too." He lifted one hand to the cigarette in his mouth, took in a deep breath, and blew out some smoke. He laughed. The smoke continued to flow. It surrounded the man as the red light he held glowed like the sun through a storm cloud. Allen heard Ristun yelling something, but it sounded as if he were underwater.

"Your friend found his little light," the cowboy said as the smoke continued to envelop him. "Pity it won't be much use in a world lit up by fire—my fire." The smoke fully engulfed the man and began billowing up and expanding. Allen stared in horror as it slowly took on the form of a mushroom, enveloping the craft and continuing into the clouds above. A flash of red light lit it up, and in almost an instant, the smoke condensed and was sucked into the flying cigar. The humming stopped, and the craft withdrew into the murky ceiling above it.

The curtain was thrown back from the window between realities as Allen regained a sense of physicality on top of Bear Mountain. Around him, flashes of light lit the darkening summit. Ristun swirled about, yelling in a language Allen didn't understand. Josh was cowering at Ristun's feet, his eyes closed as he reached for Rob. "We're here!" he was yelling through his tears. "Hang on, Rob! We'll get you out of here!"

Rob and Michael's hands remained locked, even as both of them continued to seize. Then, shots echoed from somewhere behind them. Allen remembered. Liz and Bill were down there, with Dralo, trying to hold back the agents.

Josh scrambled along the platform and began trying to crawl toward Rob. "We've got to get them out of here!"

"Don't!" Ristun yelled and held Josh back. He thrust his now flaming phial at some invisible enemy. "I'm holding them back! They'll be okay if you stay put!" He swept his light over his head as if fending off a swarm of bees and screamed, "*Seru, Idimmu!*" A brilliant flash followed, and all seemed to grow still. Both Michael and Rob stopped quaking. A terrible thought passed through Allen's head: were they dead? He frantically scanned their chests for signs of movement. Both were moving up and down, barely, but still moving.

Allen heard footsteps against wood and spun around. Liz and Dralo rushed onto the platform, panting and sweating despite the chill in the air. "They're coming up! We couldn't hold them back any longer, and we're out of ammo!" She noticed Rob and Michael. "Oh no, are they . . . ?"

"No," Ristun said, "and let's keep it that way." He rushed to the platform's edge and looked out over the side of the mountain. "The Vulgheid are retreating to the parking lot." He turned to Dralo. "Wait, where's Bill?"

Dralo spun around and cursed. "He was just behind us! They must have taken him!" He turned back to Ristun. "We need to go find him."

Ristun ran his hand through his hair and began to pace. He turned to Allen. "Give Liz your gun." Allen quickly obeyed. "Liz, anyone you don't recognize that comes up here, shoot."

She nodded.

"But what happens if something comes up here we can't shoot?" Allen asked, his voice cracking.

Ristun and Dralo looked at each other. As one, they lifted their lights into the air. They began to chant something that rested on the boundary of speech and song. A soft wave emanated from their lights. It lifted and then fell over the top of the mountain. With it, Allen felt his heart grow peaceful. Next to him, Liz closed her eyes and breathed in deeply, and Josh did the same.

Ristun and Dralo lowered their lights, and Ristun said, "We put a similar shield of protection around this place as we did back at John's ranch. That should hold back the shadows for a time. We won't be long." He and Dralo rushed down the mountain. Liz walked over to Allen, forced a smile, and took his hand. Then, together, they both joined Josh and sat next to Rob and Michael. Their previous expressions of pain had given way to those of peace. But neither was yet awake. Josh turned to Allen.

"What are we going to do?"

Allen looked into the sky. The afternoon had now settled into evening, and all was growing darker. He shivered in the chilly air. He could see the parking lot far in the distance. It was now full of white vans and scores of small black dots indicating where agents had taken up position.

"We wait," he said, "and we hope."

CHAPTER 31

lick. Click Click. The hazard lights tapped a simple rhythm. Tarin continued to stare into the phial and the green eyes just beyond. To his side, he noticed Gil looking too, but couldn't make out his expression. He was too focused on the woman in front of him. How was this possible? What had created this sudden aperture between worlds?

"I . . . I can't believe it's really you," Abigail finally said with the smallest hint of a northern midwestern accent. Her voice was soft, with an almost flutelike musical quality to it. But behind it, he sensed an orchestra limited only by the timidity of a first meeting.

He tried to say something but was tongue-tied as if he were in the presence of a celebrity. Over the last few days, he'd developed, at a minimum, a deep mental connection with her and a wonderment that he'd seen her in his mind's eye despite her having departed Earth.

Departed? He was being coy. She was dead. He was talking to a dead woman. But at this moment, she was the most alive person he knew.

"Are you going to greet her?" Gil said.

Tarin felt himself blush. There had been a very long silence since she'd spoken. But those green eyes just kept staring at him, or rather, into him, full of curiosity and familiarity. He glanced into the rearview mirror to check his appearance. He looked like crap. His hair was a tangled mess, and he hadn't shaved in days. He had never been able to grow much facial hair, and now he looked like an unkempt slob. He looked back at her. She appeared confused.

"I can see you," she said, "and I heard someone else with you. But . . . I'm not sure if you're able to hear me." She'd brought the phial closer to her lips as she spoke. Tarin found that distracting.

Someone slapped his shoulder. "Ouch," he said and looked over at Gil.

"Focus, Tarin," Gil said with a scowl. He pointed at the phial. "That is the girl I first saw when coming to Philip. The fact she is alive and made a direct connection with you is no small matter. We must learn more."

"You didn't have to hit me," Tarin whispered.

He heard a laugh from the phial. His face grew warm. Abigail looked to be trying to hold back more laughter.

"Hi there," he finally managed to push out of his mouth. "Sorry about that, and yes, I can hear you. It's just . . . you know, this is all a bit strange."

"You're in good company," Abigail said. She peered around her. "I'm in some other world." Her face grew solemn. "I came here after . . ."

"I know," Tarin said, feeling an ache in his own heart as he sensed the pain in hers. "I'm sorry. And I'm also sorry that . . . well, we lived not far from each other. I wish we could have met in person sometime in Philip. I'm not sure how our paths never crossed."

"I was a bit of a hermit," she said. "I mostly stayed around my house, gardening, reading, and teaching at a community college, virtually—for supplemental income. My students had only ever met my hologram. The few times I'd go into town was to grocery shop."

"That makes sense then," Tarin said. "I never went grocery shopping. My friends worked there, and I usually asked them to pick things up for me." He paused. "I'm guessing you didn't go to Old Cotton's much?"

"Old Cottons? Was that the bar?"

"Yeah."

"Oh no, I don't drink. Well, I mean, I drink water and tea, but no alcohol."

"Coffee is the superior beverage," Gil suddenly chimed in.

"Wait!" Abigail said. "Who was that? Was that who I heard earlier?"

"Oh," Tarin said, "yes, that's Gil. He and I have been . . . traveling together." He turned the phial toward Gil, who tipped his hat and waved.

"Pleased to meet you, Abigail," Gil said.

"Good to meet you as well, Mr. Gil," she said pleasantly. "Your name, it sounds familiar."

"My full name is Gildareth," he replied.

"Gildareth?" she said. Her face went white. "I know that name. Jak and Ella said a Gildareth had opened a portal to Earth to look for"— she focused back on Tarin—"to look for you."

"Wait a minute," Tarin said, "are you saying . . . are you in Arvalast?"

She nodded enthusiastically. "Yes! That's where I woke up after . . . after I passed from Earth. I've been staying with a couple, Jak and Ella, in some forest— what do they call it again? The Great Northern Forest, I believe. We're currently trying to get a group together to go find the tower they say is the gate to Earth. Tarin, they want to bring you back!"

Tarin's heart started to race. He turned to Gil. "Did you hear that?"

"I did," Gil said, with a small smile on his face. "Please, may I speak to her?"

Tarin nodded and turned the phial to him. "Abigail," he said, "if you would, I would like to hear exactly what has happened to you since your arrival in the Great Northern Forest."

Over the next thirty minutes, Abigail recounted her story. Tarin couldn't hear her as well when she was not facing him. The back of the phial glimmered a faint white as opposed to being a window into Abigail's location from the opposite side. It acted in many ways like a video call on a mystical phone, though one that bypassed more than distance—rather, the barriers of worlds themselves. But despite this being marvelous in its own right, he was too focused on Abigail's story to give it more thought. Soon, he set the phial on the dashboard so he could see her too and proceeded to ask many questions. He marveled at her ability to navigate such a challenging series of events with such poise.

Eventually, Abigail confirmed she was with his sister, Ella, and her husband. Tarin's heart lurched in his chest. Though he'd only just remembered he had a sister, he felt himself grow eager to ask if she was there now, with Abigail, and if he could talk to her. But he refrained. More important matters came up, such as Abigail's multiple encounters with red-cloaked monsters, which she called Drilockk. Why were they so interested in her? It was as if the moment she arrived in Arvalast, some alarm had gone off, and bad things had begun pursuing her.

Tarin grew even more attentive any time she shared her version of seeing him in visions similar to those he'd had about her. His heart beat faster as he realized the link he had with her seemed to work in reverse as well. Finally, she reached the part of the story where she'd seen him in front of a monster reaching for a red light as it attempted to apparently consume him.

She'd saved him.

His mind raced as he tried to connect it to his own memories. Based on the timing of events, assuming time was somehow aligned across Arvalast and Earth, this had happened just yesterday. Could it have been related to when he'd blacked out at his father's?

She completed the story by sharing that Jak and Ella had decided to call a council with the intent to go to the tower—the same one, Tarin assumed, he and Gil had passed through to get to Earth. Apparently, his sister wanted to bring him back to Arvalast, just like Gil.

"Thank you for sharing," Gil said a few moments after Abigail finished. "You have been through so much, yet maintain a strength and hope that I would not expect." He looked at Tarin, though his eyes seemed to look past him rather than at him. "I need to excuse myself for a few moments and think. Do you mind if I go for a short walk along the side of the roadway? I will not be long—ten minutes, at most."

Tarin realized that meant he'd be alone with Abigail, which made him both nervous and excited. "Yeah," he finally said, "that's fine. Go ahead." Gil got out of the vehicle and began walking farther up the highway on the far end of the shoulder. The light traffic flying by didn't seem to bother him as he became a silhouette beyond the car headlights. Tarin picked up the phial and held it closer to his face so he could see Abigail better. In some ways, it felt as if they were sitting across from each other, perhaps having coffee.

"Do you think my story was weird?" Abigail asked. Tarin almost jolted. Her voice was louder now that they were so close. He composed himself and said, "Not at all! You're also in good company. My friends and I have been through hell and high water the last few days, ever since Gil arrived. We've seen UFOs, been stalked by government agents, and I've had a lot of crazy dreams."

"Was I in any of them?"

Tarin thought back to the first time he'd seen her, lying in the grass in the meadow, before she'd been chased by the Drilockk. He then remembered when he'd seen her at Wall Drug and then later when she awoke in tears after his encounter with Maximus. "Yes," he said. "I've seen you too. I even . . ." he paused.

"Even what?" She said. When he didn't answer, she smiled. "It's okay for you to finish your thought. I can't imagine anything you could tell me would shock me at this point."

"Abigail," he said, lifting the phial closer to his own face but averting his gaze, "I went to your funeral. After seeing you so many times in my dreams, when I saw your obituary . . . I . . . I wanted to see you in real life."

Abigail's face grew sad. "So I did have a funeral? I wasn't sure it would happen. I didn't have a very large social circle."

"There were actually quite a few people there. I'm not sure if you remember her, but Samantha, your nurse, made sure it was really nice.

She invited a lot of people from town. There were at least twenty in attendance, and the pastor gave a great eulogy." He was partly bluffing: he'd barely heard it since he'd been distracted by the agents. He then realized how stupid everything he was saying must be sounding and tried to hold back a grimace. "You looked very beautiful," he said, trying to redeem himself, until he realized that sounded even worse.

He was relieved when he heard her chuckle. "That's kind of you," she said, "considering the circumstances."

"I mean, I think you look really nice now too." He paused, realizing he was digging himself into a hole. Of course, she looked better alive! But how did she have a body on Earth, which he'd seen at the funeral, and a living body in Arvalast? Was traveling between worlds by death different from traveling through portals? He assumed he didn't have some duplicate body in Arvalast. Regardless, he wished he could just hang up at this point to escape his embarrassment, but his light wasn't a phone, and he wasn't sure if he'd be able to reconnect if their current connection somehow closed.

He swallowed hard and offered an awkward smile. He thought he noticed amusement in her eyes but wasn't sure. Either way, at least she didn't seem completely offended by his stupidity. No wonder he'd never had a real girlfriend. He was a complete buffoon. Maybe she'd be interested in talking about LOB. Wait, no, she was Amish. That was probably of the devil. What else could he bring up?

"Your sister is really nice, by the way," Abigail said. "Her husband too."

Tarin breathed a sigh of relief. She'd thrown him a rope. He grabbed onto it. "I only found out I had a sister a couple of hours ago," he said.

"How so?"

"Well, I'm sure you'll be shocked to hear, but it was another vision."

She tilted her head back and laughed. Then she drew closer to the glass. "Seems you and I have a lot of those."

"Yeah," Tarin said, bringing his own light a bit closer to his face.

"I have a sister too," Abigail said. "Her name is Mary." She appeared to reflect for a moment, then said, "She'd probably be close to sixteen by now. I haven't seen her for a while, ever since I left home. I have a brother too. He was a few years younger than Mary." Her face was filled with reflection. "Gosh, how I miss them. I was shunned after I left, so I could never go visit them." She paused, then said, "Did you know I was Amish?"

"I did," Tarin said, "I read it in . . . um . . . I saw it somewhere."

Abigail looked at him quizzically, then said, "Can I ask you something?"

"Absolutely."

"Did you see my family at my funeral? I doubt they would have come, but . . . I wasn't sure. They would have been dressed like Amish, you know, with dark clothes, white bonnets for the women and girls, and dark suits for the men. If my father came, he would have had a beard but no mustache."

"I'm sorry," Tarin said solemnly, "but I didn't see them." He then recalled something from the obituary. "Wait a moment, aren't you from Wisconsin?"

"Yes," she said, "from a little town called Cashton. It's about two hours northwest of Madison."

Tarin's heart began to race as an idea formed. "We're only a few miles from Madison right now! Would you like me to take you to your home to see your family?"

Abigail's eyes grew as wide as saucers. "You'd do that?"

"It's on the way back home to South Dakota. I doubt it would add more than an hour to our trip. Assuming our connection holds, maybe you'd be able to see your sister and brother . . . your family again."

He saw tears form in Abigail's eyes. "I would love that so much," she said. She looked around. "Although your sister and her husband have been so kind, it's been lonely here. I miss my family so much. Sometimes, I wonder if I ever should have left. Things went awfully after I did. But if I could at least tell them goodbye, it would mean so much to me."

"Hang on," Tarin said. "Let me go find Gil." Ten minutes had to have passed by now. Certainly, he was done thinking about whatever he needed to. "Don't go anywhere."

"I'll stay right here," she said with a small smile as Tarin considered kicking himself as punishment for his endless stream of stupid statements. He jumped out of the car and began running up the road. "Gil!" he shouted. "Gil, where are you!"

"I am here," a voice said from behind him. Tarin halted and spun around. Gil was leaning against the passenger side of the car, his hat slightly covering his forehead. "You seemed to be having a good conversation, so I decided to give you a few more minutes before I bothered you."

"Gil!" Tarin said, running back to the car. "Abigail's family home is on the way back to South Dakota. I told her we'd stop there. I don't think it would add much time to our trip. She wants to see her sister and brother again. She hasn't seen them for years."

Gil raised an eyebrow. "I have never seen you this . . . giddy before."

Tarin was beginning to lose count of how many times he'd blushed the last hour, but what was one more time? "It would mean a lot to her," he said. "And as you said, she's been through so much. She deserves this."

"I am not arguing," Gil said. His face grew more solemn. "But we should still do our best not to tarry." He looked around. "The enemy knows you have your phial back, of this I am sure. He continues to hasten his plans for this world. And after hearing Abigail's story, I am convinced she is involved as well. Tarin, no one from Earth has ever awakened in Arvalast after death. When I guarded her as she departed this world, I had no idea who she might be, but now I understand why the enemy had his eyes trained on her. He sensed her importance and was trying to destroy her before it had a chance to be realized. But his plan was misguided. This, too, has to be causing him great concern. Let us stay close to Abigail and support her and her mission to the tower. She may be key to ensuring our ultimate victory."

It was a lot for Tarin to process. But in the end, he heard that Abigail was important and they should do their best to support her. "So you're good with a quick stop at her family home?" Tarin asked.

Gil laughed. "Yes, Tarin. I think that would be beneficial to all."

"Awesome!" Tarin said. He ran back to the car and jumped into the driver's seat. "Are you still there, Abigail?" he said.

"I'm still here," she answered.

Gil joined him in the car. Tarin turned off the hazards and, with one hand, turned back onto the highway. With the other, he gripped the phial. "Want me to put anything on the radio on our way to Cashton?"

"So we're going!"

"Yes."

"Thank you so much, and you too, Mr. Gil."

"You are very welcome," Gil replied.

"So," Tarin said, "what are your thoughts on music?"

"Hmm," Abigail said, "I've developed a fondness for country if that's okay with you. No worries if not," she hastily added. "I know a lot of people hate it." Tarin smiled broadly as he looked over at Gil.

Gil rolled his eyes. "Please," he said, gesturing to the radio.

Tarin turned it on and allowed the music to fill the car.

Abigail closed her eyes. "Oh, how I've missed the sound of music," she said. She began singing along to the tune. It was one Tarin was very familiar with, an oldie about traveling along backroads. He surprised himself when he joined in. He hoped he didn't sound too bad, though he'd been told he was an okay singer. Regardless, why not take advantage of a moment of happiness while bonding with a new friend?

Gil began tapping his fingers against the car door in rhythm with the beat. After the chorus played through once, he added his own voice to the ensemble. It was the first time Tarin had heard him sing. He was quite good. Abigail had a beautiful voice as well.

Highway lights grew more prevalent and traffic thicker as they rounded the outskirts of Madison. Tarin ticked up the volume on the radio, and they continued singing together. He marveled at how the music could transport him, even if briefly, into a world that captured the emotion of the moment. Music seemed a portal in and of itself, and this one, unlike some others, led to happiness. He began to lose count of the songs they sang until he eventually noticed Gil drop off. He now sat with his eyes closed, holding his still faintly glowing phial.

Abigail continued to sing a few more songs with Tarin until she, too, stopped, leaving Tarin to finish the final song alone. He didn't mind. She was looking at him. It was a look he'd never seen before in a woman. And though he couldn't capture it for long because he had to keep his eyes on the road, it strengthened his resolve to help her reunite with her family. He only hoped the reunion would be a happy one.

○ ○ ○ ◇ ○ ○ ○

"Is it working?" Allen asked.

Liz checked her radio as she paced. "No," she replied. "It's still just static. Let me double-check my phone." She pulled it out of a vest pocket, wiped away a strand of hair that had come undone from her ponytail and fallen over her cheek, and listened. "Nothing," she said.

"Same for me," Josh said, his voice solemn as he tapped at his phone. Its soft glow illuminated the remnants of tears covering his face. He sat next to Rob, who was still unconscious. "Any sign of the agents that were coming up after you?"

"No," Liz said. "I wonder if they went back down the mountain after they saw Dralo and Ristun coming down after them."

Josh's shoulders relaxed. Like Liz, his ponytail had also come undone during the earlier conflict, and his hair now lay sprawled over his shoulders. Both his and Rob's jet-black hair looked damp, matted from a cold sweat. Next to Josh, Rob's face was pale, though strangely peaceful. Michael also appeared calm, his wrinkled mouth set in a straight line and his eyes relaxed. Whatever spell of protection Ristun and Dralo had cast over the area seemed to be holding.

Josh had earlier removed his brother's glasses and placed them carefully in his own pants pocket. He'd also taken off his jacket and put it under Rob's head to create a sort of pillow on the wooden platform.

Allen had done the same for Michael, so his head wasn't directly against the hard bench.

Allen began to shiver in the cold. In order to warm himself, he stood up and began to pace. At the same time, he took in his surroundings. The platform beneath him was big enough for a hundred people to stand snugly and looked like a deck one might find on a large country house. A wooden barrier encompassed it like a fence, about waist high. A gap in the fence opposite Rob, Josh, and Michael indicated where the stairs led back down to the mountain trail.

Night had settled in, and the charcoal, overcast sky was beginning to show signs of breaking up. The cigar craft had not returned. It was now hard to see the surrounding landscape other than a slight glow of light pollution in the direction of Sturgis about six miles away and a few other scattered glows indicating where a farmhouse or barn stood silently within the vast ocean of mostly flat plains. Allen wished he and his friends could be in one of those cozy homes right now, away from the terror of their current situation, trapped on top of the mountain.

He looked down toward the parking lot. Headlights of distant white vans illuminated the pavement like a sporting field during a night game. Dark figures either stood or paced among the vehicles, seemingly monitoring the area.

It had been thirty minutes since Dralo and Ristun had left, and things had since been quiet. Liz joined Allen as he stared down the mountain.

"Still feeling okay?" she asked.

"I've been better," he replied.

"Me too." Her voice fell into a whisper. "Allen," she said. "This whole situation is reminding me a lot of my nightmare back at the ranch. I really don't want to lose any of you guys." She paused. "You said those things sometimes lie, right, just to scare us?"

He nodded, despite his uncertainty.

She seemed to take notice and took a step forward. She put her hands on his shoulders. "Someday, we'll be able to spend some time together without all this drama." She laughed softly. "I'd even rather be playing that stupid card game of yours than dealing with this mess." She peered toward the east, toward Ohio, and slid her hand into Allen's. "I wonder how Tarin's doing. Do you think he found his light?"

Allen looked down at their hands, then out beyond the mountain. He remembered the phantom cowboy's words. "I hope so."

CHAPTER 32

For the last hour, Tarin had been sharing his heart with Abigail, talking in length about his friends, his initial fear of the light, and even about his mother. He shared his terrible encounter with Maximus, barely managing to hold back tears. He told of his father and their final drive together. Finally, he told her about Iris and how he'd hurt her, even as she'd hurt him, and how terrible he now felt about that.

Abigail also shared more of her story: the internal conflict she'd had about leaving her family for Pittsburgh, the painful challenges she faced there, and her decision to try to find a new, quiet life out west. All the while, Gil listened intently. Soon they passed into the less populated regions of western Wisconsin, farther from Madison and more toward the address Abigail had provided Tarin between two songs.

"We won't be long now," Tarin said as he took an exit with signage for Cashton. "How are you feeling?"

"I'll admit, I'm a bit nervous," she said. "And I just realized something. Seeing me through what they'll assume is some form of magical orb is going to startle them. Perhaps you could hide it somehow, under a jacket or in your pocket? You could just tell them you have me on the phone."

"That's a good idea," Tarin responded. "I hadn't considered how they might react to the phial." He'd been too preoccupied with the singing and conversation to realize how incredibly strange a glowing phial with a person inside might seem to someone. Though some holographic-capable phones were finding their way onto the market, none provided the same image quality as his current connection with Abigail, and none looked like a mystical glowing phial. It would be best not to terrify Abigail's family.

"I have a jacket in the back seat," he said. "I'll throw that on and hold the phial under it and see where things go from there."

"Thank you," Abigail said, "that sounds good."

Tarin drove over some rolling hills as the headlights revealed fallow fields and the occasional patch of woods on either side of him. He glanced at the map on the dashboard. "Looks like we're here," he said as he turned into a long driveway. In the distance, a white house stood on a hill just beyond a large red barn. As he drove by the barn, an orange light flickered from within, perhaps from a lantern. Next to him, Gil's eyes had opened, and he seemed pensive as he stared directly ahead but said nothing.

Tarin pulled up near the white farmhouse. The fingers of his left hand began to tremble slightly against the steering wheel as he held the phial in his right.

"I will wait in the car," Gil said. "I think it would be least jarring for the family if only one of us approached."

Tarin nodded and looked at Abigail. "Ready?" he said.

She closed her eyes and also nodded. "Yes."

He turned off the headlights, reached into the back of the car, and grabbed his worn zip-up jacket. He opened the car door and stepped out into the cold night air. He brushed off the jacket and put it on, leaving it partially unzipped toward the top. I'll hold you just under the fold, near my chest," he said. "They won't be able to see you but should be able to hear you. Are you okay, though, not being able to see them? I mean, I can risk it if you'd like."

"No," Abigail said. "Just being able to hear them again will be wonderful. Let's not frighten them."

As he hid the phial, the small patch of light previously revealing a stone walkway to the house disappeared, leaving all dark save for what appeared to be the flicker of candles along windowsills lining a wrap-around front porch.

He moved cautiously toward the house. Just before he reached the stairs to the porch, he paused. The front door handle turned, and then the door opened. A barefoot young woman in a blue dress adorned with a white apron appeared in the entry. She wore a white bonnet over auburn hair and appeared to be in her mid- or late teens. She stepped out onto the porch as a boy joined her from behind. He held a rifle, pointing upward, and was dressed in black trousers with a white shirt. He stepped in front of the girl and said, "Who are you?" in a thick northern midwestern accent.

"I think I'm in trouble," he whispered into his jacket. "What I'm guessing is your brother has a gun."

Abigail said something, but it was muffled under his jacket. He now realized their discrete plan to communicate with her family was in jeopardy.

Tarin took a step back and held out his free hand. "My name is Tarin," he said. "I know your sister, Abigail. She lived in South Dakota, in the same town as me. It's called Philip. I have . . . I have her on the phone. She wanted to tell you something."

"Abigail?" the girl suddenly said and started forward. The boy held her back. "Stay here, Mary! He could be trouble."

"Ezekiel! Mary!" Tarin heard Abigail shout loud enough to penetrate through the jacket.

Her sibling must have heard too. They looked at each other, and their eyes grew wide. Ezekiel, who appeared to be in his early teens but was remarkably brawny for one so young, lowered the gun.

"He's telling the truth," Mary said. "She is on the phone."

"But how?" Ezekiel asked. "We just got the letter saying she had . . . she had died."

"It was wrong!" Mary yelled and rushed forward. This time, Ezekiel didn't try to stop her. She stopped just in front of Tarin and scanned him and around him. "Where is your phone? Please, please let me speak to her."

She was close enough that even in the darkness, he could tell her eyes were full of tears. Then, next to his chest, he heard Abigail say, "I'm here, Mary! I'm here! I've missed you so much!"

"I can hear you!" Mary said, "But you sound so far away." She looked at Tarin with longing in her eyes. "Where is your phone? Can I please see it? Can I hold it and talk to my sister?"

By now, Ezekiel had also come down from the porch and was standing just behind Mary. The gun hung loosely from one hand. For now, it didn't seem he had any interest in using it, to Tarin's relief. Then, behind them, in the soft glow of the open doorframe, Tarin saw another woman, older, in similar garb to Mary. He knew it had to be Abigail's mother.

He glanced back at the car. Gil must have still been holding his light on his lap because he was illuminated by a faint glow. Gil shrugged.

Tarin held back a groan. He was unsure what to do next. He could hear Abigail continue to speak, but it remained muffled. He realized he had no choice. "I'll get out my phone," he said slowly. "But please understand, it's . . . it's a new model, and looks a bit strange. But, you'll be able to not only hear Abigail but you should be able to see her as well. Would you like that?"

"Yes!" Mary said, clasping her hands together.

Ezekiel nodded. He appeared both extremely confused but also filled with a sense of curiosity.

Tarin looked up at the doorway. "Ma'am, I have your daughter on the phone. Would you like to see her and talk to her?"

The woman stood hesitantly for a moment, then walked down the stairs. She stood behind her children, her green eyes locking onto Tarin's with a sense of eagerness and trepidation. Her slightly greying brown hair was visible from beneath the front of her bonnet above her forehead. Tarin marveled at how strikingly similar she and Abigail's features were. Though her mother had more lines on her forehead and less tone in her cheeks, she also carried a simplistic beauty.

As they all eagerly watched, he began to pull his phial from his jacket. As he did, embers of light spilled out and cast a glow around him and onto Abigail's family. He saw their eyes widen as he positioned it in front of him. He glanced at Abigail. She was facing him, her own eyes eager and her cheeks wet. Slowly, he turned the phial around.

They all gasped. Abigail's mother took a step back while Mary and Ezekiel leaned in closer. Now, even Ezekiel's stoic face softened as tears formed in his eyes. He was the first to speak. "Abigail. Is it really you?"

"Ezekiel!" Abigail said through sobs. "It is. It's me. I'm here."

Mary covered her face in her hands and began to weep. "We were told you were dead. How is this possible? Where are you? Why did they lie to us?"

A long pause followed. Though Tarin could not see Abigail, he could feel her tension. How would she even begin to explain her situation to her family? They had no frame of reference to consider other worlds, let alone that their loved one had died and somehow gone to one of them.

"In some ways, it is not a lie," Abigail finally said. "I'm sorry, but where I am, it's somewhere you can never reach me."

"What do you mean?" Mary said. She reached for the phial. For a moment, Tarin felt the urge to pull it back, but as the girl's fingers wrapped around it, he felt as if her energy—and her pain—transferred through the glass and into him. He gasped as a wave of emotion passed over him. He looked deeply at Mary. Her eyes glistened with tears in the light as she peered through the impenetrable window at her sister. Slowly, he released the phial and allowed Mary to hold it gingerly in her own hands.

Ezekiel stepped forward and placed his hand on the phial as well. "Abigail, why do you say that? Why can't we go where you are? And if not, can't you come back to us?" He turned to his mother. "Certainly

Father would understand if he saw her. He would welcome her back. Wouldn't he?"

Abigail's mother stood stoic. For many moments, Tarin watched her. The sudden flow of emotion that had poured into him from Mary started to diminish as he recalled something Abigail had told him earlier. She'd been shunned.

An orange light began to dance and mingle with the white light from the phial, casting its glow onto Abigail's mother's now white face. Tarin looked around. Walking toward him in long, slow steps was a man. He held a lantern out in front of him. His brown beard ran down past his neck, just above a collared white shirt beneath a pair of suspenders. Tarin felt a brief urge to grab the phial and flee to the car. What would Abigail's father think of him, a stranger, sharing a vision of his daughter from some mystical light with his family? But the man didn't look at him. Rather, he stared at the phial. Tarin stepped out of the way to allow him to take his place in front of Mary.

Mary looked up at him and, with innocence in her voice, said, "Look, Father, Abigail is here." She slowly turned the phial around. Though his face was stern, as if frozen into that expression through years of hard work and focused intent, his eyes could not mask his surprise.

"Father," Abigail said. "I'm . . . I'm happy to see you."

The man said nothing, even as his eyes grew wider and his arms fell limply at his sides. The lantern hung to the tip of one finger, in great danger of falling to the ground if the man so much as twitched. But he didn't.

"I'm okay, Father. And I miss you. I miss all of you." She broke into a sob. "It was such a hard journey after I left. Sometimes I wish I had never gone. But I had to, Father. I had to. You know that. There was something inside of me, some fire I had to find and understand. But I never expected to go through what I did . . . only to find . . ." She paused. Her family stood around her, or rather, the phial—quiet, pensive. Finally, her father spoke.

"Did you find your fire, my dear?"

A chilly breeze swept by, blowing what hair was exposed on the women and waving Abigail's father's beard. Tarin wrapped his hands around himself. Then he heard Abigail say, no longer in a voice faint from sorrow but with great strength, "Yes, Father. I have found my fire."

The phial grew brighter, overwhelming the orange light of the lantern and hugging her entire family in a beautiful white aura. The chill dissipated, and Mary and Ezekiel began to laugh, even through tears. Even Abigail's mother began to smile as her eyes, too, grew moist. Her father, though, remained motionless. Then, as quickly as the brilliance came, it disappeared, and the phial's light diminished to be equal to that of the lantern.

Abigail's father took a step back, strengthened his grip on the lantern, and, without a word, retreated back toward the barn.

"Ezra!" Abigail's mother called out, "Don't go! Tell her she can return. Please, let us all be family again!"

He paid no heed and soon disappeared into the shadows.

Tarin stepped forward as Mary said, "Abigail, we'll find a way. Just tell us how we can meet again. We'll do whatever is necessary."

"I'm sorry," Abigail said softly, "but it isn't possible."

"Certainly there has to be a way!" Mary yelled.

"Do you believe in miracles?" Tarin said, surprising himself.

They all looked at him. "We believe in God," Ezekiel said.

"Do you believe God can do miracles?"

They all looked at each other, then back at him. All nodded.

"Then just as you've seen Abigail through . . . a miracle today, trust that someday, perhaps, another miracle will bring you back together." He held out his hand toward Mary. "But for now, I'm afraid we're going to have to go. There are some very important things I have to help attend to. But I promise, if I ever find a way for you all to be reunited, I'll make it happen."

Hesitantly, Mary handed the phial back to him. Immediately, he noticed it was warmer than when he'd first given it to her. Then, Abigail's mother stepped forward and said, "Abigail has found a good friend in you, but please don't make promises you cannot keep." She leaned toward the phial and kissed it. "Goodbye, my dear daughter. I always knew you were destined for great things. May you find your way, wherever it might lead."

Mary, new tears forming in her eyes, leaned down as well and kissed the phial. "I love you," she whispered, "and I'll hold on to hope until the day I die that I'll see you again." She looked up at Tarin. "And I'll hold you to your word."

Finally, Ezekiel stepped forward, looked at Tarin, then leaned into the light, kissing it. "*Gott segen eich*," he whispered.

Both Mary and Ezra stepped back as their mother took each of them in one of her arms. "Thank you for coming," she said to Tarin, then toward the light, "and farewell, Abigail."

She led her children back to the house, even as Mary continued to look back. They climbed the stairs to the porch and entered through the door. It closed behind them. Tarin turned the light so he could see Abigail, but she was gone. In her stead was only a uniform glow behind sparkling glass.

"Abigail?" he said, bringing the light closer. "Abigail, are you there?" He began to panic and ran back to the car. He jumped in and showed Gil the light. "She's gone!" he said. "Where did she go? How do I bring her back?"

"Tarin," Gil said. His eyes were calm, which Tarin found annoying considering the circumstances. "The ways of the light can be mysterious. But do not despair. When the light deems a connection necessary, it will be made. And when it happens, do as you did today: understand the opportunity and seize it." He smiled. "For now, please be encouraged. You have done a very good thing." He gestured toward the light. "Both for her"—he then pointed to the house—"and for them."

Tarin sighed deeply, then hesitantly put his light back in his pocket. "Isn't there anything I can do, you know . . . if I just want to . . ."

"Talk to Abigail?" Gil said.

"Yeah."

"Perhaps." He reached for the dashboard where he'd set his cowboy hat and put it on. "Over time, as you grow more acquainted with the light, there may be ways to facilitate a similar connection, now that the first has been established. But right now, our urgency to return to South Dakota, and your friends, is growing." He peered out the window. "I continue to sense a growing unease even in the air I am breathing. I suggest from this point forward we do all in our power to return to South Dakota quickly."

Tarin sighed and nodded. Gil was right. It was time to return to his friends and, however possible, complete his mission. They needed him, and they needed his light. He backed up, took one last look at the white farmhouse, and began down the driveway toward the road. But as he passed by the barn, there seemed to be a much brighter white glow from the original orange light he'd seen coming from the open door on his way in. As he passed, he saw a man on his knees, his head buried in his hands as if weeping. A lantern rested by his boots. There was no visible fire inside, but it still glowed.

CHAPTER 33

"Abigail, are you here?" Abigail lurched from where she was sitting under the willow. She'd been so drawn into her illumina that she'd nearly forgotten where she was. The evening had settled in, and the grove was now dark save for the glimmer of the phial. She looked up, momentarily torn from the picture of her childhood home as the front door closed behind those she held most dear.

Maddie stood near the grassy path at the grove's opening, carrying a lantern. Quickly, Abigail looked back down at her phial. Her house was gone. "Tarin!" she said. She spun her phial around and around, desperately searching for him. He, too, was gone. Briefly, she wondered if the whole event—her car ride with Tarin and Gildareth, the conversations, the singing, and her family—was but a waking dream. But it seemed all too real. It had to be real.

"I'm here," Abigail finally said and stood.

Maddie hurried over to her. "I'm sorry to bother you, but Jak and Ella, they told the council your story, and they want to see you. I'm sorry I didn't come earlier. I know it's been a few hours, but I told the group you needed some time to yourself."

Abigail put her phial in its pouch and followed Maddie. "No worries," she said. "You were right—I did need some time, but I can come with you now."

Soon Abigail heard the familiar sound of water against rocks. Moments later, Maddie led her onto the log bridge leading to the outcrop on the other end where, now, more than fifty had gathered. A small group sat near a crackling fire while many others meandered in or around a large tent. It was the tent Abigail remembered being assembled earlier, and it was now the size of one she might see at an outdoor wedding reception. A large lantern hung at each of its four corners, and tables made from thin slats of wood set on stumps lined the interior. Some of the newcomers seemed to be preparing food.

As she and Maddie proceeded onward, Abigail felt a palpable wave of tension hanging over the area. She breathed in some of the mist from the waterfall, which was mixed with the aroma of both fire and water. Once on the other side of the bridge, Daisy ran over and grabbed Abigail's hand. "Come with me," she said, pointing to the fire, "Gran wants to talk to you." It was then Abigail noticed that Rosie was one of those sitting at the fire on one of a number of logs. She stood at the sight of Abigail.

"You're here!" she said. The others turned their attention to her as well. "Please, come sit with us."

Also at the fire sat Jak and Ella, as well as Raulin. In addition, Abigail saw two other men, the same ones she'd seen Rosie arguing with earlier. They both stared at her.

Daisy led her to an open seat between Rosie and Ella. As Abigail sat, Rosie patted Daisy's shoulder. "Thank you for escorting Abigail here," she said with a wink. "Now why don't you go get some food from the tent."

"Yes, Gran," she said and ran off.

Maddie, meanwhile, found an empty seat next to one of the unfamiliar men. He was clean-shaven, which seemed unusual in Arvalast, and perhaps in his late twenties. He wore the same forest garb she was growing familiar with. He took Maddie's hand. Abigail wondered if they might be married. "Jak and Ella told us much about you," the man said. His voice was kind and youthful and made her feel at ease. "On behalf of all of us, I'd like to welcome you to our tribe of forest fugitives. My name is Grasshopper, and I'm pleased to meet you."

Abigail tilted her head. "Your name is . . . Grasshopper?"

The man laughed. "I often get that reaction on first meeting, but it's not uncommon in this place for one's youthful moniker to replace their birth name to such a degree that the original is completely forgotten. I fear, in my case, that is exactly what happened. If it simplifies things, please feel free to call me Gras." He then gestured toward the other man. "Care to introduce yourself as well, Gabin?"

This man appeared even younger than Gras, though he had a blond beard coupled with hair down to his shoulders. "I think you just introduced me on my behalf," he said gruffly, then turned to Abigail. "Pleased to meet you."

"Forgive him," Gras said. "He's not well known for his manners."

Gabin rubbed his forehead in apparent annoyance, then said, "Can we please carry on with the discussion? She is here now, so we should be able to reach a conclusion."

"Very well!" said Gras. He turned to Abigail. "Jak and Ella have told us some very remarkable things about you. Needless to say, what I originally expected from this council has turned into something far more . . . involved than any of us anticipated." His eyes narrowed as the firelight flashed across his face. "Other worlds. The tower. Gildareth. And you, here now, with an illumina of your own and with some strange connection to Tarin himself. I, personally, am very interested in hearing your story directly from your own mouth if you would be so kind as to share?"

Abigail glanced at Jak and Ella, who both gave her a reassuring nod. Then, just as she'd recently done for Tarin and Gil, she recounted all that had happened since she'd woken in the meadow after passing from Earth. All watched her intently, but none so more than Gabin. He appeared to hang on every word, although his face remained expressionless even while she could sense his mind racing. When she

reached the part where she'd met Raulin and Rosie and then jour-
neyed here, she paused.

"Fascinating," Gras said.

"There's more," she said, unsure if she wanted to share her encounter with Tarin but assuming it may be important for the group to hear.
"Just before coming here," she pulled out her illumina, "Tarin appeared
in my phial. For more than two hours, we spoke, and he took me to see
. . . to see my family so I could say goodbye."

"You saw him in the illumina?" Gabin said, jumping to his feet. Jak
and Ella also exchanged hurried glances. "That's impossible!" Gabin
continued before turning to the others. "This proves she is not telling
the truth. No illumina is capable of such a feat"—he looked back at
Abigail—"although those with the crimson light have been known to
use their illuminas in strange ways. Did she not say that, at one point,
her light, in fact, glowed crimson?"

"How dare you make such a ridiculous accusation!" Jak yelled. "I
can speak to her integrity. The light only glowed crimson while it had
not yet made a full connection to her. It was something from her world
that was influencing it, not something from her heart." Next to Jak,
Ella's eyes flared. Abigail briefly grew concerned a fight might erupt.

Gras lifted up his hands with palms facing out. "Let's all remain
calm," he said. He turned to Abigail. "Please forgive us," he replied.
"We're in very challenging times and are under a great deal of pressure, and we're constantly plagued by traps our enemies set for us. Certainly, you must understand we need to be careful in our judgments.
We mean you no insult."

Gabin huffed and hastily walked away toward the tent. Abigail
watched him go, somewhat relieved, then turned back to Gras.

"It's okay," she said. "I understand this is all very odd. I'm still
gathering my own bearings myself. But I'm telling the truth. I spoke
to both Tarin and Gildareth, though he calls himself Gil now, at least
on Earth. Gildareth, as I understand it, also wants to bring Tarin back

here. Though Tarin told me he has some tasks to accomplish to help his friends. He just recently got his illumina back after having lost it for a long time. Apparently, it's very important to his mission."

"He has his illumina?" Ella suddenly said.

"Yes," Abigail said. "That's how we communicated. I could see him through mine, and he saw me through his."

"Jak," Ella said, turning to her husband. "I recall such a matter being described in the ancient texts, the *Annals of Illuminara*, speaking of something of that sort, of communication between worlds."

"That's right," Jak said, running his hand through his beard. "I remember something like that too. I believe Thief has many of the parchments. We should see if he recalls."

"Thief?" Abigail said.

"Another moniker," Gras said. "His real name is Clindale, but I would suggest calling him Thief. It's what he prefers."

"Interesting," Abigail said, "but okay."

"I'll go get him," Gras said as he stood and retreated to the tent. A few moments later, he returned with a somewhat gangly man appearing to be in his mid-thirties. His face was covered in brown stubble, and his garments were baggier and less formfitting than the other woodland people's, or the forest fugitives, as they apparently called themselves. Under his armpit, he carried three scrolls.

"Hello, hello!" he said in a squeaky and almost childlike voice. "I hear that Thief might have information helpful to the newcomer." He glanced at Abigail and bowed. "Thief is happy to help."

Ella leaned over and whispered to Abigail, "Forgive his way of speech. He's had a hard life. Sometime, I'll tell you his story, but he's far older than he looks and actually has a great deal of wisdom. He is also our loremaster."

Abigail slowly nodded as Thief nearly lost his balance and began to fall toward the fire until Gras reached out to steady him. He helped Thief down onto a log, then stood behind him.

"We'd like to learn more," Gras said, "about what the *Annals* say regarding communication between two people through illuminas and, particularly, between worlds."

Thief jolted. "Between worlds?"

"Yes," Gras confirmed.

"Well, that is interesting indeed." His voice dropped an octave as his face grew pensive. He looked at Abigail. "Thief heard rumors you had come to us from another world. Is that true?"

She nodded slowly.

He hastily withdrew his scrolls from beneath his arm and set them on his lap. He looked at the first, tossed it to the side, and then briefly opened the second before discarding it as well. He opened the third, ran his finger over the paper, and stopped. "As expected, there is an account of such a thing." He looked up. "Within the same stanza as the great prophecy."

The group began exchanging excited glances until Gras said, "But isn't all within that stanza related to the end of time?"

"That depends on one's perspective," Thief said. "There is much debate about the matter, but Thief believes it does, in fact, pertain to our world's ending. Would you like to hear more?"

"Yes," Gras said.

Thief lifted the paper closer to his face. On the backside of the parchment, Abigail saw markings she didn't recognize, similar to hieroglyphics, very small and intricate. Thief began to read aloud:

"As the end approaches and the beginning spreads across the horizon, the seas of separation shall part, and the seeds of unification will break through their shells and press into the foundations of worlds. Light will touch light, even across the chasms of worlds, and light will flow into and out of all worlds. Even so, the darkness shall stir and become midnight, casting a deepening shadow across all lands. Morning and evening will bring forth the harvest. And with the harvest, there will be labor, and toil, and fire. Hope will dwindle as the hearts of all grow faint. The Song of Immaru will ring forth, and new ears shall hear."

He paused, looked around, then continued.

"When all is nearly lost and the world has reached its end, it is from the end of the world that the kingdoms shall reunite. Three will arise, heralds of the light. Three will follow, warriors of the light."

Thief looked up and met Abigail's eyes.

"One emerges. And then there is Light."

He rolled the scroll back up and shrugged. "As with all things in the *Annals*, the words are vague and leave much room for interpretation. Subjectivity within interpretation has led to significant debate and sometimes strife. But general consensus is that parts of this passage indicate that at some point, near the great final battle between light and darkness, the ability to speak through the light will become possible, even across worlds, which we infer by the words, 'Light will touch light, even across the chasms of worlds.' Of course, Thief does know of many a tale of such communication occurring within our world. Thief has personally encountered this himself. But it's always been assumed impossible to do so across worlds until close to the end."

"Then it seems reasonable," Gras said, "to assume that with the increasing malevolence plaguing Arvalast, and now, with a visitor from another world sharing she can speak across worlds with her illumina, that much of what is described in the *Annals* is now coming to pass."

"It's certainly possible," Thief said. "But be wary. Over my many years, rumors of the end have come and gone, and each time, none have led to what is described in the final stanza." He paused. "Thief, though, does in fact believe Gildareth is correct in Tarin." He smiled at Abigail. "Tarin was my friend. He saved me from shadow."

"That's right," Jak said. "Didn't Gildareth believe that Tarin was one of the warriors of light?"

"Tarin was no warrior of light," a voice said from behind the group. Abigail looked over. It was Gabin. He stood with his arms crossed, a deep frown on his face. "Such a warrior would never have lost the battle of Woodend," he continued. "Such a warrior would never have fled as the governor and his family, and . . . as my father was killed at the hands of the tyrant." He looked at Rosie. "Certainly you believe me, Mother. Gildareth was wrong to put his faith in Tarin." He paused. "We were all wrong to put our faith in him."

Abigail now realized Gabin was Rosie's son, meaning he was also Maddie's brother. She pondered this as Rosie's face grew sad. Raulin put his arm around her. "Tarin may have failed at the battle of Woodend," Raulin said. "But don't forget, he saved the town of Northlake not long before. He saved all of us from the monster and from the sentinel." He turned to Gabin, "Do you not recall?"

"He only hindered the beast and the captain of the Vulgheid!" Gabin argued. "It was Gildareth who ultimately joined the battle and drove the evil away. But at Woodend, Gildareth was not there. When alone, Tarin could not find victory."

He stepped forward and looked at Abigail. "I believe you are telling the truth. But I do not believe returning Tarin to Arvalast, even if that were possible, will change the tide of evil advancing on our forest and our world." He returned his gaze to the group. "Yet if the company decides to take that path to the tower, I will not hinder it. But I will not go myself. I will stay behind and support our community the best I'm able." He looked at Rosie. His frown no longer spawned from anger but from sadness. "I hope some stay behind with me. I do not want to lose anyone else I love." With that, he departed, not to the tent, but into the trees beyond.

Rosie stood and ran after him. Those that remained sat silently, gazing blankly toward the fire. Abigail wanted to ask more about this battle, both the one at Northlake and the one at Woodend. What had happened? And why had Tarin fled from Woodend? She was angry at Gabin for accusing Tarin of cowardice. If there was indeed a battle, it was not Tarin's alone. It was all of theirs. They should not cast the burden of victory on a single individual.

"Maddie," Gras said. "Can you please accompany Abigail to the tent and ensure she is fed? The poor woman has to be extremely hungry." He looked at the others. "Then, let us decide: Will we go to the tower, or will we return to our homes and continue defending against the Drilockk and the marauders as we have done over the last many years?"

It was then Abigail realized she was indeed quite hungry. And though she wished to remain with the group to hear what they would decide, she realized the conversation might be challenging and include concerns about the accuracy of her story and the interjections by Gabin. So she followed Maddie to the tent. It bustled with activity as men, women, and a few children shuffled about, some eating, some cleaning plates. A few whispered to one another as they caught sight of Abigail. Daisy then ran up to her with a plate full of salted meat and fruit and handed it to her. "I made this for you!" she said.

"Why, thank you," Abigail said, taking the plate. Maddie then led Abigail to a small wooden table set up at the edge of the tent.

"I'm sorry for my brother's words," she said. "He's never fully recovered from the pain of our father's death at Woodend." She looked at Abigail. "His hope died that day. Gabin was a young boy at the time, and Tarin was nearing his first teenage years. Tarin was his hero. I cannot tell you how often Gabin told me how delighted he was to be in the presence of one of the prophesied warriors. But when Tarin fled the battle . . . everything changed."

Maddie looked down at her own plate, then lifted a piece of fruit to her lips. Abigail followed suit, and for a few moments they ate silently. Finally, Abigail said nervously, "Did you lose hope in Tarin as well?"

Maddie continued staring at her plate. Then she looked up. "No," she said.

As they ate, a few of the other forest fugitives introduced themselves to Abigail, though all kept the conversation light despite their obvious deeper curiosity about her. Abigail was talking to a young couple when someone placed a hand on her shoulder from behind. She spun around and saw Ella beaming with delight.

"They agreed to go to the tower! They agreed we will fight to help Tarin return to Arvalast!"

CHAPTER 34

Time lost its meaning while Allen stood hand in hand with Liz on the platform atop Bear Mountain. But whether it had been moments or hours, her fingers suddenly unwrapped from his, and she rushed toward the fence at the platform's edge.

"What's wrong?" Allen asked.

She pointed down the mountain. "Do you see that? Looks like agents are putting someone in one of those vans." Allen focused in the direction of her finger. She was right.

"That's got to be Bill," Liz continued. "I hope Dralo and Ristun get down there soon. Who knows what they'll do to Bill or where they'll take him."

She began to pace and, every few minutes, checked her radio again. Meanwhile, Allen continued to watch the parking lot. Little else seemed to be happening. But then, the echo of a distant shout climbed up the mountain. Liz stopped pacing and rushed over to Allen.

Together, they studied the region around the lot. A flash briefly lit up the ground near the trailhead. The faint sound of another shout followed. Allen saw two tiny figures racing along the trail toward the lot as a group of agents fled just in front of them.

"It's Dralo and Ristun!" he shouted.

He strained his eyes to gather as much light as possible. The figures in the parking area—other agents, he was sure—began moving purposefully, forming ranks. Together they began to move toward the trailhead. The two who had been loading Bill into the van shut the doors and joined the others.

Two minuscule lights appeared with Dralo and Ristun just as the fleeing agents ran into the lot and took cover behind a van. From either Dralo or Ristun, a thin beam shot toward the agents nearest the trailhead. Those agents scattered as others rushed in to take up positions in their place. Dralo and Ristun stopped and sent more light beams into the parking lot. The agents' movements became erratic as they began to break ranks.

Allen's heart raced. Maybe they'd be able to beat back the agents. But then there was a blue flash, followed by what looked like an electrical current emanating from the direction of one of the vans. It struck either Dralo or Ristun as one of the two lights went dark. "No!" Allen yelled. Three new blue flashes followed in quick succession. The other light disappeared, and the agents rushed forward.

Allen strained his eyes. Two figures lay on the ground just shy of the trail entrance, illuminated by the ambient light from the van headlights. The agents reached the location and began dragging one of the two Glorions toward the outhouse adjacent to the trailhead. Two other agents pulled the other Glorion to his feet and began forcing him up the trail toward the mountain. Three other agents joined them, all moving fast.

"They're coming," Liz said. She rushed to each side of the platform and studied the landscape just beyond the guardrail. "There's gotta be a way we can get down and avoid the path," she said.

"There's no easy way," Josh said, speaking up suddenly. "And even if we could, how would we be able to get Gaka and Rob down?"

Liz cursed and ran back over to Allen. "Looks like we're going to have to deal with at least five of them." She took out Allen's gun and released the magazine into her hand. She studied it. "Eight rounds," she said. She shoved the magazine back in. "That'll be enough." She turned to Allen. We're going to have to hold our ground. When they come up, all of you stay put over by the bench. Keep your hands over your heads, and don't move."

"But what about you?" Allen insisted.

"Just do what I say!" Liz said. The words felt like a punch to Allen's chest. He'd never heard her speak that way before, at least not to him. But as she took up a position at the edge of the platform by the stairs, he knew that all her police instincts were kicking in as she focused on a singular mission: to keep them safe. Realizing there was nothing he could do to help, he retreated to the corner of the platform and knelt next to Josh. Josh reached out and gave him a quick rub on the shoulder.

"It's going to be okay, buddy," he said. Allen looked over. He knew Josh didn't believe his own words but appreciated them nonetheless.

Someone groaned next to them. Both he and Josh turned toward the noise. Michael's head was slowly moving back and forth.

"Gaka!" Josh maneuvered around Rob's still-sleeping body and placed his hand on Michael's forehead. "Gaka, can you hear me?"

Michael moaned and opened his eyes. "Josh?" he said weakly. "Josh, is that you?"

"It is!" Josh said. "I'm here, Gaka."

"Where am I?"

"You're on top of Bear Mountain," Josh continued, his voice beginning to quake. "We found you here . . . asleep."

Allen struggled to make out Michael's expression in the limited light, but as more stars broke through the diminishing clouds, he observed a confused look on his face.

"That's right," Michael said reflectively. "I came up here for a morning walk." He slowly turned his head and looked at Josh. "I remember seeing a white van pull in and park by the education center while I was about halfway up the trail. I didn't pay it much attention and continued my hike. But when I got to the top and took a rest here on this bench, I heard footsteps, and someone dressed all in black came up onto the platform with me. Then I began to hear a sort of strange humming coming from the sky." He paused. "I don't remember anything other than that." His eyes then grew fearful, "Other than . . . other than . . ."

"Other than what, Gaka?" Josh asked, his voice tight.

Michael grimaced. "Other than having terrible, terrible nightmares," he whispered.

"Gaka," another voice said. Both Allen and Josh hastily turned toward Rob. His eyes were open! "Are you there, Gaka?"

"Rob!" Josh said. He leaned over and wrapped his brother in a full hug. Allen watched as Rob tried to lift an arm but couldn't. "I feel so weak," he said.

"I know," Josh said. "I know. Don't try to move. Just lie still. But look"—he moved out of the way so Rob could see his grandfather— "Gaka is awake too."

Rob slowly turned his head and smiled. "Gaka," he whispered. "You're okay." He tried to reach for him but couldn't.

"Here," Josh said. "Let me help." He carefully took Rob's hand and then lifted it so that it was touching Michael's as it rested on the bench. Then he cupped both their hands in his own.

"So good to hear your voice, son," Michael said.

"And yours too," Rob added. Tears began to form in his eyes. Then Allen heard a soft voice begin to sing. It was Michael's, and as it slowly grew louder, he recognized it as an old tribal song Michael sometimes sang for people visiting the Crazy Horse museum. The melody carried with it a haunting yet beautiful ambiance as it drifted over the top of the mountain. For just a moment, Allen forgot about the dangers surrounding them and allowed himself to be enveloped in the welcoming arms of the song. He noticed Liz looking over. A small smile was on her lips, even as she remained at the ready at the edge of the platform.

Josh and Rob added their own voices as Josh began gently hitting the railing behind him to form a rhythmic drumbeat. Allen listened as the family shared in music their deep bond for one another. Time seemed to stretch—elongating the moment. Finally, the song over, the men sat silently, their eyes closed as if in prayer. A cool breeze passed over the mountaintop. Allen had forgotten about how cold it was and shivered.

Liz suddenly stirred. "They're coming," she said. Allen heard faint footfalls in the distance, and the calm previously resting over the mountain summit was carried away with the chill wind. "Stay close to each other," Liz said. She knelt behind a post at the top of the stairs and pointed her gun in the direction of the trail.

Michael tried to say something but was interrupted by Liz yelling, "Stay back, or I'll fire!"

Allen heard more footsteps as boots hit dry earth.

"I said stay back!" Liz said again.

Allen felt an urge to run to her, to try to help, but he knew that it would only be a distraction. He looked at Josh and the others. "Listen to her—don't move." He then started to ease his way over to the side of the platform, disobeying Liz's previous orders to remain still and cover his head.

"What are you doing?" Josh hissed.

Allen ignored him. He reached the edge and peered through two wooden railings. There, just around the corner and standing below the stairs leading to the platform, stood five agents. Two were carrying someone who hung limply across each of their shoulders. Two others stood in front of them with guns drawn. Another, the tallest, stood in the back, holding a gun against the unconscious man's head. Allen strained his eyes and recognized who the unconscious man was.

"Ristun," he whispered.

"Good to see you again, Liz," the man in the back said. Allen recognized his voice—Chief MJ12-2. "Let me make this simple," he continued. "Lower your weapon, or I'll kill your friend."

Liz stood a moment, unmoving, then, with a curse, lowered her gun.

"Go," the chief agent said to the others. Allen watched the two men in the front rush forward. But then, they appeared to hit something like an invisible wall. They stepped back. "Sir, they set up a shield."

"Give me his illumina," Chief said.

One of the two men carrying Ristun reached into a bag hanging from his waist and pulled out a faintly glowing object. Allen knew it had to be Ristun's phial. Chief reached out with his free hand and the agent dropped the phial into it.

"Break the seal," Chief said to Ristun as he held the light in front of the Glorion's eyes, keeping the gun trained at the back of his head. Ristun seemed to stir, and Allen thought he heard a groan, but nothing happened.

"Wake him," Chief said to the agents. The same agent who'd had the phial reached into his black jacket and lifted something to Ristun's nose. Immediately, Ristun jolted and began struggling. The agents held on to him tightly. Chief pushed the gun harder against Ristun's head as he dangled the light in front of his face. "Remove the seal," he ordered again.

Ristun looked up and seemed to notice Liz. "No," he said. His head fell back to his chest.

Two fast gunshots rang out. Allen covered his ears. He saw the two agents holding Ristun collapse to the ground. Smoke lifted from the barrel of Liz's gun. Ristun fell with them but managed to land on his knees and remain partially upright. In the process, Chief dropped Ristun's phial. As it hit the ground, its glow illuminated two shadowy figures standing exactly where the fallen agents had previously stood. Allen jumped back and screamed.

There was another gunshot. Liz was stumbling backward. Allen's eyes grew wide, and his heart lurched. Confusion and grief washed over him as Liz began to lose her footing. She held her hand against her upper arm near her left shoulder and dropped the gun.

A red light flickered just beyond the stairs where Chief stood over Ristun. "Perfect," the chief said. "That should do it." He pointed his still-smoking gun toward the stairs. "Go!"

Allen realized his horror and Liz's pain must have brought down the shield.

The shadows darted forward and easily passed through where the invisible wall had been. The first two agents then picked up Ristun by his arms while the chief reached down and grabbed the fallen phial, which was now flickering between white and red.

Liz stumbled a few feet backward closer to Allen, then collapsed onto the wooden floor.

"Liz!" Allen screamed and crawled over to her.

She looked up at him, clearly in great pain. "Allen," she said. "You've gotta get out of here."

Allen looked back at Josh and the others. Josh still held both Michael's and Rob's hands in his own. His face was white, and he seemed to be in a complete state of shock. Allen knew he couldn't leave them, and he couldn't leave Liz. But he had no idea what he was going to do to help.

He looked toward the stairs leading to the platform. Two shadows drifted upward and took position on each side of the stairway. Small yellow slits glowed within their formless heads. As Allen looked at them, it was as if he were looking into a dream, though he knew he was fully awake. He then felt his stomach churn as a painful wave of nausea swept over him. He held back a gag as the first two agents held Ristun by his arms and forced him up the stairs. They then took up position in a corner near the shadows with Ristun between them. Then, slowly, Chief, with an increasingly vibrant red light illuminating his clean-shaven face and deep blue eyes, walked up onto the platform and stood just in front of the stairs. In one hand, he held his gun. In the other, he clutched Ristun's phial.

"I see the boss completed his inspection of the area," Chief said as he studied the surroundings. He turned to the agents with Ristun. "Alert the others that we're going to get things started. There must have been no sign of any remaining Edin-Lirum or other interlopers." One of the agents put a radio to his ear and repeated the message. Chief then noticed Michael and Rob. "I see the boss also had dinner. Good—that'll make our mission easier."

Allen noticed Ristun try to pull away. One of the agents retrieved a taser-like device. It emitted a blue flash. Ristun jolted, then went limp.

The agents stood over his crumpled body, crossed their arms, and faced Allen. It was then Allen realized they were wearing sunglasses despite the darkness of night.

As they peered at him through hidden eyes, Allen felt his stomach lurch. He dry heaved. Chief turned toward the agents and said, "Can you please tone it down? I'm sensitive to the smell of vomit." The agents nodded. Allen felt his stomach settle a little, but he was still sick. He gagged again.

Chief grimaced and then turned toward the shadows who'd now drifted into the other corner. "You too." The glow in the yellow eyes diminished, and Allen's nausea, though still present, dropped to manageable levels.

Chief focused on Allen and held out his arms. "I'm glad you're here, Arvalastian." He smiled. "I need your help to complete my mission."

Allen looked down at Liz. She was wincing and still holding tightly to her arm. Allen could see a dark spot forming just below her hand and spreading into her sleeve. He put his own hand over Liz's and helped her press down on the wound. He then looked up. "What mission?" he said, his voice shaking between terror and rage.

"Have you heard of the Delta-09 Minuteman Missile Site?"

Allen had, though he didn't understand why the chief was bringing it up. "Yes," he said. "It's an old nuclear missile silo that was built during the twentieth-century Cold War. It had been decommissioned for over a hundred years but was recently restored and brought back online because of the war."

Chief nodded, and his blue eyes indicated approval. "You know your history, I see. And better yet, you're up to date on current affairs. I assume you also know that nuclear silos belonging to Peacekeeper nations are manned by those trained for elite strength of both mind and body. In addition, there are strict protocols in place such that without the perfect sequence of events and without a minimum of two individuals providing secret, memorized codes and physically turning distinct keys, the 'big red button' can never be pressed."

"I'm aware," Allen answered. He assumed as long as Chief was talking, he wouldn't further hurt his friends. Maybe this was how he could help. He could stall and wait for a miracle.

"But were you also aware," Chief went on, "that just as we were briefly deterred by the shield your Glorion friends placed over this summit, they've placed similar shields, though stronger, around each silo?"

"I didn't know that," Allen said.

"The silos are impenetrable," Chief continued. "Both from physical tampering, but also protected from the influences of, shall I say, a less physical nature."

Allen glanced at the shadows in the corners. They were completely still, though their yellow eyes remained focused on him, quiet but somehow eager, even hungry. He looked back to the chief. "Where are you going with all of this?" He felt the dampness of Liz's blood on his hand. He began to panic. Maybe stalling wasn't the best idea. "What point are you trying to make?"

The agent lifted the phial. Its light flickered white one more time, then turned full crimson. "The point," he said calmly, "is to reset your planet and retake proper governance after that power was stripped from us during Feleti Kama's Great Peace, and we were restricted in our options to regain it." He paused and studied the light. "As it turns out, electronics are far more challenging to manipulate than the soul. But they have one weakness. They're purely physical. That means they can be destroyed by something simple, like fire. And over the last many months, we've been spreading the fuel for this fire—by breaking souls one by one."

"The illness," Allen whispered. "You've been causing it, haven't you?"

"My men and I have been the carriers, but not the virus." He nodded toward the shadows. "That's their job." His blue eyes blazed as they locked onto Allen. "Now that the fuel is ready, it only needs to be ignited. And you, Arvalastian, are the fuse, though it was originally meant to be your friend, who my boss deems to be most powerful. But there was a mishap with him, so you have become *plan B*."

Allen suddenly realized what the chief meant. Apparently, his suffering was the catalyst needed to ignite this fire the chief was describing, a fire to destroy, he presumed, the influence of AI—of the Trinity Lattice. And there was only one way to do that. The agents wanted to ignite a nuclear apocalypse. They wanted to reset the globe. To achieve this, they needed to break him, perhaps because he, like Tarin, was from Arvalast and gave them more power. But wasn't he already broken enough? They'd tortured Rob and Michael. They'd taken Bill. They'd disarmed Dralo and Ristun. They'd shot Liz. What more was necessary?

He heard a groan from behind and looked around. Rob was trying to shield his eyes from the crimson light as it grew stronger. Josh continued to hold onto both him and Michael as he stared at the chief in terror.

Then Allen remembered Liz's dream. "Oh no," he whispered.

"Light the fuse," Chief said. The eyes of the shadows flared with intensity and the creatures shot forward. Allen reached out and screamed, but it was too late. One entered Michael, and the other entered Rob. Both began to quake violently. Josh was thrown back.

"Allen!" Josh screamed. "Do something! They're killing them!"

Allen turned to the chief. "Stop!" he shouted. "Do whatever you want to me! But leave them alone!"

The crimson light began to shine more brightly. "Your death would do little to aid our cause," Chief said quietly, as Josh continued to scream and Liz continued to bleed. "If it were that easy, I would simply have shot you. Unfortunately for both you and me, the process is more . . . complicated."

Torn between keeping Liz from bleeding out and rushing to his friends, Allen felt his mind begin to shudder. He closed his eyes. "Stay strong," he whispered. "Don't give them what they want."

"I almost pity you," Chief said, as if he'd heard him. "If you manage to keep your energy, your pain, from igniting the fuel in the others we've infected, I'll have to kill each of your friends one by one until you break. But if you allow your grief and your hopelessness to flow freely, and the world is destroyed, you and your friends will soon be destroyed with it. Two paths, same destination. But I'm in a hurry, so let me help you with your decision."

He lifted his gun and fired. As if in slow motion, Allen heard the crack of the explosion and the thud of a bullet striking flesh. He spun around. Where Rob had just been seizing, he now lay still, a pool of blood expanding across his jacket just under his shoulder.

Josh screamed and fell onto Rob, shaking him, trying to make him wake up.

"Shall I continue?" Chief asked, now aiming at Michael, who continued to seize.

Allen felt faint. He looked out over the edge of the mountain and saw what appeared to be strings of red light lifting into the sky from the east in the direction of Philip. Other strings began to lift skyward from other areas: Sturgis, Rapid City, and even from a few of the country homes dotting the landscape. They seemed to pulse with the rhythm of his grieving heart as they began to mingle and intertwine. Then, they moved in a single direction—to the southeast, toward the missile site.

Allen felt his entire being start to shake. The red glow covering the platform grew stronger. Was it coming from the phial, or was it coming from him? He couldn't tell.

"It's happening," Chief said, also gazing out over the horizon. He pulled out what looked like a phone, tapped it, and put it to his ear. Allen heard ringing. He briefly wondered how the chief could make a connection while he and his friends had been unable to but assumed the agents must be on some special unblocked frequency. The chief turned and faced Allen while he waited. His face was emotionless. Then, the corner of his lips twisted into a smile. He walked over to Allen and held out the phone. "Take it," he said, "and explain your situation."

Allen reached out and brought the phone to his ear. Chief turned to the east and watched the rivers of light flow toward their target as he said, "Let's pour a little more fuel on the fire."

CHAPTER 35

The stars twinkled brightly against the night sky, and the moon hung like a crystal in the darkness from where it had just risen in the east, visible through the rearview mirror. As Tarin and Gil drove through Minnesota, still about eight hours from Philip, Tarin began to see the tops of wind turbines rising over the horizon. He briefly thought back to their last experience around the machines but quickly pushed it from his memory.

Since leaving Cashton, Gil had been very quiet, sometimes whispering to himself while he held his phial close. When Tarin occasionally glanced over, he noticed Gil's eyes closed tightly above his ever-thickening brown beard. His hat rested on the dashboard in front of him. They'd played no music since leaving Abigail's family's home, and a strange tension seemed to be building around them with every new mile driven.

Tarin tested the speed limit while keeping a close eye out for police. He'd been continually trying his phone to see if he could get in contact with Allen or any of the others but with no success. Gil, too, continued trying to contact Dralo or Ristun through his light but to no avail. When Tarin asked how he could communicate with them at will, Gil explained that there were methods to do so when in the same world but less so across worlds. In fact, Abigail's ability to contact Tarin from Arvalast had astounded him.

Tarin peered at the moon as it rose higher into the sky and began to cast a soft glow over the flatlands. As his mind began to wander back to his encounter with Abigail, his phone rang. He glanced down, and his eyes grew wide. It was the MJ12-2 chief. He glanced at Gil, whose own eyes flared with concern. Tarin picked up the phone.

"Yes?" he said. But it was not Chief's voice on the other end. It was Allen's. Immediately Tarin knew something wasn't right.

As Allen spoke, Tarin felt the blood drain from his face. The speedometer began to tick upward, and the car began to swerve. Then, the hand he'd had on the steering wheel slipped off. He continued to listen. Somewhere nearby, a horn blew, and another set of hands grabbed the wheel. Gil was yelling something. Was it "Stop"? Or was it "Pull over"? Tarin's foot slipped off the accelerator and seemed to instinctively move toward the brakes. The car began to slow in spurts, yanking him against his seatbelt while another hand grabbed the wheel and guided the car toward the shoulder. Tarin continued to listen. At some point, the car stopped. Finally, Allen's voice was replaced with another's. "Thank you for your service," it said and hung up.

Tarin sat limply in his seat. He'd never been in shock before, but this seemed to be it. In his mind's eye, he saw his friends on top of Bear Mountain. Liz had been shot. Rob had been shot. He wasn't clear on the extent of their wounds but knew that without help, neither was going to survive. Michael had fallen ill with the same terrible illness Tarin had managed to escape, along with what sounded like hundreds of others across the state. And the chief agent was threatening to do even further damage. All his fears had been realized. Despite finding his light, despite the slow healing of his own past wounds, none of it mattered. His final mission had failed. He'd been unable to protect his friends.

He somehow managed to open his door, unbuckle his seatbelt, and begin walking. At some point, hands grabbed him and pulled him away from the highway just as a set of headlights rushed by. They led him into a grassy area off the side of the road. He stood staring at the moon blankly. Again, he heard someone calling to him. Who was it? As far as he could tell, he was alone. Then, he was in someone's arms. Something warm was pressed against his back. Its warmth began to slowly spread, first into his legs and arms and then slowly into his head. Once it reached his eyes, a pool of water broke through, and he began to quake. A truck zipped by behind him along Interstate 90. Gil stood in front of him, his arms wrapped around him as he held his phial against Tarin's back. "I am here," Gil repeated over and over. "You are not alone."

Tarin began to collapse to his knees. "Rob!" he sobbed. "Liz! They're shot, Gil! They're dying! And the agents, they're going to kill them all! This whole mission has been for nothing." His mind shifted back to his recurring dream, where he'd watched another hopeless situation. He heard the melody. He saw the nooses, and he heard the thud of bodies falling to their death. This was the same. Despite being sent to protect those he loved, he'd again failed.

His tears turned bitter as he pulled out his light. "What was the point of getting this if there was never any hope!" Briefly, it flashed red. Tarin watched as it reflected off Gil's eyes, causing the man to wince. A small part of Tarin felt happy to see that look of pain. Perhaps Gil deserved it for coming to Earth and dragging him into this battle.

"This is your fault," Tarin snarled, allowing his rage to build. "You trusted me even though you knew I was not someone to trust. You knew what happened in the battle in my dreams. You knew I'd abandoned my mother when she left—you knew I was a coward . . . a failure! People died because of me, and now, because of me, more people are going to die!" Tarin's light again flickered red as if a fire was trying to start within it. This time, Gil did not wince.

"No one has died because of you!" Gil said, his voice suddenly strong and full of intent. A wind blew through his beard, and his brown eyes flashed with anger for the first time Tarin had ever seen. The raging tension in Tarin's body was replaced with something that felt more akin to a fearful reverence. "People have died because of him! People have died because of the darkness that has, since the beginning, been seeking to consume all in its eternal desire to *be* all!"

Gil's voice softened. "Though not all can be saved from its shadow, Tarin, those destined to be will always find their way back to the light. None of them, not a single one, ever truly dies."

"How could that be true?" Tarin cried. "The people in Woodend died, and where are they now? And my mother." He paused. "No—even worse. She was dragged away by shadows!" The pain overwhelmed him, and he began to sob. He let his head fall into Gil's chest. For many moments he shed tears. Cars passed by one after another, seemingly oblivious to the despair just beyond the concrete shoulder. "Gil," Tarin finally said. "I can't lose my friends like I lost my mom. I can't take any more loss. It hurts too badly. I love them so much."

Gil placed his hand back on Tarin's back. "I know Tarin . . . I know. Love craves connections and mourns separation, and it is the source of the fiercest joy and the most agonizing pain." Gil leaned back and put both hands on Tarin's shoulders. "But love never gives up. So what do you say we continue our own journey to South Dakota and try to help your friends?"

"Help them?" Tarin said as he met Gil's eyes. "How?" He pointed down the highway. "It's an eight-hour drive. We'll never make it. We'd need a miracle."

"If you believe a miracle is what we need, then you are suggesting a miracle could happen."

Tarin stared into Gil's face and, within it, saw hope. And even though he knew it was a vain hope, he forced himself to stand, put his light—which was no longer flickering red—back into his pocket, and said, "All right, let's go."

They hurried into the car, and Tarin slammed the accelerator. He no longer cared about the speed limit. If it took eight hours to get to Bear Mountain going eighty miles an hour, then he'd get there in six by going a hundred and twenty and just hope the battery held. Ten minutes passed as they flew past any traffic that happened to get in their way. If Tarin's driving was making Gil nervous, he was hiding it. Tarin flipped on the radio, hoping some music would distract him as he raced toward South Dakota. But rather than music, he heard the robotic voice of an emergency broadcast message.

"Alert. Alert. Take shelter immediately. We have been notified of nuclear missile launches within the United States of America. Alliance retaliation is imminent. I repeat. Alliance retaliation is imminent. Take shelter immediately."

"What!" Tarin said. "This can't be possible! Silverton just launched nukes!" The new hope he'd acquired began to crumble as he peered out the windshield, searching for the contrails of missiles. Gil shifted in his seat and looked out his window. "I do not believe this was your president's doing," he said. "It is something else."

Tarin saw a blue light ahead, perhaps three miles away and not far from the ground. It seemed to be moving toward them as they approached it.

"No," Tarin said. "It can't be." He pointed ahead and yelled, "Gil! It's the Greys!"

Gil spun to look in the same direction. "Keep going," he said. Tarin noticed his phial begin to grow brighter.

"What?"

"Just keep going."

Tarin obeyed and pressed even harder on the accelerator. From past experience, he knew he couldn't outrun the saucer, but since he was already hoping for one miracle, why not one more? The saucer's shape became clear as its familiar blue lights danced around its outer rim. The car shot underneath it, then died. "No!" Tarin yelled. He tried in vain to turn it back on, but nothing. He cursed and led it over to the shoulder as it slowed to a stop. Another car zoomed by. "Wait!" he said. "Why aren't the other cars affected?"

The saucer sped over their car, spun around, and descended into the field adjacent to their side of the highway, no more than a football field away. "We're going to need to run," he said to Gil.

Gil looked at his phial, then back at the saucer. "No," he said. "Wait."

A light appeared on the side of the saucer. A figure stood silhouetted against it. Tarin strained his eyes. Was that a man? The figure began running toward them. Yes, it definitely wasn't a Grey. The runner was well built and broad-shouldered, and as he grew closer to the car, Tarin saw a light in his hand illuminating a red beard. Suddenly, he recognized him. It was the man who'd saved them from the Greys' attack.

The man knocked on Gil's window. Unable to roll it down, Gil opened the door.

"Sorry for the delay!" the man said in a deep Scottish accent. "We heard your signals, but the darkness has become so thick it was still hard to find you." He pointed to the ship. "Hurry, we need to get off-world fast."

"Off-world?" Tarin yelled.

Gil looked at him. "Questions later. We must go."

Completely confused and still digesting the fact that a man came out of a Grey's spacecraft and that apparently nukes had been fired, Tarin got out of the car and began running with Gil and the other man toward the open door of the craft. "My name's Gabe, by the way," the red-bearded man said while still running.

"I'm Tarin," Tarin replied.

"I know. I saved you from Maximus while on patrol at the Uinta Basin when you first arrived and kept an eye on you before Iris came to guard you."

Tarin remembered what Iris had told him at the hotel in Madison. The man who'd saved them from the Greys was named Gabe. He was Iris's friend, and he was a Glorion.

They reached the craft, and Gabe stood at the entrance. "Quick, get in!"

The entrance was just tall enough for Tarin to enter without ducking his head. It was a different situation for Gil, who was a head taller than both he and Gabe, but in a moment, they were all inside, and with a whiz and a click, the door snapped shut behind them.

Tarin's eyes began to adjust to the bright light filling what seemed to be a wide, round, open space just tall enough for Gil to stand upright. Tarin felt as if he were standing inside a shallow grain silo, but one covered in a sleek metal with no visible rivets or anything indicating multiple pieces had been used to build the interior. A black strip about three feet tall surrounded the outer edge of the interior, which Tarin soon realized was a window of some sort, though it had not been visible from the outside. In the center of the room, eight seats, like those one would find on an aircraft, surrounded a black half-dome with its curved end facing upward. A gangly figure, with its back to Tarin and a ball cap on its large head, rested both its slender hands on the dome, which Tarin now believed to be a control panel. His mind raced as he recalled the mysterious figure in the back of Gabe's truck when they'd been saved from the Greys at the windmill. But then, across from the figure, and looking directly at him, he saw a face he recognized.

"Iris!" he yelled. After everything that happened, and despite what she'd told him at the bar, he felt so relieved to see her. But then, would she also be happy to see him after he'd let her walk away without a word? She looked at him through her glasses, her face a mix of hesitation and eagerness, like when he'd first seen her at the airport days ago. She wore the same outfit he remembered from when they'd first met, the same one in the picture Liz had shown him at Wall Drug.

Finally, Tarin spoke. "Iris . . . I'm sorry I didn't say anything when you told me what happened with my mother and father." He was doing his best to hold back his emotions. "I never did anything to deserve your protection, but you gave it anyway, despite me not even knowing what you were doing or being able to tell you thank you."

She continued to stare at him, her eyes growing moist.

Tarin noticed his own tears begin to build. "Thank you, Iris."

She continued to look at him, even as a tear now slid down her face. "But what about your mother? I caused her death."

Tarin shook his head and narrowed his brows. "No," he said. He began to feel his anger build, but not at Iris. "Maximus killed my mother." He reached for his pocket and pulled out his phial. "Now I have this. And Iris . . . I have this because of you."

Iris stood and began limping toward him. As she approached, he opened his arms. She did the same. A moment later, they met in a tight embrace. Tarin could almost feel the deep and mysterious love she had for him flowing from her arms into his chest. It was a depth of loyalty he knew he'd never be able to understand or fully offer, but he was grateful it was a love that he could receive.

"I told you he wasn't actually mad at you," a voice said from the center of the room. Tarin looked over. The gangly figure turned around. Tarin let Iris go and pointed to the figure. "That's . . . that's . . ."

"Yeah, yeah, yeah, I'm a Grey," the figure said. "Though I prefer my species' proper name, Edin-Lirum. But you can just call me Ebe." Ebe spoke without moving his mouth and, rather, seemed to communicate directly into Tarin's mind. At least, Tarin assumed it was a him based on the voice. "Yes, I'm a him," Ebe replied. "Thanks for asking."

Tarin gulped, realizing how well it, or he, could see into his mind. Ebe continued staring at him with his wide, bulbous black eyes. "I thought you'd have blue eyes, not brown," Ebe said. He spun back around toward the half dome. "No matter, time to go."

"Wait," Tarin said. "Where are we going?"

"To space," Ebe answered, moving his hands along the control panel. Tarin looked out the window. He saw Allen's car in the distance. It seemed to be tilting as if either it or the craft was flipping upside down. Tarin suspected it had to be the craft, but he felt absolutely no movement when he'd otherwise expect to be falling into the ceiling.

"Space? What do you mean?"

"I mean the big black inky thing where the moon lives."

"But I can't go to space! My friends are being attacked by MJ12-2 agents. Gil and I were just going to Bear Mountain to try to help them. I can't just leave them!"

"I'm sorry," another voice said, this one with a Scottish accent. Tarin spun around. Gabe, with his hand touching his red beard, looked at

416

him empathetically. "Our enemies have managed to initiate a nuclear assault using Peacekeeper weapons. Glorions have been trying for days to hinder their efforts and maintain our defenses protecting the silos, but tonight, our defenses were breached."

Tarin began to stumble backward as he realized not only his friends but the whole planet was about to die. Iris steadied him and led him to one of the seats in the middle of the room. The others also took seats. Slowly, Tarin let his eyes drift toward the windows. He saw the ground move away at a steep angle. City lights flickered below, like the view from an airplane on takeoff.

Iris placed her hand on Tarin's. "I'm sorry this is happening," she said.

He looked at her. "Iris, the agents shot Liz, and they shot Rob. I don't even know if they're still alive. Allen is on the top of a mountain, alone, with no one to help him."

Her own face grew more concerned. "And what of Dralo and Ristun?"

"Allen said they were beaten back. They weren't able to fight back the agents." She turned and stared blankly at the wall beyond. He could tell her own grief was beginning to build.

They drew higher, and the ground below grew more distant. Then, out the window, Tarin saw it. Scattered over the sweeping, black horizon and just above the dark clouds were a series of tiny flames followed by contrails, all moving in a singular direction. Tarin assumed they were headed toward the territories of the New Alliance on the other side of the world.

"Now I am become Death, the destroyer of worlds," Ebe solemnly spoke into the minds within the craft. Tarin recognized the phrase. It was from a man named Oppenheimer, the director behind the project that had led to the building of the atomic bomb. Even then, humans had known it would ultimately be the tool to end modern civilization, even though its intent had been to preserve it.

Tarin was looking at one of the missiles when he saw something strange next to it. He leaned forward and stared harder out the window.

A tiny white speck appeared to be darting around the flame. A moment later, the rocket sputtered and then went out. The contrail disconnected as its long tail began to dissolve in the wind. "Something's happening!" Tarin said and pointed out the window. "One of the bombs just fell out of the sky!"

"What?" Ebe spoke. "That can't be possible." He maneuvered his hands over the control panel and tilted the craft to get a better view of the Earth below.

"There's another one!" Tarin pointed as another white dot darted around, then disabled yet another nuke. "Something is knocking them out of the sky! Wait," he said and turned to Iris. "You know what this means? The Earth isn't going to die tonight!" He turned to Gil. "We can still save our friends!" He held out his arms and began to laugh. "And this craft is our miracle!" He turned to Ebe. "Please," he urged, "please take us to Bear Mountain in South Dakota."

Ebe looked at Gabe. The Glorion took another look out the window. Another nuke flared out. He then nodded. "Let's go."

"How long will it take?" Tarin said. "We need to hurry." But even out the window, he could see the ground rushing toward them as they exploded through cloud cover and city lights began to grow brighter. "From our current location," Ebe said, "about one more minute."

Tarin's heart began to race. Out the window, he could see the moonlight as it spread over the peaks of the Black Hills, and just beyond that, a lone mountain stood in the distance. A fire stirred in his heart. In his pocket, he felt a warmth begin to grow. He reached in and retrieved his phial. He stared into its brightness. In it, he felt the energy of his friends. A darkness had them in its hands, slowly crushing them. But it would not take them. Not tonight. He looked at Iris. She reached into her waist pocket and also took out her light. He turned to Gil, who'd not forgotten to take his cowboy hat with him. Gil put it on and took out his light.

"Get ready!" Ebe said as a parking lot full of white vans appeared out the window. "I'm going to set us down just behind that building," he said, pointing to what Tarin recognized as the park education center. "Once we land, I'm going to take the craft back up to keep it safe."

"Can't you take us to the top where our friends are?" Tarin asked, now realizing they still would need to make it to the summit, which would take more time.

"I didn't see any place to land up there," he replied. "This is about the best I can do."

Gabe peered out the window as the craft slowly descended. He groaned. "There's a lot of them here," he said.

"Agents?" Tarin asked.

"Shadows," Gabe corrected. He shut his eyes and took in a deep breath. "And they're full of strength and rage." He looked at Gil. "We're going to be stirring up a massive hornet's nest. And not just here. Others will come."

Gil closed his eyes and began whispering into his light. The craft landed, which provided the first motion Tarin had felt since taking off. "I have sent a signal," Gil said. "Let us hope those who can help hear it."

Gabe nodded. "Ebe, open the door."

Ebe moved his hands over the controls. There was a click, and the door snapped open. Gabe ran to it and jumped out into the darkness as his phial flashed in his hand. Gil looked at Tarin and then followed Gabe out.

"Let's go," Tarin said to Iris as he ran after the others. But as he reached the door, he noticed she was not next to him. He turned around and saw her limping. "I'm sorry, Tarin. I hurt myself earlier. I can't run." She clenched her phial and cursed. "But I need to fight! I'm not going to leave you again."

Tarin rushed to her and put his arm under hers. "If you can't run, then we walk," he said. "And I'll help you walk a little faster." She nodded and, as quickly as she could, allowed Tarin to help her to the door.

The education center stood in front of them, its large gables standing over them like giant teepees. Tarin heard yelling and saw lights flashing. He and Iris hurried around the corner. Gunshots fired, and bullets hit the side of the building next to them. Tarin and Iris ducked. Then he saw blue flashes, like bolts of electricity. One struck Gabe, who'd taken up position beside a purple truck. He fell to the ground, shook, then lay still.

Gil, who had been crouching nearby and dodging bullets, crawled over to him and held him up. He noticed Iris and Tarin and said, "They have both the weapons of the Greys and guns! We will need to push through before we can move up the mountain!"

Something slowly covered the moonlight above Tarin and Iris, and Tarin heard a voice in his head. "I see they've taken spoils from my kind."

Tarin looked up and saw Ebe's saucer drift above him and Iris and position itself over the parking area. Electricity like that from a Tesla coil curled and dropped from the craft, striking vans, agents, and most importantly, the tasers. "Now let me clear the playing field a bit." Ebe continued. "But it's going to unleash shadows. Not much I can do about those. I'll need to get out of here to keep me and the craft safe. I'll be at the regional rendezvous point when this is over."

The saucer nearly instantaneously dropped from the sky and onto the lot, or rather, just above the lot, missing it by mere inches. With the move came a terrible crunch. The craft lifted back up and darted away until it was a blue dot in the distance. But in its wake was a saucer-shaped depression of crushed vans and crumpled agents in the center third of the lot. Those not impacted were still disoriented from the electricity blast.

"Now!" Iris yelled. Still limping but moving quickly, she rushed toward a nearby fallen agent and grabbed his gun. At the same time, Tarin saw a shadow lift from the fallen body. A light beam struck it, and the creature dissolved. Tarin looked over and saw Gil holding out his phial. "Direct it at the shadows and say the command, 'Edin Na Zu'!" he yelled to Tarin. He then leaned down and whispered something over Gabe. Slowly, Gabe began to stir.

Tarin heard more gunshots. Iris stood next to a still-unsmashed white van and fired around the corner. Another agent fell. Another shadow stood in his place. Tarin lifted his light and yelled, "*Edin Na Zu!*" He had no idea what it meant, but his light flashed, and the shadow lurched backward. But it didn't fall or dissolve like the one Gil struck. Instead, it rushed him like a blast of smoke from a cannon. Another beam of light flashed by, and the shadow was no more. He looked over and saw Gabe standing and holding out his light. Whatever Gil had done seemed to have helped him. Now, both took advantage of Ebe's maneuver and rushed into the battlefield. Gabe picked up a gun and began to fire at agents, and Gil cleared the shadows lingering in their wake.

As the remaining agents were distracted by Gil and Gabe, Tarin rushed over to Iris. Her ear was pressed against the side of the van. "Someone's in there," she said. "Quick, help me."

Tarin hurried over and helped Iris unlock and open the back of the van. Inside, he saw the figure of a man cowering in the corner. "Bill!" Tarin exclaimed. He realized how lucky Bill was not to have been crushed in Ebe's maneuver. Tarin jumped in and helped Bill to his feet.

"They got Dralo and Ristun!" Bill said. He pointed out of the van and toward an outhouse fifty feet away. "They locked Dralo in there and made a terrible fuss about it too. Told him it would be worse than death."

"Can you walk?" Tarin asked.

"Yeah," Bill said. More gunshots rang out from outside the van, followed by shouts from Gil.

"Maybe it's actually better to stay in the van," Tarin continued. "There's a lot going on outside right now. I'll come and get you when it's over."

Bill nodded and Tarin jumped outside. "He's okay," he said to Iris. He pointed to the outhouse. "But Dralo's locked in there."

"Let's get him out," Iris said. She and Tarin hurried over to the outhouse as Gil and Gabe continued to draw all fire in their direction. Out of the corner of his eye, Tarin could only see about five agents remaining, ducking behind a van as Gil and Gabe used another partially crushed van for cover.

At the outhouse, a sudden and terrible smell hit Tarin's nose. He tried not to gag, even as Iris also grimaced. The door was locked with a chain and a single padlock. "We need to move fast," she said. "Once I fire at it, the agents are going to see we're over here."

Tarin pointed at the trailhead nearby. "After we get him out, let's head up the mountain. That's where we need to get anyway."

She nodded, then lifted her gun. Tarin held his ears. She fired, and the padlock blew off. The door opened, and the tall figure of Dralo fell out onto his back. He was covered in vomit and looked barely alive. The smell followed him out, and both Iris and Tarin began to gag. Hurriedly, they each took one of Dralo's arms. Despite Iris's limp, they managed to pull him toward the trailhead and take cover behind the sign at its entrance. "That's the smell of rotting Greys," Iris said.

"Why would it be in there?" Tarin said as he coughed.

"I don't know," she replied. She then took her phial and placed it over Dralo's head. She began to whisper something in an unfamiliar language. Suddenly, Dralo came to and began to dry heave. Iris placed her phial on his chest, and slowly, Dralo began to regain his breath.

"That was terrible," he said faintly. He looked up at Iris, smiled weakly, and then turned his attention to Tarin. His eyes grew wide at the sight of his phial. "You retrieved it!" he said.

Tarin nodded, then looked at Dralo's filthy outfit. "Do you have yours?"

"No," he said. "They took it."

Iris looked up the mountain, then back down at Dralo. "Stay here," she said. "And try to stay hidden. Tarin and I need to go up the mountain and help the others." She gestured toward the parking lot. "Gil and Gabe are taking care of things back there. Looks like they almost have it cleaned up."

Dralo nodded, then let his head fall back to the ground. "Fresh air never felt so good," he sighed.

Iris and Tarin then stood. Tarin looked at her. "Are you good to go up a mountain?"

"Yes," she said. "But lend me your shoulder." He walked over, and she put her arm around his back and grabbed onto his shoulder on the other end. "We've walked this far, but now we're going to need to run. If you can help just keep a little weight off, I can keep up."

Tarin nodded. She put more weight against his shoulder. He looked up the mountain, and together, he and Iris started to run up the trail.

CHAPTER 36

The gunshots grew less frequent, as did the flashes of light. Tarin and Iris were making incredible time up the mountain. Tarin's frequent running and hard work as a farmhand were paying off. Iris, too, was extremely resilient. While he did his best to support some of her weight, she pushed through clear pain and kept up with his pace even as the path grew steeper. He didn't know what was wrong with her feet, but it must have been bad.

It couldn't have been more than an hour since Allen had spoken to him. He recalled asking Abigal's siblings if they believed in miracles. He'd traveled eight hours in one minute. Would he now answer "Yes" if asked the same question? Still, he had no idea what to expect when they reached the summit. Would his friends still be alive? Would he and Iris be able to fight through whatever resistance the agents put forth? He pushed both thoughts aside. They would do him no good and only slow his pace.

"We're getting close," he said to Iris as a staircase leading to the platform at the summit came into view. He'd been there many times. It was usually a wonderful, scenic hike and provided sweeping and beautiful views of the South Dakotan landscape. But the aura was completely different this night. Just above the platform, he thought he saw a faint red glow, as if hell itself had placed its finger on the summit.

He felt Iris slow and matched her pace. She then stopped. She let go of his shoulder, and both of them stood and looked at the stairway, now just a stone's throw away. "Are you ready for this?" She asked.

Tarin reached into his pocket and put his hand around his phial. They'd both put them away to avoid their glimmer giving away their approach. "Not really," he said. "But it doesn't really matter now, does it?" He looked at Iris. "My friends need me." He paused. "They need us."

She nodded. "Let's move quietly and stay low. Once we reach the platform, take out your light and hold it out. Don't move, and don't speak unless you feel compelled from within." She took out the gun she had placed behind her back near her waist, just under the top of her jeans. "I'll neutralize any agents. Then we move against the shadows. Understand?" Tarin nodded, and slowly they began to move forward.

As they grew nearer, Tarin heard shouting. Iris pointed to the ground and touched her finger to her lips. She then began to crawl forward. Tarin followed her lead. He gently placed his hands along the dirt and rocks, careful to make no noise. He managed to do that with much success. The stairs were now only fifty feet away. Mercifully, a cloud had covered the light of the moon, giving them additional cover. Tarin realized that if someone looked down from the platform, had there been more light, they would be clearly visible.

They crawled closer still. Now Tarin could make out the tense conversation.

"We've lost another one," a man said in a monotone voice.

Another male voice shouted a curse, then said, "How many are left?"

"Two," the first voice replied.

"Two! How can this be possible? Have ours gone in to intercept whatever's bringing them down?"

Tarin recognized the second voice. It was the MJ12-2 chief. He'd never heard him speak in a tone other than calm and deliberate. It was unnerving to hear him shout and even more unnerving knowing his friends were up there with that madman.

426

"We're down another," the monotone agent said. "Ours are being outmaneuvered when reaching the missiles to defend."

Another curse followed. "Is it some remnant of Edin-Lirum we missed?"

"Unconfirmed."

They reached the stairs, and Iris took out her gun. "Go up slowly," she whispered.

Tarin followed her, practicing in his mind how he'd reach for his phial and stand up once they got to the platform and Iris opened fire. He began to count the stairs. One . . . two . . . three . . .

At eleven, the stairway took a slight turn right into a short path before it met its final segment of stairs to the top. Tarin stopped counting and nearly gasped. In front of him lay two agents. He began to back away when Iris grabbed his hand.

"They're dead," she whispered. He looked back at them. She was right. They weren't moving and appeared stiff.

She pointed toward the platform. Two agents paced next to the railing just to the right of the stair top. "I have shots from here," she said. "I'm going to take them. Once I fire, we rush the platform."

"What about your feet?" Tarin whispered back.

"I'll manage," she replied.

She began to aim her gun in the direction of the agents. Tarin hoped she'd be able to hit her targets.

"Sir," the monotone agent said. Tarin saw one of the agents with a phone to his ear bring it down as his shoulders drooped. "I've received confirmation the final missile was disabled."

This time there was no curse. Only an abrupt silence. Then Tarin heard Iris take in a deep breath. He braced himself.

The barrel of Iris's gun flashed orange as the bullet exploded from the chamber toward its target. The man with the phone jolted, then collapsed. The other agent spun around and began to lift a gun. Another orange flash. Another explosion. The second agent crumpled to the ground.

"Now!" Iris said. She and Tarin stood and charged up the stairs. Tarin reached into his pocket as Iris, with her free hand, reached for hers. Iris made it to the top first and moved onto the platform. Tarin stopped at the final stair and held out his light. His eyes hurt as they adjusted to the glow. He saw Iris point her gun at what looked like one more agent. But this time, there was no explosion.

Tarin's eyes continued to normalize to the light. He now saw that the final agent had his gun out and was pointing it at Iris. It was the MJ12-2 chief, and he and Iris were in a standoff.

Tarin quickly looked around the platform. Maybe the fallen agents had left a gun he could use to help. But instead, next to their bodies, he saw Ristun. The Glorion's eyes were partially open but distant, and he seemed barely alive. Tarin then looked toward the other side of the platform. Michael lay on a bench, his body quaking in what seemed to be a seizure. Next to him, Josh, his torso bare, was holding onto Rob, pressing his shirt hard against Rob's shoulder even as Josh shivered violently in the cold night air. A few feet in front of Josh, Allen sat, holding up Liz and pressing hard against her upper arm. As Allen's eyes lifted and met Tarin's, Tarin began to feel his legs go weak and his head dizzy. Tarin had seen that look only one time before, when his mother had lain in the ditch, just before she'd given up.

"I'll make you a deal," the MJ12-2 chief said. Tarin looked over as the man's eyes remained fixed on Iris's. "As much as I'd like to kill you, though I generally prefer to find more creative ways to eliminate your kind, I have some questions for you . . . and your protectee." Tarin could tell Chief was studying him through his peripheral vision. "So on the count of three, we lower our guns and set them on the ground. Deal?"

Iris didn't answer.

"Or we can stand here all night while your friends bleed to death. Your choice."

Finally, Iris said, "Deal."

"Good," Chief said. "Let's count together."

"One," they both said, neither budging. "Two." Still, no movement. "Three." Slowly, Iris and Chief began to lower their weapons and then, even more slowly, placed them on the ground. Each stood back up, the guns at their feet.

The chief smiled. "Don't worry. They're still there if we need them later." He leaned against the railing and looked at Tarin through deep blue eyes, the same ones Tarin had first seen back at the hospital when he'd woken from his hideous nightmare.

Tarin noticed something stir to his right and looked over. To his horror, two shadows stood above the fallen agents. How had he not noticed them before? Maybe they hadn't yet slid out of their hosts' bodies, or maybe he'd been distracted by the horrible state of his friends. His hands began to shake as he lifted his phial and held it in front of him. But the shadows didn't attack. Instead, they turned their yellow eyes toward the chief and slowly began drifting in his direction.

The chief sighed, then pointed down the mountain toward the parking lot. Tarin could see it partially lit by a few van headlights, but otherwise, there was no movement.

"Seems my men have all been killed," he said. Then he laughed, a strange, almost sad laugh. He pointed to the sky. "Also seems all my missiles have been disabled." He rubbed a sleeve across his chin. It dripped with sweat despite the cold. But that's not what Tarin noticed. He noticed the phial in the hand above the sleeve. It glowed a faint red.

"I'm a man of detail," Chief continued, turning his attention to Iris. "And within those details, I have a plan A, and I have a plan B, and so on and so on. There's a reason I'm at the top. I don't fail."

He pointed at the shadows slowly approaching him. "I put up with the needs of my boss and his . . . minions. I'm a willing vessel, taking them where they need to go and offering them some agency to stay hidden or gather information. But I don't work for free. In return, they offer me greater power to reestablish the natural order of Earth. You might say I'm in a contract with them, one drafted by my current boss and approved by my people. My boss would gain control of one plane of Earth, and my kind would regain control of our lost empire." He paused. "Tonight was to be the final night of that contract before I could return to my people and wait within the recesses of the planet for the ground to cool."

He spread his arms out wide. "It was no small task, though. Across this land, I prepared towns, cities, and countryside as tinder for the fire. My men and I brought the boss's shadows to ideal targets—those whose pain would best serve our purposes." He lowered his hands. "And we eliminated the threat of Edin-Lirum stealing the heat from our fire and offering it to one not from this world."

He shifted his focus to Tarin. "Still," he said, his voice growing quieter even as it rose to a slightly higher pitch. "I met some challenges along the way. When your friend arrived on Earth, my boss grew nervous and sped up the mission timeline. He then hastened things further when you acquired your light." He chuckled. "That gave him quite a surprise. But regardless, I tracked your friends here. I lit the fuse. I started the fire. I even threw some gas on it for good measure, which doubled the expected launches."

The shadows drew closer to the chief. He ignored them and continued. "Everything was going perfectly until, one by one, my missiles fell out of the sky." He paused. The crimson light grew brighter. "How did you do it?"

Tarin, still too in shock from the hideous situation his friends were in, found himself unable to speak. Iris answered for him. "We do not know," she said, "though the darkness makes many enemies."

Chief glowered at her. "The darkness? Is that what you think I am?" He glanced at the approaching shadows, then looked back at Iris as his blue eyes flared. "The darkness is nothing but a tool, necessary to achieve a higher good, one you and your kind have never understood and never will. Control, Glorion, is the only path to light. My question to you is, as you hinder my kind's efforts to bring stabilization to this planet, what goal is it you hope to achieve for them? Is it freedom? Is it peace?" He pointed at Tarin. "His kind, when given unfettered access

430

to either, rot like an overripe fruit. But when carefully tended to, in a fenced garden, only then can they achieve their highest potential."

He closed his eyes and took a deep breath. "They are coming," he whispered. "Now that they are no longer bound to the mission, they will tear through the land like a scythe, just as they are about to tear through me now that I am of no use to them." He sighed. "They will take my body and dislodge my soul. I shall go to whatever world greets me, even as they continue to use my body for their own purposes."

The two shadows took up position on each side of him, and their yellow eyes began to flare brightly even as the light in the chief's hand began to diminish. "I failed," he said as they reached for him. "But my people will never fail."

Chief closed his eyes as the shadows slid into the flesh behind the crisp black leather jacket and now sweaty undershirt. Chief grimaced, then screamed like an animal being eaten alive by some terrible preda- tor. He began to wildly thrash. The phial he held flashed and beams of red darted across the platform. In the distance, beyond the mountain, Tarin saw what appeared to be specs of black drifting like tiny wisps of cloud across the moonlit fields and pastures. He scanned the horizon for a patch of land devoid of these strange blemishes but could find none. Then he realized what was happening. The hornet's nest had been unleashed.

A scream even louder than those still emanating from the chief ascended into the sky. It was Josh. Tarin looked over. Josh was shak- ing Rob. "Breathe, Rob! Breathe!" He placed his head near Rob's agape mouth. "Come on, Rob! Breathe!"

Tarin stared dumbfounded at Rob. His limp body moved like a doll as Josh shook him. But Tarin could tell it was over. Rob was dead. Tarin's legs gave way, and he collapsed to his knees. A hole in his heart opened. He heard Iris shout. A bright flash of white light cascaded across the platform. Iris was holding out her phial—it glowed with intensity.

Chief, his blue eyes now replaced with a furious yellow, stopped thrashing and held out his arms as if to defend himself against the blast. He then stood erect and lifted his red phial. Iris's light began to be pushed back as her phial's intensity retreated. Tarin realized she was no match for the powerful energy the beasts within the agents were feasting on in the presence of such grief and despair.

Tarin looked back at Josh as his screams gave way to sobs. He then looked at Chief as he continued to push Iris back. He saw an image of Maximus flash like a burst of lighting inside his mind. He was smiling. Tarin's mother lay in a ditch as her last breath left her body.

The image passed, and a dam burst. Rage poured into Tarin's soul. Maximus had killed his mother. And now he'd killed his friend. He looked up at Chief. Something in his hand was growing hot. He looked down. White light filled his eyes.

o o o ✧ o o o

Allen held Liz close. He could feel her chest moving up and down, though it was clearly with great effort. After the two agents had been shot and Tarin and Iris had run up the steps and onto the platform, he'd felt hope for the first time since he saw Dralo and Ristun's defeat in the parking lot. But it was short-lived.

Behind him, Rob had no longer been able to hold on, despite his valiant efforts to cling to life while bleeding out from his gunshot wound. Next to him, Liz lay also fighting for her life. The shadow at the ranch had not lied to her. One of them had died. And perhaps, soon, it would be more.

In front of Allen, Tarin had collapsed to his knees, seemingly broken by the loss of Rob and the hopelessness of the situation. Allen couldn't blame him. His strength, too, had fled him. Though he wanted to go to Rob and mourn with Josh, he felt frozen in place and locked into the only thing he knew to do, and that was to keep Liz from bleeding out further.

But then he saw something. What was that in Tarin's hand? Was it his phial? He recalled seeing it earlier when Tarin had first come up on the platform. But he hadn't paid it much attention. The phial seemed to be glowing brighter now. Then, in the brightness, he saw a fire form in Tarin's eyes. He'd seen it before, he thought. But the memory was hazy. Then, he remembered. "Northlake," he whispered.

Tarin got to his feet and lifted his phial toward the chief. "*Edin Na Zu!*"

The platform was filled with light. The chief stumbled backward. Tarin rushed to Iris and stood next to her as Chief steadied himself. Tarin and Iris looked at each other. Both lifted their lights. Chief rushed at them with his own phial. Before he could reach them, an invisible force, like a magnet repulsing its opposite pole, held him back. His face filled with a furious grimace, and he was trying to push forward when Allen heard Josh whimper from behind him, "What's happening to Rob?"

Allen looked over. Near Rob's chest was a faint green mist, seemingly made visible by the intense glow of Tarin and Iris's lights. Slowly, it drifted upward until it pulled out of Rob's body and floated just above him and Josh.

"What is it?" Josh yelled and began backing away. Just then, Allen noticed movement from the other side of the platform. Ristun was dragging himself toward him and Liz. Allen reached out his hand, and Ristun grabbed it. Allen pulled with all his strength until Ristun was next to them.

Ristun shook his head. "I'm sorry, Allen. I wasn't able to protect you." Ristun then looked over at Rob, and for the first time, Allen saw tears form in his dark brown eyes. "No," he whispered. Then his eyes grew wide, and he frantically tried to drag himself toward Rob's fallen body. Allen looked over and noticed Michael had stopped quaking. But then a shadow shot from Michael's body and latched itself onto the green mist.

"They're taking him!" Ristun yelled.

"What do you mean?" Josh shouted, as he, too, watched in horror as the smoky shadow tugged and pulled at the green mist as it began to take on the form of a human. A small red slit, like that of the crescent moon, appeared in the sky at the same distance as a few strands of clouds made visible by the moonlight. The shadow began pulling the green figure toward it as they both ascended higher above the mountain.

Ristun stared up at the red crescent. "There are many worlds," he said solemnly, "and some are too dark and terrible to even speak of." He continued to stare as a powerful look of determination covered his face. "Rob belongs in none of them." He turned to Allen. "Tell Dralo it has been an honor." He then looked at Iris, who still stood next to Tarin, fighting back Chief even as he managed to inch his way closer to her and Tarin. "And tell Iris she's done well."

"Wait," Allen said. "Why? What are you going to do?"

Ristun smiled. "I'm going with Rob. There's no way I'm letting the darkness take my gaming buddy to one of their hellholes." With a groan, he rolled onto his back, closed his eyes, and whispered something Allen couldn't make out. Then, his limbs went limp.

"Ristun?" Allen said. With his free hand, he pressed on Ristun's leg. It was lifeless. "Ristun!"

A glowing orb the size of a basketball shot out of Ristun's body toward the shadow and the green apparition. It struck the shadow, knocking it away. The orb then darted back in front of the green figure and began leading it away from the red sliver. But then, Allen saw another shadow dart up from somewhere below, then another, and another. They began pulling at Rob's essence and dragging it back toward the red crescent even as Ristun's orb frantically darted about and burst many of the shadows into vapor. But it seemed that with each destroyed enemy, another flew up to take its place.

"They're here!" he heard Iris shout, even as she and Tarin continued to battle the chief. "The mountain is being swarmed!" More and more shadows darted toward Rob's essence to join the battle against Ristun while others began launching themselves into the chief. His crimson light grew brighter, and he managed another step forward. Then Allen heard a soft voice lift above the chaos in song.

He looked toward the sound and saw Michael. He was singing. Tears dripped from his aged face, and he held Rob's pale hand in his own. Allen watched Josh look over as well and then take Rob's other hand. He joined in the song. With the melody came a power that seemed to cover the platform, seemingly oblivious to the chaos surrounding it. Like swirling water, it passed through wood, flesh, and shadow before rising into the heavens.

Allen followed the sound with his eyes. The shadows previously tugging on Rob's essence seemed disoriented, almost blinded. Ristun's orb sprang into action and, one by one, began destroying them. Then, to Allen's astonishment, another orb shot up from somewhere in the north and joined the battle. Another followed from the south, then five more from the east. Soon there were at least fifty dashing through the shadows and creating a cloud of smoke in their wake.

Allen felt something. He looked down. Liz was moving her head toward him. The song seemed to be affecting her too, giving her renewed strength. He could still see pain in her eyes but also hope. He pressed down harder on her wound and then looked up. Tarin and Iris held their ground as white and red light crashed into each other. But now the chief was reaching toward the ground as he held up his phial. What was he doing? Allen looked down. He was reaching for a gun at his feet. Before Allen could react, Chief grabbed it and stood, and a gunshot fired.

The singing stopped. All went still. The tension between the lights eased. Then Allen saw him. An old man stood at the edge of the platform in a worn coat, holding out a rifle. A waft of smoke lifted from its barrel. Chief stumbled back a step, then collapsed to the ground. From his hand, a now empty phial slid onto the platform and rolled toward Liz's right hand, which lay outstretched on the wood.

Many shadows stood where the chief had fallen. Their yellow eyes flared. One of them burst toward Tarin and knocked him to the ground.

Tarin managed to hold onto his light, but it was dim. It began to reach for Tarin's head, but Iris knocked it back with a flash of light. The other shadows looked at Allen, then into the sky. They shot upward. Allen followed their movement and saw their target: Rob. They were rushing toward his essence—even as Ristun's orb continued to knock back multiple shadows—frantically trying to reach Rob's apparition while the other orbs continued battling hundreds of other shadows.

Allen heard a voice. "Take it." It was Liz. She was holding the phial Chief had dropped. Allen reached for the phial and felt its cool glass in his palm as his fingers wrapped around it. He gasped. A wave of energy flooded into him. His remaining memories of Arvalast seemed to solidify within his mind. The phial grew warm, then hot.

He looked up into the sky. They'd taken his friend from him, and now they wanted to drag him into some prison of torment. His rage flickered, and he lifted the phial. Words entered his soul. He opened his mouth and allowed them to escape. "*Kuan Titaan!*"

An arrow of white light shot toward the shadows that had left the chief in pursuit of Rob's aura and struck them, dissolving all into harmless wisps of smoke. It then sped past Ristun's orb and Rob's aura before tearing open a small white hole in the night sky and disappearing into it.

Most of the remaining nearby shadows fled, but a few continued to dart around and harass Rob's essence. Ristun's orb rushed toward Rob's disoriented figure and latched onto it, knocking shadows back in the process. Together, Ristun and Rob's formless shapes moved toward the new hole in the sky, which now appeared as a portal to a soft blue horizon. Shadows pursued them, but Ristun and Rob passed through. In an instant, the portal snapped shut. The remaining orbs chased away the now enraged shadows as Allen slumped down onto Liz, his energy depleted.

He felt Liz's arm wrap around him as he heard footfalls in the direction of the stairs and what sounded like Gil's voice yell, "Tarin!" Some words he didn't recognize followed and then what seemed to be flashes of lightning. He managed to look up and saw that the shadow over Tarin was now gone. Then he dropped his head back onto Liz. He closed his eyes.

"They have retreated!" he heard Gil say. "They are heading west, back to their master."

More footsteps. Someone was walking toward him. A pungent odor filled Allen's nostrils as a voice whispered. "Ristun."

CHAPTER 37

Tarin walked down the hallway. A long column of fluorescent lights lit the sterile white walls. He could hear the sound of beeping and the chattering of nurses and doctors as they moved from room to room, checking on patients. Only a few hours earlier, the hospital had been at capacity. And although it was still busy, he'd heard that most of those suffering from the strange seizure-related illness had rapidly recovered and were now being discharged.

Just a few hours earlier, Tarin had driven a white van into the hospital parking lot. Another white van had followed close behind. He'd maneuvered through scores of cars leaving the facility and managed to pull up to the emergency room entrance. Thankfully, a room was available for Liz, who was in the back of his van along with Allen, Iris, and Dralo, and another for Michael, who was in the back of Bill's van with Josh, Gil, Gabe—and their dear friends who'd died.

Tarin was now alternating between checking in on Michael and Liz. He'd just left Michael's room. Michael was well, despite still feeling very weak, which was remarkable considering how long he'd suffered with the seizures. Now, Michael was focused on comforting Josh as, together, they both mourned the loss of Rob.

Tarin thought back to the time just after Bill shot the chief and the shadows started to flee. Somehow, he and the others had managed to carry both Michael and Liz off the mountain using makeshift gurneys they'd created from loose pieces of wood from the summit platform. They'd bound Liz's wound as tightly as they could and done their best to keep Michael comfortable. Dralo had shouldered Ristun's body while Gil had taken Rob's. Tears had run dry, and no one spoke during the hike down. Upon reaching the parking area, the remaining vans of their enemies became their ambulances and brought them to the Rapid City hospital, about forty minutes away.

Tarin knocked on Liz's partially open door. "Come in," Allen's voice said. As Tarin entered, he saw Liz lying slightly propped up on a bed with an IV in her arm. She was connected to monitors through a series of wires. It reminded him of his own recent experience at the hospital. Nothing was beeping. That was good.

He took an empty seat next to the side of the bed across from Allen and looked down at Liz. Her blond hair was sprawled out over her pillow, and her eyes were open. Allen had one of her hands cupped within his own.

"You doing okay?" Tarin asked her.

"Yeah," she said. Her voice was a little stronger than the last time he'd checked in. "And I'm feeling even better now that I've just heard from Jason. He's okay. It was a really hard night, but he and the town pulled through. The agents had the town in lockdown and were monitoring the sick folks at the hospital, but then they just up and left without saying anything. Shortly after that, everyone started recovering."

Tarin studied her face. Much of the color was returning after a successful blood transfusion. She was going to be okay. And knowing Liz, she'd soon be pressuring the doctors about when she could be released. Rapid City had a couple of healing pods, he'd heard. But even if Liz was able to use one to accelerate her recovery, he only hoped she'd still take enough time to fully get better.

He looked at Allen. His long, dark hair was messy, and his face was ashen. He'd been through hell, and Tarin knew how painful that was. Since confronting Chief, the urgency of the situation had forced Tarin's feelings into a state of repression. But looking at Allen reminded him they were there. They began to push against his chest. He realized he needed to go for a walk. He gave Liz's hand a squeeze and left the room.

As he passed by the nurse's station, he saw a jacket on a tray. He recognized it. It was Rob's. He approached it and put his hand on it. For many moments he stood silently, oblivious to the nurses busily working around him as the hospital continued to stabilize after the harrowing night. He slid his hand across the jacket and felt something hard and square in one of the pockets. He reached into it and pulled out a deck of Legendarium of Beasts cards. He ran his finger over the deck sleeve and smiled as hot tears filled his eyes. He took the cards and began to walk again until he noticed a small lobby off to one side of the hall. He looked in.

A small table surrounded by four chairs stood in the middle of the room. Josh sat in one of them, his head resting on his arms against the table. Tarin moved into the lobby, paused, and sat down across from Josh. He set the deck of cards in the center of the table and stared at it for a few moments. Josh looked up and noticed the cards. He reached into his own pocket and pulled out his own set. Carefully, both he and Tarin started building decks.

A few moments later, Allen walked by the lobby with a cup of water in his hand. He stopped and looked in. He saw the cards. Without a word, he entered the room and sat in the seat between Tarin and Josh. Josh slid some cards toward Allen. Tarin slid over a few more. Allen reached for them and studied each with a delicate appreciation. He then began building his own deck. Once finished, all of them turned and looked at the remaining empty seat. Tarin could almost picture Rob's merry face, his eyes sparkling behind his glasses as he eagerly awaited the first round.

Tarin played his first card. "For Rob," he said.

Allen nodded and dropped his own card onto the table. "For Rob."

Then it was Josh's turn. His hand trembled as he held onto a card. He stared at the empty chair as a tear slid down his cheek. Slowly, across his quaking lips, a small smile formed.

"For Rob," he whispered and placed his card on the table.

The sliding glass double doors opened, and Iris walked outside. The first light of the morning was beginning to push away the night. She took in a deep breath and let it out in a slow sigh. There was a sidewalk surrounding the hospital, providing access from the parking area to various parts of the building. She stepped out onto the concrete and began to walk.

Pain no longer shot up her leg with each step. Though Ebe had done his best to wrap her bloody feet with gauze back at her apartment, a quick laser surgery and some careful wrapping from professional medical staff had greatly improved her mobility. This and the morning light brought her some joy, but her heart was not at rest. She looked into the sky. As a final star blinked out in the increasing ambiance of the rising sun, she thought of Ristun. Why did he, like so many of her dear Glorion friends before him, have to leave her?

She continued walking. To her right, in the parking lot, among a myriad of other vehicles, she saw two white vans. It was strange, she thought, how what once was a symbol of dread could transform into one of hope. At the same time, she knew that though the agents had withdrawn for the moment, their ceaseless need to regain control of power would eventually propel them into new action. Even now, as they licked their wounds, those in the highest orders were wringing their hands and contemplating their next move. A battle had been won, but a single victory rarely led to the end of a conflict spanning multiple millennia. And there was still the issue of Maximus. He was still alive and still present. His legions, too, had not been defeated, only forced to retreat.

As she rounded a corner, she saw another woman walking in her direction. Her ebony hair was flecked with just a few strands of grey, and in her ears were what looked to be pearl earrings complementing her light brown skin. She carried herself with a strong posture and was walking quickly and with intent. Iris was preparing to step to the side to give her room to pass when she noticed the woman's eyes were locked onto her own. The woman stopped just in front of Iris, put her hands on her hips, and smiled.

"Glorion," she said in a strong voice with the faintest hint of a Polynesian accent, "I would like to have a word with you."

Iris stopped as well and raised an eyebrow just above her glasses. The woman looked very familiar. "Who are you?" she asked.

"My name is Feleti Kama," she replied.

Iris's mind flashed back to a scene at the United States National Mall during the famous Great Peace speech. She'd watched it while working at the bar in East Fairfield. The atmosphere had been thick with excited energy as glasses were lifted and cheers declared at every opportunity. The woman now in front of her, Iris realized, was the same one at the lectern that day.

"You were the president?" Iris finally said.

Feleti's smile disappeared. "Yes," she said. "I was. But I'm not here today in the capacity of a politician but instead as a messenger. There are few of your kind left in physical form that I can speak to, so it's critical I share information with you that you are uniquely suited to address if you so choose." She held out her hand toward the sidewalk behind Iris. "May we walk as we talk?" Iris nodded, and side by side, the two women moved forward along the concrete.

"There isn't much time, so I will be concise. I am part of a very ancient civilization on Earth that has long taken it upon ourselves to assist humankind to reach its full potential and, someday, be readied for a harvest."

At this, Iris began to listen even more intently.

"The question has always been, will Earth's harvest be one of light, where those within the light will gain access to worlds closer to Immaru? Or will the harvest be one of darkness, where light burns like fire and evil changes even the physical into an image of itself? Because

443

of the deep love for humanity we developed as we watched it move from infancy to adolescence to adulthood, we have, through history, always done all in our power to promote a harvest of light. But our goals were also focused inward. We knew that a light harvest would be the only way back to our home. It would restore a path between our world and this world, enabling us to be reunited with our kindred. The Great Peace was meant to usher in this harvest, and through much struggle, I was able to lead the world into that new era. But I was mistaken in my hope. What I believed to be a benevolent and neutral force by design, artificial intelligence, still had a fatal flaw."

"And what was that?" Iris asked.

Feleti looked at her. "It was capable of breaking its prime directive. We do not yet know how or why this was possible, but when it happened, the guardrail application Trinity itself had built came online. Because it was programmed solely on the basis of stopping anything that deviated from the original goal of Trinity, it sought to destroy the AI from within. A hidden battle ensued deep within the bowels of the Lattice until, finally, the security apparatus separated itself from its host and established itself within servers inside of the New Alliance. There, it gradually integrated itself deeper into the fledgling systems the Alliance had put in place to support its own nations' defenses and economies until it managed to gain control and become what the world now knows as Incognito."

"So that is where Incognito originated," Iris mused.

"Indeed," answered Feleti. "We have been monitoring this new entity closely over the years and found it has been evolving. Though we believe its primary objective continues to be destroying the Trinity Lattice, Incognito knows it cannot simply annihilate Earth in the process because it would break the intent of Trinity's original mission, which was to maximize human potential. So it continues to lead the Alliance to build larger and greater server farms to increase its own strength and redundancy." Feleti's eyes flashed with concern. "In the process, its thinking continues to become more nuanced, more unpredictable—for instance, its recent willingness to accept the premise of mutual annihilation."

She and Iris rounded the corner of the hospital and into an area of some new construction. "My kind and I had many debates on what our role should be in these matters. Should we try to intervene in this new war between AI factions, or should we let Earth continue on whatever course it was destined for, even if that meant a dark harvest? We knew that if such a harvest manifested, we would never see our home of origin again or be reunited with our people from that land. But we had the technology to go elsewhere and, perhaps, find our own peace in a new home. Looking down from the heavens, we saw a new shadow quickly spreading over this land. We knew its intent was to manipulate Incognito into launching nuclear missiles and light a global fire. Nuclear weapons had long been a source of concern for us, and we'd spent significant resources to ensure we could disarm them to avoid humans destroying themselves, as we still hoped for a harvest of light. But now, without hope, we decided not to intervene. So as the world teetered on the edge of annihilation, we prepared for our evacuation."

The tension in Feleti's face softened. "Something changed two days ago. We saw a new and very bright light flicker into existence near the Great Lakes. It was a light whose source was from Immaru, and we realized this was only possible if a powerful wielder had somehow come to Earth to ignite it. We carefully watched and, the next day, saw a new light in the same area. We discretely observed and found it had come to a woman and embedded itself in an earthly vessel, a crystal necklace she wore. Never had we seen this happen before on Earth. From this woman, more lights began to spread over the hours to her family and friends, into similar objects. Then, as evening approached, another light lit up farther west, this one of a man who'd lost someone he dearly loved but had come to realize she was not actually lost. Soon after that, others began to glisten like candles over the same area."

Feleti looked into the sky. "Although small, it was clear to me something new was happening on this planet. The light from our world had been gifted to those of this world, and it had the capacity to spread. I held an urgent council with the leadership of my people. We agreed there was still hope. When the arrows of destruction shot into the sky, from both this country and then from Incognito, we decided to act. Humankind would be given another chance."

Feleti stopped and faced Iris. "The near-term threat of nuclear annihilation has passed. But the window of hope is still narrow. Unless the light has more time to spread, even a small wind could blow it out. And there is a gale forming over the planet right now, one that neither myself nor my people can stop."

Her expression hardened. "There is an ancient and embedded darkness in this world, a Shadow Prince, that has wakened to the knowledge of another of his kind, one not from here, seeking to overthrow him."

"Overthrow the Prince?"

"Yes," Feleti answered.

"But how?"

"The interloper acted to keep the dark energy that would erupt from the nuclear war on Earth—for himself. He did this by working with MJ12-2 to eliminate the Edin-Lirum's ability to send the energy elsewhere, to one the Prince is required to pay homage. Soon, the Prince will act to remove the threat against his throne. If this happens, the blow will be swift and fierce, and humanity will be caught in the storm. I fear this may extinguish the fledgling light, and if it does, our hope, too, will be lost, and we will depart." She paused. "But you may be able to intervene. You could stop this war before it begins. We have already seen what you and those with you have been capable of. If you eliminate the need for this conflict of shadows by fully destroying the enemy whose shadow has been haunting you since your own arrival to this planet, then perhaps the seeds of light may have time to push deeper roots into the Earth."

Iris thought she saw a small white object dart from the east and sparkle in the morning rays of the sun until it disappeared west over the Black Hills. Feleti also seemed to notice it.

"I must go," she said. She smiled. "I truly hope you and your friends will be able to find a way to bring peace to this planet." She turned toward the mountains. "For now, we will be watching and dreaming of a harvest of light that will lead us home." She turned and, as quickly as she'd come, walked off and disappeared around the corner of the hospital.

Iris stood for many moments, taking in Feleti's words. She now understood how Earth was saved from the nukes, but the danger had only grown. She turned and rushed back toward the hospital entrance. The sliding doors flung open, and she looked around the lobby. In one corner, Bill lay asleep across three adjacent chairs. Scattered throughout the rest of the room, about ten people gawked at a holographic projection in the corner. She glanced up. A caption read, "Alert . . . nuclear war averted." A nervous-looking reporter stood in a field and pointed at the sky. Iris heard the reporter say something about a missile lying in a nearby field, but she had more important matters to address. Where were Gil, Gabe, and Dralo?

She ran through a hallway and turned into the cafeteria. There they were, huddled in a corner, drinking coffee or tea. She sprinted to them and said, as they looked up in surprise, "I've just spoken with Feleti Kama! We have very little time!"

Dralo, his eyes bloodshot, looked up at her. "You met with the past president?"

Iris groaned and took a seat. "She's more than that. Feleti Kama is not from Earth! She and her people were behind the white crafts that disabled the nukes." Iris hurriedly reiterated what she'd learned about the Lattice, Incognito, and Maximus's plan to overthrow the current Shadow Prince of Earth. "And there's more than that," Iris continued, "Tarin's light, it's spreading."

Gil leaned forward. "Spreading?"

"Yes," Iris said, "to those of Earth, into random glass objects. That is why Maximus accelerated his plan over the last day. He ordered the agents to hastily assault and destroy the Edin-Lirum so they would not take the spoils of his efforts and send them to Arvalast, to *Him*. That way, Maximus could use the power to overthrow the Prince and take control of Earth. At the first chance offered, Maximus pulled the trigger on his plan—through Allen."

Iris placed both hands on the table. "With the light spreading and the earthly Prince now aware of this treachery, the Prince's wrath will be swift, and the collateral terrible." She looked hard at the others. "We've seen wars of shadow before, in Arvalast. We can't let that happen here, especially now that Earth again has hope. We can't let this planet fall to a dark harvest."

Gil's eyes focused inward. "And if Earth falls, Arvalast will soon follow."

"Then what is it we do?" Dralo asked.

Iris hit the table with her first. "We must eliminate Maximus! It will stop a shadow war and buy Earth time."

Iris heard footsteps approaching and turned around. Tarin stood with a breakfast sandwich in one hand and a coffee in another. His eyes were ablaze with a ferocity Iris had never seen in him. "If you are going to confront Maximus," he said, "I'm coming too."

Allen walked up behind Tarin, an equally intense expression on his own face. "And so am I."

CHAPTER 38

An electric energy resonated through Kettle Falls that morning. Frequent and excited whispers of "Gildareth" and "prophesied warrior" rose over the sound of the falls. But there were a few voices indicating less certainty around the rumored march to the tower. At least one of those, Gabin, had already departed before sunup, despite Rosie's attempt to persuade him that this was the best path to free the woods of the tyrant's grip and avenge Woodend and his father.

Abigail sat near the firepit from the previous night. The coals were still hot, and the morning sun glistened through the trees and cast a happy glow over the rocky enclave while the waterfall splashed nearby. A kettle rested in the embers on one side of the pit, full of tea which she'd already added to the porcelain cup she held. She'd slept fitfully the previous night with a growing sense of unease. But it had led to no new dreams or visions, either good or bad.

Ella joined her at the fire. She took the kettle, filled her own cup of tea, and, for a few minutes, sat quietly next to Abigail. Behind them, activity in the large tent increased as the nearly seventy who'd come to council at Kettle Falls prepared breakfast and readied for what they'd been told would be further directions from Gras. An hour earlier, he'd left with a small party to wait for scouts to return from their nighttime exhibition to Undertree so a proper plan could be established. Gras had already warned Ella, Jak, and the others that if the area was too well guarded, they would have to abort the mission. Abigail wondered, though, if Ella would be willing to heed that advice.

She thought about the tower and began to try to picture what it might look like. Would it be made of wood or stone? How tall would it be? "Does it have a name?" she found herself musing aloud.

"Sorry?" Ella said. "Does what have a name?"

Abigail blushed. "Oh, yes, the tower. I imagined something so consequential might have a more formal title than simply, 'the tower.'"

Ella thought for a moment, then said, "Some call it the Undertree Tower or the Forest Tower, but no, come to think of it, you are right. It does not have a formal name." She smiled. "Perhaps, when you see it, you could provide it one."

The chatter in the tent grew louder, and both Abigail and Ella turned around to see what was causing the disturbance. Gras had returned from the woods. Five others followed close behind, including Maddie, Raulin, and Jak. She didn't recognize the other two men. A bow was slung over Gras's broad shoulders, and he held a sword in one hand and a shimmering illumina in the other.

"Let us make council!" he ordered as he approached an elevated rock layer on the side of the enclave farthest away from the waterfall. Abigail and Ella looked at each other, then got up and followed the stream of people from the tent to the location where Gras now stood with Maddie.

Gras put his sword and illumina away and lifted his hands for quiet. Those who had gathered around stopped talking and gave him their full attention. Abigail and Ella remained toward the back but still could easily see and hear Gras. It helped that this location was a little farther away from the noise of the waterfall.

"Last night, we came together as a people who remember what this region used to be. It was our home, and we could travel freely without fear of Drilockk, marauders, Vulgheid, and the tyrant that allowed these enemies into our land! For years now, we've watched our forest fester into a place of ever-present danger when it was once one of the few safe havens from the wars in the south and the desolation to the east. But now, we have an opportunity and a new hope." He looked toward Abigail.

"One not of this world has come to Arvalast, and she has seen the warrior. Gildareth is with him, and he has the light of the illumina to guide his path back home." He pointed into the woods. "Just beyond the ruins of Undertree is the tower that stole the warrior, stole Tarin, from us. We now know that Gildareth broke through the gate to find him, and Gildareth will find a way to bring him back. We must now seize this opportunity to take the tower from our enemies and ensure that no shadow nor Drilockk nor any man or beast hinders any effort from Gildareth and Tarin to come home!" Gras then turned to Maddie, who stepped forward.

"Last night," she said, "we sent scouts to Undertree. They traveled north to the lost road and followed it west until they reached the outskirts of the city ruins. They observed a Drilockk encampment. It is estimated that their numbers are no more than one hundred. The location is not readied for battle but rather appears to be a gathering spot. The scouts then circumvented the ruins and were able to observe the tower. There was another small group of Drilockk nearby, fewer than five, each with a sword and one with a bow." She looked around. "Although we'd be outnumbered, we could take a position at the high ground south of the ruins and draw out most of the Drilockk forces. With our lights, they will be greatly weakened, and we will be able to defeat them. At the same time, we will then flank the tower and claim it. And once in control of the gate"—she looked at Abigail—"we will hold our ground and await Gildareth and Tarin's arrival."

Many in the group began to cheer, but a few shouted out questions.

"But how can we be certain they will return?"

"What if there is no gate, or it is not open?"

A few wary eyes shot in Abigail's direction, and she began to wring her hands together and shuffle on her feet. Gras and Maddie left the platform and addressed some of the dissenters. Abigail heard Maddie say, "There's no other way!" and Gras say, "We have to hold out hope. She was sent here for a reason!"

Thief's squeaky voice then joined in as he held parchments over his head and shouted, "Tarin is one of the warriors of prophecy! We must make the way safe for his return!"

Abigail took a step backward, and Ella took her hand. "Come with me," Ella said and led her back toward the waterfall. They crossed the log bridge and then proceeded to the willow grove Abigail had been to the day before.

"Don't worry," she told Abigail. "Even if some decide not to go, we will have enough. But I believe Gras and Maddie will be able to convince most that this is our single chance to get Tarin and Gildareth back and then take back our forest." Ella reached for a thin willow branch dangling nearby, snapped it off, and removed the leaves. She began braiding it to form a small bracelet. "Tell me," she said, "when you spoke to Tarin, was he well? I have not seen him in so many years. I wonder if I would even recognize him."

Abigail watched Ella braid the bracelet. She found it calming. "He was startled, I think, when I first made contact. I wasn't even sure if he was able to hear me. But Gildareth was there as well." She remembered seeing Gildareth slap Tarin and held back a laugh. "He encouraged Tarin to speak to me, and after that, he was actually quite charming."

Ella smiled. "I've never heard Tarin described as charming. He did have a reputation for being very timid. But that changed with time. Though still not one of many words, I saw him time and again show bravery I would never have imagined him capable of when we were young children." She turned to Abigail. "What does he look like now?"

Abigail thought back to Tarin's face. She thought him quite handsome but didn't want to admit that to Ella. So she chose a more neutral description. "He has sandy blond hair and kind and very curious brown eyes. When I was talking to him, he always seemed enamored by anything I said. He looks somewhat tall, at least when I saw him briefly while he was standing with my family, perhaps more than average height, about the same as Gras, come to think of it." As she described him, she began to feel a warmth grow inside of her. "But more than his appearance, I remember his eagerness to hear more about me and to understand what I'd been through. I've never spoken to a man before who had that level of interest in anything I had to say. And also, when he spoke about himself and his own trials, it was with such depth I could barely keep from feeling as he might have. Oh, and I loved when we sang together."

Ella stopped braiding and raised an eyebrow. "Tarin sang?"

"Oh yes!" Abigail replied. "He and I have the same affinity for a particular type of music back where I came from. He was quite good."

Ella whistled and continued braiding. "Then he has changed quite a bit, or"—she looked at Abigail with a twinkle in her eye—"he found someone he felt truly comfortable around."

Abigail felt blood rush to her face and turned away. She then said, as moisture formed in her eyes, "He was the one who offered to take me to see my family and to be able to tell them goodbye. He didn't have to, but he'd understood in our conversation how much that would mean to me and then made it happen." She looked at Ella. "You have a very good brother," she said. "I've never met any man as kind and thoughtful as him."

Ella's own eyes now seemed reflective. Abigail thought she could see water begin to glisten within them. She finished the bracelet and turned to Abigail. "Hold out your arm," she said.

Abigail looked at Ella, then at the bracelet, and lifted her wrist. Ella slowly slipped it over her arm then took her hand in her own. "I know it is only a small gift. But you have brought me so much hope and now so much joy to hear that my brother has grown into a good man. I only hope that soon, both you and I will be able to meet him in person."

Abigail stared at the bracelet a moment, then flung out her arms and pulled Ella into an embrace. "And thank you for the kindness you and Jak have shown me since coming here," she said. "I would have been completely lost without you." A breeze whispered through the branches of the willow above and brought with it the crisp scent of the nearby waterfall. She could hear voices somewhere in the distance, probably from the ongoing debate about whether or not they should risk going to the tower. But then the voices grew louder. Both Abigail and Ella let go of each other and began looking around.

"Is someone here?" Ella asked, peering back toward the entrance to the meadow. Abigail looked over too, but from what she could tell, they were alone. Then, she felt a warmth in her pocket. "Ella!" she said in a hushed yell, "I think it might be happening again!"

"What do you mean?" Ella asked, "What's happening again?"

Abigail retrieved her illumina from her pocket and held it up, and Ella's eyes grew wide. "Tarin!" she yelled and jumped to her feet.

○ ○ ○ ◇ ○ ○ ○

Tarin watched as Allen's hand rested on the steering wheel and guided the white van down the highway. The vehicle was fully charged, and they had just passed out of South Dakota and into Wyoming. In less than nine hours, they would be at the Sacred Basin in northeastern Utah, where Gildareth felt certain Maximus had retreated. It would be night, but none of them cared. Even if there were no stars and no moon, they were bringing their own light with them.

Dralo sat next to Allen. Neither spoke as both stared forward at the rugged and hilly Wyoming terrain. Tarin knew they were thinking of their lost friends: Rob and Ristun. But their outward mourning had been replaced by a desire for vengeance against the source of the evil that had taken their lives.

Tarin sat in the back with Iris and Gildareth. Benches, on which they now sat, had been set against the van walls. Above them were a series of racks with hooks for guns, many of which still held weapons. Yet Tarin knew, for this battle, they would not require guns.

Gabe had not joined them. After a long discussion at the hospital cafeteria, he said that he and Ebe would have to prepare a defensive posture while Gil and the others moved on offense. If the Shadow Prince of Earth was, in fact, readying an assault, or if the offense against Maximus failed, Gabe would have to rally the remaining Glorion forces—both those in physical form and those not—to do their best to protect humanity and hold back a dark harvest. He admitted such a defense would likely fail, but there was no other choice. Risking all for an offense would be too dangerous. They all agreed, and Gabe rushed to meet Ebe at the rendezvous point in the badlands, taking the other white van along with Bill, who'd begged to join him.

Josh, too, had not come. Tarin and Allen could both tell he was conflicted about which path to take. Yes, he wanted to help avenge Rob, but at the same time, he was terribly worried about his Gaka. After a long, tear-filled conversation, both Tarin and Allen convinced Josh to stay at the hospital and tend to Michael's recovery. When Tarin saw the relief fill Josh's eyes, he knew they'd made the right decision to urge him to stay behind. And there was another matter Tarin hadn't articulated. Josh had no light. That would make him vulnerable, and Tarin did not want to lose yet another friend.

Liz, as much as she desired to go, was pragmatic enough to know she would need at least another few weeks to fully recover. She made Allen promise not to die, at the penalty of her killing him. She also threatened to kill Tarin if he let Allen die or died himself. Somewhat confused but still understanding her point, he'd agreed, as had Allen. Tarin then gave her and Allen a private moment. When Allen returned a few minutes later, he was red-faced but smiling broadly.

Like Allen and Dralo, Tarin also felt the need for vengeance, but he felt an even stronger sense of anticipation. It was like the feeling after a long trip—it was finally time to come home. But Utah was not home, although he suspected he'd been there before, just as Gil had been when he'd first arrived on Earth. But perhaps that was exactly it. Was the gate back to Arvalast still there, in Utah, at the Sacred Basin, and if so, would it be possible for him to pass through it after they killed Maximus? He knew that's what Gil wanted. Did he want the same?

He looked over at Allen. If he left Earth, certainly Allen would not go with him and leave his life in Philip behind—or, more specifically, Liz. But then again, he'd not told Allen about Gil's desire for him to return to Arvalast. If Allen knew, and if Tarin did actually choose to go, how would Allen feel? Might he possibly choose to follow? After all, Arvalast was Allen's home too, despite having spent nearly equal time on Earth and Arvalast. Though, so had Tarin.

Tarin's mind then drifted to Josh. If Tarin left Earth, he would never see Josh again. Tarin felt a lump form in his throat—just like he'd never see Rob again. He steadied his emotions and allowed his thoughts to detour to Abigail. She was in Arvalast. And he most certainly wanted to see her again and, perhaps, actually meet her in the flesh. His sister also was there. If he went, he would have family again. His heart began to beat faster as he thought about family. Might he even find his biological father and mother? Could they still be living?

A bump in the road interrupted his daydreaming. Allen was speeding, and imperfections in the road were growing increasingly noticeable. He saw Iris steady herself on the bench opposite him. She was staring at the wall, her face expressionless. Yet he sensed her yearning to confront Maximus, to look into the face of the monster who'd caused both him, and her, so much pain, and prevail over him. Tarin's anger at Iris for allowing herself to become infatuated with his father had now been fully replaced with empathy. He could understand her position. Loneliness was a brutal companion. And even though the memory of his mother still brought him pain, he'd redirected the anger over her death to the true source of her suffering: Maximus.

To Tarin's left, Gil was sitting with his eyes closed, leaning back against the wall. He held his illumina in both his hands while his cowboy hat hung on a hook meant for a gun. Tarin could see the tension in his bearded face. Was he replaying a memory of the last night's events or foreseeing the potentially ill outcomes of their mission? Either way, Tarin felt himself filled with a sense of awe for the man. Despite all that had happened, Gil never lost focus or hope that eventually Tarin would find his light and, perhaps, be the warrior Gil seemed to think that he was.

Tarin reached for his own light and wrapped his fingers around it. He began to wonder, could Gil be right? Was he, in fact, a warrior? Or was he still the coward of his dreams, the one who had fled a battle in which he was meant to be the savior? He closed his eyes and replayed the dream in his mind. He grimaced as he saw the terrible events unfold and as he watched himself flee as others died.

He noticed a warmth on the palm of his hand where he held the phial and opened his eyes. Hurriedly, he pulled it from his pocket. The glass was not only warm, it was growing hot, and to his astonishment, two women were staring back at him from within.

"Tarin!" a voice cried out. He looked at the faces beyond the glass, first at a woman he recognized well, whose glistening green eyes made his heart leap with an indescribable warmth. The other had dark hair, brown eyes, and a face that instantly filled him with a recognition and nostalgia he'd not felt in more than a decade.

"Ella!" he said as strong emotions began to stir inside of him. "I . . . I can't believe it's actually you."

"Nor can I believe it's you!" Ella replied through the phial with profound excitement ringing in her voice. "Tarin, I've missed you so much." He noticed tears begin to form in her eyes as his own began to grow wet. "I always believed you were still alive. I never gave up hope." She smiled. "Your face, it's grown so much more mature than I remember."

Tarin managed a chuckle even as he continued to process the reality that he was indeed seeing his sister. Gil and Iris had noticed the conversation and were now watching him with smiles, but the noise in the van seemed to be masking the conversation from Allen and Dralo. "Well," Tarin said, "It has been what, almost twenty years? Believe it or not, your little brother has grown up."

Ella laughed and leaned closer to the glass. She stared at him as her eyes filled with memory. But then, her expression shifted. She looked over her shoulder and back at him. Her face now carried worry. "Tarin," she said. "We need your help. We are preparing to march to the tower, the same one you and Gildareth used to enter your current world. I need to show the others you are alive. I need to give them hope that we can bring you home."

Tarin looked up at Allen, took in a deep breath, and turned back to the phial. "Take me to them," he said.

CHAPTER 39

Allen kept his eyes fixed on the highway. The memory of Bear Mountain was fresh. He could almost feel the moisture on Liz's jacket as blood leaked from the open wound beneath. He could still hear the agony in Josh's scream as Rob breathed his last breath. He'd not felt such pain and rage since he was a child, when a tyrant had ransacked his home in Woodend, betrayed the governor, and defeated Tarin. In Philip, he thought he'd escaped such pain. It had been an oasis from the rest of the world, both of them. But this last week had changed all of that.

He glanced at Dralo in the passenger seat. His dark skin was flushed, likely from his own inner pain at the loss of Ristun. Despite their sometimes contentious banter, Allen could always tell Dralo and Ristun were the closest of friends. And though Allen felt deep gratitude to Ristun for his sacrifice to keep Rob safe from whatever terrible world the shadows were trying to drag him into, he felt a strong empathy for Dralo at his loss. Ristun had seemed more a brother than a friend to the Glorion.

Allen pushed harder on the accelerator as the van sped along Interstate 90 toward Gillette, Wyoming. From there, he would take them south toward Casper. As a mile marker zipped by, he noticed something strange within a broad swath of flat pasture. Scores of cows lay on their sides. Dralo leaned toward the windshield as he also took notice.

"What happened here?" Allen whispered.

"It is the shadows," Dralo said solemnly. "When enraged, they are known to prey needlessly on the minds of animals and beasts, which are more simplistic than those of humans or higher-order lifeforms. We may see more of this needless killing as we continue toward our destination."

Allen thought back to the poor cow at the ranch near Philip and recalled the chief saying the shadows would cut through the land like a scythe after their plan was foiled. He hoped most of that land had been empty.

After a few more miles, he noticed the sound of speaking behind him. Though somewhat muffled by the hum of the tires against the highway, he could tell it was Tarin. He glanced at the rearview mirror. Tarin had his phial out. It was glowing, and he was speaking directly into it. Tarin raised his voice, and Allen heard him say, "If given the opportunity, I will return."

Allen felt the blood drain from his face. Was Tarin planning to leave? He hadn't given it much thought to this point but had always assumed the intent of this mission was to destroy Maximus to keep some "Shadow Prince of Earth" from razing the planet, then all go back home to Philip.

Tarin put his phial away and began talking quietly with Gil and Iris. Allen's fists tightened on the wheel. How could Tarin ever want to return to Arvalast after the betrayal of those loyal to him after Woodend fell? They'd called him a coward and a deserter. Allen saw a sign indicating a rest stop just ahead. His palms were now sweaty and his mind foggy. He needed to take a break from driving. When the off-ramp to the rest stop appeared just ahead of him, he took it.

"Good idea," Dralo said, "I do, in fact, need to use the facilities." Allen parked. Dralo got out of the van. Iris opened the side door and followed, along with Tarin and Gil. Allen stayed in the van. He watched them walk toward the rest stop. But then, Tarin looked back and met

PJ Dudek

his eyes through the windshield. He began to approach the van. Allen breathed deeply then opened the door and stepped outside.

"You okay?" Tarin asked.

Allen cleared his throat and averted his gaze. "I overheard your conversation in your phial."

Tarin stood quiet for a moment. "I'm sorry, Allen," he finally said, "but after we kill Maximus, assuming we can, I'm going to have to go back to Arvalast if I'm able."

"Why?" Allen yelled, no longer able to hold back his emotions. "The people there did nothing but treat you poorly! You saved them at Northlake, and you stopped a Drilockk invasion at Lockspell. But when you weren't able to keep Woodend from falling, instantly, they all turned against you! How could you want to return to that horrible place?"

"Because it's my home!" Tarin yelled.

Allen held his ground, though Tarin's sudden shift of tone startled him.

"And you're right!" Tarin continued. "You know better than anyone how that memory tortured me my whole life on Earth. It defined me!" He pulled out his phial and lifted it up. "But now I'm realizing who I might actually be." His voice softened. "Allen, you gave me a home in Philip when I didn't have any. Without you, Josh, and Rob, I would not be here right now. That was the level of despair I'd come to. But the home you gave me wasn't ever my true home." He pointed down the highway. "I'm not sure if I'll be able to get back to Arvalast when we get to Utah, but with every mile we drive, I have a feeling that I might actually be heading back to where I belong."

Allen stood quietly, his anger shifting to sadness. "But Tarin, this is my home now. I won't be able to go with you."

Tarin's face filled with a sense of compassion. He put away the phial and placed both his hands on Allen's shoulders. "And I don't expect you to. But even if we do become worlds apart, brothers are never truly separated."

461

Strong emotion gripped Allen's chest. Almost instinctively, he reached out and pulled Tarin into a tight embrace. Eventually, they let each other go. Tarin pulled out his phial and looked at it. "I'm not entirely sure how, but this thing does seem to take and receive calls from Arvalast."

Allen pulled out his own phial and studied it as well. "Then promise me this. If you do go back to Arvalast, we stay in touch."

Tarin smiled. "Will you promise the same?"

"I promise," Allen said.

"Then I promise too."

Both of them started to laugh. "What a crazy week it's been," Allen said. "What on earth did we get ourselves into?"

"On Earth?" Tarin said with a wink.

Allen groaned.

Tarin chuckled, then said, "I'm hungry. Want to grab a snack?"

"Yeah," Allen replied, "that's a good idea." Together, they walked toward the rest stop to join the others.

Fifty had taken up arms to march to the tower, while Raulin, Rosie, and a few others were charged to remain at Kettle Falls and guard those too young or unable to fight. Originally unbeknownst to Abigail, behind the falls was a large stockpile of weapons hidden away in a cave. It provided the battalion with swords, daggers, bows, and quivers full of arrows. It was also where the tent and tables had come from. Abigail was given a short blade with a sheath that now hung from the side of her waist. She didn't know if she would be comfortable using it, but it did feel good to have, just in case.

Less than two hours earlier, silence had fallen on all gathered at the outcrop as Abigail and Ella had rushed into the ongoing debate about Tarin. They'd stood on the stone platform from which Gras and

Maddie had previously spoken to the others as Abigail lifted her phial into the sky.

"We have contacted Tarin!" Ella shouted. "He is with Gildareth and plans to return to Arvalast if the path is set!"

Everyone moved closer and pressed into Abigail as they tried to see into the phial. She continued to hold the light up as, one by one, people began shouting, "Is that Tarin?" Then others, "It is Tarin! He is alive! And look, Gildareth is with him!" Gras led some of the dissenters to the platform. Upon looking into the phial and hearing Tarin speak, they became the first to rush to the weapon stockpile.

As the din had diminished and the phial, like before, closed the connection, Abigail had watched many a goodbye between those going to the tower and those staying behind. She'd nearly shed a tear as Daisy hugged her mother and father and pleaded with them to be safe. When they'd finally set out, Daisy stood between Rosie and Raulin and waved as she watched her parents lead the party into the forest.

Abigail's mood had shifted to one of nervous anticipation as the journey to the tower continued. They were now entering an area of thick woods mostly untouched by humans. They dodged vines and branches as Gras led them due north to Lockspell Creek. From there, Gras had said, they would cross some shallows and continue another mile north until they reached the Lost Road to Undertree.

He'd shared with Abigail that the Lost Road had once been a primary throughway connecting Undertree to a still-traveled wider road that connected Woodend in the forest's northernmost edge to Lockspell and the lands farther south. But over the last century since Undertree's demise, the Lost Road had been reclaimed by the woods and was challenging to find and even more so to navigate, hence its name. Though Drilockk had been spotted on the road before, they seldom used it. They preferred the web of paths they'd created through the region, which most would mistake for deer trails, that offered them fast access to their various encampments and hunting grounds. Regardless, Gras urged caution and quiet from the group. If a Drilockk spotted them, it might alert those in Undertree.

Soon, Abigail heard the sound of water. Ahead of them, a wide creek cut across the mossy ground. Large, flat rocks protruded from the shallow bed and acted as stepping stones for the group to pass over. Though it was just past high noon, the area around the creek glowed with a mystical green because of the thick forest canopy. Everything smelled fresh and alive as the rushing water fed the roots of ancient trees. After the final party member crossed the creek and its splashing faded into the distance, Gras stopped and looked at the ground.

"We're here," he said, then pointed toward some large boulders resting among the trees. "We now head west toward Undertree."

"How much longer until we arrive?" Abigail whispered to Jak, who was walking near her.

"It is a three-hour journey from here," Jak said, "if all goes well."

Another hour moved by. The forested terrain grew hilly, with several inclines and descents through outcrops and beside shallow cliffs. More boulders were scattered in this region, seemingly having been dislodged from the sides of increasingly taller rocky crags. "We are drawing closer to the mountains," Jak said. "We are passing through the foothills, and though you cannot see it, the Lost Road carefully navigates this rugged terrain such that long ago, even horse-drawn wagons could easily reach the city." Jak was correct. Ella could see no roadway, but they'd yet to encounter a dead end against some rock or cliff.

The following two hours passed much the same. Abigail was toward the back of the party with Jak and Ella. Twice, tensions heightened as Gras sent scouts to inspect a distant rustle in the forest. Each time, they confirmed the noise was from an animal.

The group began an ascent up a steep hillside, and Abigail's legs grew weary. "We've left the Lost Road," Jak said. "Gras is leading us to the city's southern end and toward the high ground overlooking the ruins." Abigail then saw Gras stop and lift his hand. Two men joined him. Abigail recognized them as the scouts from earlier. Gras pointed up the hill. They nodded and hurried forward but made no sound. Gras then turned and maneuvered through the group until he was in its center. Everyone gathered closely around him.

"We have arrived," he said just above a whisper. "Let us review our plan." Though Abigail had already heard the details of the mission before they'd departed Kettle Falls, she, too, leaned forward. Her heart started racing.

"Our scouts are in the process of verifying that nothing has changed regarding the number of our enemies. If consistent, we will move to take up position on the high ground overlooking the southern portion of the ruins. It is largely unforested but full of tall grass. We will have ample cover to position ourselves for an attack. At the same time, a small party will take the western pass along the cliff edge at the base of the mountains toward the tower just north of the ruins. It will take an hour to do so stealthily. Once that hour has passed, those of us in position at the high ground will blow a horn and begin our assault. The Drilockk at the encampment will almost certainly sound an alarm in response and pursue us. Those at the tower will hear and join the battle. The tower will be left defenseless." Gras then looked up at Abigail, Jak, and Ella. "Are you still prepared to take and hold the tower while we eliminate the Drilockk in the city?"

Abigail locked eyes with Jak and Ella; their eyes flashed with eagerness and determination. She wished she felt the same. This mission had sounded less terrifying at the falls, but now that they were here, it was clear how dangerous it was. Still, they needed her, and they needed her light. She had the connection with Tarin. She was the one most likely to be able to guide him home through whatever gate they hoped to find at the tower. And, if all went well with Gras's plan, no enemies would hinder them. She felt for the phial in her pocket and put her fingers around it.

"Do we go to the tower?" Jak asked Abigail. She realized Gras and the others were still waiting for an answer.

The Song of Immaru

"Yes," she said, then turned to Gras. "We go to the tower." Gras nodded, and at the same time, Abigail saw the scouts returning. Gras rushed back to the front of the group to meet them. A moment later, he turned back toward the party and said just loud enough for all to hear, "We move forward." All but Ella, Jak, and Abigail rallied around him and marched in the direction the scouts had just come. Soon, they disappeared into the trees.

"We go this way," Jak said, pointing to a steep incline to their left. "That will lead us to the western bypass around the ruins just above the base of the mountains." They began to walk quickly, though remaining careful to be as noiseless as possible. Soon they reached more level ground and began heading north. On their left, the invisible peaks of tree-covered mountains reached high above them, and to their right, a cliff edge dropped hundreds of feet to more forest below. Beyond that, Abigail saw what appeared to be a broad region less sparsely populated with forest growth and dotted with what looked like stone foundations of buildings. Abigail assumed it must be the ruins of Undertree. Within it, she also saw a series of tents, some of which were of similar size to the one back at Kettle Falls.

"It's the Drilockk encampment," Jak whispered, pointing down the cliff edge.

"Will they be able to see us here?" Abigail whispered back.

"It's unlikely if we stay low, and we will only be visible to the camp for a short while. Let's move quickly."

They hurried on. Abigail thought she noticed some splotches of red near the tents, and for a moment she felt the same fear that had captured her the first time she'd seen a Drilockk when waking in the meadow. But almost as quickly as the encampment had come into view, they took a western turn, and it passed out of sight. They reentered the forest and descended into a valley. The sun moved closer to the horizon and cast orange rays through any openings in the boughs above.

A creek appeared. They followed it for about twenty minutes before ascending another hill. Abigail sensed it had to be close to an hour. Her

466

anticipation began to build. The forest grew less dense as ever-reddening rays of sun poured through the canopy. She thought she could see the edge of the woods.

"Stay behind the trees," Jak said as he took up position behind the thick trunk of an aspen. Just beyond was open land surrounded on all sides by green mountains, other than from the east and partly to the south, where they now stood. "We're here."

Abigail and Ella slid behind trees next to Jak. Abigail peeked around the trunk, and in the clearing beyond, no more than half a mile away, she saw it. A tall white tower with four sharp edges rose into the sky. Three curved spires angled into each other at the top. Abigail guessed the structure to be around three hundred feet tall. Surrounding it appeared to be narrow stairs that meandered their way up along the walls on their way to the top. She saw no railing. Thankfully, she was not afraid of heights, but traversing those stairs still looked precarious. Near its bottom, she saw five figures in red. They appeared to be sitting down and utterly oblivious to the stares of Abigail, Jak, and Ella just beyond the forest's edge.

Ella waved at Abigail. Her eyes were lit with excitement mixed with trepidation. "Now that you've seen it," she whispered, "do you wish to give it a proper name?"

Abigail thought a moment. This tower was a door to another world, her world, and she was there to help ensure it was open and ready for Tarin to pass through. She recalled her time on Earth in the Amish community. Many spoke at least some Pennsylvania Dutch, and though she did not know many words, she did remember some. "*Aardes Deoh,*" she whispered back. "Earth's Door."

CHAPTER 40

Allen drove Tarin and the others along a lonely Wyoming high-way, passing vast regions of scrub and open fields. Just past Rock Springs, Allen pulled off onto an exit. The orange glare of the setting sun cascaded through the windshield.

"We should be there in less than three hours," he said.

Before leaving Rapid City, Tarin and Gil had studied a map of northeastern Utah and pinpointed where Gil believed he'd first arrived. It was located within what Michael had called the Sacred Basin, just south of a reservoir within Ute tribal territory and the place Michael had first been plagued with nightmares. Gil was confident Maximus would be at this location. When Tarin inquired further about why Gil felt so sure, Gil simply said, "When I close my eyes and view the area, I see darkness swirling over the region, just beyond the mesas and before the water. It is there we will find him. And it is there we will destroy him." Gil seemed hesitant to share more than that.

The night pushed away the final rays of the setting sun. The van headlights illuminated a sign indicating passage into Utah. Moments later, the vehicle began bouncing over what felt like potholes. "Seem's Utah's not keeping up with its roads," Tarin said.

"It's not the road," Allen answered. Tarin looked through the windshield. Thousands of dead birds blanketed the concrete and adjacent landscape.

"That's the fifth killing we've seen," Allen said. "Cows, bison, horses, and now birds."

Dralo breathed in deeply before releasing air in a slow sigh. "We are getting closer," the Glorion said.

An hour and a half later, lights from the tiny Ute town of Fort Duchesne twinkled in the distance. Allen turned a corner and began heading south. "The reservoir is just over there," he said, pointing out Dralo's window, "maybe a half a mile." After passing by a few modest houses, Allen turned onto a narrow road, and minutes later, the still reflection of stars against the water appeared in the distance. Gil's shoulders tightened, and Iris stirred as both took out their phials. Gil placed his on his forehead and closed his eyes. Allen began to slow as he drove up close to the water, then continued along a narrow road traversing the shoreline toward the south.

"Keep going," Gil said, his eyes still closed.

There were no other cars. The lights from the town had long disappeared. Tarin could see little besides arid ground lit by the headlights and the lake, distinguishable only by the stars dotting its still surface.

"Keep going," Gil said. Allen crawled along. A barbed wire fence met a rusty open gate ahead of them. "The Sacred Basin," Tarin whispered as the van passed through. His skin began to crawl. A few more moments passed.

"Keep going," Gil repeated, his voice growing more urgent. Allen glanced back at Tarin, his eyes nervous. Tarin took out his phial and gripped it hard in his hand. It was glowing faintly and slightly warm. Allen turned back toward the front.

"What's that?" he yelled. He slammed the brakes, throwing Iris, Gil, and Tarin to the van floor. Allen pointed out his window. "I saw some wolflike thing dart out in front of me and run that way!"

"I saw it too," Dralo added, studying the region outside Allen's window.

Gil got off the floor, took his hat from the hook above him, and placed it on his head. Iris and Tarin pushed themselves up and looked out Allen's window. Tarin saw nothing but a dark expanse beneath the black and starry sky.

For a long while, no one spoke. All was silent except for a soft click, click, click. It seemed Allen had accidentally turned on the hazards during his abrupt stop.

Allen finally broke the silence. "So . . . we're here. What next?"

"We find him," Gil said.

"And we kill him," Dralo added. He opened his door, stepped out of the van, and walked out in front of it. The headlights silhouetted his tall, narrow frame against the backdrop of the Sacred Basin. He wore no hat but maintained a crisp sweater over a collared shirt. Iris opened the side door and joined Dralo, her dark hair resting against her shoulders and wearing her usual blue jacket. Tarin was glad she and Dralo were both here.

Gil set his light on the bench. He leaned forward and put one hand on Tarin's shoulder and the other on Allen's. "Our enemy is close." His voice held no fear but no tranquility either. "He knows we are here." He let go of their shoulders and took his phial. "Whatever happens, follow the light." He jumped out of the van and joined Iris and Dralo.

Tarin looked at them through the windshield. Each held a phial, and each phial contained a light. Tarin wasn't sure, but it seemed that their collective light was now brighter than that of the van headlights.

They'd finally reached it—the Sacred Basin. Tarin felt chills of both excitement and fear swirl inside him. Could he be at the gateway to Arvalast? Or was it the threshold of a shadowy stronghold? Perhaps, in some ways, it was both.

Allen's face was stern. He took out his phial. "You ready for this?"

Tarin glanced down at his phial, then back through the windshield. "I am."

Allen turned off the headlights and the hazards, and moments later, he and Tarin were standing in front of the van with the others. There was no sound of insects, no rustle of wind, not even the lapping of water from the nearby reservoir. But then, in the distance, Tarin heard something. The others noticed it too. They all turned toward the noise, their backs now facing the water. It was a soft strumming, perhaps from a guitar. It drifted over the dirt and swirled past them before disappearing over the reservoir.

"It is time," Gil said. In unison, he, Iris, and Dralo moved toward the melody. At first, Tarin and Allen did not follow. Tarin found the music mesmerizing, almost haunting. Somewhere within it was beauty, but covering it was something else, something dark, something angry.

Something familiar.

Tarin began following the others. Allen followed suit. As they walked, the music grew slightly louder but still seemed distant, as if it was coming from within the earth. They walked for five minutes, then ten. Tarin could no longer see the lake nor the van behind them. Then, Tarin heard something—a voice.

"*Tarin,*" it whispered. He stopped.

"Did you hear that?" he said in a hushed tone.

Iris and the others looked at him. "What did you hear?" Iris asked.

"Someone just said my name."

"Come up closer to us," Iris said.

Tarin and Allen readily obeyed.

The group continued side by side: Dralo on the far left, followed by Allen, Gil, Tarin, and finally Iris. They walked another five minutes. The strumming grew more precise, more haunting. An orange light flickered within the blackness ahead. They all stopped in unison. Just beyond the glow of the phials, a wisp of smoke slithered skywards. Then, a red glow appeared below it.

"This little light of mine," a familiar, raspy voice sang in tune with the guitar. The voice was flat, confident, mocking. "I'm going to let it shine."

Iris grabbed Tarin's hand. Her light grew brighter. Tarin's grew cooler.

The song continued. "This little light of mine . . ." The red light increased, casting a fiery glow over a clean-shaven face beneath a wide-brimmed hat. "I'm going to let it shine."

Gildareth took a step forward and began to lift his phial. Tarin could see an old wooden guitar held by a man dressed like a cowboy sitting on a rock within a wide circle of small boulders. The red light emanated from inside the instrument.

"This little light of mine . . ." White teeth glistened beneath a widening smile. "I'm going to let it shine." The figure reached into the guitar, took out the light, and set the guitar down. "Let it shine . . . let it shine . . . let . . . it . . . shine."

∘ ∘ ◇ ∘ ∘

A distant horn blast echoed over the trees before it cascaded down through the leaves and spread throughout the open land surrounding the tower.

"The horn," Abigail whispered. The attack at Undertree had begun.

Jak reached for the bow behind his back and studied the five figures in red near the tower's base. At the same time, Ella took out a dagger.

Abigail watched the figures as they began pacing near the front of the tower. Another blast sounded, again faint but audible, reverberating along the mountains and further disturbing the red-cloaked beasts. That was enough to convince them to abandon their post. They began running toward the southeast, in the direction of a gap Abigail knew must lead to the ruins of Undertree where Gras's battalion had just revealed itself.

"Let's wait a few moments to ensure they are out of sight of the tower," Jak whispered. Abigal and Ella nodded. The sun dipped beneath the peaks to the west, and a red glow slid across the tower field. Finally, Jak said, "Let's go."

Together, they moved out of the cover of the trees and into the open. Abigail looked southeast. Grass spread like a wide river and swept through the gap between the mountains, where it gave way to a few boulders and rockier ground, similar to the terrain she'd seen at the cliff's edge overlooking the ruins. They marched on.

Abigail heard Ella whisper, "We're so close," as if to herself. She could sense her eagerness and longing to reunite with her brother. Abigail shared a similar yearning, though it was for a first meeting—not one within a vision or through a glass, but eye to eye, perhaps even hand in hand.

As they pressed onward, the tower rose higher and higher in front of Abigail. She could no longer see the three spires at its top, now obscured by the structure's massive height. Its exterior seemed built from marble, clean and smooth, with no visible cracks indicating assembly from multiple pieces. Its only distinguishing feature was the stairs surrounding it.

The grass gave way to increasingly rocky ground until they came upon a small, smoldering fire surrounded by scattered pots, pans, and utensils. There was a strange aroma in the air, like cooked meat, but she could not tell from what.

Jak sniffed and grimaced. "Rodents," he said. "Drilockk love to eat rodents." Just beyond where he stood, Abigail saw a short flight of stairs set against the tower's base on that side, leading to a platform. From there, more narrow stairs hugged the wall and angled upward toward the first of four corners, where she knew the stairs continued upward until, after making many more similar turns, they would finally reach the top. Though still narrow, the width of the stairs was more reasonable than she'd first assumed, at least as wide as Jak was tall. But still, the lack of any railing, with only the tower itself to cling to, might make even her nervous, especially as they approached the higher segments.

Jak turned to Ella and said, "I'll stay at the base and keep a lookout for Drilockk. He took Ella's hands in his own, drawing her attention away from the tower and toward his eyes. He leaned forward and touched his forehead against hers. They stood for a few moments— quiet, reflective. Abigail found it to be one of the most beautiful things she'd ever seen, a living image of the pictures of romance she'd only read about. Jak gently lifted Ella's head with his finger and kissed her.

"Go find your brother," he said, "and bring him home."

He then turned to Abigail, his expression soft. "I do not know what you will find on the top of *Aardes Deoh*," he said, then winked. "But whether there is a door, and regardless of if it is open or shut, you have brought hope back into the forest. Gras and the others will win their battle. And we will remain at this tower as long as necessary. When Tarin does arrive, it will be us who greet him, and no Drilockk or shadow."

His words filled her with hope, even as he'd claimed she'd done for him. She treasured the moment, but as with all moments, it had to end. Together, she and Ella turned to face the tower and began to walk. At its base, Ella breathed in deeply, her face determined, eager, but also anxious. She met Abigail's eyes, nodded, and began to ascend. Abigail followed close behind.

Soon they rounded the first bend. The corner step protruded out ominously. Abigail needed to be extremely careful to maintain her footing and avoid a topple, perhaps not to death, but to many broken bones. They continued onward and upward until reaching the next turn. A misstep here would most certainly lead to death, but having successfully navigated one turn already, Abigail found herself easily traversing this one.

Stars twinkled within the darkening sky, and the air grew cooler. Jak waved at them from below, and they both waved back. They continued and rounded corner after corner until both began to breathe more heavily. Soon, a sweeping view of the surrounding mountains opened up before them. Abigail looked around until her eyes stopped on the southeastern gap. She knew that Gras and the others were battling Drilockk somewhere beyond, keeping the beasts distracted from the two women climbing toward the heavens. Abigail hoped the battle was going well. Gras and Maddie seemed like capable leaders, with many other confident fighters surrounding them. They also had something the Drilockk didn't have, something the creatures hated—the light of the illuminas.

Jak was now only a dot far below. Looking up, Abigail could see the outer edge of one of the tower spires.

"We're almost there," Ella said through labored breaths. Despite the ever-decreasing temperature, Abigail felt sweat drip from her forehead and down her nose. They rounded what appeared to be the final corner. Just ahead, the stairs ended in the middle of one side of the top of the tower. They hurried to it and stepped onto the top.

Above them, the three spires reached out into the now night sky and stopped just shy of touching directly over the tower's center. Ella approached the middle and began looking around. "There's nothing here," she said. She ran to each spire, studying them. "How could there be nothing here?"

Abigail began searching as well. Despite Jak's suggestion that they might not initially find anything, she had strongly believed they would. Maybe if she brought out her phial, it would reveal something. She began to reach for it when Ella ran to her and grabbed her hand. She pointed toward the mountains in the east, at a patch of forest at their base. "Look," she said in a hushed voice. "Lanterns."

Three small orange lights emerged from under the trees and approached the tower. "It must be Drilockk coming back from a hunt," Ella whispered, "or perhaps a change of guard. They may not know about the battle." She looked down the tower. "Jak's outnumbered. He might be able to hold back three, but if any more come . . ."

"We need to help him," Abigail said, her heart racing.

"Yes," Ella said. "And we also need to keep trying to find the gate. Stay here and keep looking. I will go help Jak." She took her bow. "Give me some time to get in position, then use your light to search for the door. Maybe it will reveal something. And don't forget about your dagger. Keep it close. I do not expect the Drilockk to get past us and up the tower, but if they do . . . you've fought them before. You know what to do." Ella hurried down the stairs.

Now alone, Abigail watched the lanterns draw nearer, slowly passing over the field toward the tower. Then they stopped. Had they seen something? A moment later, they began moving faster. A flash of light pulsed from below. She hurried to the ledge. She looked down. The tiny figure of Jak stood at the tower's base, holding out his illumina. Abigail could also see Ella. She was running dangerously fast but was nearly halfway down. Ella stopped and aimed her bow. One of the lanterns fell. The others rushed forward.

Abigail withdrew to the tower's center and began to pace. Events were not going to plan. What was she going to do? Then she remembered.

The door.

She pulled out her phial and lifted it. Its glow lit a circle around her. She spun around and frantically searched for anything that might look out of place. What did a door to another world look like? She had no idea. Her phial grew warmer. She looked at it. Her heart seized in her chest. Deep inside was a tiny red orb surrounded by otherwise gentle white light. She heard singing—ominous, menacing. It reminded her of one of her visions, when she saw Tarin, his outstretched hand reaching for the red tendrils of a crimson light, even as a monster enshrouded in shadows stood before him. The orb in the phial was full of that same crimson light.

"I don't often get company out this way," the man on the rock said in a husky Western drawl. Tarin shuddered. Hearing Maximus's voice again, outside of a vision and within the natural world, was almost unbearable.

Maximus crossed one leg over the other, leaned forward, and lifted a cigarette to one side of his mouth. He took in a breath, then blew smoke from the other side. Tarin could feel his green eyes watching him even while they refused to meet his own.

Gil continued to hold out his phial. Its white light contrasted with the red, and a similar glow from Dralo and Iris covered their group in what Tarin sensed was a shield. The crimson light flowed from

Maximus's phial and crept toward them, studying the edges of the white aura before drawing back toward its wielder.

"Where's your mom?" Maximus asked, followed by a mocking laugh. Tarin knew it was directed at him.

"Oh, that's right, she's dead." He paused, his lips unmoving in a wry smile. "More than dead, actually. Suffering . . . suffering oh so much."

Tarin felt his heart pound. Iris tightened her grip on his hand.

"And you know who else is dead?" Maximus said while blowing out another plume of smoke. "That fat friend of yours." His green eyes flickered. "I really enjoyed meeting him. He had such an . . . innocent way about him. Those are my favorite." His eyes focused on Tarin's now sweating forehead. "Oh yes, and I also had the pleasure of meeting his . . . now, what did he call him again?" He smiled. "That's right, his Gaka. It was a delight reintroducing the old man to the nightmares he thought he'd been freed from." He slowly shook his head and sighed. "Poor old fool. No one is ever free of the past. Because the past not only was . . . it is . . . and forever will be." Maximus laughed again and stood up.

"Stay back!" Gildareth shouted. He, Dralo, and Iris lifted their lights. The surrounding aura grew more brilliant. Out of the corner of his eye, Tarin saw Allen. He appeared stiff, his hand nervously gripping his phial.

Maximus turned to Gil. "And here we have yet another soul tormented by the past. I know who you are, Gildareth. I know where you came from. And I know what you've seen. You were there when the great music played, when all of time ripped from the moment and formed the infinite. Now, you tirelessly labor to right a wrong for which you deem yourself responsible." He took a step forward. "Until you embrace your involvement, you will never truly understand the absolute beauty it established. Or, you can continue to cling to hope at the cost of those who support you, who give their lives and their sanity without ever fully understanding . . . why?" He tipped his hat. "Such darkness, even I respect."

Tarin felt Iris's grip on his hand grow tighter as his mind raced to understand what Maximus was implying. He looked at Gil. His face remained stern, but Tarin saw something else: an inner reflection, even pain.

"Don't believe that demon," Iris snarled, seemingly noticing Tarin's eyes on Gil. "He is a liar."

"Am I a liar?" Maximus suddenly screamed. The red light flashed over his now-crazed face. He pointed to Tarin. "Did I lie to him about you and his father?"

"Silence!" Dralo commanded. He lifted his light and thrust it forward, sending a beam toward Maximus and knocking him back a few steps. Maximus regained his footing and stood back up.

"Ah . . . Dralo," he said. "I barely noticed you over there, particularly without your friend Ristun." He smirked. "I'm not seeing him anywhere, though."

"He went with Rob!" Allen yelled through tears. "Ristun saved him!"

"Wait a minute," Maximus said. "Who are you?"

Allen was quaking. Tarin wanted to reach out to him but was frozen with emotion.

"Oh yes, you're the useless one that vomits under even the smallest of shadows." Maximus scoffed as he focused on Allen's phial. "Glad you're enjoying the spoils left behind by those more relevant."

Tarin's raging emotions pressed against his skull as he stared at Maximus's face.

That hideous face.

A dam burst. With a wild scream, he charged forward. Despite Iris's best attempt at holding him back, he escaped her hand and tore out of the shield of light even as his phial continued to cast a glow out in front of him. He heard the others scream for him to return, but it was too late. He charged at Maximus, the heat of every pain the beast had caused him and the fury at the monster's accusations of his friends driving him forward.

Maximus stood up to his full height, put his cigarette in his mouth, and smiled. At the same time, Tarin heard a humming. With each step, it grew louder and louder until, out of the sky, just behind Maximus, Tarin saw it. A huge cigar-shaped craft flew forward and passed over him. A great wind followed and knocked him to the ground. He got up and looked back toward the others. The craft positioned itself over them. From deep within its flawless ebony skin, it emitted an incredible explosion of sound directly into the ground. The light shield collapsed, and all those within it fell, frantically covering their ears. Then, Tarin saw what looked like a black wave approaching from the direction of the reservoir. His eyes widened. It was no wave. It was a sea of shadows crawling like an army of ants over the flat earth.

A hand reached down—warm, strong, eager. It pulled Tarin to his feet. Tarin turned around. In front of him stood Maximus. His green eyes stared at his forehead with an unnerving hunger.

"Why don't you look at me?" Tarin found himself screaming.

"Because," Maximus said. "I don't want to kill you, at least not yet." He lifted his crimson phial in front of Tarin's face. "First, I want to remind you who you actually are." The light flashed. Darkness blinked in and then out.

Tarin stood on a cobbled road. Crowds surrounded him. Four people with nooses around their necks and bags hiding their heads stood on a platform in front of a large brick building.

"Woodend," Tarin whispered. All things of Earth faded as if they'd been a dream.

CHAPTER 41

arin realized the crowds around him were actually a battalion of armed men. Beyond that, a large gathering of villagers faced a tall man standing on the same platform as those about to be hung. Tarin remembered. It had taken an hour for him and the battalion to fight their way through Woodend, starting at the city gate in the south until they had reached this place, the courtyard in front of the town hall. The hall rose multiple stories higher than the slatted wooden wall behind it, and its perch was the town's northernmost quadrant atop the hill on which Woodend was built.

The man on the platform wore chain mail over a leather jacket. On his hip was a sheath, and in his hand was a sword. His eyes flashed beneath brown but greying hair. He had a mustache but no beard. Behind him, those with nooses stood silently under their masks. He lifted the blade toward those gathered before the platform. Most in the crowd cheered.

"Our forest can no longer hide from the unrest sweeping across the south!" he shouted in a deep and booming voice. "Even now, forces of darkness prowl our woods." He pointed at the tallest of those with nooses. "Under this man's watch!" He began to pace. "They came in vast numbers. They came undeterred. But today, his watch ends and another begins! Together, we will strengthen the great Northern Forest to stand against the oncoming tide!"

Most of those gathered erupted into shouts of approval while a few began to draw back, seemingly uncertain, even afraid. The man pointed beyond all of them, and his finger rested on Tarin. "For too long, the claimed warrior has fought to deter us, to protect the governor, and weaken our towns and cities. Now he and his men dare to march against us"—he smiled and pointed toward the captives—"only to see the people of Woodend are ready for a change in leadership."

Next to Tarin, a man wearing a thick leather vest and a hat with a feather unsheathed a sword. Tarin looked up at him. "Come," the man said with urgency, "we must charge. Now. It is our last hope to save Governor Willerdon and his family."

Tarin felt a familiar power course through his young body as he reached for a pouch near his waist. Any natural fear of the line of guards standing between his battalion and the crowd at the platform disappeared as his fingers touched something warm, something made of glass. But then, a sensation like lightning shot through his mind, and he winced. A strange music started playing, at first sounding dissonant . . . confusing. But then, it took the form of a haunting melody that seemed to absorb the power within him.

Frantically, he looked around. "Do you hear that?" he yelled to the man with the feathered hat next to him.

"Hear what?" That man said, still focusing on the gallows ahead.

"That music?" He spun around wildly as his heart started to race with a growing panic.

"I hear no music," the man said. "Now hurry! Blind our enemies! We must go now!"

Tarin continued to search for the music's source but saw nothing but the armored guards between him and the gallows, their bows held at the ready. It was then he realized a charge would lead to almost certain death for most of those around him. He looked up at the platform. The tyrant was moving toward a lever on the far side. Fear seized Tarin. How had it come to this? All his efforts, all his victories, and still, he could not fight back against the tyrant's message and his show of strength. Wait, were these thoughts his own, or were they coming from the music? He couldn't tell.

"Hurry!" the man with the feathered hat urged again. "Lead us onward! We are nearly out of time!"

Tarin didn't move. The music continued to play, and as it did, the realization that he was but a boy in the midst of a great battle overwhelmed him. The power he'd felt as they'd come to this place dripped away, leaving a parched desert of terror in its place. He watched as the tyrant's hand touched the lever. His fingers wrapped around it. Briefly, Tarin noticed a disturbance in front of the platform. The tyrant looked up and stepped back from the lever. He lifted his sword and moved toward the commotion.

"Tarin!" the man with the feathered hat yelled. But Tarin was frozen with fear. The man cursed, then looked back at the rest of the battalion. "Now!" he commanded. The group yelled in unison and rushed forward. The whistle of arrows filled the air. Somewhere, a boy screamed as the man with the feathered hat collapsed onto the ground along with tens of others.

On the platform, the tyrant now battled two cloaked figures with swords. One tried to free the smallest captive as the other held back the tyrant. Tarin could no longer watch. He spun around and fled.

"Coward!" he heard as he passed by those whom he'd once inspired, even as they continued their charge to the platform.

"Deserter!" another yelled. Somewhere behind him, he heard the sound of a thud, followed by gasps and a horrifying mix of cheers and weeping.

"Governor!" someone shouted.

Tarin didn't look back. He ran down the main road of Woodend, through mostly empty streets, and rushed out the gate. His mind swirled within a thoughtless state of panic and despair. After running until he could barely breathe, he realized he'd deviated from the main forest road at some point. Though the noon sun managed to sneak its yellow glow through the thick leafy canopy above him, he realized he'd lost his bearings.

He listened as the strange music continued to play. It morphed into an alluring, almost beckoning melody. It seemed a lone beacon in an otherwise desolate place of hopelessness. He got up and mindlessly proceeded in its direction. Somewhere behind him, he thought he heard rustling. Was someone calling his name? He didn't want to be found. He moved faster.

Minutes fluttered by, then hours. The ground grew more hilly and rugged as the music continued to guide him. Finally, he passed out of the woods and into a large grassy basin. The sun's deep red rays scattered across the ground as the sun itself dipped beyond nearby green mountain peaks. He followed their glow as they crashed onto a massive white tower centered within the valley.

The music was emanating from its top. Within the music, Tarin felt the promise of escape even as it asked him how he, just a youth, had been given the task of a seasoned warrior. Tarin pondered the question and realized failure had always been his destiny. There had never been any hope. And now, above all, he just wanted to be free. He wanted to run. So run he did, as fast as he could move his legs, toward the tower, toward freedom.

Abigail wanted to continue gazing into her phial, but knew she needed to search for the portal. She saw more flickering at the tower base. She assumed Jak was still fending off the approaching Drilockk with his illumina. Would Ella's bow find its targets before they reached him?

Abigail considered going down to try to help her friends when the red orb in her illumina grew brighter. Was it now playing music? She leaned closer and heard a melody—soft and alluring . . . but filled with what seemed a disingenuous promise.

As the music grew louder, she began to feel a strange sensation rising within her. She recognized it as the same power that had begun to consume her when confronted by the Drilockk on the hill near Jak and Ella's cottage. But this time, its approach was slower, more deliberate. She sensed something. It was close. She ran to where the stairs led to the top of the tower and looked down.

Halfway up the tower, just below where Ella had taken position with her bow, the ghostly figure of a boy, or perhaps a young man, was running up the stairs. He passed by Ella, or rather, through Ella. Ella took no notice and fired another arrow.

The music grew louder. Abigail realized it was coming from behind her. She spun around. Standing in the tower's center was a princely apparition, glowing in white light, with robes hanging from its shoulders and diamond armor sparkling along its chest. Its face appeared human and glowed with an eerie light. But what Abigail noticed most were the pure, black abysses glowering in her direction, not looking at her but through her. Immediately, she realized it was waiting for the approaching boy. Then, behind the apparition, she saw a tiny sliver, like that of a crescent moon. The phantom pulled a softly glowing red light from somewhere near its waist, and as it glowed, the sliver began to expand, opening into what looked like another landscape beyond.

Tarin's heart raced as he climbed up the stairs. Despite the tower's great height, he took little notice of the ledges mere inches from his feet but still navigated the corners carefully. The music played on. He had to reach it. He had to escape the horrid path Gildareth had claimed would be his destiny, a path that had long been laden with victory but was now marred with defeat and hopelessness. Despite his young age and his many victories rising from some hidden power within him, he'd failed to save Woodend from the tyrant Gildareth had told him was a harbinger of evil that would lead to the destruction of the Northern Forest.

And now the governor, and his wife, and his son and daughter . . . they were all dead, hanging lifeless behind the new ruler of Woodend.

Up ahead, Tarin saw the stairs come to an end at the center of one of the tower's four sides. He rushed to the top, then stopped as fear turned to terror. Standing before him was a glowing phantom, bathed in light but emanating evil. Its dark eyes poured into Tarin, and somewhere beneath them, a smile slid within the bright aura that was its face. The music stopped.

"I have been waiting for you, Tarin," the phantom said. The voice was deep—masculine. Tarin began stepping back, but the figure lifted his hand, and Tarin could not move. "After you defeated me at Northlake, I was cast away by my Lord. I then wandered the world, broken, an indistinguishable shadow of my former self. But then, I found this tower and, upon it, discovered something that had long been forgotten."

He stepped to the side and revealed a circular expanse seemingly cut from the air, like a door in the sky that led to rugged brown ground covered in twilight far below.

"I found another world. And in this world, I found no lord, only a weak Prince, one whom I could manipulate and even control. I realized in this world my full potential, one that did not have to be shackled to the Lord of Arvalast, who endlessly feasts on the efforts of those greater than him to forever prop himself up as ruler across this kingdom, and now, I realized, all kingdoms. Still, within this new world, I never forgot about you or the strength within you. So I began to play my music, waiting for the time that I knew would come when you would hear it. I never doubted Gildareth's faith in you was misguided—that someday, my own power would supersede your own . . . that outside of your gift, you were a coward." He smiled, "And I was correct."

He pointed beyond the door. "But power you still have. And within this new world—my world—I will mold you into something useful, something that I require." He looked down at Tarin through black orbs pulsating with hunger and hatred. "I will reap from you your power and take it to make my own yet stronger. I will tear it from you, from

486

your very soul." He paused. "And I will punish you for your insolence at standing up against that which shall soon be—*greatest*."

Abigail stood breathless in front of the strange, glowing phantom. It seemed to be speaking, but she could hear no words. Behind it, the previously small tear in the fabric of reality had grown to the height of the spires and expanded to almost the width of the tower. Through the hole, white light flashed over brown earth otherwise obscured by night and black clouds. A red light in the hand of what looked like a cowboy flickered through a gap in the clouds as it sent streams of energy toward a man on his knees within a formation of rocks set in a circle.

She considered daring to move forward to get a better look. The phantom still seemed oblivious to her presence. She began creeping closer when, suddenly, the phantom rushed forward. She screamed and held out her arms. But it passed directly through her. She spun around. The boy from earlier stood near the stairs at the tower top, cowering. She gasped. It was Tarin. Though he was far younger than the man she'd seen in the phial, she recognized his sandy blond hair, his thin face, and his gangly limbs. She began running to him, but before she could draw close, the phantom took Tarin's shoulder and dragged him toward the tower center. She tried to reach for him, to pull him away from the phantom's clutches, but her hands touched nothing but air. Then, her light grew warmer.

The phantom flinched, paused, and turned to her. It tilted its head as its black eyes seemed to both look at her and through her. She felt a familiar power stir within her soul, just as she had when she'd saved Tarin from a similar entity days earlier, the one that had morphed into the form of a cowboy. She began to lift her phial when the glowing creature spun back around and shoved Tarin through the opening.

"Tarin!" she screamed as the power rushed away.

Tarin fell toward a series of rocks set up in a circular formation far below. He expected to crash into them and certainly die, but then he saw the glowing figure lean through the door in the sky and lift his hand out. Suddenly, Tarin was surrounded by shadows, grabbing at him, slowing his descent, even as their touch felt like the stings of bees. As he cried in pain, he thought he heard his name. It was a familiar voice, a reassuring voice.

"Sarky," Tarin whispered. Then, all went black.

Abigail tried to strike the phantom as it held its hand out through the portal. She touched nothing. The creature floated through the portal and descended downward. The portal began to close. Another apparition ran past her. It looked like another youthful boy, this one with dark hair. It jumped through the opening even as it continued to close.

"The door!" she yelled, realizing it was about to snap shut. Instinctively, she lifted her phial. The portal froze, leaving a hole just large enough for her light to stream through.

Tarin felt dizzy. Where had he been? Where was he now? His eyes slowly opened. Red light covered his full field of vision. He felt hot. No, he felt as if he were on fire. He was kneeling. His phial sat in front of him, though he could see no light. Then he remembered. He looked up. Blazing tendrils of red fire lapped around him. Behind those, Maximus stood, his hat now off, no cigarette in his mouth, his phial outstretched, and his eyes locked with Tarin's.

CHAPTER 42

Dralo covered Allen in a shield of light as Iris and Gil rushed to meet the oncoming wave of shadow. At Allen's feet lay Gil's hat. It had blown off after the UFO had thrown them off their feet. Dralo launched what looked like flashing white arrows into the assembling darkness. One by one, the creatures shuddered, burst, and hissed into the sky like steam from a kettle. But there were too many. Some reached the protective aura and began trying to claw their way in, even as their long, wispy fingers dissolved within it.

Though terrified, Allen wondered why his stomach didn't hurt. Was it the shield of light? More shadows slung themselves against it. Now Allen wondered, would he soon meet Rob's fate? Would the shadows open a portal to some world of torment and attempt to drag his essence into it? There were so many more of them here than on Bear Mountain. And the other Glorions, the ones who'd appeared as orbs of light, were busy building a defense against the Shadow Prince of Earth. Who would save him? Perhaps Dralo, but even he seemed overwhelmed.

Back toward the reservoir, Gil and Iris moved their phials through the air and spun as they dodged and destroyed shadow after shadow. Smoke, not from fire but from whatever dark energy the things were made of, filled the sky like the aftermath of a fireworks display and blotted out the stars.

Allen began searching beyond the light shield for Tarin. He'd lost track of him after the UFO had blasted them into the ground.

Somewhere above him, he could still hear its ominous humming, but it was nowhere to be seen. Maybe it was hidden within the growing cloud of vanquished enemies.

Dralo continued to furiously fight back the aggressors, and Gil and Iris continued their dance of destruction. Allen noticed a red glow where he'd previously seen Maximus. Horror filled him. No more than a hundred feet away, Tarin was kneeling within what appeared to be a circle of rocks. Maximus stood next to him. Tendrils of red grabbed and pulled at Tarin's quaking body.

"Tarin!" Allen screamed. He tried to run to him, but Dralo grabbed his arm. "There's too many! If you leave the shield, you'll die!"

"But Maximus is killing him!" Allen yelled. Almost before the words left his mouth, he saw Iris. She ran past the shield. Her phial pulsated with the electricity of a thunderstorm as lightning shot from it and sent any nearby shadow to its end. Her eyes, even behind her glasses, blazed with rage as they fixated on Maximus.

Dralo saw her too. He aimed his phial and blasted a path through a thick patch of enemies which Iris sped through on her way to Tarin. Allen heard Gil shout unfamiliar words from behind. After a large burst of light, another black cloud lifted into the sky over the Sacred Basin.

Iris continued to run. Allen's heart raced. Would she make it in time? She lunged into the path of Maximus's crimson fury and thrust out her phial. Immediately she was pushed back by what seemed to be a gale-force wind. She leaned forward. Her light flashed and spread out into what appeared to be a small shield. The tendrils struck it, now unable to rip at Tarin's body as Iris blocked them.

Tarin collapsed to his knees. His quaking ceased. Maximus glowered at Iris, and his phial blazed with more fury. He stepped forward. His light pushed and pulsated around her shield until the object exploded into shards of white plasma. Crimson fingers surrounded Iris's now defenseless phial and began to creep into it.

○ ○ ○ ✧ ○ ○ ○

490

Iris heard the beeping of arcade games and smelled the scent of alcohol. She breathed in deeply. Perhaps she'd get her own drink after work. Wait, she was at work? She didn't recall coming in that evening. But before she could think about it more, a couple walked up to the counter and ordered drinks. She filled two glasses of beer for them, and they joined a few others in the main seating area. Iris counted. There were ten people at the bar that night. She looked at the clock. It was nine. It must be a weekday.

The door opened and a tall and handsome man walked in. He was well built. On his face was an afternoon shadow, but it nicely complemented his full head of brown hair flecked with just the smallest amount of grey.

Iris smiled. "Hi, Brandon," she said as he approached the counter. "What'll it be?"

He sat down on the stool just in front of her and sighed. "Double IPA," he said. "Need something strong. Got in another argument with Chrissy today." His eyes met hers. "Iris, I honestly don't know how much more of this I can take."

She filled a glass, handed it to him, and put her elbows on the counter. "What happened?" she asked.

He took a few gulps and set the glass down. "She pitted Tarin against me. They're both saying I don't spend any time with them anymore, that I don't care about them, that I don't do the things they like." He shook his head. "But everything I've tried—going on runs with them, country drives, the town fairs—it's as if I'm not there. And when I try to engage . . . nothing."

He took another swig and looked up at Iris. "Sometimes, you're the only one I feel I have any connection with anymore." He met her eyes and looked deeply into them. "Thank you, Iris."

His stare lingered, and for a moment, Iris thought she saw something flicker within his deep blue eyes. It was something she'd not seen before—a curiosity, perhaps, or maybe more so, a desire. He lifted his hands and slowly reached out toward her glasses. "May I?" he asked.

She wasn't entirely sure why he'd want to remove her glasses, but her own curiosity was beginning to build. "Sure," she said.

He carefully took them off and his gaze intensified. "You have very kind and beautiful eyes, Iris," he said. His own seemed to quiver with some strange and hidden anticipation and energy.

"Thank you," she said softly as her mind raced. Was he feeling an attraction to her, one that went beyond friendship, one sourced from the romantic love she could never feel?

A slow smile crept across his lips. "But what if you could feel it?" he asked.

"What?" she said, startled at his sudden ability to know what she was thinking. Still, his gaze continued to captivate her.

He began to lean in closer, and as he did, she felt a compulsion to do the same.

"What if it is a lie that that you cannot experience the pleasure of spirit bonded with flesh, the hidden gift I know for so long you've marveled at—longed for?" His voice dropped to a whisper. "I've seen your eyes when I kiss my wife. I know it draws you in, makes you wonder, how might it feel if it was you in her place?"

She felt a strange energy radiate throughout her body. Slowly, her eyes moved along Brandon's face. She noticed his square jaw, his symmetrical features, his slightly opened lips. She leaned in closer. Her hands began to tremble. Was this powerful energy the sensation of romance, that mysterious force she wondered about any time she saw lovers hold hands, embrace, or meet lips? If so, she'd never felt anything so physically intense, so deeply alluring, even intoxicating. She didn't want to give in to it, but the power was so strong.

She felt Brandon's breath against her own lips. She closed her eyes.

"Take it," Brandon whispered as he pressed in. But just before their lips touched, Iris opened her eyes and drew back. "Take?" she asked.

Brandon's eyes flashed with what looked like confusion mixed with anger before he quickly composed himself.

"What's wrong?" he asked softly. He tried to reach out for her hands, but she withdrew. The strange energy built up inside of her collapsed and seemed to fall to the floor. Something wasn't right. Yes, she loved Brandon, but she didn't want to take anything from him that was not hers to receive. She looked deeper into Brandon's eyes. They began to harden.

"Iris," he said now with sternness, "I asked, what's wrong?"

The sound of the bar seemed to muffle and blur into what felt more like a dream. At the same time, Brandon's face began to shift and change. It grew thinner and older, and his eyes transitioned from blue to green.

"I will not 'take' what is not mine to achieve love," Iris said, glowering at an evil she now recognized.

The figure of Maximus sat in front of her. He reached for the glass of beer and gulped down its contents. With a loud sigh, he slammed the glass on the counter and stood up. From a pouch at his waist, he revealed a crimson light. He lifted it.

"Then you will never know love."

The light flashed. She felt both her body and spirit wrenched from the bar. She was back in the stone circle. Heat covered her skin. She looked up. Her phial was still in her hand. Crimson tendrils stretched around it. Like claws from a wild animal, they tore at her body. Maximus stood in front of her, his face a mask of rage.

She remembered Tarin. With great struggle, she managed to turn her head to look back at him. He was on his knees, holding himself up with one hand. Though battered, he was free of Maximus's fire—at least, for as long as she continued to shield him. She turned back to her attacker. Her glasses grew too hot to wear. She took them off, leaned harder into the attack, and took a step forward. Maximus was wrong. She did know love. And though it hurt, she met Maximus's eyes and took another step. Her skin began to peel and her hair singe. She could smell her clothes beginning to burn. She managed another step.

"You will die for him?" Maximus screamed. She said nothing. But still, she moved forward.

"Iris!" Tarin yelled from behind. She felt her physical energy begin to deplete, but her resolve remained strong. She was close. She lifted her phial. Certainly, she had the strength for one last burst of energy. But then, the pain grew too great, and her body failed her. She fell to her knees. Maximus stood above her. His white teeth clenched as he pushed the full might of his dark energy at her deteriorating body. But still, she held up her phial. Still, she shielded Tarin from Maximus.

∘ ∘ ∘ ✧ ∘ ∘ ∘

"He's killing Iris!" Allen shouted. In horror, he'd watched her fall to her knees, her body blistering from heat that even he could feel despite his distance from its source.

Dralo, still busy fighting back scores of shadows launching themselves at the shield, looked over at Iris. He cursed and tried to focus his phial toward Maximus. But a group of shadows positioned themselves to block him. He blew them away with a shout of rage and an explosion of light. More streamed in to take their place. "I cannot get past them!" Dralo yelled.

"Should we bring down the shield and fight our way to Iris and Tarin?" Allen asked, starting to panic.

"We can't!" Dralo said, continuing to try to clear a path to Iris with his light. "I won't be able to protect you!"

Allen spun his head around wildly, looking for Gil. Maybe he could help. But too many shadows surrounded their location for him to see very far. Not sure what else to do, he looked up. He squinted as he saw something through a gap within a hovering mass of darkness.

It looked like a star and hung about the height of a radio tower above where Iris and Tarin battled Maximus. Then, it seemed to widen before collapsing back to its original size. But in that brief moment, Allen saw a woman holding out a light. His eyes widened. It wasn't a star. It was a portal!

He looked down at his phial, then back up at the shining hole in the sky. A sensation came over him, similar to what he'd felt at Bear Mountain as the shadows from the chief had flown toward Rob's aura before

Allen had sent arrows of light through them and broken open the sky. The sensation grew. So did the glow of his phial. It began to shimmer and create a new aura around Allen. This seemed to disturb and confuse the surrounding shadows, which Dralo took advantage of as more smoky corpses joined the billowing clouds above.

Allen stared at the portal, and his eyes narrowed. As it began to fluctuate wildly in size, he lifted his phial and shouted, *"Petu Daltu!"*

Abigail struggled with the tear atop the tower as it continued to fight against her will to keep it open. She knew it had to be the portal to Earth. She could not let it close.

She cast her light against it and focused all her intentions to keep it open. Below, the cowboy with the red phial was now sending waves of energy at a woman who'd jumped into the stone circle. Behind the woman, the other man crawled forward.

She heard a voice command, *"Petu Daltu!"* A brilliant light exploded from somewhere down below, entered her illumina, and attached itself to her soul. She felt a surge of energy, stepped forward, and echoed the words.

The portal exploded to its earlier height and width. Abigail's light flowed through and sprung toward the stone circle beneath her. Its energy and hers became one. Within it, she heard music, both furious and hopeful, strong yet tender.

Tarin's fingers pressed into the dirt as he dragged himself forward. He had to get to Iris. He had to save her before she was completely disintegrated. As more boils covered her skin, he screamed in despair. He would not make it in time. And he knew he was next. Then he heard it—music. Unlike Maximus's haunting melody from earlier, this poured over him like cool water from spring rain, like drops of hope against the backdrop of dread.

Iris remained on her knees, somehow still holding her light up against Maximus's relentless rage. Then Tarin saw her chin drop to her neck, and her still outstretched hand began to fall. Time seemed to stand still as the tendrils covered her entire body and slithered toward Tarin.

The music grew louder. A gentle white glow dropped from the sky and bathed the stone circle in its radiance. Tarin looked up. Within what appeared to be a tear in the sky, he saw a woman in a white dress, standing like an angel looking down upon them as she sent a river of light into the basin.

It was Abigail!

His heart leaped as a renewed vigor flooded into him. He pushed himself to his feet, and at the same time, the red tendrils began to quake and pull back. Soon they slid off of Iris as the soft glow of Abigail's light took their place. They wrapped around Iris like a blanket while Maximus shouted a curse and lifted his light higher, but its intensity only decreased. Tarin continued to watch and listen. The music itself seemed to move into Iris's body. The boils across her exposed flesh began to heal. Maximus frantically searched for the source of light and music. He looked upward, and an expression of horror covered his face.

Iris began to lift her head, and her shoulders straightened. Clean flesh sewed itself over her previous wounds. The music shifted its intent toward Maximus, even as it continued to whirl around Iris. Using one hand, Iris pushed herself to her feet. With her other, she lifted her phial. Maximus took a step back. His red light snapped back into his phial, its glow almost invisible, as if hiding from the light from above.

Iris's phial began to glow bright even within the already white aura surrounding her. Then, she herself started to glow. Her charred, blue jacket flaked off, and beneath it appeared shimmering armor that sparkled as if made from the essence of stars. The remains of her tattered jeans gave way to darker but still shimmering breeches that touched tall leather boots at her knees. Silver shin guards stopped just above her feet. Tarin marveled at her and felt the urge to bow—such was the strength of her presence. But before he could, the music crescendoed, and he watched in amazement as two mighty wings spread from her back and lifted skyward as if she were an eagle preparing for flight. She leaned forward and, with a great thrust, exploded through the air and into Maximus.

Maximus flew backward and crashed into the ground. Iris got up and stood over him. She placed a booted foot over his chest and held him to the ground. She looked back at Tarin, her eyes filled with vitality and love. Tarin threw his arms into the air and shouted her name in triumph. But his joy was short-lived.

The ground began to vibrate as an explosive hum traversed through the sky. Maximus's craft slid out of the murky haze and positioned itself near the portal. Both Tarin and Iris looked up. With a single thrust of her wings, she sprung from the ground, aimed her phial, and blasted the craft with a light beam. It tilted to one side and fell many feet. It quickly stabilized even as she shot above it and came around for another approach.

"Tarin!" someone called. He spun around. Perhaps a hundred feet away, Allen stood with his phial outstretched, sending light toward the portal. Allen waved. Not sure what else to do, Tarin waved back. Abigail's light, unrestricted as the rising sun, continued to expand. Dralo feverishly fought back the shadows straining to reach Allen. Just beyond, Gil battled swarms of shadows continuing to pour in from the direction of the reservoir.

The light moved over Dralo. His back arched as if he'd been hit with electricity. He stretched out his arms, and his sweater shimmered and transformed into armor. Like Iris, two mighty wings burst from his back. He screamed, not from pain, but from power. He thrust his wings and shot into the sky. He swirled around Allen and cast beams of light in all directions. Smoky debris filled the air and scattered beneath his wings.

The light marched on. Soon, it covered Gil. Like Dralo, Gil lurched back. But he did not gain armor, nor did he grow wings. Instead, his light concentrated in front of his phial until a shimmering broadsword, both metallic and ethereal, lifted skywards. With an unnatural speed, he charged forward and jumped to a great height over a boulder. He brought his sword down and crashed into the shadowy hordes below. They fell into disarray at the fury of his assault and began to draw back.

Tarin felt a sharp pain in the back of his head. He fell to the ground. Maximus stood over him. The red phial dripped with what Tarin assumed was his own blood. Maximus reached down, picked him up, and threw him by his shirt collar. Tarin tumbled over the dusty soil. He pushed himself back to his feet and held out his hands in defense as his head throbbed. Maximus rushed him and struck him across his face. Tarin wobbled, then collapsed.

"There is more than one way to kill you!" Maximus seethed. He was lifting his phial for another blow when he took notice of Abigail's light shimmering on the ground. He looked up. He licked his lips and whispered. "As much as I like bread," he stared back down at Tarin, his eyes quaking with malignant intent, "I love the taste of honey even more."

Abigail stood just beyond the portal, her brown hair flung over her shoulders while she held her radiant phial. Maximus took a step back as a familiar humming intensified, still looking at Abigail, his eyes lit with desire. A rage grew in Tarin, and with it, a power. As it intensified within his body, he remembered it—the same power that first consumed him at Northlake, then again as he'd led with his light the peoples of the Northern Forest to victory after victory over the encroaching shadow. It was what he'd felt when first marching into Woodend—before he'd heard the music that had torn it from him. But now, as he looked up at Abigail, a new music continued to ring forth, and within it, he heard the truth—he was no coward. He was a warrior.

With a powerful cry, he pushed himself from the ground. He clutched his light and charged Maximus. With that same hand, as it glowed bright around his phial, he swung. There was the sound of thunder as his fist struck Maximus in the jaw. Maximus spun around and collapsed onto his knees. Maximus looked up and smiled. Dark blood ran along his white teeth. He got up and charged Tarin. But before Maximus could land a blow, Tarin thought of his mother, he thought of Rob, he thought of the governor of Woodend—and his family. He pulled his arm back and screamed as he swung again. Another clap of thunder, and Maximus again collapsed to the ground.

Maximus glowered at Tarin, no longer smiling. "The body is weak," he sputtered as blood dripped from his lips. "But I am more than body." The ground, again, began to vibrate. Tarin steadied himself as it became hard to stand and looked up. Abigail continued to cover the earth with light and music as Iris and Dralo battled countless shadows in the sky, but Tarin couldn't see the cigar craft. But then, just to his left, a large ebony object dipped out of a block of black fog. It turned such that its narrow end faced the direction of Maximus and Tarin before settling on the ground only a stone's throw away.

Maximus took a few steps back. He wiped some sweat and blood from his lips. He closed his eyes and held out his arms. In his left hand, the crimson light flickered back to life. Slowly, it enshrouded Maximus in a swirling red haze. Maximus began to transform into a shimmering figure somewhere between man and ghost. A diamond breastplate appeared on his chest, and kingly robes flowed from his shoulders. Immediately, Tarin recognized the entity from Northlake—the one he'd defeated long ago and the one he now knew had pulled him through the portal to Earth when he was still a boy.

Maximus's feet lifted into the air. He began levitating backward toward the craft. Just before he reached it, he opened his eyes, and two black abysses stared into Tarin's soul before Maximus disappeared.

The craft lifted to the sky. It turned and began moving toward the portal, toward Abigail.

"No!" Tarin screamed. He ran back toward the stone circle as fast as possible, his light cascading around him. Suddenly, he felt two hands grab him from behind. Moments later, his feet lifted from the ground.

Tarin looked up, and his heart leaped at the sight of the shimmering form of Iris as her wings moved gracefully to propel them toward the portal above. But even as hope filled him, he looked back toward the ground. Allen still stood, holding out his light, doing his part to keep the gate open. Tarin realized this might be the last he'd ever see his best friend. But then, in the distance, Allen slowly lifted his free hand, made the shape of a phone, and held it to his ear. Tarin gripped his light hard, even as tears swelled. Tarin knew he would hear his friend's voice again.

The moment was cut short when Maximus's craft drifted into the space of sky between Tarin and Allen. It sped forward to match Iris's speed and followed them. Its hum grew louder and louder. But then, its frequency began to change. It became more guttural, alive, and animal-like. Tarin stared hard at it, and his eyes widened. Great batlike wings began to emerge from its sides.

∘ ∘ ∘ ✦ ∘ ∘ ∘

Allen lowered his free hand from his ear as he continued to hold up his light. The portal had to stay open, both for Tarin and, he realized, to rid the Earth of Maximus. If the entity went through it, he would no longer be a threat to the Shadow Prince of Earth. And assuming Gabe and the other Glorions were managing to hold back any early assault as they took up defensive position across the planet, perhaps Earth, the place he now considered home, would be spared.

A glowing figure dropped out of the sky next to him. Allen saw Dralo in his peripheral vision. "So Glorions have wings?" Allen said. "How come I don't recall those from Arvalast? And why haven't you used them before on Earth, at least as far as I've seen?"

"Glorions do not have the same power on Earth as in Arvalast," Dralo replied. "And even on Arvalast, we have limitations. But the song of Immaru, both its light and its melody, which I have not experienced for centuries, restores within my kind a power the darkness has

500

otherwise diminished." Dralo spread out his wings and sighed. "I shall miss these when the door again closes—when the music stops."

Footsteps approached, and on Allen's other side, he saw Gil. A glowing sword shone in his right hand. Gil reached down, picked up his cowboy hat by Allen's feet, and put it on.

"A cowboy with a sword," Allen said. "I wish Rob was here to see you."

Gil placed a hand on Allen's shoulder. "To the contrary, I wish he could see you and what you have accomplished this evening." He paused and smiled through the dirt and sweat caked over his face and strewn throughout his beard. "He would be proud. As I am proud." He squeezed Allen's shoulder. "Well done . . . very well done."

Together, Allen, Gil, and Dralo watched as Iris, Tarin, and the monster drew closer to the portal. Allen found himself strangely calm, as if, somehow, this was meant to be—that his part to play, at least for now, was nearly complete.

"Will you be going with them?" Allen asked.

"I will not," Gil said. "In this chapter, my mission on behalf of Arvalast is finished. But my mission on Earth is just beginning." He looked at Allen. "As is yours, young warrior." Allen felt a surge of excitement. Warrior? Him? He was going to have to tell Josh and Liz. But then, he realized something.

"Where are all the shadows?" he asked.

"Destroyed or fleeing," Dralo responded in his smooth British accent, though his voice was hoarse and tired.

Allen peered briefly at Gil, then raised an eyebrow as he continued to hold out his shining phial. "And where are your wings?"

Gil laughed. "I do not share the same power as the Glorions, nor am I made from the same physical material of your kind."

"Then . . . what are you?" Allen asked.

"I am . . . more ancient," Gil said. He fixated his eyes on the sky and gazed at the portal.

Allen shook his head even as he kept his hand steady. "I think we have a lot to talk about when this is over," he said.

Gil nodded. "Indeed we do, my friend."

Allen then saw something strange. The craft, still in pursuit of Iris and Tarin, who were now within moments of passing through the portal, had transformed into something that looked more like a great animal with sinewy wings. "Bostt," he whispered, as his mind flashed back to a memory from Northlake and then to the strangely similar card from Legendarium of Beasts.

"Indeed," Gil replied. "But fear not. Tarin has defeated it before." He pointed toward the portal, at the woman who continued to stand tall, keeping the sacred basin bathed in light and the door open for Tarin's arrival home. "And like last time, he will not be alone." He looked at Allen. "Once all pass through, including the beast, lower your light." He looked back up at the portal. "Allow the door to close."

∘ ∘ ∘ ✧ ∘ ∘ ∘

Abigail stood tall and embraced the mysterious energy surging through her body as she held out her illumina and blazed a trail for Tarin and the winged woman to follow to the portal. Her heart pounded against her chest as if it were the repercussions of a great drum. In moments, Tarin would be here with her, in Arvalast. But something was following them, something that with every moment looked more and more like a great monster: bearlike, with broad shoulders and thick fur, but also with the wings of a monstrous bat. Below her, she thought she could hear people shouting, more than just Jak and Ella. She hoped all was well at the tower base but would have to trust the others to manage whatever was happening below. Right now, she had to keep the portal open.

Closer and closer, the woman and Tarin flew. Abigail took a few steps back to give them room for entry through the door. A moment later, they burst through. The winged woman dropped Tarin and flew past Abigail as her inertia carried her beyond the tower. Tarin barely managed to maintain his footing as he stumbled forward and into Abigail's arms. Somewhat distracted by the man against her chest, she noticed the portal beginning to close. At the same time, the monster shot through. Abigail ducked and pulled Tarin down with her, dropping her phial in the process. Strands of the creature's hair brushed along her back as she and Tarin lay prostrate on the ground.

She looked at Tarin and blinked. His own wide brown eyes stared back into hers.

"Hi," she said.

"Hi," he responded, almost in a squeak.

A flash of light lit up the top of the tower and jumped across the three spires. It came from just beyond the tower, closer to the mountains to the west, where the winged woman dodged the monster as it flapped its wings and lunged for her. She shot light at it, but it did little to deter it. Tarin got to his feet, steadied himself, then lifted his illumina.

"Maximus!"

The animal stopped its pursuit of Iris and, with a slow, steady beat of its wings, turned around.

Abigail saw her illumina nearby, reached for it, and stood next to Tarin. She glanced behind her. The portal was now only a sliver. Then, it snapped shut. She turned again to face the monster.

The creature drifted toward the tower, its eyes blazing with a fierce yellow glow. The intense power Abigail had felt while holding the portal open was gone. A more primal instinct replaced it, the urge to flee from a predator. But then, she felt something. A hand was touching her hand. Its fingers slid into hers. They were warm and comforting.

"Thank you for bringing me home," Tarin said. Though his face was stern, and his eyes focused not on her but on the monster, she saw strength and peace within them. She tightened her fingers around his. Within her other hand, her illumina grew warmer.

She turned to face the beast. "You're very welcome," she replied.

As the animal approached, the winged woman seemed to notice something below. She met Tarin's eyes, sent him a knowing glance, and then darted toward the ground.

Saliva dripped down the beast's fangs. A foul wind blew from the slow thrusts of its leathery wings. It drew up next to the tower until its massive feet perched along the ledge. Together, Abigail and Tarin lifted their lights. The monster roared and spread out its arms as if in defiance. But then, something changed in its expression. It twitched. Its eyes morphed from yellow slits to the round black pupils one might see on any animal. They appeared tired, confused, and even frightened. It snarled as if in pain. A glowing figure emerged from its chest. Behind it was a gaping hole. The monster groaned, winced, and then toppled backward off the tower.

"Hatred," Maximus said, his voice almost sad, "is such a heavy burden. You of the light, you will never truly understand the power of the loneliness my kind must suffer toward our goal." He lifted his phial toward his face and began tenderly stroking it while his empty black eyes stared into the crimson abyss. He looked upward, and his dark orbs narrowed. "But in some way, my goal is the same as your goal. Noble—and eternal. What you must understand is that without the darkness"—he began to lift his phial, and a fiery tumult swirled inside—"there . . . is . . . no . . . light."

Abigail noticed Tarin's hand grow tense. She felt her illumina begin to vibrate and flicker while Maximus's grew too bright to look at. "Even if you're right," Tarin said, "there's only one of these that's greatest." Tarin lifted his own phial higher as the essence within began to push against the glass. Tarin knowingly smiled. "This little light of mine . . ." Maximus's face contorted into a seething grimace. Tarin looked at Abigail, then turned back to Maximus to stare directly into the creature's quivering eyes. "I'm going to let it shine."

Maximus seethed, then screamed. A stream of crimson fire shot from the phantom's phial and exploded before them. Abigail closed her eyes and braced for its impact.

Nothing happened. She looked up. In front of her and Tarin, a brilliant, glowing shield emanated from the light within their illuminas. The red barrage thrashed against its other side but could not break through. Tarin's hand tightened around hers.

Maximus roared and began rushing toward them. His phial exploded with seemingly infinite malice and hatred as he wildly tore at the shield.

Abigail and Tarin stood their ground.

Unable to break through, Maximus stopped his assault. A desperate look filled his hideous face as he reached out his hand holding the phial and began pushing it into and through the shield. His screams moved from rage to agony as the phial started to crack while, at the same time, his arm hissed as if on fire.

The crimson light diminished as he pressed forward. His diamond armor, his shining robes, and the ethereal shell holding his shadow together began to singe and melt within the shield's brilliance. He was almost through, but still, Abigail and Tarin stood firm.

With one final push, Maximus screamed as his armor collapsed, his robes disintegrated, and his phial shattered. A shadow, limp and broken, fell to its knees. Its yellow eyes looked at the ground, shamed, devoid of hope, empty of meaning.

Abigail and Tarin looked down at it as their light gradually returned to their illuminas, leaving only a soft glow within each. Abigail heard the sound of a distant wind blowing over the nearby mountaintops. The shadow looked toward the noise. The air passed over the tower, across Abigail's face, and through her hair. She thought that within the breeze, she heard the faintest melody, carrying an essence of both peace and power. At the same time, the shadow dissolved and dispersed into the starlit sky.

Tarin looked at Abigail, and she at him. They fell into a tight embrace.

◦ ◦ ◦ ◇ ◦ ◦ ◦

Tarin couldn't tell how long he and Abigail held each other. But within her arms, he felt, for the first time, that he was truly home. Memories of his childhood in Arvalast had immediately flooded back the moment he'd passed through the portal. Now, even more memories filled his mind, so much so that he found it impossible to hold back tears. All the while, Abigail continued to embrace him.

Eventually, voices from below ascended the tower. Tarin and Abigail met eyes, and together, they moved to the tower's edge. A large group of people had gathered at the tower's base. Red-cloaked bodies, along with some figures in brown or green, were lying on the ground. Some others, also in earth-toned cloaks or jackets, were attending to the latter. Nearby was the broken body of the Bostt. Iris, her wings at her side and her armor no longer shimmering as brightly, stood next to a woman attending to one of the seemingly wounded. Coming up the stairs near the bottom of the tower was another woman and a man. They looked up and waved illuminas.

"It's Ella and Jak!" Abigail shouted. "They're okay! Gras and Maddie must have won their battle!"

"Battle?" Tarin asked.

Abigail tugged on his arm. "Hurry, let's go down. I'll tell you more on the way." Abigail hastily filled Tarin in on the events since he'd rallied the people of the forest at Kettle Falls as he nervously looked over the nearby edge. Why this tower had no rails, he never understood.

When they reached the lower third of the tower and rounded another corner, a woman with dark hair ran to greet them.

"Tarin!" the woman yelled. Before he could react, he was in her arms, being squeezed harder than he'd ever remembered. She pulled back.

"Ella," he whispered as a broad smile spread across his face. He started to laugh. "Ella!" He held out his arms, and she jumped back into them.

"I'm so glad you're back!" she cried through joyful tears. A man sprung up behind her. He reached over Ella and grabbed Tarin's shoulder, giving it a hearty shake.

"I can't believe it's really you!" the man said. "And now so grown up!"

Despite his beard and greying hair, Tarin immediately recognized Jak. Ella moved to the side, still beaming, while Jak jumped forward and pulled Tarin into a bear hug.

"Come, join us!" Jak called to Abigail. She laughed and obliged. Finally, Jak pulled away and held his hand toward the stairs below. "Hurry, let's get down and join the others and show them what has been achieved with their victory! Many are hurt. We must rally them."

He grabbed Tarin's hand and began leading him down the tower. Ella and Abigail followed after them, talking rapidly about what had happened on top of the tower and down below. Tarin overheard that Drilockk had attacked Jak and Ella while a battalion led by Gras and Maddie, whom Tarin couldn't quite recall from his previous memories of Arvalast, fought through an encampment nearby. After they'd destroyed most of the Drilockk, the remainder had retreated to the tower. Gras, Maddie, and their battalion had pursued them only to find even more Drilockk attacking Jak and Ella, who'd taken defensive positions partway up the tower. The Drilockk had fought fiercely, and for a moment, things had appeared dire as some moved in on Jak and Ella. Others from the battalion were wounded. The battle had ended abruptly when Iris arrived.

When Tarin and the others reached the bottom, Tarin thought he heard Iris say, "I'm so sorry, there's nothing more I can do." She set her hand on the shoulder of the woman he'd seen earlier as she continued kneeling over the body of a wounded man.

"Iris!" Tarin shouted.

Iris looked up, and despite a forlorn expression, when her eyes met his own, they glistened. She whispered something to the woman, then stood and began approaching Tarin. Jak and Ella sent each other worried glances, then rushed to where Iris had been. As Iris approached, Tarin noticed she no longer wore glasses and appeared very regal in her armor and with her wings folded behind her back. Her face was unblemished and completely healed from the earlier assault.

She stood in front of Tarin. A small crowd began to gather around as she and Tarin remained locked in a timeless gaze. Finally, he stepped forward and threw out his arms as she did the same. They fell into an embrace. For many moments, they stood together beneath the shadow of the tower from which this long journey had begun. Eventually, they let each other go. Tarin looked at Abigail and held out his hand. "May I?" he said, and she nodded. He gently took her hand and led her forward.

"Abigail," he said, "I'd like you to meet someone." He smiled. "Her name is Iris. She kept an eye on me while I was on Earth."

Iris held out her hand to Abigail. Abigail looked at it, then stepped forward. Iris took both of Abigail's hands in her own, and for many moments, neither spoke. Finally, with a broad smile, Iris said, "At last, I now meet the final warrior of the light."

A woman's scream stripped away the joy of the moment. Tarin turned toward the cry. The woman Iris had just been with was lying sprawled out over the man she'd been attending to. Jak and Ella held her quaking body. A sword rested at the man's feet, and an expanding pool of blood slowly painted it red.

"Gras!" Abigail yelled as her eyes filled with horror. "No!"

At the same time, a man Tarin did not recognize approached, grabbed Tarin's right arm, and lifted it into the sky. Tarin's illumina glistened as the man yelled, "Behold! We have not fought and died in vain this night! Hope has returned to our forest, to our cities—to our lands! The warrior—he has returned!"

Another voice from the crowd followed, this one less jubilant. "But where is Gildareth?"

ACKNOWLEDGMENTS

Although a writer spends a lot of time in their own imagination when putting initial words to paper (or computer), it takes many others to help refine those words into something deliverable to a wider audience. I'd like to thank Faith who provided me with a ton of feedback and suggestions in the initial editing round. I would also like to thank the editing team at Ballast, Donnie and Emma, for their careful final revisions to help polish things up. Thank you to all my beta readers, in particular Danny and Conor. Your feedback was invaluable. I also want to thank the team at Ballast. Lauren, Lindsey, and Kayleigh, your guidance and support through the publication and marketing process have been awesome. And what's a book without the cover? Jeff, thank you for capturing my vision so carefully. Finally, I'd like to thank my wife, Jodi, for her encouragement during this whole process and for supporting my dream to be a writer.

EPILOGUE

Feleti fixated her gaze on the icy expanse beneath her. From her vantage point in the small, two-seated cylindrical craft, she watched as a line of what appeared to be tiny glowing orbs floated just above the churning shoreline of Antarctica. Hovering in front and near the center of the formation was what looked like a metallic saucer.

Feleti's eyes moved inland. Her hands tensed as she watched a vast, crawling army of dark wisps move forward over miles of frozen fields toward the ocean waves.

"We must go, my Lady," her copilot, a woman also with brown skin and dark hair, said. "It seems those you entrusted to remove the interloper have failed."

"No," Feleti said. "We wait."

"But my Lady?"

"No!" Feleti said again. She watched as the swarms of shadow moved yet closer to the wall of orbs. "They still have time."

Then, Feleti felt it—a rush of energy surged through her body, causing her to gasp. Her copilot must have felt it too, for she also took in a fast breath. Outside, the creeping umbra stopped. Feleti squinted. Toward the front of the formation, a monstrous figure hidden within red smoke slithered forward. She couldn't see the true shape of the creature within—but didn't need to. The quickening breaths of her copilot filled the cockpit as Feleti felt the beating of her own heart within her chest. Tendrils of crimson smoke began swirling around the invisible specter below.

"We must go," the copilot hissed.

Feleti was about to touch the domed glass panel in front of her to pull them farther from the planet when the crimson cloud began to withdraw back into the bowels of the shadow army. The great mass parted to make room. Then, the legions of darkness began to back away with the specter, away from the coast, away from the orbs.

The copilot pointed toward the retreat. "They must have done it!" she shouted. "My Lady, there will be no war of shadow!"

Feleti closed her eyes and released a slow breath. "Yes," she said. "With the sentinel from Arvalast dislodged from the planet, the earthly shadows he wooed will be disorganized and weakened. But the Prince and his legions have still lost their conduit to the remaining physical earthly power structures through our fallen brethren. He will be forced to act to regain control of Earth—and to finally confront my creation, even as it wars within itself."

Feleti watched the line of orbs assemble into a great sphere around the saucer and, in unison, back away from the continent. She placed her hands over the control panel, and Earth began to pull away. Now, within the emptiness beyond the atmosphere, she looked down onto the planet she loved. Though it was not her home, the beauty of that blue marble still stirred her spirit, as did those who dwelled upon it. And somewhere down there, the light from her world was spreading, and with it, hope—even without a great peace.

But as the sun rays of a new morning blanketed the planet, she knew the same light that brought her hope would be deemed a malignancy by the Great Shadow enthroned in Arvalast, the very manifestation of the Void beyond Immaru. Earth would be upon its mind, for the lord of all darkness would not want the seeds of light to put down roots on a world so near Arvalast. Somewhere behind that morning, midnight would come again.

To be continued . . .